Praise for

The Virgin's Daughters

"Jeane Westin's *The Virgin's Daughters* takes the reader on a poignant journey into the hearts and minds of three dynamic Elizabethan women, including the queen herself. Intimate characterization and beautifully rendered settings and customs make us realize that the tumultuous Tudor times are both unique and yet not so very different from our own. A compelling, unforgettable historical novel."

—Karen Harper, author of *Mistress Shakespeare*

"Two well-crafted love stories set against the backdrop of the court of Elizabeth the First create high drama and at the same time paint an unforgettable portrait of the last Tudor monarch. Jeane Westin writes powerful scenes that not only pack an emotional wallop but also transport modern readers directly into the minds and hearts of members of the queen's inner circle."

—Kate Emerson, author of *Secrets of the Tudor Court: The Pleasure Palace*

"In *The Virgin's Daughters*, Jeane Westin has given us a suspenseful tale of royal power and the grip of an iron queen on the destiny of her ladies-in-waiting. Vivid characters and compelling dialogue illuminate the Elizabethan court where danger lurks in the shadows, love can be treason, and every step could be the last. You'll find yourself looking over your shoulder in this engrossing read."

—Sandra Worth, author of *The King's Daughter*

"Jeane Westin has brought the Elizabethan court vividly to life. Her heroines walk a delicious knife-edge between love and disaster. I couldn't put it down."

—Anne Gracie, author of *The Tudors: The King, the Queen, and the Mistress*

The Virgin's Daughters

 IN THE COURT OF ELIZABETH I

JEANE WESTIN

NAL
NEW AMERICAN LIBRARY

NEW AMERICAN LIBRARY
Published by New American Library,
a division of Penguin Group (USA) Inc.,
375 Hudson Street, New York, New York 10014, USA
Penguin Group (Canada), 90 Eglinton Avenue East, Suite 700, Toronto,
Ontario M4P 2Y3, Canada (a division of Pearson Penguin Canada Inc.)
Penguin Books Ltd., 80 Strand, London WC2R 0RL, England
Penguin Ireland, 25 St. Stephen's Green, Dublin 2,
Ireland (a division of Penguin Books Ltd.)
Penguin Group (Australia), 250 Camberwell Road, Camberwell, Victoria 3124,
Australia (a division of Pearson Australia Group Pty. Ltd.)
Penguin Books India Pvt. Ltd., 11 Community Centre,
Panchsheel Park, New Delhi - 110 017, India
Penguin Group (NZ), 67 Apollo Drive, Rosedale, North Shore 0632,
New Zealand (a division of Pearson New Zealand Ltd.)
Penguin Books (South Africa) (Pty.) Ltd., 24 Sturdee Avenue,
Rosebank, Johannesburg 2196, South Africa

Penguin Books Ltd., Registered Offices:
80 Strand, London WC2R 0RL, England

First published by New American Library,
a division of Penguin Group (USA) Inc.

First Printing, August 2009
1 3 5 7 9 10 8 6 4 2

 REGISTERED TRADEMARK—MARCA REGISTRADA

LIBRARY OF CONGRESS CATALOGING-IN-PUBLICATION DATA:
Westin, Jeane.
The virgin's daughters: in the court of Elizabeth I/Jeane Westin.
p. cm.
ISBN 978-0-451-22667-9
1. Elizabeth I, Queen of England, 1533–1603—Fiction. 2. Hertford, Katherine Seymour,
Countess of, 1540–1568—Fiction. 3. Great Britain—Court and courtiers—Fiction. I. Title.
PS3573.E89V57 2009
813'.54—dc22   2009003373

Set in Simoncini Garamond
Designed by Elke Sigal

Printed in the United States of America

FOR MY HUSBAND, GENE, AND MY DAUGHTER, CARA

ACKNOWLEDGMENTS

I am grateful to my friend and fellow writer Shirley Parenteau for her helpful advice and sustained enthusiasm, and to the many librarians and old booksellers who helped me find long-out-of-print research books. My appreciation also goes to the staff of the National Maritime Museum in Greenwich, England, who found for me a sold-out copy of their wonderfully illustrated tribute to Elizabeth I, published on the occasion of the four hundredth anniversary of her death in 2003. In addition, I'm thankful that my agent, Danielle Egan-Miller, is such an enthusiastic Queen Elizabeth fan.

Writing this book would not have been possible without the help of my computer tech, Ashley Lucas, a Renaissance-costume fan, who can always get me back up and running. Thank you, "Lady" Ashley.

Finally, and always, I must acknowledge my superb editor, Ellen Edwards, who sees what I need to do and knows just how to tell me.

BRIEF GENEALOGIES *of* HISTORICAL CHARACTERS

Tudor Succession

Henry VIII
B. 1491—D. 1547

|

Edward VI
B. 1537—D. 1553

|

Mary I
B. 1516—D. 1558

|

Elizabeth I
B. 1533—D. 1603

Grey-Tudor Family

Mary Tudor
(SISTER TO HENRY VIII)
B. 1496—D. 1533
MARRIED CHARLES BRANDON

|

Frances Brandon
MARRIED HENRY GREY
DUKE OF SUFFOLK
(EXECUTED 1554)

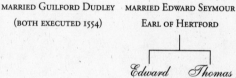

Jane Grey
MARRIED GUILFORD DUDLEY
(BOTH EXECUTED 1554)

Katherine Grey
MARRIED EDWARD SEYMOUR
EARL OF HERTFORD

Edward   *Thomas*
(WILLIAM)

Harington Family

Sir John Harington
MARRIED ISABELLA MARKHAM

|

Sir John Harington
MARRIED MARY ROGERS

Dudley Family

Sir Edmund Dudley
MINISTER TO HENRY VII
B. 1470—D. 1510
(EXECUTED)

|

John Dudley
DUKE OF NORTHUMBERLAND
B. 1501—D. 1553
(EXECUTED)

|

Robert Dudley
EARL OF LEICESTER
B. 1532(3)—D. 1588

ELIZABETH'S SOUTHERN ENGLAND

WANSTEAD MANOR

TILLBURY

WHITEHALL
GREENWICH

RICHMOND

ELTHAM MANOR

LONDON

HAMPTON COURT

NONSUCH

OATLANDS

WINDSOR

READING

River Thames

OXFORD

MAP SYMBOLS

Map Not To Scale

- Towns
- Palaces
- Manors

Somerset

BRISTOL

BATH

KELSTON MANOR

ROGERS MANOR

TAUNTON

Part One

FIRST LOVES

CHAPTER ONE

January, 1562
Whitehall Palace

The queen's voice raged above the din of smashing crockery as Lady Katherine Grey sped through the presence chamber toward the royal apartment just beyond. She stopped and pressed a hand to her painful side, catching her breath. Though fragrant Christmas boughs of yew and laurel, draped with holly and bright with red berries, hung everywhere, all the greenery remaining in the snow-covered palace gardens would not make this a good day for her, or for any lady of the bedchamber.

Kate took a deep breath, preparing herself to dutifully accept the queen's Tudor temper . . . any threat, any blow. She would never defy Elizabeth and jeopardize her place as chief lady-in-waiting. If she were sent from court, she would be forced home to Bradgate in disgrace. By Christ's cross! Her mother, Frances, Duchess of Suffolk, would despise her daughter more than ever for losing a last opportunity to advance her family. All Kate's life she had been pushed beyond her desire, forced to bow to the will of her family, no one caring what she might want for herself. The only dream she had ever held had been denied her years ago.

Kate hurried on, stumbling on a marble tile, recalling her

mother's sharp voice, all her angry disappointment at Kate coming down on her head again: "You stupid girl! You have once more failed your family. The crown is next yours by blood, by birth and by your uncle Henry VIII's will! Your sister, Jane . . . now, there was a queen to make me proud."

And did it make you proud, Mother, when the Tower ax fell on her girlish neck? Kate knew better than to say it, but not even her duchess mother could govern her thoughts. Oh, yes, far better Elizabeth's temper than her mother's fierce ambition. Kate's hand went involuntarily to her own neck, long, slender and . . . vulnerable.

Taking in a deep and much-needed breath, Kate walked on toward the queen's apartment, her step resolute. Never would she be sacrificed by her mother, as she and her father had schemed and sacrificed Jane to gain a throne.

Kate stopped for the gentlemen ushers to open the high double doors to the queen's apartment. But stopping proved to be a mistake. Lord Secretary William Cecil stepped in her way and bowed. "A word in private, my lady," he said softly, "if it please you."

Kate nodded. "My lord." She couldn't deny him without risking his enmity. She allowed him to guide her across the vaulted stone hall, half-afraid and alert to what he might say.

"Some on the council, my lady, believe that the queen will never marry."

He paused for a response, but Kate did not allow an eyelid to flicker.

Forced to proceed, Cecil added, "Of course, I do not believe the queen really wishes to remain a virgin maid. Any young woman, even a great queen such as Elizabeth, must have a man's near guidance to . . . uh . . . keep her from those natural follies that are part of a woman's God-given nature."

Kate remained silent, being well versed in what men thought women needed.

Cecil, his sober face just a bit flushed, spoke again. "My lady, there is much support for you to be named her heir. You are seen as a woman who would welcome a husband and children."

"If you do *not* believe the queen will remain an unmarried maid, I wonder, my lord, why you think an heir must be named." She added to soften her response: "I do thank you for your care of me, Lord Secretary, but you may tell those counselors who would promote my name that I am a loyal subject to Her Majesty. She is England's greatest queen and I am proud to serve her. Tell them, too, that since I do not seek the throne, therefore I do not need their aid."

"My lady," Cecil said, his voice now holding an edge, "I must advise you that they have your lady mother's full agreement."

"But never mine," she said, the words wobbly despite her resolve to steady them. "I need not remind you, my lord, that it is for Her Majesty to say who is heir to her realm, not my mother. As for me, I will follow my queen's will, and not my sister to the block." For the first time, Kate felt the seeping winter cold in the hall and wrapped one arm across the other.

Cecil bowed, but his face showed clear disbelief. "We will speak again on this matter, Lady Katherine."

"You may speak, my lord, but my answer will remain the same."

"Then what *do* you want?" he asked, his voice almost a whisper.

Jesu, he had asked the one question she could not answer. She had wanted only one thing, one happiness in her life, and that had been denied her. With a quick curtsy, she stiffened her shoulders and walked inside the queen's outer chamber.

"Down! Down upon your knees, my lord!" The queen's commanding voice penetrated the walls of her privy chamber as if they were so much fine Flemish paper.

A man's deep voice answered the queen. "I will always kneel to my queen, though I see nothing of the Bess I first loved as a playmate these twenty years gone!"

Kate knew that male voice to be Robert Dudley's, her brother-in-law since his unfortunate brother, Guilford, had married Jane. Both had lost their heads on Tower Green for daring to occupy the throne for nine days, followed to the block by Kate's father, Henry Grey, the Duke of Suffolk, who had escaped the ax once, but rebelled again and lost. So much for family ambition. Thanks be to heaven above, she had inherited none of it.

Beyond, in the privy chamber, another priceless vase or mirror was thrown. Robert and the queen often had such bitter arguments, slamming hurtful words into each other like lances against shields in a hopeless joust of love that neither could expect to win. Or they closed themselves away from the world for long hours, raising rumors that they were lovers and the queen was pregnant.

Kate's nails dug into her gloves until she felt them almost pierce her flesh and she swore an oath to go to the Royal Chapel at her first opportunity. She must pray the queen did nothing so rash as to make the council pounce on her, Henry VIII's next Protestant heir by his will.

An eerie silence had followed the last outburst and raised more fear in Kate. Was the queen pacing angrily? Whispering a regret in his ear? More? In spite of Kate's alarm, she could not help such romantic thoughts as they came into her head ... and though she pushed them away, they came again. She was a young woman, after all, a woman whose heart still ached, would ever ache, for a lost love. She did not blame her starved heart for desiring what every woman needed.

Dudley and the queen were madly in love. Anyone could see that. Their explosive behavior was the talk of court. Indeed, gossip about them had reached the Continent, though everyone said the English people would never accept Dudley as king. Elizabeth knew all this damaging tittle-tattle, had princely suitors from every kingdom in Europe and yet could not break from Dudley. What was it like to be a woman grown and to love a man so much? Kate felt a familiar warmth as her imagination took hold. Once, just on the border of maturity, she had known such a love. She thrust a vision of his young face from her, though she knew he would return in her night's dreams, as he always did.

Voices in the privy chamber rose, and Her Majesty's ladies halted their duties to gather in the anteroom and listen. Mistress Parry, Lady Saintloe, Lettice Knollys and the others stood about biting their lips and rolling their eyes, trying to busy themselves with embroidery, or continually smoothing the wrinkles from their satin gowns.

Forcing herself to a calm demeanor, Kate moved to study the antechamber wall. Ordinarily, she avoided the great Hans Holbein picture of the queen's father and her own uncle, Henry VIII. The painter had captured the king's cruel little mouth set in a red face bloated with indulgence, his monstrous codpiece, trumpeting an incredible virility, thrust through his short cloak, all atop legs like tree trunks that seemed to bestride England. He had terrified her as a child when her father had taken her to Richmond Palace to be presented. The king was a huge man, old and scowling, his swollen leg propped on many soft cushions. The ghastly odor of the leg's pus-seeping wound filled the huge presence chamber and frightened her. She had started crying.

"My lord Duke of Suffolk," the king had roared, "if you cannot quiet your daughter, remove her." She'd clung hard to her father's leg, fearing the Tower. That was where His Majesty sent girls who did not please him. Everyone said it was so.

Her father had gripped her shoulder and she had felt his shaking anger, though he would cut off only her supper tart, not her head.

As a pretty girl child of the blood royal, she was expected to please the king and to be invited to school with the royal children, Elizabeth and Edward. Kate's older sister, Jane, was already shouting out her Latin verbs with them. While Kate was not so clever at her books as Jane, the duke had said it was not beyond reason that she could be betrothed to Prince Edward and eventually become queen. Kate had overheard her mother telling her father: "If not one daughter, perhaps another, and Kate is our beauty, though not as biddable as Jane."

But seeing the king's mood on this visit, her father had not broached either subject. Kate retreated with nothing but her father's anger at her poor showing in a first court appearance. That evening, her mother had ordered her beaten and refused to speak to her for days. Kate remembered how she had waited in her rooms, content with her loving nurse, Sybil. But she couldn't buy safety for longer than a few days. Though she hardly understood her transgression, she went to her mother, knelt and begged forgiveness for her failings, earnestly promising to be a better daughter in the future. The Duchess of Suffolk offered her a cold forgiveness, and Kate ran back through the castle halls to her waiting nurse for the tenderness she needed.

Kate heard Mistress Ashley speaking. "She will faint if she continues in this much anger. It was so from her early years." The former governess, small and fleshy, had cared for the queen as a child and was now a lady of the bedchamber pacing outside the closed doors, clasping and unclasping her hands as she listened to Elizabeth's rising voice. "I must have vinegar cloths," Ashley said, and stepped to the hall doors to order them made ready.

Lady Saintloe edged toward Kate before she could escape the lady's unwanted attention. Saintloe bent close in confidence. "I see you admire the late king's portrait. A true likeness, my lady Grey?"

Uneasy, Kate answered without looking at Saintloe. "Yes, though I was only a child when presented at his court."

"I believe I heard of it." Saintloe smiled, encouraging a confidence, which she would swear to hold close, then pass on to half the court until it came back to the queen's ears. Kate, seeming engrossed in the picture's details, moved slightly away from the lady. She would not satisfy Saintloe's need to pry into her thoughts.

The queen would allow no ill word spoken of her father, though

Kate could not understand why, since Henry had not treated Elizabeth well. Royalty must have its reasons.

Kate forced herself to appear intent on Henry, towering wide-legged over everyone in the antechamber as if he were still ruling. She counted herself lucky to have escaped his court. This king had decreed Elizabeth a bastard after beheading her mother, Anne Boleyn. He'd banished Elizabeth from his sight for long periods, bringing her back to court for a time, then sending her away again, owning her completely as his daughter only in his last will. Being in the succession had saved Elizabeth's life from her older sister Queen Mary's revenge. Mary had never forgiven Elizabeth for her mother, the beautiful, spirited Anne, who'd caused Mary's own mother, Catherine of Aragon, to be set aside, and banished so cruelly that it hastened her lonely, painful death.

Snatching Kate back to the present, Elizabeth's regal voice rose again even louder. "Stay on your knees, my lord! Do you forget who is sovereign here?"

"How could I, Majesty?" Dudley responded, his voice as dramatically loud. "Your rank is what will part us forever as it parted us as children."

"I told you then that I would never marry."

"I thought it but the talk of a willful girl child who had not yet felt a woman's needs . . . as you have felt them, Bess."

Kate heard the smacking *pup! pup!* sound the queen made with her lips when she was so annoyed she could not use her tongue, though she made her usual quick recovery.

"My lord, these are now the words of your anointed sovereign and, as you see, a woman full-grown." The spaces between the hard-bitten words resounded with frustration. "It is amazing to me that my council, Parliament and you, sir—the baker, the glover, every man in my realm—trouble me so for a quick marriage. I think it most unusual in your sex"—she halted, needing breath—"unless a woman be a ruler. Do you know me so little? Elizabeth Tudor needs no man's guidance!"

Dudley's voice was calming, though his words were underlined in hurt. "That is unjust, Bess. I want you for no reasons of state, but for yourself . . . as I always have."

Elizabeth responded with softer words, but just as stabbing. "Then, my lord, you would not be a king?"

Kate drew in a sharp breath of surprise, inhaling the bay leaves and rosemary strewn among the rushes on the chamber floor. Dudley had been neatly trapped, for he surely wanted to be king. It was rare for her brother-in-law to be ensnared by his own words. Kate felt sorry for his misstep.

"I will take my leave then, Bess. I can do no good here when I am much suspected."

Kate heard real sorrow in Dudley's words. He had pulled back just in time, though he seemed to move closer to success each day. Kate longed for him to win the queen. If Elizabeth gave in to her heart and married him, Kate would be safely out of the succession as soon as a child and heir to the throne was born. Still, she had to admit that Dudley's many enemies might lead a revolt, using the Lady Katherine Grey as their reason. Could she be forced to the Tower and the block for a treason she did not support? She shivered, since that question had been answered by many falling heads, including her sister's.

All the ladies leaned forward, breathless to hear the queen's answer to Dudley's challenge.

If there was an answer, it could not be discerned, not a sound, not a sigh.

Certain that Elizabeth was about to collapse, Mistress Ashley rushed into the hall to wait for the doctor and his vinegar cloths, a sure cure for faintness.

Kate came as near to the bedchamber door as she dared, listening hard to what she thought sure to hear. Always she wondered, what was it like to be a woman and a man grown and so much in love? How many times in the two years since Amy Dudley's death had she heard Lord Dudley openly seek the queen's hand and she refuse him, while holding him ever closer? Kate thought the tension between them now tighter than a lutestring.

All the ladies were teetering forward when the queen's next words reached them, calculating now, but just as forbidding. "Remain as you are, my lord. I have given you no leave to rise. I will have *here* but one mistress and no master!"

"Bess, I have not earned such contempt as you show me," Dudley said, not humbled, though his voice shook with thwarted feeling. Yet he spoke in so rich a timber that even his hard words held a thousand caresses.

Kate turned her face away from the others because she knew it showed her own thoughts. Robert might yet tame this queen. He had half the court ladies in love with him, and he made certain Elizabeth saw it at every banquet and masque, knowing her quick to jealousy.

But Elizabeth's answer revealed no compassion or regret. Kate knew both would come soon, as they always did, but so far the queen seemed to resist her own desires. "Then, my lord, if you wish for my continued favor, I command you to cease this constant plaguing me. You know that I cannot marry a subject whom the people suspect of killing his own wife!"

Kate marveled that Elizabeth could switch from one argument to another with such apparent ease, and knew that was no skill of her own. Was it a skill she should learn? She would need more than empty bluster to resist the combined forces of Cecil, the council and her mother.

Dudley's voice rose again in wounded anger. "Amy was ill unto death, some evil growing in her breast. She died from mischance, a fall on the stairs, or even a suicide to stop her pain, and so said the commission of inquiry, all true men. You know that well, Bess."

Kate heard nothing but silence then, yet in her mind's eye she saw that the queen drew near to Dudley. His piercing dark Gypsy eyes would propel her to him.

Finally the queen spoke in a more reasonable voice. "How can you claim to love me, Robin, when you know the people, seeing my regard for you, even now may believe I conspired in your wife's death? And my council is set against you, even to favoring my own servant, that traitor Suffolk's daughter Katherine, citing my father's will that named my Grey cousins to succeed me. Would you see me undone?"

Kate's stomach churned. Were there no secrets from Elizabeth?

"The people are ever changeable, Bess, and they adore you and will love you more when you are carrying our child—"

"You are so sure, my lord. Your late wife had no children."

"Because I could scarce lie with her, Bess." He paused and then his lover's voice vibrated through the wall. "How could I make love to her when it was your face and form I saw beneath me?" His voice grew strangled, but still man-sure. "The people will do as you tell them. As for your council, grant me a position among them and I will change their minds. Bess—"

"God's death, Robin!" The queen was pacing again, her voice going away, then returning. "You ask for too much. Have I not made you master of the horse and of my revels, given you a pension and levies on cloth and sweet wine, openly shown my favor in every way?"

"In all but one way, Bess, and that way alone would heal my sore heart . . . and yours."

Elizabeth's voice was weary when she answered, but held some pleading. "Be patient, Rob. Someday, perhaps . . . Now, I need you to rise, and to be my sweet Robin again. I am sore troubled by these hard words between us."

Lady Saintloe nudged Kate slyly. "She gives him both hands. He stands and has an advantage."

Kate did not respond, shivering. It was all too alarming to be amusing. Every time the queen denied Dudley or any of her princely suitors and remained unmarried, Katherine felt her own head wobble.

Dudley was not finished. His anguished words rang clear in the antechamber. "Majesty, if you will not have me, let me leave court and go to the country, where I can have some heart's peace."

"Never, Robin!" Elizabeth said, her words holding a sob. "Everything is amiss with me when you are not by my side."

"Then, if not husband, what would you have me be . . . your little dog to pet and fondle on a mood?"

With a low laugh, Elizabeth made light of his bitter jibe. "A little dog always runs near its mistress, and all the court will know that I must be near you."

Kate shivered at this effort to jolly him. Though the answer was confounding, the queen's voice held the tremor of desire. Even Dudley in his anger could not miss such feeling, nor lose the opportunity.

Saintloe tried to engage Kate again. "I would give up my triple strand of pearls for a peephole at this moment. Richmond Palace is full of peepholes. Why not here?"

Kate did not need a peephole. She could imagine the scene, like a romance played on the court theater stage between quarreling lovers. Robert Dudley had risen now to his full six feet, his dark Gypsy looks overwhelming the queen's anger, for anyone with eyes could see that she loved him to near madness. The queen would be in his arms now. All would be quiet for a time. And playful, too, for Kate heard Dudley make little yapping sounds and the queen laughing softly, her laugh catching on a moan before all was silence.

Kate felt a tremor come from deep inside, a memory of urgent love, a love that did not allow her to tell it. No lady present dared speak a word of what they were hearing, though they would later, their imaginings traveling throughout Whitehall with faster speed than one of the queen's favorite Irish horses. Kate would not discuss this with anyone. She would give the queen no reason to doubt her loyalty, no reason to send her from court to her mother's tender care.

But there was already gossip in plenty, Kate knew, especially since Elizabeth had granted Robert Dudley an apartment next to her own. Half the court thought the queen pregnant, some foreign ambassadors even bribing the washing women to report if the queen's monthly fluxes failed to appear. Others whispered that there was a secret passage between their rooms, though one of the ladies of the bedchamber, often Mistress Ashley, sometimes Kate herself, slept on a trundle at the foot of the queen's bed. Unless Dudley was a night spirit, he could not enjoy the queen's body, although who could deny the heat between them that seemed likely to burst into flame at any time? And the queen knew it, Kate thought. Though, as princess, Elizabeth had escaped every cunning trap laid for her, outwitting all who came against her. First, Lord Admiral Thomas Seymour, her stepmother Queen Catherine Parr's husband after Henry VIII died. Thomas Seymour tried to seduce Elizabeth at fourteen; second her sister, Queen Mary, near forty and plain, jealous of Elizabeth's youthful beauty and popularity. Later, she was vigorously questioned by many privy councilors and finally the judges in the Tower, all longing to find her guilty of treason. She had cleverly outwitted them all. Yet Elizabeth now seemed helplessly drawn to the certain danger of Lord Robert Dudley.

Kate knew that if Dudley won her and took the throne at her side, there would be uprisings against a king whose father and grandfather had been executed for treason. Foreign Catholic princes, who already thought this queen a bastard, would never honor such a king. The people would believe the queen bewitched and the court licentious. Then the council would come for Kate to rule and do her duty. She trembled at the thought of the throne, with all its dangers, so close to her, with only Elizabeth standing between them. Kate would pray that God put marriage to a foreign prince into Elizabeth Tudor's heart, and that she, Katherine Grey, be given the strength to withstand men, who thought to order all of a woman's life.

Surely even desperate love could not overcome the obstacles Elizabeth would face if she chose Dudley, and the queen knew it, when she allowed herself to know. Yet, what if the queen married him and had a child of Dudley? Would France or Spain have reason to invade to set a Catholic on the throne, forcing Englishmen to rise up against a Catholic ruler in favor of the next Protestant heir, Katherine Grey? The memory of Bloody Mary, Elizabeth's sister, was yet fresh in the people's minds. Kate's thoughts swung back and forth between so many possibilities. Everywhere she saw great problems with and without royal marriage. What would be the queen's fate? And her own? She was as ensnared in royal politics as Elizabeth was.

Mistress Ashley rushed in with a tray of vinegar cloths.

"I think there is no need now," said a smirking Saintloe. "Her Grace seems quite at rest and recovered."

"My lady, it is amazing to me that you can know what you cannot see. Yet I do not require instruction regarding Her Majesty's health, since I have cared for her from the cradle."

This was a familiar refrain in Ashley's Devon accent, and Kate knew this old governess had great privilege. It maddened Saintloe, who looked to Kate, but she did not come to that lady's aid.

The doors to the queen's privy chamber opened and Lord Dudley filled the space, tugging at his rumpled black velvet doublet with jewel buttons, pressing down on a gold thread come undone from the intricate embroidery, his short scarlet-lined cape swung back over one shoulder, his right hand on his sword hilt, a prideful peacock feather sweeping the air above his cap. He stood for a long moment, one leg thrust forward, perhaps the better to show his mauve-colored close hose and red-heeled boots, or to show more clearly that he needed no false codpiece. Was he practicing to play a king? There were audible sighs from the overdazzled ladies who, even in well-practiced modesty, could not lift their admiring eyes from such a manly display.

"Her Majesty is at her prayers," he said, bowing to the ladies and again to Kate, who felt a blush rise to her cheeks and received a brilliant, impudent, even triumphant grin and a slow wink in reply. He was a man, after all. What man could believe a woman, especially one of Elizabeth's hot nature, needed no husband, and rather urgently at that?

Kate sometimes regretted being able to see behind words and faces all the way to what people were truly thinking. She'd told no one, knowing well what happened to women who were too clever at divining. . . . They were named witches. Still, she knew that Elizabeth would dine alone today. It was so like this changeable queen to give Dudley opportunity with one hand and take it away with the other, keeping him off balance. And she liked to dine alone except for state banquets. Dudley was one of a few favorites for whom she'd break that habit. But not tonight. He had already been shown enough favor . . . perhaps too much. The thought of what that could have been sent a surge of heat to places in Kate that an unmarried maid must keep cold.

Kate could only imagine what happened between a man and woman in the marriage bed, since her own marriage at not quite fourteen to elderly Lord Herbert, the son of the Earl of Pembroke, had been annulled, unconsummated. Before she had had her first fluxes and was beddable, her father was beheaded for scheming to make his daughter Jane queen for nine days. Within weeks of his marriage to Kate, Pembroke promptly ran from such an attainted connection, leaving her with no future save banishment to a country manor house, alone with her bitter mother, who blamed Kate for all their troubles because she could not blame herself.

Now, as a woman of twenty and three, Elizabeth's lady-in-waiting for three years, Kate had seen and heard much of loving in the crowded court and suspected more—quite enough to fuel thoughts of sinful pleasures that kept her from restful sleep, thoughts of Edward Seymour, son of the Duke of Somerset, as he had been that bright summer morning near the water gardens at Greenwich, back when King Edward held the throne.

Her mother had allowed her nurse, Sybil, to take her for a healthy walk away from the noisome odors of the crowded castle. Choosing a graveled path alongside a tall yew hedge, Kate became aware of a figure moving on the other side.

"Lady Katherine?" a man's voice asked.

"Don't answer, my lady," Sybil warned.

"It would be discourteous, Nurse," she whispered, recognizing that voice as that of a youth who had been in and out of her life for years at court.

"Ah, you know, nurses are not always right," the amused male voice responded.

Two hands parted the hedge and a blond head full of twigs and leaves above a grinning face thrust through. "My lady, I recognized your voice, though it has been two years since last we met."

She curtsied. "As I knew yours, my lord, though I did not know you had returned to court," she said, hoping to sound much older than at their last meeting. She did not say aloud that he had also returned much taller, and even more handsome with his shadow of a beard. He must be sixteen now, two years older than her near-fourteen years.

He cocked his head, still grinning. "I have finished my studies at Oxford and now King Edward has commanded my presence. He has forgiven my family for my father's . . . treason."

She did not say it, but she thought it. *After your father paid with his head there's not much more to take.*

"I am saddened to find the king so ill he cannot leave his bed," he added.

"I pray for him," Kate said, though she could not help a small smile at all this polite speech for the benefit of her nurse.

He started through the hedge.

"My lord, you will rend your clothes."

"A small price, my lady, for your company."

Sybil cleared her throat energetically.

Edward pulled back and Kate heard him walk on. He waved a hand thrust through the hedge at intervals until she could not help laughing aloud, though Sybil pinched her arm.

Kate walked faster toward him as he rounded the hedge into a restful bower at the far end, smoothing his hair and doublet, his voice raised to reach her. "When I saw you today, I could scarce believe how much the lady you'd become. You were in the presence chamber in a dark blue gown the match for your eyes." He grinned. "But my lady Kate, you look too far from the nursery to need a nurse . . . much too far."

Sybil interrupted, her voice stern, though Kate saw her mouth purse to keep from smiling. "My lord Seymour, you are too forward. Lady Katherine is betrothed to the son of the Earl of Pembroke, so it is proper she have a companion to protect her reputation."

"From forward young men come down from Oxford?" he asked, laughing. "But surely, Mistress Sybil, you trust me as an old playmate."

Kate held out her hand, her eyes full of him.

He bowed and, kissing her fingers, whispered, "I followed you when you left the great hall. Wait for me. I have a gift for you."

Kate's lips parted to allow her a deep breath. Ned had always been her favorite of all the boys at court, and she'd feared never to see him again when his father fell from power. He disappeared behind the hedge and appeared once more carrying a caged bird. This time he bowed low to Sybil, his arm bent to her as if she were a grand lady. "May I offer you my protection, Mistress Nurse?"

Sybil giggled and lowered her eyes, blushing.

He walked with Sybil a few steps until she was utterly captivated. "My lady Katherine," he said to Kate, bending to her so close she should have stepped away, "let us sit here in this bower and talk the while you get to know your bird."

Kate's eyes pleaded with Sybil to permit it. For months, she had spoken to no one except dull old courtiers and her schoolmaster.

Not even her betrothed had cared for more than the usual formalities of greeting and leavetaking, though she had been glad of his inattention and happier still when he was most often closeted with her father, scheming for some new advantage in the court of a dying boy king.

Sybil continued to giggle at Lord Seymour's show of courtliness and she almost danced behind the bower bench.

"Does your chaffinch have a name?" Kate asked, curious, looking close at the russet-breasted bird with the gray head.

"It is not my chaffinch, my lady. It is your bird now. Do you want to know her name?" He looked down at Kate, his gaze conveying seriousness and something more thrilling, though she had no name for it. "I think the bird's name should be Kate, and so it will be to me."

She was embarrassed, but also delighted. They sat on the bench for shade under an overarching great lime tree. He sat beside her, Sybil standing behind them, making sure there was ample space between them. He held the birdcage on his lap, stroking one side of the bird's downy breast through the bent twig bars. Tentatively, Kate leaned to stroke the other side as the chaffinch sat very still, its eyes closed. Her fingers brushed Ned's and he captured them. She raised her gaze to his and held her breath, knowing she should pull away but unwilling to leave his warmth. As they ceased stroking, the bird chirped an objection, breaking their connection.

Other birds began to rustle and twitter in the hedge, and the chaffinch picked up her yellow beak and sang a greeting.

Pity stirred inside Kate. "Poor bird. It wants to be free."

"You have kept your kind heart, Kate, even in this cruel court, as I knew you would."

"I know how she suffers in her cage."

"Then we must rescue her, sweet Kate," he said, and she didn't know if he spoke of the bird or of her, perhaps both.

He opened the cage door and, when the bird did not move, he took it out gently and threw it into the air toward the hedge. It circled the bench once and flew into the yew branches, where it received a dozen greetings.

Kate looked at Edward and saw in his face a tenderness that she had never known before.

"There," he said, his light brown eyes a little sad, though he smiled at her. "One Kate is free."

"Thank you, Ned," she said, using his boy's name, her heart too choked for more. He knew her heart. . . . Somehow he knew.

She leaned toward him, and Sybil, vigilant again, moved in to separate them, tut-tutting. "Christian names, indeed, now that you are both near grown? Decorum, please you, I beg."

They were quiet for a time, and Sybil walked a few steps away to pick some lilies at the water's edge.

Ned began to speak softly. "My father wanted me to marry your sister, Jane, before he lost his head these two years past. But it was you I wanted even then."

Kate tightened her hand on the empty birdcage and decided on a polite response, since a betrothed girl had no right to another, truer one. "The Duke of Somerset . . . your father . . . I'm sorry, Ned." His father had tried to kidnap the boy king to gain full power, and his rival, John Dudley, had taken his place as Lord Protector. Ambition had killed him. Ned must know that, too. She could not look at him until a happier thought came. "But you are now Earl of Hertford."

"Aye, the king has restored that title to me, remembering our youth together." He looked at her, his eyes pleading. "As I have always remembered you, Kate, most beautiful and most sad."

She lowered her eyes, her heart pulsing in her ears.

"Meet me, Kate, here after supper," he whispered. "There is so much I would tell you. From the moment I saw you in the presence today, I knew what would fill my empty heart."

She stood quickly, alarmed, but he held her hand tight. "I will wait for you, no matter how long."

Not knowing how she would escape her watchers, just knowing that she would, she'd whispered, "Yes."

"Yes!" And now, coming from her waking trance, she said the word aloud, and all the ladies who had gathered outside Elizabeth's bedchamber looked a question at her. She could give them no answer.

Since the queen denied her ladies male company lest they commit marriage, Kate could see that many of them were openly content that Elizabeth would sup this day without Robert Dudley. Her Majesty called them all her daughters and claimed that denying them the temptation of men was part of her motherly care. But Kate was skeptical of such a fine reason. She thought it more likely that Elizabeth, knowing passion too well, denied weaker women what she could resist herself. Before she had more such disloyal, heated thoughts, Kate joined the strict ritual of preparing the queen's table, thankful for the cooling distraction of work.

Two gentlemen ushers entered bearing a white cloth rolled on a rod, knelt three times and carefully unrolled the cloth upon the table, then retreated and knelt once again. Two more gentlemen came with a tall silver saltcellar, a silver galleon at full sail on its pedestal, several gilt plates and bread, placing all upon the table and kneeling in their turn.

Kate approached the table with the same ceremony, always the same, and rubbed the clean plates with the salt and bread to clean them further, then retreated with her face toward the table, kneeling as if the queen herself were seated there. She knew that Mistress Ashley was always on watch to make certain royal ritual was observed in all its fine details.

The hall doors opened again and in came twenty-four yeomen of the guard by twos, dressed in scarlet with golden Tudor roses on their backs, each carrying a dish for the table. To prove it wasn't poisoned, each yeoman took a bite of the dish he'd brought. The queen had French, Spanish and Scottish enemies as well as some northern

Catholic nobles who would not weep at her death, though it brought ruin to the realm. Even some Protestants thought she had not gone far enough to change the new church ritual laid down by her father. Elizabeth had enemies in plenty, Kate knew. Every ruler did.

The trumpets and kettledrums sounded in the hall outside. The doors to the queen's privy chamber were opened and Kate carried in the first meat dish. All the dishes would eventually be taken into the queen's privy chamber so that she could choose the food she wanted. The rest made a cold dinner for her ladies and grooms, then for her private kitchen servants below and, finally, for the poor who were always at the gates, waiting for their humbles.

Kate knelt and raised the dish for the queen's inspection, while a groom poured her watered wine.

Elizabeth sat carefully regal, in part due to her natural height and dignity, but as much the fault of her close-tied farthingale. Even at prayer, Her Majesty did not truly rest, since it was her duty to pray vigorously for England. Only at her virginals or lute, singing for herself in a clear musical voice, was she at her ease.

By custom, as an unmarried maid, Elizabeth wore her red-gold Tudor hair draped down one shoulder. This supper hour her usually pale complexion was replaced with higher color. Her cheeks glistened damp from recent tears, her dark blue, almost violet eyes shot through with black sparks, now brimming large beneath their fair, almost invisible eyebrows and lashes. Kate tried not to stare and rouse her cousin to anger, which could be easier to use against a forward lady than a handsome favorite.

Kate fought to keep all her thoughts to herself, even the ones caused by Elizabeth's melancholy, since the queen's eyes saw everywhere and understood everything. She was quick to any mood, laughing easily and raging in frustration on a moment's turn. Kate expected the latter treatment today.

"Choose my gown and jewels well for tonight's masque, cousin," the queen commanded. "I will carry the ivory-handled feather fan my lord Dudley gave me, the one bearing his emblem of double ragged staff and bear."

"Yes, Your Grace," Kate replied, holding the dish higher for inspection, her arms beginning to ache.

Her Majesty waved the dish away, wrinkling her nose. Kate couldn't help but feel some small satisfaction. A lark pie covered in honey was her favorite, and there was usually little left after she finished serving.

Kate backed away from the queen and past Saintloe, near the door, who whispered, "When you are queen you will have your fill of lark pie; is that not so, Lady Katherine?"

Passing through the door, Kate frowned. "All the lark pie I wish I will have now!" she said, not bothering with a smile to take the sting out of her retort. There was too much inward amusement in that lady.

And why shouldn't she be angered? Must she always be reminded of her birth? If the queen followed her threat never to marry, half the court expected Kate would be named heir presumptive. Her grandmother was daughter to Henry VII, sister to Elizabeth's father, Henry VIII, who had placed Jane's and Kate's names next after Elizabeth in his will. Although the queen was not yet thirty years, plague, the sweat and small pocks carried off many younger. And Elizabeth had various faints and nervous headaches. Many feared that it was not likely the queen would make old bones. Kate determined to pray harder for the queen's long life, lest Katherine Grey be ensnared by men's dreams of power. Nothing could tempt her to sit on the throne that had destroyed her sister and father.

Later, in the antechamber, Saintloe spoke again in confiding tones. "My pardon, Lady Katherine, if I speak on too delicate a subject. Because of your youth, I wish to caution you for your protection. I remember well the tragic fate of your older sister, Lady Jane Grey—who wished to be queen. Wasn't she but sixteen when she went to the block?"

Kate made her voice as frosty as the wintry Whitehall gardens. "My lady, since you have reached the age of thirty and five, I will grant that your memory has faded. It is known by all that my sister never wanted the throne and died a martyr to her Protestant faith and my parents' aims."

"A pretty speech, my lady. I hope it will serve you when you need it."

"And why would the truth not serve? I do not wish to be queen and so have nothing to fear."

Saintloe looked even more calculating. "As Elizabeth learned when she was a princess, plots form around anyone with a claim to the throne. Whether they wish it or not, their name is attached to every scheme. It would be suicide for Her Majesty to name an heir, for her and for you. Do not wish it. You could never lie easy in your bed."

Kate lifted her chin higher, unable to keep a calm tone. "In that case, my lady, I have no worry. Never speak of the throne to me again." She walked to the table, stuck her forefinger into the lark pie and licked it thoroughly.

"Ah, well, you have the Tudor temper; perhaps that will serve you." Lady Saintloe, laughing softly, moved to take another dish to Her Majesty, leaving Kate still angry, but satisfied that she had allowed no disrespect from that she-cat who waited to pounce from around every corner.

Costumed as the god Mercury, with wings on his gilt boots and flakes of pure gold scattered in his small pointed beard and on the backs of his hands, Robert Dudley approached Kate at the masque. She was standing with the other white-satin-clad ladies of the bedchamber gathered near the throne where Elizabeth sat in sumptuous marigold silk, covered in rubies, her head haloed with a high golden ruff of at least sixty pleats. She tapped her foot to the music, obviously longing to dance. Dudley bowed and reached for Kate's hand as the opening chords of a lavolte announced the wildly popular dance, which was so difficult that Kate had practiced many afternoons with the dancing master. The queen wanted all her ladies to dance well. But not better than herself.

Kate shrank back. "My lord," she said, a bit breathless from a recent galliard, "I cannot accept. You lead out the queen in this dance."

"I seek easier company tonight," he replied softly. He stepped into the remaining space between them, coming very close.

"You seek to cause the queen envy and make me a part of it. The lavolte is always hers. I have no wish to—"

"Tonight the dance is yours, sweet Kate." He grinned, and she was close enough to see if humor filled his eyes. There was none. Not for the first time, she realized that what could be seen was nothing to compare with what couldn't. She pulled away, knowing she would not want to see Robert's emotions escape and involve her, as they surely would. And she could not bear to see his pain. It was too familiar. How could the queen, who loved him, hurt him so?

Torches flared to light the walls and the white plaster cherubs smiling from the ceiling of the great hall. Servants renewed spent candles until the bright, flickering lights caught in the folds of whirling silk and satin to flash out at every dancer's turn and leap. Jewels dazzled from wigs and pearls gleamed at throats turned pure cream in their reflection.

Kate wore a modest amethyst hanging at the curve of her breasts above a kirtle sewn with very small seed pearls, careful to outdo Her Majesty in no way. She would never jeopardize her place at this court, while, by showing her loyalty, she had a small chance of erasing the taint of usurper from her poor sister, Jane.

Dudley grasped her hand so hard she flinched. Everyone was watching, including Elizabeth. That was his game.

There was nothing for Kate to do. Perhaps it was enough that the queen had seen her refuse Dudley. Was hesitance ever enough for Elizabeth? It had to be. Kate repeated that thought, hoping to invest it with some truth, as Dudley, not to be denied in any scheme to reach Elizabeth's heart, gaily pulled her firmly forward.

The lutes, pipes and viol de gamba struck the quick notes of the lavolte, and Kate stepped onto the floor with Robert, turning to face him, frowning.

They moved once to either side, clapping loudly, their heads held proud. He placed one gilt-covered hand on her side and the other on her back. She put a hand on his near shoulder, poised for the difficult turn and spring into the air. She came down into two fast steps, not yet daring to glance toward the queen sitting on her throne. There was no need. Kate knew she would see through the queen's unconcern to jealous anger. Giving in to Dudley's scheme was a mistake. Next time, she'd fall to the floor in a faint, and all the vinegar cloths in the palace would not revive her.

Although breathing rapidly after successive leaps as the dance brought her and Dudley near the throne, Kate needed to be heard to rebuke Robert, hoping to steady her voice. "My lord, have I no friends on this earth? You need give the queen, my cousin, no more reason to be angry with me. My birth and all the talk of succession are quite enough."

He grinned and replied, intending to be heard as well: "If you were queen you would marry me, wouldn't you, Kate?"

She recoiled from him, because even his teasing manner held great danger. "I beg you, Robert, watch your tongue, especially when you mean not a word."

Not completely the fool, he lowered his voice. "Why should I not say what the whole court, even the queen's council, talks of—that you will succeed as queen?"

Kate caught at her breath, as if it were her last one. "Robert, we should never again dance together. It only reminds everyone, especially the queen, that your brother and my sister were beheaded by Queen Mary for taking the throne."

"And my father later. And myself in the Tower for years waiting daily for the headsman," Dudley replied, his compelling eyes staring hard from behind his mask, though they just as quickly softened. "Ah, Kate, these are new days. Bess is not so quick with the ax as was her brother, Edward, and sister, Mary."

"I would not have my neck put to that test."

Dudley threw back his head and laughed so long and loud that everyone stared.

"I've said nothing to so amuse you."

"But Bess doesn't know that."

"You are a fool and will have a fool's end. I will not allow you to take me down with you! Why won't anyone believe that I do not want the throne?"

Robert dismissed her words with a wave of his gilded hand. "Kate, fair Kate. Who can deny their birth, and who under heaven knows what fate has written in their stars?" He held her up high, delaying the next leap, so that no one could possibly ignore Dudley raising Lady Grey above every head. He slowly let her slide down his body, his mouth to her ear. "But, dear Kate, I do truly love her, you know, always have and always will, to my death . . . and beyond."

Kate was anxious and fuming. "You love her so much you make this spectacle!"

"Yes, and a hundred more if need be. I know what brings her running to me."

His eyes shone with what looked suspiciously like tears, and she could not berate him more. "Robert, I beg you, do not use me this way, or you lose a friend."

His voice caught in his throat, as if he could not catch an easy breath. "I will use Jesu himself to gain Elizabeth."

She could not help feeling sympathy. "I have heard desperate love never hides its face, not even behind a mask."

"Remember those words when it is your time to hide again, as you did from young Edward Seymour. I remember the near scandal."

"That was long ago. I love no one now. And no one loves me."

"Good!" he said loudly, his face close to hers, laughing again as if he'd heard a great jest.

The dance finished, Robert Dudley bowed, kissed her hand and led her to a group of ladies standing opposite the queen's maids of honor.

"Have you met Lady Jane Seymour, namesake of the late queen who bore a son for Henry when the Boleyn could not?" he asked, playing his dangerous game again as he stopped in front of a rather plain-faced young woman.

"Sweet Jesu, Robert! Again you fool with your head. It is forbidden to mention the name of the queen's mother. Elizabeth will not forgive that."

"Oh, but you're wrong, lovely Kate. I've known Bess as girl, princess and queen. She always forgives me. She would even forgive me"—he dropped his voice to a whisper—"murder."

Kate recoiled. Was this a confession that he had killed his wife? A warning? Though he denied doing the deed, he could have ordered it done for love of Elizabeth. Kate stepped back from him, since she doubted that she, or the queen, would ever know the truth. Feeling stifled, Kate pulled her mask off to give air to her face. Sometimes she felt as if she had always been in hiding. No one knew who she was in her heart. Only Edward had ever known, and she couldn't remember him without pain.

Robert smiled down at her, as secure as any man who practiced his seductive masculine art with such apparent ease and success. He murmured, "Thank you, my lady, for your care of my head," and then spoke for all to hear: "But now I would introduce the Lady Jane Seymour, recently come to court. The heir of one queen and the niece of another should have much in common."

Kate could have cheerfully throttled Dudley with his own wired ruff, but as usual he escaped before he was in serious danger. His timing was impeccable; she hoped it was always so, for he was a fascinating man. Who could deny it?

Jane sank low, acknowledging the introduction. "I've longed for this meeting, Lady Grey. Indeed, since I first heard of you from my brother."

Kate reached out to the limit of her strength, for dimly she had known that someday she would meet a Seymour at court. "And I to know you, Lady Seymour," Kate said, having learned this polite lying court language even before she was schooled in prayer.

"I would serve Her Majesty as you do," Jane said, her voice plaintive.

"There are no present vacancies among the queen's ladies, Lady Seymour."

Jane looked downcast. "That is what the Lady Saintloe tells me, but I would appreciate a tiny word from you in Her Majesty's ear. I do not expect to be a lady of the bedchamber; the presence chamber would do, or a place among the maids of honor who walk out with the queen in her private gardens of a morning. For one little word, you would have more than my gratitude, dear Katherine. And call me Jane, for I know we shall be great and good friends, since we would have been sisters, if my brother Edward had had his dearest wish. You remember him, of course."

Kate did not have to remember; his memory was always with her, a breathing thing.

"He was much in love with your miniature as a lad after you married Lord Pembroke. He wore it for years, even as he departed for Italy and the wars."

Kate's heart skipped under her shift. "Oh, surely not," she said, making her voice light, as if she had never thought of him since that day.

"Indeed so, Katherine, and I saw that he wears it still when he returned from the Italian wars."

Edward has returned!

Lady Jane prattled on, but Kate was slow to process her words.

"I do assure you, Lady Katherine, I have warned him that you are no longer a young maid, but grown in beauty celebrated by every man at court. I cautioned him that if you are named heir, as I hear you will be, princes and kings will court you."

"You flatter me, Lady Seymour." But before Kate could coldly turn away from any further such talk, there was a stir at the doors; a trumpet sounded, followed by drums that stopped the stately French pavanne in progress.

"My brother Edward, Earl of Hertford," Lady Jane said with a satisfied smile.

Kate turned her gaze to the splendidly dressed, tall young lord with blond curls falling from under his velvet cap. He was followed by a large entourage, crossing the marble floor in long strides to kneel before the queen.

"Is he much changed?" Jane asked, her eyes steady on Kate's face.

Kate did not answer. How could she? All her senses were at once engaged, holding back the memory of that last wrenching good-bye on her wedding day, yet missing nothing of the moment. The man she saw before her contained the shade of the boy she'd once known and lost, though he was now a man grown in all his parts, strong and strikingly fine-featured.

All the dancers parted as he approached the throne. As any noble newly come to court, he roused stir and murmur about the great hall, perhaps more so since he was the son of the beheaded Duke of Somerset. And there by the throne stood Robert Dudley, son of the Duke of Northumberland, who had engineered Somerset's execution. But sons could not bear grudges for past political affairs, or half the court would not speak to the other half.

As the nephew of Queen Jane Seymour, who'd replaced the queen's mother, he had the dancers' complete attention. How would the queen greet him?

"Did I not tell you, Lady Katherine?" Jane said, tugging Kate's sleeve insistently. "Is he not wonderful?"

"Yes." It was the only word Kate thought could possibly slip past the lump in her throat.

"My lord earl," the queen said from behind her fan, motioning him to rise. "Though you disrupt our masque, we welcome all our peers to our palace of Whitehall."

Kate, who knew the queen in her many moods, did not hear pleasure at this vain interruption, though curiosity was there.

"Your Grace," Edward Seymour replied, his hand on his heart, "it has always been my dearest wish to be near and to serve you. I came with all speed on my return from the Italian wars and count the trip nothing if I may kiss your hand and remain always near to you."

Looking well pleased at such expression of courtly love, the queen gave the earl her hand, on which he pressed a lingering kiss. Elizabeth lowered her fan. "We have heard of your bravery before the French in the northern Italian cities, my lord. England needs all her warriors."

A servant approached the earl and handed him a box. He opened it slowly. "Most gracious queen, I have brought a poor Christmas gift, and though it is past Twelfth Night, it holds no less a subject's love. I humbly beg you with all my heart to accept it."

Kate could see that the silver-embossed ebony box held the largest black pearl she'd ever seen. It was a rare teardrop shape, the size of a robin's egg, nested on white velvet. The gift was magnificent and costly, Kate thought, but not as valuable to the heart as the gift of a freed caged bird.

Many courtiers pressed closer to see, then turned to tell others what they'd glimpsed.

The queen bent forward, extremely pleased. "Hertford, we thank you and will grant your wish to be near to us and find you good occupation in our service . . . to begin at once with this pavanne."

Elizabeth glanced in triumph toward Dudley as she carelessly dropped his fan to the floor.

"Your Majesty, I am deeply honored."

Kate watched as Dudley lounged near the throne, observing the queen and her handsome new courtier, his face impassive in a vain effort to foil the gossips. It was a skill she'd learned early, too.

All the court stood to one side as the Earl of Hertford led the queen in the slow processional, lightly touching her fingers with his, showing nothing if not grace and a well-turned leg, both of which Kate could see Edward also now had in great measure. This was the man full-grown whom her father had turned away as a stripling to give her to Pembroke, who had been no man at all.

Kate did not want to relive those days. It had taken her years of painful nights to forget Edward, an effort that had never been fully successful, since he always returned in her dreams.

From Elizabeth's delighted expression, the queen had taken good account of the earl, too, for she loved dancing and handsome men in equal measure, as did the masked ladies round the room, each closely watching him for any casual glance in their direction. Indeed, as Kate did, despite every desire not to do so.

"My lady Katherine," Jane said, "the ladies think him handsome, do they not? And he is the best brother. You must meet Edward at once. Surely he will want you for a partner next, for you are prettiest of all and dance quite as well as the queen." Jane leaned closer and whispered from behind her fan, "And I know that Edward has never forgotten that you were almost betrothed to him."

Kate's reply was heavier than she meant it to be, weighed down with memory. "Lady Jane, my father the duke promised me to Lord Pembroke, and the dowry was settled before your brother asked for me. We were very young and thought we could overcome all obstacles." God's bones! She must not be a pawn both to old memories and to the queen's jealous nature this night. But Kate couldn't make her feet follow that thought to the safety of the cluster of ladies of the bedchamber. Instead, her eyes followed Edward's every practiced move on the dance floor, her face like any mooning milkmaid's gaze before a handsome man. Dudley had a rival, indeed, and not just for the queen, but for many of his conquered court ladies, judging from the clear invitations cast in Hertford's direction. Kate tried hard to show better restraint and no concern as the dance ended and Edward approached as she had feared . . . and hoped.

Though the height was there, gone were the rounded features of the boy of sixteen. He was now almost too fine-featured for a man, though he had a short, curling light beard with flecks of youthful blond threading through it, and a horseman's sturdy body beneath, wide shoulders enhanced by a tight quilted satin doublet, and long legs showing their strength under striped hose. He bowed over her hand and his warm lips imprinted on her skin, rousing remembrance, while his soft mustache prickled in a most pleasant way.

For something to say, she said the usual: "Why have we not seen you at court before, my lord?"

"My lady, I waited until I might claim what I once wanted for my own."

She was trapped in his gaze and lowered hers to escape. Jesu! Another threat? Had he any idea how dangerous such talk was, coming from the nephew of Henry VIII's third queen to the next in line for the throne? More dangerous now than when he defied only her father. His brash answer needed a clear response. Before she could gather one, he frowned and looked to his sister.

"Fie and for shame, sister," he rebuked Jane. "You wrote that the lady Katherine had most pleasant eyes, and here I see two priceless jewels. You said her face was very pretty, and now I find her not as you wrote, but grown in beauty, with curving cheeks and delicate pointed chin." He bowed to Jane to remove any sense of reproof. "I think that it is her very heart she wears for her face."

Without asking, Edward clasped Kate's hand, and she realized her rapt attention and silence had invited this familiarity. She must reverse it.

She retrieved her hand. "Pardon, my lord, but I am taken with an aching head and will withdraw."

"A sudden aching head is the worst misery for a lady." He bowed, as she saw a smile pull his mouth awry. "I am obliged to escort you to your rooms."

Kate felt her heart being squeezed and realized she was holding her breath. "My lord earl, the queen would not allow it."

He smiled easily. "Then it would seem that, aching head or no, we must dance or give everyone cause for gossip. I will have great care of you, I promise."

She felt swept from shore into a swift stream tumbling toward a wild, rolling ocean as he led her into the madly popular gavotte recently come from France. The dancing master had only just begun to teach it, so many courtiers left the floor to watch. Kate and Edward formed into a small circle with two other couples, skipping forward and backward, exchanging kisses as they came together. Kate turned her face just in time to miss Edward's kiss, but at the next circling he caught the corner of her lips with his.

Kate felt warmth seep from under her bodice and mount to her face. "My lord, you have been long from court in warmer climes and must learn to have a care"—she shook her head, stepping about the circle until they came together again—"or you will ruin us both."

He grinned, showing good teeth against a face tanned from Italian summers. "Am I mistaken, or do they not call this the kissing dance?"

"Yes, my lord, but you—"

He looked down at her, serious now. "I remember, my lady, when kissing was not an annoyance to you. But you are older now and perhaps you are tired of kissing."

"You are mistaken, my lord Hertford," she said, not trying to conceal her anger.

He pursed his lips and made a soft kissing sound.

Were all men like Dudley, reckless and heedless of this queen, who would have every man adore her alone? He needed a stronger warning.

"My lord Hertford, you must have a care for the queen's—"

"You used to call me Ned and come flying to me, though your father forbade it."

Kate turned her eyes from his face so that she could speak hard words. "Nine years have passed, my lord earl, and you must forget childish imprudence, as I have."

"Have you? Well, lady, I have not. I see only you, have seen only you all these years."

His voice, so much deeper than she remembered, though as caressing, frightened her. How many dangers could she face down in one day? It seemed the world, past and present, was arrayed against her.

"My lady Katherine, what I need in great measure is your instruction. Of all the queen's ladies, you are the one I most longed to see . . . again. Reports that you were yet a maid without a husband—and of your loyalty to the queen, your strong godly faith and growing beauty—have reached Hertfordshire and well beyond." His voice was low, for her alone, his eyes steady on her face as if he would memorize its every change. "And I am in no way disappointed, when I feared I might be after such a time. We were cheated of love once, but never again, I vow it, Kate."

"My lord," Kate replied, "you have too many desires for this palace . . . and one too many memories. We were never betrothed, so do not claim it."

"Then do you count love as nothing? If so, meet me in the garden by the sundial at midnight, where my memory can be made right—and you can tutor me in proper thinking and court ritual."

"Edward, you seem to have grown into a natural talent for this court. But you are in every way as bold as the boy you were when you ignored my betrothal."

"And did you not ignore it, too?"

Her face flamed with embarrassment and confusion, though she kept longing at bay. "Lords may conduct themselves as you do in Italy and Hertfordshire, but not in Elizabeth's court. The queen watches me with a motherly eye fiercer than my father's."

"Then I must bring Italy and Hertfordshire to Whitehall at once."

He was laughing at her as she circled again, seeing they were left alone on the dance floor, the entire court staring at them. "Even if I thought it wise, my lord, which I do not, I have no wish to meet you later—"

"Do you not?"

He bent and put his lips near without touching hers, pretending to a great distress. "Then some poor gardener will find a frozen statue in the morning, looking the very portrait of me."

She pressed her lips hard to keep from smiling or agreeing. She was not sure which, then or later. The dance ended and he led her to his sister. Bowing, he strode away, looking back over his shoulder at Kate, probably to see if her gaze followed him. *Damn the devil!* she thought, using one of the queen's favorite curses. Of course she was looking at him.

But she would *not* meet him. It would be folly. Madness! She would not go through that heartache again. Anything more than casual acquaintance was impossible and, she suspected, more dangerous than it ever had been all those long years ago.

Kate, as mistress of the robes, carried the queen's gown, stomacher, stiff lace ruff, silk stockings and satin-covered cork shoes to the wardrobe chamber. She then placed Hertford's black pearl into its velvet cushion and then into the queen's large jewel box, with her brooches, necklaces and a diamond thumb ring. She locked the box with the key about her neck until she could return all to the guarded jewel room on the morrow. When she stepped back to the bedchamber, the room had been freshly sprinkled with rose petals to cover any creeping odors of a royal residence housing more than a thousand people and not enough jakes and closestools. Her Majesty had been bathed from a bowl of fresh rose water and had donned her embroidered fine linen night shift.

The tall case clock struck midnight, and Kate waited to be dismissed to her room. There were only prayers to do and then . . . No, she would not go to the Earl of Hertford. She knew folly when she met it. Such heartache could not be endured twice in one life. And surely a yeoman guard would see her and report to the queen. Unless he had a sufficient bribe.

Prayers. They were next. All the ladies would kneel at the queen's bedside, while Her Majesty leaned against her pillows and led them from her own prayer book. Then Kate would be free to go. To her chamber. Not to the garden.

Yet, the queen did not prepare for prayer. She announced to her ladies' surprised faces, "You are dismissed. I will need you no more this night."

Her ladies sank low and, each lighting her way with a candle, moved toward the outer chamber.

"Lady Katherine will remain. You have urgent need of prayer this night."

Kate's hand closed on her candle, almost snapping it in two. She bowed her head and waited until the door was firmly shut. She could imagine the pleasure on Lady Saintloe's face at the queen's fuming tone.

Elizabeth began to pace about, her slippered feet stomping the floor, releasing a cloud of scent from scattered herbs.

Finally, she whirled to face Kate, tiny bits of lavender and rose petal clinging to the lace bordering the queen's shift. Tall for a woman, she took a wide stance, one hand on her hip, looking much like her father in the Holbein picture. "Am I betrayed by my own?

Have I not shown you great favor, cousin?" The queen assumed the harsh tone that had made the Spanish ambassador cower.

Kate kept her eyes modestly lowered. "Yes, Your Majesty, and I have tried to serve you well. In what duty have I grieved you?"

"Humble words, indeed, for a lady of the blood royal who flaunts herself before every man at the masque. You will create a scandal to send even the French court into sniggering at my realm."

"Your Majesty—"

"Do you dare deny my eyes?"

"No, Majesty. But I would correct my fault with your instruction." A queen was never wrong. Kate must endure in silence, whatever came, as she always had.

The queen raised her hand as if to strike, her face flushed with anger.

Kate steeled herself for the blow. She was highborn, but still a servant to be chastised as a mistress thought best. She tried to bring all the submission in her belly to her face.

Slowly, Elizabeth lowered her hand, looking wounded. "Have I not been to you as a mother to a daughter . . . raised you high from your family's disgrace . . . shown you the favor of great appointment among my ladies?"

Kate did not say, *And satisfied your need to keep an eye on me*, though it was true. Instead, she said, "Yes, Your Grace, a blessing for which I meekly thank my God each day."

The queen's face slowly resumed its normal pale shade, her beautiful long, tapered fingers pressed against her heart. "I do remember the gossip about you and Hertford before you were given to Pembroke, and I have heard Hertford has since resisted every suitable offer. Do not wish to marry, Kate. Marriage is death, and well I know it. Live and die a virgin, as I will do."

Kate didn't dare look up, but bit her tongue for suspecting that *virgin* had broad meaning for this queen. There was Dudley, of course, and before him Lord Admiral Thomas Seymour, who was said to have romped in fourteen-year-old Elizabeth's bed and even cut her gown from her in raucous sport. Scandal said she was pregnant by him when he went to the Tower block, but she proved them wrong in that, at least.

"Husbands," Elizabeth continued, her voice grating on the word, "are master of your body and all. You can have no thought of your own, and in too short a time they love another and then another. What if you could give an earl no sons? Think you he would not rid himself of such an impediment to his hereditary title?"

It was plain the queen was thinking of her father and her own early years. How could she not have learned those lessons well? It was time for the words that Elizabeth wanted. "Majesty, I am past twenty these three years and soon to be counted an old maid. But more than age, my affection and admiration for you allow me to hold no desire to leave you for marriage . . . or for the throne. I vow that I wish only to serve you for all my days."

Elizabeth's eyes narrowed. "You would make such a vow before God?"

Kate's stomach twisted and she wished herself in any other place but where she was. An oath before God could not be broken without putting her immortal soul in grave danger. She could languish in purgatory for eternity, and pleading with all the old saints together could not pray her out.

But there was no choice. Elizabeth was Elizabeth and not to be thwarted. "Yes, I would make such a vow, cousin."

"Kneel with me, Kate."

Kate knelt beside the queen at her bedside and spoke aloud: "I swear before God almighty, His crucified son and His holy Church, to serve Elizabeth, queen of England, for all her life, faithful and true."

The queen rose, pointing to a trundle at the foot of her great bed. "Stay tonight, Lady Grey. It would please me to have you near if I require a little wine for sleep."

"I am grateful for the opportunity to please Your Majesty."

Elizabeth yawned. "There will be more, many more such opportunities."

Kate took herself to her bed. She did not want to sleep. If she did, she would dream of being a girl again, desperately in love, frantic to escape her fate, the fate of so many women of ambitious families, marriage to an older man who frightened her and who did not love her beyond her dower lands. But sleeping or waking, she could not escape the memory of Edward Seymour and of their hurried, tremulous, stolen kisses, their young bodies pressed urgently together. Once more she was taken back to the night she was to stand before the altar to be married to Pembroke with Guilford Dudley and her sister, Jane, in a double wedding.

Edward, taking a terrible risk, had sought her in the great stone hall and pulled her behind a huge pillar, away from the torchlight and her own wedding revels. "Sweetheart, I have a carriage waiting at the Holbein Gate to take us to a ship bound for France. The king is ill to death and the government will surely change to Queen Mary unless the king chooses to make a Protestant heir . . . your sister, Jane, who marries Guilford Dudley tonight. That could put your family in great danger. Escape such intrigue with me. We can return later and all will be forgiven us."

She clutched his arms, longing for them to enfold her, to hold her safe.

He pulled her roughly to him and she felt him shaking against her, whether from fear or passion she could not know. She knew only to cling to her only hope for happiness.

"Come with me now, Kate, lovely Kate . . . or I die. I swear it."

He kissed her until she leaned against the rough stone pillar, limp with passion and fear. "Ned, my father would follow us. You know that our rank makes us pawns." He must know that it was the joining of titles and lands that determined a suitable marriage.

He bent to kiss her breast swelling above her gown. Struggling for breath, she choked out the words, "Ned . . . Ned, we have no will of our own against our families' wishes. That is the way it is and has always been." But she clung to him, fearing to let him go.

He kissed her wildly, her tears falling on his lips.

"They will follow and capture us. Ned . . . they will take you to the Tower and throw me to Pembroke to do as he will."

His voice came to her in a ragged whisper. "If he beats you, I will kill him!" He shook, his mouth twisted in misery. "Kate, what life *will* you have if we are not together? What life will I have?"

He had crushed her against him again so that she could not speak. She fought to keep her sobs from turning to wails.

Torches suddenly flared in their faces. Her father and mother glared at them.

The Duke of Somerset wrenched Edward away and her mother clawed at Katherine. "You young Seymour whelp!" her father yelled. "If you were a man grown, I'd challenge you to the death."

Guards ran up and forced Edward down the hall, his arms twisted behind him.

Kate heard his choked voice grow fainter. "I'll come back for you . . . my love!"

And there the memory always ended. She was back in her cage.

Tonight, a man grown, he had come back, but not to the girl. She was a woman now and no longer thought that love would always win. A tear ran down her cheek to the small bolster on the trundle at the foot of Elizabeth's bed, the last of the tears she would shed for the past, she swore.

But she'd sworn that before.

Her eyes were becoming heavy and closing when she felt the warmth of a presence and looked up to see the queen in her white night shift bent over her, a guttering candle in her hand.

"It is wounding to give up the man you love. I know it well," Elizabeth whispered, her voice catching on the last word. "But duty for a queen must come first." She stood straighter, taking a deep breath. "The throne of England demands everything of a woman. I've sacrificed my beloved Robin."

Kate needed to understand such sacrifice, because it was demanded of her, too. "Why, Majesty?" she asked.

"To redeem him . . . and my mother, Anne Boleyn. They called her the Great Whore and a witch and took her young head. They call my Robin a murderer, saying he killed his wife to marry me. Whether it's true or not, I must deny my love for him, for what would confirm their opinion more? But I will stay on my throne and rule this realm, make it greater than the country my father left to me. No foreign prince will ever share my throne." She drew herself to her full height, the candlelight flickering across her pale face and slender shoulders. "I am a prince of England; my people are flesh of my flesh, blood of my blood. They will be husband and children to me, and it will be enough. It *will* be enough."

Kate rose up on an elbow. No Englishman would believe for a moment that a woman could rule a lifetime without a man. "I understand, Majesty," she said, although she did not understand, nor ever would.

"Old loves, new loves," Elizabeth murmured, "both can be pleasing, even more than pleasing, but they are not necessary."

Elizabeth receded with her candle into her cavernous and empty bed.

Kate closed her eyes to make her own dark night. Would she dream? Of Ned? She had sought to put away hope long ago; now was no time to allow it back into her heart. She must try to be as resolute as the queen. It was her only protection.

Still, the memory of young lovers intruded. In all these years, no one, not even her family, had cared a whit whether she lived or died unless she served their purpose.

But Edward Seymour had remembered her with love and never sought to use her. And he had kept his promise to come back . . . all these years later. She hugged that thought until finally she slept.

CHAPTER TWO

"Let this stand you in good stead . . .
never tempt too far a prince's patience."
—Elizabeth Regina

Candlemas
February 2, 1562

*H*er skirts gathered up for swifter passage, Katherine hurried from the jewel room down the long stone passage that led to the presence chamber. She was tired and it was not quite midday. The queen rose early and her ladies earlier.

Kate had been on an errand to return the golden crown worn by the queen at her morning audience with the Scots emissary from his queen, Mary. When the clock struck the eleventh hour, Kate must be in her place to serve Elizabeth her dinner meal. Since the night of her oath, Kate had achieved a perfection of service to please even this demanding queen. And she could not fail now, especially while wearing a valuable silver brooch containing the queen's miniature . . . a recent gift to mark her special favor. The court was filled with rumors of Lady Katherine Grey being named heir, while she denied and denied, disbelieved by all.

Kate pushed hard on her stomacher, reminded by a rumbling emptiness that she had not broken her fast with the least bread and ale this entire morning.

Ahead, two pikemen threw open the doors to the daylit presence chamber. She saw workmen everywhere on ladders removing the last reminders of Christmas and mounting the first signs of spring. Deep violet pansies, the queen's most loved flower, forced open by the royal gardeners, were everywhere in pots, woven into vines and strewn about the dais already being arranged for tonight's banquet to honor the Scots queen Mary's ambassador. Elizabeth intended to impress him with her brilliant court, a sure contrast to Mary's in the bleak north.

As Kate neared the entrance, the Earl of Hertford appeared around the doors and lolled against the wall, one outthrust elegant leg barring her way. The guards did not blink.

Startled, Kate suppressed any pleasure that might show, forcing herself to look fully into Edward's face, something she'd tried hard to avoid since the masque, though of late avoiding him had become more difficult and at this moment impossible.

He bowed, smiling with his easy grace, and stepped into her path, his hand over his heart.

Now she was well stopped and much too close to him. She sank down in a hasty curtsy, not low enough for his rank and much too fast to be well-done. She thought to step around him, but that would be unpardonably rude. *God's bones!*

"Good morrow, my lady Grey."

"A good morrow to you, my lord earl," she said, as formal as she could manage, "but I must beg your leave to quickly pass. The queen needs my service for the dinner meal and the banquet tonight." She lifted her head and kept his gaze. Any weakness of spirit was an invitation to bold men. It allowed them to serve up their protection without being asked. No woman could remain a virgin at the virgin queen's court for long without learning well the ways of forward young lords, especially ones who thought to claim a right they might once have had, but now had no more. *No more.*

Though Elizabeth pronounced her court the most virtuous in all Christendom, Kate knew the queen was self-deceived. Under a righteous exterior, love of every hue and stripe roiled. *Remember your oath to the queen*, she cautioned herself severely, then commanded: *What you once felt is gone*. She realized that her lips moved as with a private prayer. The more she thought it, the more it would become true.

Edward dipped his head to follow her gaze, while she tried to slide from under his intense watch. "I am pleased that you are so eager at your duties, my lady. It recommends the woman as innocent tenderness recommended the girl." His face asked her a thousand questions. "Yet, my lady, is duty a cause to be brusque with a longtime . . . friend?" He bent closer. "What have I done to so deeply offend? It is rather I who could find offense when denied as boy and man . . . when I have so little fault and so many obvious virtues." He smiled at his self-flattering, the smile growing.

It was a change from the serious, desperate boy he had once been when they stole moments together in dark corners or an empty chapel, or rounded a lonely staircase to suddenly find each other and desperately embrace. Now his was a light humor she usually admired. All the more reason, she knew, to be on her guard. She clenched her small hands into harmless fists.

"Or, my lady," he continued, serious now, "is it my admiration and the truth of my words that cause offense? Would you have me lie and deny my delight in the face and form that I fought for years in Italy to forget? And could not forget." He bent closer and murmured, "Deny what my eyes witness and my heart yet feels?"

Kate had heard such courtly words before, but none she'd wanted to believe as she wanted to believe Edward Seymour this minute. She made her voice blunt to stop him . . . and herself. "You take much for granted, my lord. I doubt not that you've had great success in warmer climes and even in Hertfordshire with such designed poses, but not in this court . . . and not with me." Edward's face looked so instantly and completely dejected that she was ashamed of herself and offered a slight smile. "When I did not come to the garden, I see that you did not freeze, Edward."

He brightened at her friendlier offering. "Oh, but, Kate, your eyes cannot truly see me as I was on that night, hoarfrost covering my hair—weighing down my very eyelashes. I must have paced a thousand leagues to keep warm, and I would have walked one thousand more for the sight of you coming into the garden—and along the hedgerow where I always see you in my dreams."

Her breath quickened at that deliberate remembrance. "A long way to walk, Edward, even for a very forward lord. I am happy you seem none the worse for your journey." She made a desperate move to pass, but he stepped in her way, easily refusing her passage. She turned to his other side and he sidestepped again with the agility of the practiced swordsman he must now be, a pleasant smile on his face. A man well grown, he did not lose composure for long.

"I still think it worth the trip, Kate, though you give me no reason why I should," he said, adding, "I remember when you called me Ned, when you whispered it at every passing."

"Ned," she said, surprised to hear her voice say that name again. *Jesu Christo!* She bit her tongue to keep from saying the deliberately forgotten name again, pulled along by a strong current of memory she had to fight. She backed away from him.

How had they so easily fallen into the use of Christian names as if nine empty years had not passed? She stepped resolutely forward, hating to look the fearful child. She allowed herself to glance into his eyes and found them teasing, but convincing, despite their sparkle.

She had known much flattery and many attempts to seduce in Elizabeth's court, but none like this. Was he playing a young man's game to brag on later? Did he wish to even an old score, as in a game of tennis? She could not believe their youthful affection remained with him as it did with her. Men were quick to forget, finding love again with another woman. Yet, if true affection lingered, she must have greater care than she ever had. But while she wanted to be resolute, as her vow to Elizabeth demanded, her body leaned forward, drawn by something remembered.

He saw her move and yet did the opposite of what she might have allowed, stepping aside with a formal hand flourish. "Take pains when you pass under the queen's much loved pansies in the presence chamber," he whispered. "The country folk in Hertford-shire do say the juice of pansies is a love potion. I had no care and you see the result, a man before you quite overcome with unchanged devotion."

Kate had to laugh, though she tried to cover it quickly. Had he clung to his boyish dream, when she had wanted to firmly set her own aside, or was he become a most accomplished rascal? She dared not imagine his was a living passion. Dared not! Her heart could not sustain another assault.

He grinned. "Kate, you are most beautiful when amused. I will seek to amuse you at every meeting."

Her voice soft, but as firm as she could make it, she replied, "There can be no future meetings, Ned."

"This court is not so large that we cannot meet by happenstance. I could sit near you in the great hall for supper."

"I rarely dine there."

"Then I could follow you into the maze when you are lost."

"I'm never lost . . . or alone."

"How fortunate you are, my lady, for I am always lost near a hedge and always alone there."

"The queen would not allow us . . . a friendship."

"Her Majesty has preceded you in that warning, sweetheart, when I petitioned her to court you." He took her arm, not hurtfully, but firmly. "Though she be the greatest queen in all the world, I think she cannot stop love in this court, nor clutch it all to herself."

Kate put a finger of her free hand to his mouth and hastily with-drew it as if burned. "Say no more, for such words are treason to her." For the first time, she noticed the white line of a scar that trav-eled down his cheek to disappear under his beard. Without thinking, she traced it with her finger.

Ned stepped nearer and put his face almost to hers. "It was this wound that kept me away in Italy so long."

She was drawn into his sparkling light brown eyes with golden lights, his beard smelling of the oil of Spice Islands sandalwood trees, and the salt ocean between. Underlying that fragrance, she breathed in the scent of wine on his breath, and horse on his clothes. *Beware, foolish maid*, Elizabeth's voice echoed inside her. *You are led to disaster by a nose.*

"Kate, I mean to gain the queen's permission to court you. Our families, those who are left," he added ruefully, "could have no possible objection, for we are well matched in rank and age. As we always have been."

"My lord, there was no agreement between our families, and as a dutiful daughter, almost fourteen, I married as my father commanded." She'd been no dutiful daughter, but frightened and beaten for days before she agreed to stand at the altar with Pembroke. Kate tried to lean away from Ned, but she was held in place by his warm hand on her back and his next words.

"And now both our fathers have lost their heads for their ambition, and though your mother, Lady Frances, lives she seldom sees you. We have little family left . . . but we can have each other." Pain showed briefly on his face; still his voice became more gentle. "Hear me, Kate. Before God and as I stand here, I intend to win you, to have you lawfully in my bed. I will take you to Eltham, my manor in the green countryside, and make you my wife."

Surely this was enough to capture a woman's heart, any woman but one of the blood royal. "Know this, Ned. If you are ambitious for the throne, you will not reach it through me. I do not want to be heir and the queen will never name one. She says naming an heir is like choosing her own winding sheet."

His eyes flared with anger. "Do not judge me by other men. Do you think ambition is why I want you? Do you think that is the reason I came to court when I have not come before? I waited until I was assured Elizabeth planned no marriage for you . . . that you were at last free. God knows I have never been."

Kate laughed almost feverishly. Summoning more strength than she'd thus far shown, she broke away. "Do not, for pity's sake, go to the queen again on such a matter. You are a man and cannot understand Elizabeth's mind."

"I know mine. And I know yours."

"Again, you take much on yourself, my lord. I have vowed to stay in the queen's service for my life long, to live and die a virgin in Her Majesty's image. Don't you see? Only then can I survive." Kate slipped from his hold and swept past him into the presence chamber.

"Have a care for the pansy juice," he called softly after her.

In the flame-lit banqueting hall a troop of dwarfs, including Thomasina, one of the queen's fools, was dancing a lively morris dance. They wore oversize wooden clogs and stomped to drum and fife with first fluttering handkerchiefs and then pounding sticks, finally tumbling into a merry heap, to the queen's great entertainment.

Kate clustered with the other ladies of the bedchamber to attend the queen behind the high table. Elizabeth sat on her throne in the middle, the Earl Marshall, Duke of Norfolk, and Howard family kin to the queen on one side and the dour Earl of Lethington, the Scots emissary from Queen Mary, to her right. Edward was far down the lower table, staring at her. She shook her head in slight warning and turned her gaze away before Elizabeth, who seemed to have eyes in the back of her head, could notice their exchange.

When the Royal Chapel boys' choir began to sing in their sweet treble voices, the queen, who usually gave complete attention to music, turned to the Earl of Lethington, raised her wineglass and said in a voice loud enough for many to hear, "My lord, we wish you to convey our best wishes to your mistress for her very good health and to propose a meeting between us. The business of queens should be done by queens. There is no better understanding in the world than would be between our cousin and ourself. Any problems would be quickly resolved in goodwill and like minds." The queen bent her head, heavy with wig, crown and jewels, to better hear his answer.

The Scots earl nodded graciously. "I will convey your generous proposal to Her Majesty immediately upon my return. May I also say that Your Grace is ready to name Scotland's Queen Mary and the lawful sons of her body as your rightful heirs?"

The hall fell into total silence, cups and knives in midair.

"My lord, we always consult with our council and Parliament about the question of succession."

Kate could not help admiring the queen's accomplished sidestep. Elizabeth could not be trapped by any ambassador.

The queen continued after a satisfied moment. "My lord, we confess surprise that our cousin Mary must have a declaration from us, when she has already declared herself to be queen of England and quartered my arms with her own."

Lethington shifted uneasily, but the queen wasn't finished.

"Does your queen not know that my father named Lady Katherine Grey in his will to follow me?" Elizabeth waved her hand over her shoulder in Kate's general direction.

Lethington found his ambassador's voice. "But, surely, Your Grace, that lady's claim is invalid because of her father's treason."

Holding her body rigid, Kate controlled her shock at hearing her father once again accused, since he had long ago paid the ultimate price for placing Jane on the throne. Was he never to be forgiven? Though anger surged through her, she did not allow it to reach her face. Realizing that she was holding her breath and might well faint, she slowly began to breathe deeply. Surely Elizabeth spoke the lies of diplomacy when she reminded the Scot of her father's will. Later, before bed tonight, the queen might explain . . . but Kate knew that was unlikely. Elizabeth never saw the need to explain her actions. Kate looked out to the lower table at Edward. He understood what she was feeling: trapped again. She could see it on his face.

Elizabeth tapped Lethington's sleeve. "My lord, they tell me your queen is tall for a woman."

"That is so, Majesty."

"Taller than me?"

"Yes, Your Grace."

The queen struck the table for emphasis. "Then she is *too* tall."

Many in the hall hid their amusement. Elizabeth was jealous of the Scots queen, a celebrated beauty.

Before the ambassador could respond, Robert Dudley stood at his seat at the table immediately below and bowed to the queen, a wide grin of approval on his face.

"Master carver," the queen called for a servant from her flesh kitchen.

The servant approached, stood over a meat course and, removing artfully placed feathers, expertly laid a slice of peacock on Her Majesty's gold plate.

Elizabeth speared it with her knife and, half standing in her turn, she reached far and dropped it on Dudley's plate. Dudley grasped her wrist and kissed the inside of it, though the knife was at his throat.

It was a confident lover's move and brought audible gasps from around the table and a frown from Lethington.

Dudley's head remained close, almost touching Elizabeth's, and indeed the small space between them was heavy with a palpable yearning.

Astounded by an act that both ignored an ambassador and rewarded a favorite of lesser rank in such a way, Kate watched Robert retake his seat, look well pleased, bite off a large chunk of pheasant and chew with obvious enjoyment. His pleasure wasn't to last long, for the queen, laughing, almost immediately cut another slice with her own hand, motioned to the server and sent the generous piece down the table to the Earl of Hertford, who picked it up, kissed it, ate, and licked his fingers one after another.

Kate was beyond surprise now. Aware that half the room was watching the queen and the other half watching her, or trying not to, she allowed nothing to reach her face. She marveled that men continued to encourage the queen's vanity, which needed not the slightest support. Though Her Majesty ruled as a king, she must be the queen of hearts to every man at court. Such behavior by any of her ladies would mean a berating if not a beating. Though she knew that the queen used her treatment of handsome courtiers to impress Lethington and ultimately the beautiful Queen Mary, she also knew the story would be repeated in such a way as to bring Elizabeth's virtue into question. Kate dug her nails into her hands, feeling pain through her gloves. She was not jealous of the queen's attention to Edward. She truly thought only of her country. She forced her fingers to relax.

Elizabeth had been under Kate's close attendance for all these three years in her service. She had seen Her Majesty in every one of her moods. This flirtatious mood was the one she liked least and saw often. It dared too much even for a queen.

"My lord," Elizabeth said, turning once again to the Scots emissary, "I would have you try this sweet comfit from my confectionery, so that you will return to your mistress with well-sweetened words."

Lord Lethington, looking a little sour at the queen's jest, was presented with a sugar plate full of colorful marzipan fruit sparkling with gilt. It brought *ah*s from the crowd, but Lethington took only a bite and fastened his eyes on jugglers who were tossing large curving knives, their blades catching the torchlight.

The feasting and mummery lasted until midnight. When allowed to sit, Kate ate little, talked less and longed for her bed and sleep, if there was any to be had this night. What did the queen's attention to Ned mean beyond an effort to bring Dudley to heel? Surely, Elizabeth did not mean to name Kate as heir. That talk was mere diplomatic evasion. She murmured a prayer and crossed her fingers to ward off the devil.

Later, walking in processional behind the queen to her chambers, drums beating, trumpets blaring, Kate tried to push away a growing recognition: Edward was still the only soul in this world who might offer her real caring, comfort for herself alone. He had declared himself free of royal ambition. Could she believe him, especially after the queen had all but named her? As she hoped for it, she knew herself a fool. Still, she warred with her need to trust that one man alive on this earth truly cared for her. Was that so wrong?

Waiting in her room was an invitation to sup next evening with Lady Jane Seymour. "Who brought this, Sybil?" she questioned her old nurse.

"A servant wearing the Earl of Hertford's livery, my love," she answered, holding out a warm posset. "Is there something you need to tell me?"

"Nay, Nurse." The risk of a meeting with Ned, even with his sister attending, was too great. Kate went to her writing table, wrote a quick excuse, citing duty, on a sheet of foolscap, folded and sealed it with hot wax and pressed the wax with her signet ring.

Sybil approached. "Take this to my lady Seymour," Kate said.

"Please, my lady, tomorrow morning. It is not safe for a woman abroad in the palace at this hour. I could see something that I should not around any corner and be punished for it. Even be poisoned," she said, her eyes wide.

Sybil was obviously in earnest.

"Quiet yourself, Sybil. On the morrow, then, and mind you, early, please." She drank her spiced milk, was bathed, dressed in a night shift and tucked into bed as Sybil had always done. It was the only soothing ritual of a long day. Kate lay quiet in her bed until anonymous sleep claimed her.

❧

The next evening Elizabeth met with a high member of her council, the Lord Secretary, William Cecil, and Lethington in her privy chamber. Kate heard everything from the queen's linen closet.

The queen had clearly regretted her hasty words of the night before, especially when the Scots lord hinted that Queen Mary, with France's help, could easily send an army over the northern border and take the English throne by force, since the northern lords were always restive, and resented a woman on the throne.

Since Elizabeth had inherited a bankrupt kingdom, she tried to appease the ambassador with hints of favor toward his queen, gestures of endearment and jewels, though not her best ones. At almost any cost, Her Majesty must avoid war and the drain on her treasury, even to hinting that Kate could be sent to the Tower to appease the Scots.

Kate had groaned inwardly all day to think that the court would have their eyes on her as heir, approaching her for favorable mention in the queen's ear—until this minute. She knew that when the news of her sudden abandonment by the queen reached the court, they would no longer know her. She was a pawn being moved about the chessboard at whim.

Dismissed to her room by Mistress Ashley, Kate escaped to her chamber to find a servant in Ned's livery waiting there to escort her to Jane Seymour's apartment. Almost without clearly thinking, Kate followed him. At that moment, she did not care if the queen frowned at her association with Edward Seymour's sister. Elizabeth, the queen of all deception, had used her in a game to hold off the Scots. The queen commanded everything of her. It was the right of a sovereign, but it meant that Kate could believe nothing, always being on the edge of Elizabeth's caprice.

But she approached Jane's rooms with some unrest. It was one thing to be silently angry with a sovereign, quite another to defy her.

As Kate had expected and, had to admit, silently hoped, Edward rose when she was ushered inside. As she had not expected, Robert Dudley rose as well.

Ah, ambitious Robin. He had not heard that she could as easily go to the Tower as to the throne.

Lady Jane came forward, her arms open in welcome. "Dear sister Kate—may I call you sister?—I am so happy to see you with a free hour or two. I had thought to have a quiet supper of women's talk."

Edward bowed over her hand and pressed his lips before Robert could reach her. "Kate, do not blame Jane for my presence. I could not allow two lovely ladies to dine alone without protection."

"From whom, my lord?" Kate smiled politely at his compliment.

Robert laughed. "Probably from me, sister-in-law," he said slyly, invoking his family privilege and kissing her on the cheek.

She laughed as if she thought Robert joked, though she knew he probably did not. He was a man who allowed no opportunity for improvement to pass him by. She could not hate him for wanting power. It was as natural for him as it was unnatural for her.

She was seated across from Ned, the only man in this Tudor court, if she could believe him, who did not seek advancement through her. She wanted to believe him.

Their supper was served on a richly carpeted trestle table. A salad of boiled capers with vinegar came first; then in quick succession a beef pie, porpoise for the fish course, woodcock for a game pie and a sweet fruit tart were served, with Jane apologizing for the scant meal from the palace kitchen, which could not compare with Kate's usual fare from the queen's private kitchens.

Kate graciously pleaded delight with the supper while Ned, seated across from her, transferred tempting tidbits from his plate to hers. She tucked her feet together to keep from accidentally touching him and then having to explain it was not meant to encourage him. Though she tried to avoid eating what Edward served, her appetite got the better of her. Emulating the queen's frugal eating left her always hungry, though her farthingale, as usual, kept her from overindulgence.

Edward leaned toward Kate, dropping a honeyed bite of woodcock on her plate. His voice was low, meant only for her. "I am gladdened that I can make amends for the night you missed your wedding supper."

She came close to kicking him, or worse, having to acknowledge her tears.

He turned to his sister. "Jane, I think your supper is finding much favor with Lady Katherine."

Kate was happy for the change of subject and groaned in mock discomfort when Ned added to her plate. "I thank you for your kindness, my lord, but I beg you—no more."

At this exchange, Robert left off telling Jane a rollicking tale of a lonely countess compromised by a night-roaming country squire. "Exercise, Kate, is the best antidote to the table. I have planned a hunt tomorrow for the queen. We ride to Epping Forest and the queen's hunting lodge. The deer have been driven into enclosures and the queen will have the first kill. Will you be riding out?"

"My duties may keep me at Whitehall, Lord Robert, as I must oversee the packing of Her Majesty's gowns and jewels. She could signal a move upriver to Richmond at any time now that Candlemas is passed." She twitched her nose. "The court has been at Whitehall too long and the palace is in need of a good sweetening."

Robert laughed. "Her Majesty is also known for her dainty nose, but in truth the common jakes are overflowing."

Edward grimaced at Robert's crude words, though his gaze did not leave Kate. "I will hunt tomorrow," he murmured for Kate alone. "My flag will fly from the lodge."

"As will mine," Robert said, no conversation being private to that lord.

"Oh, you must go, Kate," Jane added. "I will ride, though I will make a poor showing next to Her Majesty, who rides—"

"—like a prince," Robert said. "In the saddle, she is a match for any man. I have brought the fastest horses from Ireland for her stables."

He's proud of her, Kate thought, *as if she were his creature and he had a hand in her making. Maybe he did, or maybe he thinks he did, which is more dangerous.* Elizabeth would not be willing to acknowledge any man her maker but King Henry VIII.

The evening was short, but there was time for a game of backgammon before a messenger from the queen called Dudley away. Vowing to gain an invitation for all the queen's ladies to hunt tomorrow and swaggering as ever, he kissed Kate's cheek again as he left. To Edward's obvious displeasure.

While Kate had ridden with the queen many times, she was not a rider who could match Elizabeth and was often left behind. But the Great Standing lodge the queen's father had built for his hunting pleasure was famed. It would be glorious to see it and to get away from Whitehall for a day.

"I will be in the queen's party tomorrow. Will you ride with me?" Edward asked Kate as he and Jane escorted their guest by means of a lantern through a little-used servants' hall to her chamber.

"My lord Edward, you know I cannot, but I will try to finish my duties early and join a later party. Her Grace likes for all her ladies to ride for exercise."

He placed her hand on his forearm and held it there.

Two of the three torches had burned low and the hall was dimly lit. Kate could barely see his face shining in the lantern's light, but she felt the urgent pressure of his hand on hers. She tried to draw away, bumping into Jane at her side. "My lord, I have no room to walk." She had meant the words to be impatient, but they sounded pleading and desperate to her ears.

Jane quickly dropped back as if by design, and Edward pushed Kate gently against the wall, the lantern swaying, sending light bouncing up to the vaulted and painted ceiling. The queen's coronation portrait hung on the wall half in sight, probably to prod the servants to their duty and having a similar effect on Kate.

"My lord, you must not."

"Do not fear me. I would do nothing to harm you."

Kate gathered courage from the unyielding wall at her back. "You do me harm already, Edward, waylaying me like any road rogue. The queen would have you in the Tower for molesting one of her ladies."

Edward laughed softly. "As much as you say for me to stop, yet I hear no true complaint in your voice."

Kate was shocked at his bold certainty, and suspected he had too easily read her heart. She was even more shocked as she pushed against his shaking arms. He was not as composed as he seemed. There was still something of the desperate boy in him. Edward's body was barely touching hers, and yet she could sense his heart beating and hear his breathing quicken, as if he had been running toward her all these years. She was frightened by the power of such feeling, even more afraid of the heat building in her own body.

She fell back on raillery, which sometimes cooled a man's blood and might help her own. "What do you hope to gain? Kidnapping is long out of fashion, my lord. You will surely be mocked."

He quickly placed the lantern on the floor and wove his arms about her. She forgot to breathe. Kate felt his warmth down the length of her body and more comfort than she could remember since he'd last held her. No one, save Sybil, had eased her in any way since that day, only weeks before her sister, Jane, had been taken to the Tower.

Edward bent and laid his cheek atop her head. She regretted weaving a pearl string through her hair and adding Spanish combs, which must surely press most cruelly into his flesh.

"Will it harm you if I speak love for your ears alone?"

She did not answer; could not answer. He could speak love, but Kate doubted she would understand. Her father had been intent his whole life on obtaining a good marriage for her to the advancement of his family, and seeing her gone; her mother was so strict a parent, her bedtime kiss hurt. As for Kate's first husband, the Earl of Pembroke, he could not wait to be rid of a frightened girl whose father was attainted for treasonous plotting and beheaded, losing all his lands and her dowry. She had come from Pembroke still a royal virgin.

She had a desire to bury her face against Edward, but she could not, choking out words that brought tenderness to his touch. "The girl you once knew is lost," she said, her voice full of anguish.

"Though you try to deny her, I see her hiding inside the woman," he murmured. Edward lifted his cheek from her hair, bent farther and kissed the tip of her ear.

No man had ever done that, not even the young boy she'd loved so desperately. Edward's lips moved slowly down her cheek and took her mouth. Only Elizabeth could take a man's warm kiss and resist such urgent love.

Kate was full of longing and near lost. It was a rare yearning she'd never heeded as a woman, never wanted since a girl, always rejected before that yearning was lost. Edward drew the heat of her body into his own and returned it a thousand times.

"Ned. Ned, do you . . . oh, do you not . . . know what you do?" She was surprised to hear her own broken words.

"We must marry at last," he whispered. "I will take you honorably, as I promised, take you away from this court where you may be traded for advantage . . . or given nothing at all."

"Ned, you do not know the forces arrayed against us. . . . The queen, her council, my mother . . . all have plans for me. The queen uses me to threaten the Scots queen's claim to the throne. The council uses me to threaten Elizabeth lest she persist in living and dying a virgin. . . . My mother just uses me to regain her power at court and to recover the lands returned to the crown after my father's death." Kate was near desperation. "Ned, don't you understand? The queen will never allow me out of her sight, unless it be to the Tower."

"I will petition her as a peer of this realm."

"If I am a threat to her alone, think you she will want my Tudor and your Seymour blood to combine?"

"What do *you* want?"

She stared at him, amazed. It was unthinkable to have a desire of her own.

"What? Tell me," Ned insisted.

"You," she said, her voice strong enough to surprise her.

His arms tightened. "Sweetheart, I *will* petition the queen. I am of Dudley's party and he will help."

"Do not be so certain he will ever go against Elizabeth."

"With him. Without him!"

This was a new Edward. There was nothing of the carefree gentleman's drawl, just purposeful determination. But such purpose frightened her. "You do not really know me now, Ned. I am changed, wanting nothing. Empty. It is too dangerous to want what is not easily given. I cannot risk your place in court, if not a trip to the Tower, for you."

He raised his head to the vaulted ceiling and spit out the words. "Hang my place in court! I hate it as much as you do. For years, I have been a soldier, leading men, free of all this flummery." He lowered his voice. "Sweetest, it could never come to the Tower. Being heir saved Elizabeth from her sister's wrath and it will save you, though I know you have no desire to succeed, as the queen did." He grinned boldly, now an arm's length from her, his teeth white in the light. "Do not forget that the queen likes me. I am a new favorite and I pay her all that a prince is due."

"She will demand more," Kate warned. "The queen is not like other women. Admiration is not enough for her. She will not take you, but she will not share you. And she will never set me free."

"As a peer, I have a right . . . a duty to marry and have an heir."

His surety almost swayed her into belief, but she knew only a fool would think Elizabeth would celebrate the union of two people each with a strong claim to the throne. Still, when she was in Edward's arms she felt a fool, a complete and alive fool without a brain to resist.

Edward handed Jane the lantern as she came up to them, looking very pleased. Well, if Jane could not be one of the queen's ladies on her own, Kate thought rather uncharitably, she could conspire to create a vacancy.

Edward withdrew two miniatures from beneath his doublet. One was of a very young Kate.

Had he kept it against his heart all these years?

"Look on this," he said to Kate, holding up the second small portrait of her.

Astonished, she said, "I did not sit for that."

Jane looked very pleased. "Oh, but, my lady, you did. I paid a court artist to draw you in secret as you are now. You were sitting for this portrait every time you appeared in the queen's entourage."

Edward nodded, admitting his part of the conspiracy. "I asked my sister for this favor. When I heard that you were yet free and the loveliest of the queen's ladies, indeed the supreme beauty at White-hall, I had to see for myself if you were worth the possibility of another broken heart."

"Ned . . ." She couldn't go on. All these years that she had thought herself forgotten and alone, she had been on his mind and next to his heart.

Edward knelt as if to the queen.

He looked up at her, his expression adoring, everything she could want from any man, all she had ever dreamed.

"At night, during those years in Italy, it was your young picture that I kept on my pallet beside me, your face the last I saw before sleep. Now I am as you see me, lady—with two portraits but without you, and I cannot live so. If I lie, let me die now!"

He fell sideways to the floor, motionless, his eyes closed, until Kate, laughing and crying, too, knelt beside him. "Ned! Dearest Ned, get up. I am convinced."

A smile slowly widened his mouth, though his eyes remained closed. He did not rise and she was compelled to bend and kiss his lips. He pulled her to him.

Jane had moved off with the lantern, leaving them in shadow.

Kate pulled back as Ned reached to hold her closer. "No, Ned. If someone came upon us, how would we explain it?"

"My sweet, I think there would be no need."

He leapt to his feet and raised her up to him. "From this day we will never be parted."

With that promise, they proceeded to Kate's room without being detected.

"Tomorrow," he whispered, reluctantly letting her fingers slip from his. "Come again to Jane's chamber."

She heard herself agreeing, then added, "We must be careful to draw no attention." She responded to his back, hoping he heard.

Kate was one of the last of the hunting party to arrive at the Great Standing the next morning.

"My lord," she began as Robert helped her, breathless, from her horse, "I fear the queen will kill herself riding so fast."

Dudley disagreed. "She is God's anointed and afraid of nothing."

"Except love," Kate couldn't resist saying.

Robert bent to untangle a stirrup before summoning a boy to walk the sweating horse. "You don't know her as well as you think," Dudley said, annoyed, and for the first time Kate suspected that he had bitter doubts of his power over Elizabeth.

"Then why does she first seek the love of so many men and then run away from it with you?" This was not mere rhetoric, but a question that Kate longed to have answered.

"You misread her, my lady. Bess does not run away because she is afraid of love. She is angry at love. It's the only thing she cannot control. Anger is what fuels her resistance to me and all the princes of Europe. It will keep you and Edward apart . . . especially if she sees you in love with him."

"I am not in love with him," she said, hoping to convince him.

"Are you certain?"

Kate's voice was unsteady. "I am not in love with him."

He grinned. "That smacks of a confirmation, Kate."

She nimbly changed the subject back to him. "My lord, if you know the queen is angry at love, why—"

"Why do I love her?" he answered, his voice less than steady. "Better to ask why I breathe. Ask why you are about to doom your chance for the throne with Edward. We cannot help ourselves."

"God's bones, Robert! Does no one believe that I do not want to succeed?"

He continued adjusting the stirrup to disguise his advice. "Who could believe it? And never think she will believe you, or consent to your marrying the nephew of the woman who followed her mother into her father's bed. And, if not for that reason, she knows how plots form around heirs. Such conspiracies sent her through the Traitor's Gate and into the Tower in great fear of her mother's fate. I know, I was a prisoner there, too, at the same time, but managed to get messages to her. She waited every morning for the sound of hammers building a platform for her block."

Kate took a long step back. "I fear you are mistook, brother-in-law. Your advice is quite unnecessary. The earl is but the brother of my friend Lady Jane."

"A mistake, Kate. Don't ever take me for a fool. I remember the whispers when you two were young. And the scent of lust is heavy on you both." He sniffed the air.

She tried to turn away but he took hold of her arm. "Eventually, Bess knows everything. She will not allow you to marry and have children." Grinning and nodding for observing eyes, he handed Kate on to a gentleman usher with his customary swagger and motioned a boy to take the reins of her horse. Kate, somewhat unsteadily, climbed the stairs to the second floor of the hunting lodge open on all sides and walked to the queen's shooting box at the rail. She wondered if Robert was capable of believing that Katherine Grey had no thirst for rule. Could a man who loved a queen ever believe that? He had seen four Tudor sovereigns in his life, all unhappy in their own way. Yet he loved Elizabeth deeply, defying history.

Many lords' banners were flying from all three levels of the lodge, and the queen's from all four corners. Kate wondered if a fair wind could send the building sailing over the Forest of Epping to confound the people of London, but before she had a chance to form an amusing question, the queen bent over the second-floor railing and cried below, "Loose the deer, my lord Dudley."

Dudley looked up at Elizabeth, splendid in his green velvet hunting suit, and flourished his cap. At his command the deer ran from the forest into the clearing below.

Elizabeth gently handed her favorite little dog to Mistress Ashley, picked up a crossbow, the quarrel already loaded, took aim and sent it through the neck of a doe, dropping it as it leapt. "Well shot, Your Grace," Ned cried, taking the quarrels from the Master Archer to swiftly reload the queen's crossbow himself.

Now that the queen had shot, others began shooting as the deer ran pell-mell for the cover of trees, only to be turned back, frightened by boys waving large sheets. They were met with a hail of arrows and bolts.

Kate did not mind the hunting so much as long as the deer died instantly from a good shot, though she'd never confess that the sight of a deer mortally wounded, flailing its legs in its own pooling blood, made her stomach sick. And certainly she would never reveal that the smell of hot venison pie would offend her nose for weeks to come.

The shooting lasted for two hours, with the queen bringing down six does and given the honor of slitting the throat of her first kill. The deer carcasses were loaded on wagons, some to go to the queen's kitchens, some to London's poor hospitals.

Edward trailed the queen's party as they left the Great Standing lodge. Kate alone heard what he said when she passed. "I can see that your heart is even now with the caged bird," he whispered. "That is your glory."

As the weak winter sun rose to its height, the queen and all her ladies were led down the stairs and walked to the forest. Dudley led the queen along a carefully swept path covered with sweet-smelling herbs and lined with frolicking pipers and drummers making music to move feet. Kate saw Her Majesty's eyes shine when she looked up at Dudley, and did not dare to stare at Ned for fear that her eyes would shine even brighter. She wouldn't be able to help herself. Being loved by a man like Ned was exhilarating beyond anything she'd known, beyond even her cherished girlish love for him. Her body had not shrunk from him, but melted into his perfectly. For two heartbeats, she wondered what it would be like to dare what Elizabeth dared.

"Robin, you are indeed a master of my revels," the queen said with a special warmth, leaning against him.

Dudley looked down at the queen, a half smile on his kiss-me lips. "Thank you, Your Majesty. I would be master of your *every* pleasure."

Elizabeth laughed softly, like the young girl she'd never been allowed to be.

Everyone looked straight ahead for fear that Elizabeth would read their shock at this direct enticement. But all heard, as the least scullery maid at Whitehall would by evening.

Kate felt her bile rise. The queen did not keep her feelings to herself, while she herself must.

They reached the forest glade readied for the picnic. Sweet-smelling boughs draped the pavilion, complete with warming braziers and steaming food laid on low tables, almost as lavish as the banquet for the Scots ambassador. Dudley produced ermine-trimmed robes to cover the queen as a light snow began to fall, the flakes sizzling as they landed on the burning coals. A dozen musicians blew on their fingers, then began a rollicking roundelay and, at the queen's request, Kate and the other ladies began a circle dance, skipping with a garland for Her Majesty's pleasure, as if spring could be commanded to come.

In a minute, Elizabeth in high spirits threw off her fur robes and ran to join the dancing, grasping Kate's hand, raising it high. The queen danced faster and with more abandon than any of them, a wild winter dance among the snowflakes, laughing so that every dancer was infected with her sheer physical joy.

Finally, Kate clasped her breast, sucking in air, and broke the circle. Dudley collected the queen, who laughed and danced on his arm back to her warm robes.

Ned, following Kate, whispered, "Are you ill?"

"No," she answered softly. She could not reveal her thought: that she must imprison her tortured feelings, while the queen could let hers free.

Kate walked to the pavilion, huddling next to a brazier for warmth. She did not look at Ned, though she knew he was attending the queen. She held her breath when she saw him approaching her. He bowed and offered her his heavier winter cloak.

"Take this," he said in a low voice, placing it about Kate's shoulders. "I'll not have you shivering to keep some pretense of not caring."

Kate smiled, nodding graciously, and replied for all to hear, "A kindness, my lord of Hertford." Kate glanced at the queen as Ned returned to her side.

"My lord earl," the queen said, her face unreadable, "you take gallant care of my lady Grey when all the morn you scarce glanced her way. Do you devise some secret bed sport, my lord?" She smiled as if her spies had already shared Kate's secret. Then the smile was gone. "Never tempt too far a prince's patience, my lord Seymour, if you would remain in favor."

Ned apologized for his offense, but Kate decided at that moment to ask the queen for leave to visit her mother. Even the Duchess of Suffolk would be a relief, and while at Bradgate, she would have time to sort her thoughts, find a way to achieve the impossible or the strength to forever hide her desire. In her heart, Kate knew there was no way to hide from Elizabeth at court. She was too schooled in deception, having practiced it since scarce out of the cradle after her mother's beheading. Avoidance between maid and man to the queen was as significant as a swelling belly.

That night as Kate helped prepare the queen for her bed, she asked for a month's leave.

"Pish!" Elizabeth said, catching Kate's hand in a strong grip. "You ask the impossible, Lady Grey. We are moving the court to my warmer palace of Richmond in two days' time, and as mistress of the robes, you must be at your work . . . if you would continue in it."

"Of course, if you wish it, Majesty," Kate said, sinking to the floor, her face turned away, holding back thoughts that Elizabeth would never forgive.

CHAPTER THREE

"Better beggar woman and single, than queen and married."
—Elizabeth Regina

February 4, 1562
Whitehall/Richmond

Twenty-four rowers dipped their oars into the Thames, pulling the royal barge smoothly away from the water stairs at Whitehall. The morning mist rose and the winter sun shone on the gray river. Kate leaned back against the cushions in the rear cabin, smiling to herself: Even the weather, which had been all blustery wind and snow, bowed to Elizabeth of England.

She was out of the queen's sight, needing to rest from the labor of the frantic packing of everything in Her Majesty's apartments for removal to Richmond Palace: a thousand gowns, and twice as many oversleeves, jewels, pictures, her huge bed and all the royal apartment's furnishings. Catching the tide on the flood, the barge was moving with some speed upriver, the lap and surge of the water against the craft lulling Kate into a deeper rest.

They sailed past Westminster Abbey and the Star Chamber and were soon in more open country. It was a false spring day, warmer than it would be for weeks ahead, but it brought eager husbandmen into their fields to clear and plow furrows, preparing the earth for seed. Parish bells rang out their greeting as villagers came to the water's edge to kneel. They shouted, "God save Her Majesty!" and pushed their children to the front to see their queen.

Kate heard Elizabeth's cheerful reply to them: "God save you all, my good people!"

Elizabeth was always at her happiest in public, while in private she was too often melancholy. In spite of her strength and majesty, the queen seemed happy only when she could display those qualities to her subjects. Otherwise, she was again the lonely, withdrawn princess banished to country houses, surrounded by tutors and nurses, some of whom reported her every word to her enemies.

Staring through the many-paned, leaded window with its jewel-tone roundels, Kate felt some of the same loneliness until at last she caught a glimpse of Ned. She had known him as a woman for less than a month and yet she counted a day without seeing him as one of miserable hours. Could love rekindle so fast, or had it been smoldering all these years, a love that could mean her undoing and his? And though it felt to her as anything right should feel, could it be the devil's doing, tempting her to trouble?

She shook off the fleeting sense of apprehension as she watched Ned riding with other nobles alongside the river as guards for the queen's lumbering wagons. All four hundred of them were packed to overflowing. As the wagons, coaches and gentlemen came fully into her view, it had not been difficult to espy Ned. He sat a richly caparisoned horse of at least seventeen hands and spirited, prancing about as well as had his master at the masque that night he'd come back into her life. Kate softly hummed the tune of the gavotte they'd danced, clutching a pillow she should be embroidering. Ned was everywhere in her mind. She flushed with the memory of his most recent stolen kiss. And in the queen's own jewel closet!

Yesterday, she'd passed the guards and walked into the closet to retrieve a brooch for Her Majesty. She'd expected to find the jewel room empty, but found Ned instead. "What are you—"

"My lady Grey, I am doing what any man in love would do."
He'd spoken formally, bowing, his brown eyes shining with warmth
that did little to reduce her anxiety.

"Not in this court, my lord," she whispered. "Are you run mad?
This will reach the queen before I return to her apartments."

"I have bribed the guards."

"They are not loyal to you. If they do not tell the queen, they will
tell it in the postern guardhouse tonight and—"

"—and they will not receive the second and larger part of their
bribe."

He stepped closer to her.

"Do you always think of everything?"

He reached for her. "No, I have not always been such a seer. For
long years, I thought I'd lost you, seeking you in other women and
never finding you. But, Kate . . ." He swallowed compulsively twice.
"I had to see if you yet thought of me in the same way as—"

"—two nights ago at Jane's supper, when you kissed a queen's
lady without permission while escorting her to her room?" she said,
in a futile attempt to sound severe. "Or this morning in the stables?"
she added quietly. "Or yesterday, in the garden maze?"

"I cannot resist a yew hedge."

She closed her eyes, remembering him as a boy on the brink of
manhood, but with a man's needs already upon him. He touched her
cheek and she opened her eyes to find his face very close.

"Kate, I always find it surer to kiss first in hopes of permission
for another." His humor faded suddenly to anguish. "We should not
play at such love games, Kate. I'm too far gone for such."

He had come so close his breath brushed her cheek when he
withdrew the womanly miniature of her that he carried in his doublet. "Kate, please, a lock of your hair." He tapped on the back of the
portrait locket and it sprang open.

She pretended alarm, teasing him. "So you can take the lock to a
necromancer and have me bewitched?"

His arms had wrapped tight about her. "Turn and turn about. I am completely under your spell."

She felt safe in his strong arms, safe to do as she wanted and not always to do as she was bidden. His hands had slid to her buttocks and pulled her into him. She wanted to go farther . . . such a short distance . . . and close the last gap. Although she was near to losing any resistance, fear told her to back away from him. "How can I believe a lord who is so easily bewitched by a small portrait?" she asked, trying to speak lightly.

Edward had dropped his hands and stepped back, his brows drawn together in hurt by her mistrust. "You think all I see is your beauty?"

"What other?" She could not stay her curiosity.

He raised the miniature, looking into it . . . inside it. "I saw utter loneliness and yet compassion. I saw a longing for gentleness and laughter, a true laughter not prompted by any command. I see the girl of long ago who wanted to fly free."

She drew nearer to him. "You saw all that in my face?"

"That and more, or I would not have come to you. I see all those things now, or I would not remain here."

"Ned, you are mad." Standing on her toes, she kissed him.

"Most mad." He'd grinned, and, withdrawing his jeweled dagger, he'd cut a small reddish blond curl that had escaped her hood.

The lap of water against the barge pulled Kate back to the moment, and she looked about the cabin for fear that someone would see her trembling with the memory of his body pressed against hers. The other ladies, even the observant Lady Saintloe, were busy with their embroidery, occupied as Kate should be, yet this morning she could not force her fingers to their task.

She sought the warmth of the memory of his kiss again and again, wondering at the need for her body to repeat the heat of it, linger over it, and amazed that she could call up the stir of what she'd felt in the candled shadows of the queen's jewel closet. It had been the same for years after they'd been forced apart by their fathers. Was this to be her life, all lived in remembrance?

"Her Majesty requires your presence, my lady." A gentleman usher spoke loudly in front of Kate.

She was aware from the heavy emphasis on each word that they were being repeated, and now she must hurry. Could Elizabeth see through the barge walls and read a maid's mind? She couldn't smile at such a witchy thought. The queen was not in any part a fool, and surely she and Ned would give themselves away to her. Although Elizabeth had said nothing to Kate about denying Ned's earlier petition to court her, this queen did not forget.

Ned was a strong man in a court that feared strong men. Every man was less than the queen here, a queen who was more than a woman. One forgot that at the peril of one's head. She must warn him again to have exceeding care, and heed that warning herself.

Kate stepped out onto the gilded, painted deck strewn with herbs and boughs, the many oars splashing in rhythm. "Yes, Your Majesty," she said, drawing her cloak closer against the river air.

The queen looked young and excited, happy to be on the move, her light complexion dewy and glowing from the river mist. She had removed her hood, her hair a red-gold cloud about her shoulders. "My lady Katherine, we wish you to read to us." The queen pointed to Plutarch's *Lives* that she'd just translated from the Greek into Latin into English, weeks of enjoyable winter evenings for the queen.

"Of course, Your Grace." Kate opened the English translation slowly, thankful she would not have to test her Latin before Elizabeth. Her pious sister, Jane, had been the scholar.

As she began to read, the barge sailed around a bend in the river and into an explosion, a puff of smoke rising from the bank. An oarsman screamed and fell from his bench to the deck, bleeding and clutching at the splintered bone in his arm.

"Assassin!" As the cry was out of her mouth, Kate moved to

shield the queen, only to be shoved aside by the sergeant of her guard, his sword drawn.

"To arms!" The cry went up from every throat.

Ned! Was he in danger? In the whirl of action on deck, Kate gripped the railing and saw both Dudley and Edward leap from their horses on the riverbank into the cold water and wade toward a fowler's boat in the reedy shallows. They grabbed the man's fowling piece and dragged him roughly from his boat to the shore.

Although the sergeant begged the queen not to pull to shore in case rebellion lurked there, the queen laughed. "Pish! A queen of England does not cower before her fowlers." She added prudently, "But we have a care for our servants, so bring the wretch here. And bring our two wet lords, who have saved our life." A boat set out immediately.

But Kate saw that Ned had not waited. He was swimming strongly for the barge.

The queen stood and went to the wounded oarsman, kneeling beside him, careless of her gown and person as he groaned on the deck in a startling amount of blood. "Come, good fellows," she commanded the cringing oarsmen, who seemed to be without wits, "bandage and tend this brave man who took a bullet into his own body for his sovereign. We will have our royal physician tend him when we arrive at Richmond, and he shall have a pension of a hundred . . . of fifty a year." She made comforting sounds to the oarsman, whose pain seemed somewhat relieved by his queen's words, then stood and returned to her pavilion with the cheers of her rowers resounding on both sides.

Kate knew Ned would arrive momentarily, but she couldn't help watching Elizabeth, guessing that the tale of kindness to her wounded servant would be told and retold in London, adding to the adoration of her. Kate believed that the queen, without thought of popularity, had truly meant to comfort the man, though she would not overprotest the good results to her reputation.

Ned pulled himself up over the rail, water sluicing from him, as the queen returned to her throne under the canopy. He spoke to Elizabeth, but he was looking at Kate with relief. "Thank God you are safe, Majesty."

Kate, her eyes wide with warning, went immediately to Elizabeth's side.

"Quite safe, my lord," the queen replied sharply.

A set of dripping wet hose came over the side, and Robert Dudley followed. "Bess?" His worried gaze swept her and observed the bloodied rower. "Jesu be praised," he said, and hauled a terrified fowler, like a large bag of grain, up and over the rail, throwing him prostrate on the deck before Elizabeth. The fowler pressed his cheek against the wood, and Kate could see him wishing to plunge through the deck to the better death of drowning. He knew very well what he faced for endangering the queen.

"Up on your knees," the queen commanded. "Look at your sovereign!"

The man, whose stained leather jerkin pointed to a morning ill spent over a wine flask, opened and shut his mouth like a giant gawping fish.

"Did you mean to kill your queen?" Elizabeth asked sternly.

The fowler, still struck dumb, could only shake his head and make gargling noises.

"You have endangered our person, master fowler, which is treason under England's law."

Robert Dudley picked up the limp man by the clothes on his back. "The penalty is death, rogue."

At last the fowler found his voice. "Nay! Yer Majesty, I be never bringin' harm to ye. As I hope for heaven, 'tis God's whole truth."

Ned yelled to make even Kate jump: "You shot at the queen's barge!"

"Nay, not so, good lord. The gun fired—" More gargling noises.

The queen raised a hand. "Hold, my lord of Hertford. The man is beyond his tongue with fright." She leaned forward. "You were hunting our swans, Master Fowler." It wasn't a question. This queen knew.

He hung his head. "Aye, Yer Majesty."

Lord Dudley frowned. "Your Grace, he deserves a traitor's death for his carelessness alone."

The queen laughed aloud, showing no fright, nor had she ever. "If we were to hang all our careless people, we would have no tree limbs vacant in our realm. We will show mercy. Fine him his boat and fowling piece and give him a time in Bridewell Prison to regret his desire to take my swans and sell their feathers. We think, then, in future he will not be so good a patron of his wine merchant." She laughed and waved the stumbling fowler away into the sergeant's custody. Surely he would count his great good fortune for the rest of his days.

Kate admired the queen's forbearing humor. Her father would have had the man racked all night and hanged for a traitor the very next morning at Tyburn, cut down alive, drawn and quartered, his last tortured sight that of his own entrails roasting on a brazier.

Ned carefully avoided looking in Kate's direction, and she turned from him. As he was going over the rail, back to his escort duty, they both looked away at the same time in the same direction and she saw him suppress a grin. How could they avoid all contact under Elizabeth's gaze when they were both serving her? How long could a lady sworn to her service hide what she felt at every sight of a man? Kate sensed she was trapped like a bear at a baiting, tied on a short lead to a stake while a pack of dangerous mastiffs circled.

Soon enough, to Kate's relief, they rounded another curve in the river and saw the magical, faerie-wrought, onion-domed and crenellated towers and cupolas of Richmond immediately ahead. Kate had been there many times, but the beauty of this palace always thrilled her. Rich water meadows, green and teeming with heron, surrounded the brick-and-stone mass—a most perfect place to be in a new spring, far from the plagues and odors of London. She knew that its gardens and enclosed walks offered cover for lovers, and she shivered with imagination more than the chill air surrounding the great fountain in the entry quadrangle.

Elizabeth was welcomed as they walked through the high stone entrance in the curtain wall. The first wagons were already being unloaded.

"Majesty," the palace chamberlain said, kneeling with all the household, the carver, cup bearer, porters and chaplains behind him. "While your apartments are readied, your privy kitchen has laid a dinner in the great hall."

"We thank you for this welcome, but we will first to our chapel, and take our meal in our chambers later. An eventful trip, Master Chamberlain, our life saved by the hand of almighty God. It is our Lord in heaven who must be shown our gratitude first."

As Elizabeth went in procession to her chapel to praise God for protecting her from the fools in her kingdom, Kate, with the other ladies, rushed away to see that the queen's apartment furnishings were arranged exactly as they had been at Whitehall.

The Earl of Hertford dismounted just inside the curtain wall, amidst ordered chaos. The Lord Steward directed porters to unpack wagons, grooms struggled with all manner of chests in every direction and stable boys led sweating horses away. "Mind you, boy, walk him out, rub him down well with straw and hold the cold water. And," Edward added as the boy took the reins, "only water from the cistern house, not water from the river flowing under the main jakes."

Dudley tossed the boy his reins, slapping his horse on the rump. "My horse will have the same and the best stall. Tell the stable master that I'll be down to see to the queen's mounts as soon as I have eaten and changed clothes."

Edward dismissed Dudley's high-handed behavior. It was a typical test to Edward's greater rank, but he wouldn't be provoked, not today. He needed Dudley's influence with the queen, and soon. He did not know how long he could force himself to honor Kate's virginity. Their last kisses in the jewel closet had told him that and more; they had shown him her willingness. "My lord, I would have urgent speech with you on a private matter."

Dudley looked interested, but Edward thought it a shrewd interest. "Come to my apartment with me and we will talk privately while I change. I must attend the queen after chapel and see that she wants for nothing. Like her father before her, Bess does not tolerate waiting."

Edward followed Robert into a large brick building off an inner garden courtyard and down a labyrinth of halls barely passable amidst a flood of goods moving toward the queen's apartments.

When they were inside Lord Robert's rooms, Edward waited for Dudley's servant to bring fresh clothing and then he could wait no longer. "I must have your help, Robert."

Dudley put up a hand to stop further speech until he had dismissed his servant and the door was shut behind him. "If this is about Lady Katherine Grey, I beg you to go no further."

"But, Robert, I—"

Lord Dudley stepped forward and lowered his voice. "Don't be a fool, Edward. You know that I should tell Bess every word of this speech. If she thought I was involved in that which is against her will . . ."

Edward saw Dudley swallow hard and turn his face away, but not before his expression could be easily read. Dudley did not shrink for fear of the queen's anger, but from his love for her, a love he must know in his heart was more hopeless than Edward's own. No sign now of the clever courtier, the charmed lord who'd escaped the ax that had taken off the heads of his father and brother. Now he was only a man denied the woman he desired above all others, his heart despairing. Still, Edward knew Dudley kept a tiny flame of hope flickering. Edward knew because he had done the same all these years.

Yet he was not content to wait, as Dudley must. "My lord, I must beg your attention. The queen has ignored my petition. I need to know how best to proceed in my suit for Kate."

"Best *not* to proceed!" Dudley's face showed annoyance. "You have already followed bad advice, and I expect it came from your sister, the lady Jane, who wants Kate's place in the bedchamber."

"Naturally, my sister, as niece of Henry's queen, wants her rightful place, but also my happiness, happiness that will be purchased only by marriage to my Kate. I have waited years and can wait no more." He stood straighter and tried to make his voice proud, but he could not keep the pretense. "Robert, you *must* speak for us!" Edward said, all sense of civility lost as he grasped Dudley's arm. "If Kate and I could marry, we would leave the court behind and retire to the quiet of my manor of Eltham. I have seen cities in foreign lands. I have fought in battles on sea and land. I desire nothing more than to spend my life with Kate and our children in the green country far from intrigue and court affairs of state. On my honor, we would never betray the queen."

Dudley pulled his arm away so quickly that Edward was rocked forward. "You fool! Others would betray your honor for you, hatching plots, naming you in letters—the lieutenant of the Tower would be building a scaffold for both of you in less than a year." In earnest, Dudley continued: "I will forget your words, Edward, as you should." Robert laughed bitterly. "Henry wanted a prince, and by all that's holy, Bess has become one. Do not allow her female body to deceive you. Her head rules her."

Edward heard a heart aching in those words.

"Hark to me, Edward; there is no appeal to the queen's fear of an intrigue to take her throne."

"But she cannot think we—"

"Are you so blinded by lust that *you* cannot understand? You both have royal blood, which makes you a threat even unmarried. That's why she accepted you so readily at her court and keeps Kate close—to maintain an eye on both your doings. She could never tolerate the joining of both Seymour and Tudor lines with the possibility of male heirs. Think you she endured a life of almost endless fear and loneliness waiting for the throne to be hers to lose all now to her cousins?" He smoothed his doublet and settled a cap on his dark hair. "Now, my lord, excuse me to my duty as the queen's master of horses. She will want to ride out on the morrow. Say no more to me on this matter, or by the good Lord, I'll see your head on a pike myself."

Edward's hand went to his sword. "No man threatens me—"

But Dudley had flung himself away, his servant in the anteroom caught unready, racing to catch him.

Edward stood silent, staring at the open door, clenching his fists, his heart thundering. If he challenged Dudley for his arrogance, many in the court would approve. As with most favorites, Robert Dudley had truer enemies than friends. But Elizabeth would be sure to send Edward Seymour to the Tower, where he would never see Kate again. He stood for a moment, quieting his breathing to somewhere near to calm.

Though he was disappointed and angered, he knew his anger was unreasonable. In his way, Dudley was truly trying to help him. Indeed, there was too little difference in their troubles for Edward to hold resentment and, with understanding, anger flew swiftly away.

As well, he knew Dudley's immediate troubles: desperately opposing each foreign prince's marriage proposal that came before the queen and her council in every way he could, knowing that a princely consort would not only erase his own hopes for marrying Elizabeth, but would also strive to separate them completely.

But there must be a way open to Kate and him. There must be! Dudley could be wrong. Squaring his shoulders, Edward walked, head high, toward the queen's apartments, next to Dudley's own. He hoped to catch sight of Kate, but trumpeters and drummers were at the doors announcing the queen's dinner. The doors opened and with a quick glance he saw Kate, surrounded by yeomen with steaming food, kneeling before an empty table. Then he heard the queen's laughter, followed by Dudley's. The doors closed, but not before Lady Saintloe saw him, her eyebrows raised with interest.

He flicked dust from his doublet sleeve, all unconcerned. He was wary of her, but he would not allow it to show. She was wily and rich, having buried three husbands, and was a great gossip who loved to agitate already aroused tempers. Were she a village shrew instead of a wealthy widow, she would have long ago owned the ducking stool. He must warn Kate to have great care with that lady looking on.

A little disheartened but trying to hold disillusion at bay, Edward made his way to his own rooms in the next hall to Dudley's, and, finding that one of his servants had unpacked dry clothes that did not smell of Thames water, he quickly changed, was shaved and his close beard trimmed and oiled. His spirits lifted, he made his way to the great hall, aromas of game pies rising from the laden tables making his belly growl. If he could not feed his heart, for the moment he would have to nourish his stomach.

After riding in the fresher air of the countryside and his forced swim in the Thames, he feasted heartily on quail pie with a high, crispy crust set inside a moat of gravy with a good Portuguese wine and an eggy custard to follow. He'd just risen from his stool when a groom in the royal livery found him.

"My lord, Her Majesty commands your presence in her privy chamber."

Edward followed the man, smoothing his velvet doublet and adjusting his ruff as he went. He hoped for the best, but if Dudley had reported their conversation, he set himself to face her well-known temper as well as he could. Although there was little any man could do if the queen were well and truly displeased.

He was shown into a luxurious withdrawing room with greater decoration than at Whitehall. A large, elaborate fireplace gave off heat that reached into the corners; the walls were of carved oak paneling. High windows let in the waning winter sun to illumine the ceiling with its intricate plaster decoration covering every inch. All the queen's paintings and tapestries were hung. The rest of the palace was helter-skelter, but here everything was in perfect order. Edward knew it had taken fifty grooms supervised by her ladies to settle the queen's belongings so quickly.

Removing his cap, he knelt. "Your Grace, I am yours to command." He didn't look about him. He'd already noted that only the queen's ladies were with her, including Kate, her eyes cast down in modesty. Dudley was not there.

"My lord of Hertford?" Her Majesty's voice lifted, as if she were surprised to see him.

"You commanded my presence, Your Grace." Edward's tone was apologetic until he realized the queen knew very well why he was here. He would not be caught off guard and begin babbling uncalled-for excuses until he knew how much Dudley had told her, or if he had. Dudley was no fool. Bad-news messengers were rarely well received.

"The Lord Steward has given you adequate accommodations, my lord Edward?"

"Perfectly so, Majesty. I thank you." He breathed deeply and kept his eyes steady on her, forbidding his face to show turmoil. She had the same slender face and changing eye color as Kate, pupils blue in light, but so large they turned a dark slate color in shadow. There was no question the same blood flowed in each.

The queen was speaking: "My palace of Richmond is not so great as Whitehall, and I will be certain to hear near endless complaining. My lady Katherine Grey, for example, is not so happy, we believe, to share a room with Lady Saintloe. Yet, I think it well met when youth has the advantage of older guidance, don't you, my lord earl?"

Edward did not look away from the queen toward Kate, but he began to sense a cat-and-mouse game, and he was the prey.

"I have heard it to be so, Your Grace, though I have also been well taught by the young, who have often retained an appealing innocent curiosity that is sometimes lost by age." He said the words lightly as wit and not as a question of the queen's judgment, since everyone at court was there at Her Majesty's pleasure, whatever that was, or however it changed.

The queen smiled slightly as the mouse nibbled the cheese but escaped the trap. "My lord, I see nothing of the child left in you. But I am gladdened to hear the loving boy I first saw in my brother's court remains in the man's heart."

Edward did not allow himself to breathe. She remembered earlier gossip about him and Kate, and of course the queen remembered his petition of just days ago to court her lady-in-waiting. He'd escaped the visible trap to fall into a hidden one.

Elizabeth reached to her side table and picked up a sheet of vellum hung about with red seals and signed in her distinctive hand, *Elizabeth R.* "This is our letter to the French queen, asking for reasonable toleration of her Protestant subjects and protection from the excesses of the Duke de Guise's anti-Huguenot policies. You are to deliver it to the French ambassador, presently residing in London, and then you may look to your house in Westminster on Canon Row. Stay as long as it pleases you to settle your affairs, which have surely been neglected of late. Wait there, holding yourself in readiness for our further pleasure."

"Thank you, Majesty. I'm most happy to have your confidence."

Elizabeth slipped the rolled parchment into a leather tube, sealed it and handed it to Edward, who held it against his chest.

The queen turned to some other papers and began reading them. Edward stood and bowed his way to the antechamber. He walked swiftly to his own chamber. It was obvious that Dudley had told her something, or at the least suggested his name for this mission. Separation was supposed to be the cure for unsuitable lovers. The queen would find more than one reason to keep him in London, or on numberless missions that he could not refuse. His throat burned with angry—even treasonous—words he couldn't help. But angry words had no power here. His legs moved stiffly, like a puppet's, taking him away from Kate without his having looked at her or reassured her with an unspoken message.

He exited the hall at the presence chamber, the queen's great canopied chair being heaved onto a stage that dominated the great room. God's bones! He'd forgotten which hall to take to his sister Jane's rooms. He slammed a fist against the stone wall, scraping skin from his knuckles. Sucking on the sore hand, he asked a gentleman usher where Lady Jane Seymour's rooms were located.

He rushed to the right exit. Somehow, he must see Kate before he left. His sister could get a message to her.

Jane was busy directing her own maids in unpacking and airing her gowns. "Edward, these rooms are smaller than at Whitehall. If I were one of the queen's ladies—"

"You might have to room with Lady Saintloe," he said in a low voice.

Jane dismissed her maids to another room and drew Edward to a settle near to the fire, waving a hand in front of her face. "This smoke from the sea coal burns my throat," she explained, waiting for the door to close. "Edward, dear brother, are you saying that the queen has placed Lady Katherine with that gossip?"

"Yes, and there is no way I can see her unless you help me."

"You know I would do anything for you, Edward, but it is terribly dangerous. Half the court knows of your love."

"I have told no one but you and Dudley!"

"Edward, you have never been able to dissemble. You are compromised a dozen times each day. You can't hide what you feel, although this urgency puzzles me."

"Urgency!" he growled. "You think nine years not long enough to wait? She was meant to be mine and well you know it!" Edward's voice was more impatient than he had intended, so he sweetened his tone. "She was forced to marry Pembroke when she wanted me."

"But that marriage was annulled, so she is yet a virgin of the blood royal. Have a care, Edward. You know that taking an heir to the throne without the queen's consent is treason."

"I lost her once, but not again. I could not count myself a man if I allowed it."

"You can't go against the queen of England," Jane said, alarmed.

"I would give up my life's blood for the queen, but not Kate . . . not Kate." He bent forward and sank his face into his hands.

Kate followed the queen in procession through the palace to a meeting of her council. Along the way, Lady Jane Seymour slipped a note inside a slash in Kate's sleeve. She curtsied briefly and walked on, glancing hastily at Lady Saintloe, who walked behind, but appeared to be in deep conversation with Mistress Ashley.

"My lady Grey," the queen called when they reached the council chamber.

"Yes, Majesty." Kate hurried forward past the Lord Chamberlain to the queen.

"We would have you attend us in council. It will provide you good experience."

Kate stiffened. It was like Elizabeth to say nothing in advance to prepare Kate. But for what? Kate kept her face blank, although the queen must surely know that her unusual request had put Kate in suspense.

For fear the paper inside her sleeve would crackle, Kate was careful to keep her arm relaxed, one hand in the other, while holding her head high in regal attitude. Now was no time to have the queen discover secret correspondence.

Liveried yeomen opened the door to the council chamber, the council members standing to bow as the queen walked quickly to her large upholstered chair at the near end of the table. The Lord

Secretary, William Cecil, stood at the other end, his white staff of office in his hand.

There could not be a greater contrast between ruler and servant. The queen was royally attired in bejeweled golden satin hung about with ropes of pearls, with matching embroidered slippers, her long white fingers flashing with diamonds and precious stones. William Cecil, past forty years, was dressed in somber black, befitting his strict religious, near Puritan, beliefs. He faced his young sovereign seated opposite.

The queen smiled pleasantly. "You may acknowledge the lady Grey . . . my beloved daughter."

The assembled men bowed, as astonished as Kate at the thought that Elizabeth claimed to be her mother, and not in jest, nor in general, nor in private. Kate caught her breath. She had dismissed a palace rumor that the queen planned to adopt her as just wild gossip. Yet what game was this? Was it another maneuver to confuse those who urged her to marry or name an heir?

But Kate's overwhelming worry was what Ned's note said.

The queen opened the meeting. "Rest yourselves, my lords and gentlemen." She waved her hand for them to sit. "We have here a fair copy of our letter to the French queen regarding the Huguenot troubles. The Earl of Hertford is sent to London to deliver it."

Kate bit down on her tongue. Was Ned already gone from Richmond? Was the note in her sleeve from him, or from Jane, saying he was gone? She dared to touch it to make sure it was still there.

"Majesty," Cecil spoke in his steady, unemotional voice, "we have received a petition from Parliament regarding your earlier promise to communicate your future marriage plans during this session. Your Grace, there is yet the possibility of a Hapsburg match."

The queen stamped one foot under the table, making an irritated *pup! pup!* sound with her mouth. "Better beggar woman and single, than queen and married."

The grim-faced council members looked to Cecil, while Cecil inclined his head, indicating he had heard.

Yet the queen had not completely vented her displeasure. "Is there no other business before our Parliament except our marriage? Tell the gentlemen that we will reply in good time." Her angry voice rang throughout the chamber: "My lords, we think it monstrous that the feet do attempt to direct the head!"

"Majesty," Cecil intoned soothingly, "it is our given duty to advise the Crown, though I admit many think a foreign Catholic prince would rouse your Catholic subjects against the English church."

"Aye, Your Grace," the Duke of Norfolk agreed, "there is concern that such a prince would put his own people in powerful court positions."

Since the duke was thought a secret papist, Kate thought the response deceitful.

Elizabeth was more than angry with all of them, her face red with unexploded frustration. "And such a foreign prince would drain our treasury for his continental wars, or demand we go to Austria when he succeeds to that throne"—she inhaled deeply—"and as a wife subject to a husband's rule, we would have to obey." She pounded the table with her free hand. "Yet you would not have us marry an English lord for fear of offending other English lords, who would raise revolts!"

By this time, Kate was certain she knew why she had been invited to accompany the queen. She had known in advance of Parliament's marriage demands and planned to use Kate to calm them if necessary. Kate moved slightly toward the door, out of range of Her Majesty's strategy.

"My lords, there is no way we can please, so we will not seek to do so. Elizabeth of England will marry when moved to do so by God . . . not by Parliament, or a council of wavering opinion!"

"Majesty," Cecil said evenly, glancing at Kate, "there is a desire amongst the commons for an heir."

Elizabeth sat even taller in her great chair. "God will provide an heir for England when the time is right." She glared at her councilors to see who would dare to doubt that her word came directly from God. "My lords, we think that our father was not so much reproached for his many marriages as we are for none!" The queen stopped for a much-needed breath.

Kate wondered if there was a vinegar cloth at hand.

All the councilors remained mute where they sat, some obviously wishing to be elsewhere.

After an audible sigh, Elizabeth smiled at them and crossed her hands against her heart, saying in her most cajoling voice, her eyes sparkling with humor, "Yet, my good lords, we would have you pursue this Hapsburg match, if it please you so."

Even though Kate nearly wilted with relief, realizing the queen could have named her at that moment, she pinched herself hard to keep from laughing aloud. Still, she smiled inwardly at her own mixed allegiances. Elizabeth was monstrous, but wonderfully and unpredictably changeable. When in a temper, she was like a channel storm blowing up from nowhere, and just as suddenly as the sun forcing its way through to calm the waters, she was beautifully radiant. And irresistible, judging from the rapt faces of the men around the council table.

Watching them bask in the glow of the queen's change of heart, Kate could not help but wonder if Anne Boleyn's supposed witchery had descended to the daughter. But that was a treasonous thought, even in jest, and Kate pushed it away.

Elizabeth's commanding words shifted the topic. "Now, my lords and gentlemen, there are more pressing problems than matrimony in our realm to occupy our attentions." She leaned forward, tapping her fan on the long table, although her council was all attention. "Last year we sent our armies to aid the Scots Protestants. Can we do less for the French? We would discuss that situation and what opportunity it provides to regain our port of Calais, lost by the late queen, my sister. It is a stain on the honor of England. We *will* have it back, my lords!"

While Kate tried to listen as first one man said this and the next man said the opposite, she found it impossible to follow talk of troop levies, taxes, and Parliamentary demands when her heart ached to know if it was truly Ned who had written the message hidden in her sleeve.

"My lords!" the queen said through tight lips, finally exasperated, "if no two men can agree here, from whom do we take our counsel?"

Though the words caused Kate to shrink away, as she knew too well that rage could follow and be aimed at her, the paper in her sleeve seemed to burn with more urgency than the queen's annoyance or her motherly surprises.

If Ned were leaving court, he must want to see her. But what if the note said farewell, finally acknowledging the risk to them both? She would be alone, and this time forever. She could never trust love again.

Her heart and head were still at odds when the queen stood, the council members quickly getting to their feet and bowing. Cecil remained serene as Her Majesty swept from the chamber. She murmured over her shoulder to Kate, "My lady Grey, *that* is what it is to be queen. Do not wish to leave your womanhood in such a stinking stable midden."

It is not my wish, but yours that commands. Kate did not say the words aloud. Elizabeth would do what she wanted, when she wanted. That was what it truly was to be queen, and Kate wanted none of it. The deception, the constant meetings, the scheming—a queen's life was no match for the green fields of Eltham.

As all Her Majesty's ladies flocked into procession behind her, trumpets and drums began their notice to the court that the queen approached and to stop pissing in the corners and begin doing what would please her most. Kate's mind was awhirl with all she'd heard.

She felt a growing cold, not sweeping down the wintry halls of Richmond palace but from inside her own body. Elizabeth would never marry, never allow Kate to know what a queen rejected. She offered hope to her council in any way she could, from naming a daughter to agreeing to marriage negotiations. But she meant none of it. Kate would grow old and ugly waiting and hoping for Ned.

Minutes later, alone in the queen's linen closet, Kate withdrew the note, sensing how warm it was to her touch. She could not help but wonder if it was warmth from her own body, or warmth sent from Ned's. She quickly read the words written in his hand: *Tonight at my sister's apartment.*

Pleading her monthly flux and a gripping in her stomach after supper, Kate announced: "I must visit the court apothecary to obtain some tansy water."

Mistress Ashley nodded. "Some women do take their monthly bleeding hard. Tansy water has been a cure for Elizabeth, princess and queen."

Kate quickly made her way to the apothecary and obtained a vial of distilled tansy water. Looking both ways, she walked toward Jane Seymour's apartment, until, certain she was being followed, she doubled back to allow Lady Saintloe to rush past her hiding place. Then Kate hurried on down another hall.

Ned was waiting alone inside a partially open door. No servants and no sister were in sight. He pulled Kate inside and kissed her fiercely. She gave a little cry of pain. She put the back of one hand to her mouth, thinking it bruised with the violence of Ned's kiss, although while it stung she felt its heat more than its hurt.

He stepped back while still holding tight to her arms, his face showing concern. "How did you get leave?"

Blushing, Kate said, "I told Ashley that I was unwell."

"Dearest," he said, worried.

Kate shook her head. "It's nothing. An excuse to escape, nothing more."

Relieved, he rushed on. "Kate, forgive me. These last hours, knowing I must leave you and may not soon be invited back to court, have made me near lose my wits."

"What do you want of me? What can I do?" She was surprised at how steady her voice was, though her heart was not.

He pulled her to a settle by the fire, seating her on it and then sitting close beside her, imprisoning her gown under one leg. "Warm yourself, my love. You're shivering."

She nodded, not daring to look in his face, or tell him that she was not shaking from cold, but from his nearness.

"Kate," he said fiercely, "I will be no martyr to love. My feelings are too hot and my heart too empty without you. I will have you as part of my life, part of my morning's waking and my night's sleeping. Kate, I cannot be the man I must be without you. I thought I'd lost you once, but now that I have you again, we must marry, queen or no." His voice shook. "I have sworn to God that I will not take you without his priest's blessing on us."

His words drew her to him. How could any woman not respond to such a man? Kate looked at him and felt her face flush as the import of his words became clear. He was not afraid to say what came from some desperate place that she would have been afraid to enter alone. But with Ned, she would dare, though when she tried to say yes, her courage failed her. She swallowed hard and tried one last time to deny him. "There is no way, my lord. As you know well, she will not consent. Elizabeth called me *daughter* today, trying to ward off more calls for her marriage, although it did not work."

"Listen to me, Kate." He had never sounded more urgent. "When the marriage is blessed and consummated"—he slid his hands to either side of her face as she began to shake her head—"when *blessed and consummated*, what can she do?"

"She can send us to the Tower. Do you forget that her father's will put me in the succession and also named it treason for an heir to marry without their sovereign's consent? By law, she could demand our heads."

"No!" He spat the word. "That would outrage the people, and she values her popularity above all. They would take it ill if Elizabeth harmed a queen's nephew and her own blood cousin for falling honorably in love and receiving the blessing of the Church."

There was truth in what he said, though Kate did not know if the queen would forgive their defiance. But she wanted to believe it. She needed desperately to believe it. "Maybe, Ned. I don't know—"

"You do know!"

At that moment she realized, opening her eyes wide, that the chance of a life with Ned was worth any risk. She would have no life without him.

"Don't you love me, Kate?" His words were laden with anguish.

No answer came from her mouth because Ned was kissing her again, taking the breath she needed to say no, taking the immense will she needed to produce that lie. Her lips released, she spoke: "Yes, I love you . . . oh, many times yes!"

He leaned away, his mouth wet with her kiss, joy lighting his face to the brightness of a hundred candles. "What matters a few months in the Tower and then all forgiven with our lives joined? Far worse, sweetest, to be together in the same palace, yet miserably apart, eventually to lose each other forever."

"She might invite some foreign suitor to come for me," murmured Kate as she sank her face into his doublet, inhaling the scent of him that had never quite left her nostrils since their first meeting. "I couldn't bear it."

"You won't have to bear it as my wife," he said, his voice as confident as ever.

"But, Ned, I am watched constantly here. How will I . . . How will we—"

"Tomorrow, the queen will hunt from early until late. Continue your illness. Make your excuse to remain in the palace and come to Jane. She will do the rest. Will you come to London, Kate? Will you marry me before God and be my wife?"

Kate hesitated, her mind racing.

"Say yes, Kate, or we must part forever. A man cannot live this way."

"Nor a woman, Ned. I say yes with all my heart. I will be your wife."

He stood, helping her up on her feet, twirling her about as if he heard the queen's consort playing a dance just for them. "You won't regret it, Kate. Tomorrow we will be together before the priest and in my bed, husband and wife, never to part again. Whom God has joined—is that what you want?"

"More than anything." As she heard her own words, she realized for once and all that she wasn't like Elizabeth. She wanted Ned more than she wanted Elizabeth's transient approval, her mother's blessing, or the revels of the court. . . . She wanted him more than anything in this realm. Ned could be right: Elizabeth could never deny a marriage, twice joined, once by priest and again by body.

CHAPTER FOUR

"A clear and innocent conscience fears nothing."
—Elizabeth Regina

The Next Morn

The queen finished her morning prayers for England at her *prie-dieu* and rode out toward the main gate of Richmond Palace shortly after the larks awakened. With hounds baying and trumpets blaring to alert every deer in Surrey, Robert Dudley rode beside Elizabeth, both on magnificent, black, high-stepping hunters.

Kate stared through the swirling dust kicked up by the stallions, for Elizabeth would not have a gelding. "Man or horse. What challenge in that?" she'd once jested. Despite herself, Kate had been amused and smiled now in memory.

Below, Elizabeth and Dudley, faces glowing in the mist, were laughing in anticipation of a breakneck ride over every obstacle in their path.

Kate watched them go, standing behind the mullioned windows in the queen's bedchamber. They were so obviously of the same heart, Kate could not doubt that the queen would one day regret her choice to remain without Robin as her husband. That was not a regret Kate wanted, or could bear. The idea of living without Ned created an instant emptiness in the deepest corner of her soul. And she no longer cared if an imp of Satan planted that thought. She was loved. For the second time in her life, she was truly loved, and she would not give it up again for mother, council or queen. Since she had been a child, she had been told what was wanted of her; now she would tell herself. Ned's love had given her that strength. Ned had set her heart free.

Hastily, she gathered the queen's nightclothes and linen, gave them to the mistress of the body for washing, informed the master groom that she had a toothache, and went to her chamber for her fur cloak. Lady Saintloe was riding with the queen, so Kate was safe enough for the day. But she knew her absence would be immediately reported when the hunting party returned. The countess would question Sybil, then rush to question Jane and, finding her gone from the palace as well, would issue a hue and cry through the hundreds of chambers. When they were both known to be gone, Kate didn't doubt that the queen would dispatch yeoman guards to Ned's Westminster residence.

She felt her heart thudding against her breasts with part apprehension and part excited resolve as she changed into her best gown, one of the queen's of last year's design, minus the jewels, but still fine white velvet with exquisite cutwork. She settled her best fur cloak about her shoulders as her nurse opened the door.

"But, my lady," Sybil asked, "what be I saying to—"

"I returned to the apothecary," Kate prompted.

"In yer fur cloak?"

"Say as you're told," Kate said too brusquely, and then took time to kiss her nurse's cheek and hug her.

"Aye, love. I be seeing you grieve Lord Edward in secret all these long years."

Inhaling deeply, Kate stopped and removed a coin from the pocket hanging from her wrist and handed it to Sybil. "Buy a dainty at the bakehouse, Sybil, and thank you," she said, then whirled out the door before she lost her nerve. As she raced through the presence chamber, Kate sensed that Elizabeth was there even though her throne was empty.

This was a mad thing she was about. Maddest of all, she could not stop herself.

Jane waited in her rooms, cloaked, hooded and nervous. "Come swiftly," she said, tugging at Kate's hand.

They followed one of Ned's grooms down a private, steeply narrow stone staircase and out upon a wooden planked walkway to a little-used dock, downriver from most castle windows, covered by fog that crept silently along the marshy ground. A small barge waited.

"Ned hired the rowers from a nearby village," Jane explained. "They are well paid to keep their silence."

Kate nodded, too anxious to make conversation, or argue that few men kept their silence on the rack.

There were several early fishermen on the river and two small barges taking early lambs to the Smithfield market. Lambs to the slaughter, Kate could not help but think with some empathy. She was relieved to see that their own boat was shrouded from sight in the mist. As she huddled within her cloak, her emotions ran between fear of Elizabeth's revenge when she returned, and longing to see Ned and be safe for any time at all in his arms. She prayed that he was right and Elizabeth would have no choice but to acknowledge their marriage. Then she prayed the same prayer again, her hands clenched together in reverent attitude.

Jane chattered all the time the fast-moving barge made its way back to the Westminster water stairs, mostly talking about Dudley, praising everything to his fingertips. She was as taken with that dashing, lusty lord as were half the court ladies, but without their chances of any return. Though loyal to her brother and of the royal Seymour family, she was plain and dull-witted, with nothing to truly attract a man like Lord Robert. Women were such poor creatures, Kate mused, either helpless in their love, or hopeless. She laughed a bit cynically, because she'd described herself as well as Jane, though she smiled reassuringly at her future sister-in-law, who looked hurt because she'd said nothing remotely humorous.

Ned, dressed splendidly in rich, sable brown velvet, with gold slashes on his doublet sleeves, stood on the stairs, his tall form rising out of the swirling mist like a sea god's. He bade the rowers wait, and after a tender kiss he helped Kate and Jane up the slimy stone steps, where his servants stood with lanterns to light their way through the fog still clinging to the dark, muddy streets.

They walked quickly past the looming stone mass of the abbey and through the alleys made dim by overhanging many-storied houses. The narrow passages were thronged with geese picking at refuse and fish sellers pushing their barrows on morning rounds, shouting their fresh catch to the upper stories.

Ned kept tight hold of her waist and hand until they came to an open square. Every few steps he whispered in her ear, "Do not doubt, my love; all will be well."

Did doubt appear on her face, when she was most careful not to let it escape her tongue?

They exited the square onto Canon Row. The first large stone house was Ned's, welcoming lights shining from every window.

"Hurry, Kate," he said. "The priest and witnesses are waiting."

"You've thought of everything."

"I hope so."

His voice held concern, and Kate glanced behind her.

"No, sweetheart, I swear there is nothing to alarm you. All is in readiness."

A ladies' maid took her fur cloak away for drying and brushing as Kate stepped into the great hall hung with large arras tapestries, huge apple-wood logs burning in the stone fireplace, pushing February's cold into the far corners and replacing the chilled air with a fruity, springtime scent. An oak-paneled gallery circled above the hall with many doors leading to bedchambers. One of them, Kate knew, was Ned's bedchamber. And soon it would be hers. She trembled and he tightened his hold, leading her to a small chapel off the great hall.

A few trusted old servants had gathered to witness their master's wedding, and were clustered in a group around the door. The chapel and stained-glass windows were lit with the soft glow of lanterns and braziers. Lifting her eyes, Kate could see the mark behind the altar where a large cross had hung during Elizabeth's Catholic sister's reign. Mary Tudor had brought back the old faith and burned at the stake all the outspoken Protestants she could find. They were going to burn in hell for their heresy, so why not a few years earlier? she had reasoned.

Ned led Kate to his family altar and they both knelt.

The priest wore tattered black robes, and looked windblown and not altogether sober. "My lord," he mumbled, "you say no banns have been published; then I cannot—"

Ned's stern look as he drew a folded document from his doublet silenced the priest. "This is our marriage bond signed by the bishop of London, giving us permission to marry without banns. Now, no more delays. There is no time to lose."

These words dropped the priest's gaze to Kate's belly to see if birth was imminent. Kate met his puzzlement with her own. Did Ned expect the queen's guard to break down his door?

"Begin!" Ned commanded when Jane was in her place behind them.

"Dearly beloved friends, holy matrimony, as a remedy against the sin of fornication—"

"No, good priest . . . to the heart of the service, quickly." Ned looked at Kate, his gaze troubled. "I'm sorry, my love. I would that this were not so hurried—"

"Remember, Ned, I have heard it all before when it meant nothing, less than nothing to me. Now the smallest word with you before this altar means everything."

He tightened his grip on her hand.

The priest coughed, his eyes searching the rear of the chapel, mentally finding his place in the wedding service. "I require and charge you as you will answer at the dreadful day of judgment that if either of you do know of any impediments—"

"There are no impediments," Ned said impatiently, his arm going reassuringly about Kate's slender shoulders. "Get on!"

The priest had to think, having lost his way again in the service he usually offered. Finally, he began: "No impediment being alleged . . . Edward Seymour, Earl of Hertford, wilt thou have this woman, Lady Katherine Grey, to thy wedded wife, to live together under God's ordinance in the holy estate of matrimony and forsaking all others keep thee only unto her, so long as ye both shall live?"

"I will," Ned said in a very steady voice.

The priest repeated the words for Kate and she said, "I will," adding, "and thereto I plight thee, Edward, Earl of Hertford, my troth."

His sister, Jane, handed her brother a ring; then Ned, following the priest's words, placed a gold circlet centered with a ruby on Kate's fourth finger, saying: "With this ring I thee wed. With my body I thee worship and with my worldly goods I thee endow."

The priest pronounced them married, then seemed to lose his way and mumble, but found his place in memory again, saying loudly, "May you ever remain in perfect love and peace together."

A servant handed the priest a cup of wine, which he gratefully accepted. "And now to the wedding feast, my lord."

"No feast, good priest."

"No feast?"

Ned handed him several silver coins. "Sign the wedding contract and you may feast at the inn in the square where we found you"—he added a gold royal to the priest's hand—"and swear you will ever after keep secret what has passed here. Now raise your cup to the Earl and Countess of Hertford."

"Aye, my lord," the priest said, eagerly complying. The cup

drained, he was shown by a servant to a side entrance, where he clutched his robes about him for warmth and was gone into the darkened day of rain and fog.

There was a scurry of feet behind Kate as the servants pressed forward to sign or make their marks as witnesses to the marriage contract, and together they chanted their best wishes for a long life. After a rousing "Huzzah!" they went to their duties with a blessed coin for good luck.

"It's unseemly, I know, Kate," Ned said softly, his face gentle, "but I would have you returned to Richmond before you are missed."

As he led her, preceded by his chamberlain holding candelabra, to the gallery stairs, she asked, "How can I possibly return to the palace before—"

"Robert will keep the queen's party out until nightfall."

Kate shook her head, disbelieving. "Dudley is aiding us?"

"Yes, sweeting, he is."

"But why, Ned?"

He shrugged. "Because he listens to his heart for once."

"Perhaps he would like to see love triumph so that Her Majesty would more likely turn to him."

"Who knows why Robert does anything?"

Kate frowned. "He does nothing that will not further Robert Dudley. Next to Elizabeth, he loves Robert most."

"He is arrogant and proud, I grant you, but do not judge him too harshly, Kate. He will put it about the court that I am to make a marriage contract with the daughter of a knight in Hertfordshire."

"He would deceive the queen?"

"I will be recalled to court, and I will also own to it, so no blame can come to him."

Kate frowned. "He ensures the queen never forgives us for a double deception."

"Sweetheart," Ned said, his courage flowing to her through the taut muscles in his arm, "we must take aid where we find it, when we need it. I require time to prevail with Cecil or Norfolk to intercede with Her Majesty on our behalf."

Kate did not argue further. She wanted to forget the queen and Dudley, if only for this short time they had together. She wanted to forget everything that would not speed her into Ned's arms, the only place in life where she had ever felt loved and safe. It no longer mattered to her that the queen would be in a rage when she discovered Kate's deception. She had known Elizabeth's rages, had felt their fury on her own body with many a slap. Kate knew the queen's anger would matter later, but at this moment, with Ned's arm tight around her, she felt safe from any earthly punishment, for surely God had blessed them, and He was the higher power.

She mounted the stairs, unwavering. This was her chance for love and a happy life, her first chance, perhaps her only one. Elizabeth's heart would come to understand. How could a woman who loved not understand another woman's love?

When they reached Ned's privy chamber, the servant opened the heavily carved door and Kate stepped inside, while the chamberlain went about the dark-paneled room that shone with newly applied beeswax, lighting each candle. Kate had never known lighting a room to take so long.

All candles lit, she found herself standing in the center of a large chamber already warmed by a coal fire in the hearth, not knowing what to do next. This was unlike her other wedding night, in that it was scarcely after twelve of the clock in the day, and she had long ago started the flux that released the foul womanly humors that made her ready for a husband. After her wedding to Pembroke, she had gone to her bed crying for Ned and alone save for Sybil in the trundle bed, shushing her. At this moment, near a decade older, she was blissful and eager for Ned's touch.

"Kate?" Her name was a warm breath against her neck. Ned stood against her back, slipping his arms tight about her waist and resting his chin on her shoulder.

"Yes," she whispered, and she meant *yes* in every way she could mean *yes*. "I acknowledge you as my lord husband and lover, till death us do part." She did not add, *Or until Elizabeth parts us*, but she believed they both thought it.

"Sshh," he mouthed, turning her body toward his own, which even through his doublet radiated heat. "I need no more pledge from you than the one you made before God." He kissed her, a slow, enveloping kiss that lasted until she was breathless.

She trembled, her heartbeat fluttering in her throat.

"I wish we had endless hours, but . . . I won't hurt you, Kate. Not more than I have to. You know that."

She touched his lips with the tips of her fingers to stop his stream of words. "Ned, for years I have lived and seen much at court, and my sister, Jane, told me of her wedding night." Kate's face must have revealed what her sister had confessed about her young, unfeeling husband.

Ned smiled and his lips parted and, slipping two fingers beneath her laces, he began to undo her stomacher. "Then, my heart, you know nothing but what is hidden or hated. You will know better, much better, I promise you."

When the laces hung open, there were yet gown, sleeves, ruff, farthingale, shift and hose to remove. Ned looked at his hands. "These hands have not the patience for this work, Kate, and I would not frighten you with my fumbling hurry."

"You don't frighten me, Ned, but you do keep me waiting. Is it because I bring you no dowry but my name? You forget that as the queen's chief lady, I am paid forty marks per annum."

He laughed. "A princely sum. I have in my arms a woman of great wealth."

She laughed in her turn. What had made her so bold? She did not know, but whatever it was, it continued. She moved toward the wide, towering bed that could hold several couples, a bed to match the famed Bed of Ware said to contain six loving couples at once. She pulled aside the heavy tapestry curtains.

She heard him shedding clothes behind her as she slipped from her gown, shift and farthingale. She hated the abomination the Spanish had brought to England, but no woman could be seen in a gown in public without it. The leather harness and bone structure crashed to the floor, leaving her hips and her womanhood free.

Ned picked her up gently and laid her on the fine linen sheets and swansdown pillows that smelled of sandlewood, smelled of him.

Ned shed his breeches and hose. In the crowded life of the court she had seen other naked men being sluiced with water during summer baths and at river plunges. But Ned surpassed them all. His powerful soldier's body had been hardened by battle and outlined with the scars of healed wounds. A smile tugged at his mouth, softening his face almost to the innocence of the boy she'd first loved. She tried not to stare, but time and again she failed, her gaze traveling from his wide shoulders to his narrow waist and hard hips to . . . Her eyes widened. Ned needed none of the padding Elizabeth's courtiers used to give themselves inflated bodies and manhood. "You are . . ." She searched for a word, but could only breathe, "Beautiful."

Ned laughed. He waited for her to look her fill, until he could wait no longer. He lay beside her, his hand reaching for her golden red hair loosed from under its hood onto the silken pillow. He combed his fingers through her curls, thinking she looked like a sea nymph floating on white water. He touched her breasts, spreading his fingers across to capture both in his one large hand. "I promise to be easy, Kate," he murmured against her cheek, his lips scalding.

She raised her hand and touched the fine brown hair on his chest. "You worry overmuch, Ned. I am no rag doll; I will not come apart."

His cock was hard against her leg, and he thought she might have good reason to soon disown her own reassuring words.

But Kate had no sense to disown, to speak, to think. Falling to little pieces was what was happening to her at this moment, soft pieces of her body collapsing and melting into him at his touch. She closed her eyes, holding her breath as they were slowly, ever so little by little joined more completely in his bed than by any priest with all his ceremony. At his first thrust, her pain was sharp but brief, and followed by a molten rush mounting from his deepest touch, their passion rising higher and higher until each spilled love into the other.

Above her, he cried out her name. "Kate . . . Kate! My only love."

As he said it, she believed him with all her body. He shook, his breathing ragged. God had saved her for Ned, through her false marriage, through her family's disgrace. She was sure this was the Lord's doing. Not even Elizabeth Tudor could stand against God.

He collapsed on top of her. "Are you—"

She threw her arms about him, holding him even closer. "I am very well, husband, never more well." Kate gasped, drawing in needed breath and with it the unfamiliar musky odor of after-love. She was deeply filled and emptied by him, aware she'd been holding her breath, for how long she could only guess. She smiled up at the sound of his voice above her, thinking that her childhood punishments had hurt far worse than the sundering of her virginity.

Kate opened her eyes wide to find Ned looking down at her and, through a crack in the bed hangings, the chamber illuminated by the sun, newly burst through the fog, thrusting through thick glass oriel windows to cast a greenish light into every shadowy corner of the room.

Ned inclined his head to the glow. "God is smiling on us, Kate."

The door creaked open. "Your pardon. Is it done?" Jane asked hurriedly.

Ned laughed, and Kate quickly hid her face in his chest. "It is well-done, sister." Then for Kate's ears, he whispered, "Though not for as long or as often as I would wish."

The door opened wider. "Should I call a maid to help the lady Katherine dress?"

"No," Ned responded. "I will be the Countess of Hertford's maid this day, sister." He swung his legs through the curtains and out of bed. "Wait in the hall, unless you wish to see me as God made me."

"Edward, there is no time to lose," Jane replied rather severely. "I am at risk, and I would have you both remember me."

"Wait in the hall, sister," Ned said, no teasing in his tone. "Sisters can be nettlesome," he said, winking at Kate as the door closed, but at the lost look that swept her face, he took her in his arms. "I beg pardon, sweeting. I forgot about your own dear sister, Lady Jane Grey."

"She would be happy for me, Ned, and there is no reason for you to remember. She is quite forgotten by all," Kate said, her words wobbling with sudden remembrance of her kind and gentle sister. "It will be different with us." She clasped him closer. "Won't it?"

"Very different. Never doubt it. The queen would not dare to . . ."

"Take our heads?" Kate finished the sentence he was too loving to complete.

"Come, my countess," he said, standing and raising her to her feet. "The sun is up, making this no day for gloom or doubt. Remember, whom God has joined together, let no man put asunder."

Nor queen, echoed Kate as she stepped into her farthingale and Ned, laughing at its complications, tied it around her waist, then let her gown fall down to cover it.

They retraced their steps to the Westminster water stairs along with Jane, the chamberlain and two grooms, Kate keeping her warm, glowing face well in shadow under her hood and her hand in a tight hold of Ned's arm.

He helped Jane into the waiting barge, then kissed Kate, clasping her so tightly that she groaned.

"I will see you soon?" she asked, not wanting to leave him without that promise.

"Yes, love. You will. With news of my betrothal, there will be no reason for the queen to keep me away from court. When I return we must be careful to be polite, but no longer caring."

She clung to him. "That will be past enduring."

"I know, my heart, but my sister will help us come together whenever it is safe."

He put a hand inside his doublet and passed the marriage contract to her. "Just in case . . ."

She clasped him tighter. "In case of what?"

"Nothing will happen to me, but this belongs with you now." He kissed her scarcely less ardently than he'd kissed her in their marriage bed, then gently placed her in the barge and shoved it away, the rowers beginning their rhythmic dipping and pulling, their doublets stretching tight across their backs.

Kate looked over her shoulder, waving as the sun went behind a cloud and a chill breeze swept round her hood. Ned's figure disappeared quickly into the dark background of the mossy water stairs.

They had rowed about halfway back to Richmond when two huge barges crammed with soldiers, their upright pikes shining even as the afternoon light faded, a drum beating time for the oarsmen, came swiftly toward them.

Kate pushed Jane to the bottom of the boat, then crouched over her, hardly daring to breathe, and shushing Jane, who was mewling in fear.

The sound of drumming and splashing oars came closer. The bargeman at the tiller behind them complained: "M'lady, yer lord ne'er paid us to dodge the queen's pikemen."

"Be assured, he will pay you in far poorer coin if we are taken!" She made her voice as severe as she could, though she could not remove every tremor. She pressed her hands against the deck to stop their shaking. Dread covered her more surely than her cloak.

Had Dudley played them false? Were these yeomen guards on their way to arrest Ned and take him to the Tower? She prayed for strength and gathered some courage from the prayer for what might face her when she returned.

Kate spent the trip back to Richmond Palace calming herself, losing calm and finding it again. When they disembarked out of sight of the palace, Kate, holding fast to the faltering Jane Seymour, linked arms and came swinging down the boardwalk as if returning from a stroll.

She would not wear her guilt for all to see, and that was easier than she imagined. Before God, she had done nothing outside His ordinances.

Courtiers stopped to bow as they passed. "Give you good day, my ladies."

Kate curtsied in return. Surely, if there were a hue and cry, these gentlemen would know of it.

"Sir," she said, "did we miss . . . a ceremony that brought out the guards?"

"Indeed, my lady," a gentleman answered. "Her Grace is sending them to honor the French ambassador on his departure."

"The queen is returned from the hunt?" Did she utter her own sentence for treason?

"Nay, lady, not as yet."

She smiled her thanks, clasped Jane's arm and half carried her down the path. Kate put some menace in her voice: "If you faint—"

"I'm quite recovered, sister," Jane said, but her voice was a squeak.

They passed the tiltyard and entered the castle full of scurrying servants and courtiers about the business of preparing for the queen's return, Jane going to her apartment. Without another word, Kate returned to her room to change her gown.

Did the loss of her chastity show clearly on her face? Did others see that she had left the palace a maid and returned a bedded wife? God was said to see everything and know each grain of sand on His earth. He must know what she and Ned had done this day in defiance of His anointed queen. Shaking herself, Kate refused to dwell on whether He approved or not.

She would face Elizabeth before she faced God.

Elizabeth and Dudley returned long after dark, cloaks and boots muddied, faces high-colored, eyes bright, calling loudly for their supper and mulled spiced wine. Both threw themselves down on the cushioned hearth before the fire in the queen's antechamber, laughing, talking loudly, as if the wind were still in their faces.

Elizabeth threw off her cap, letting her red-gold hair fall about her shoulders as a mark of her unmarried state.

Kate knelt to serve a dish to the queen, Ned's wedding ring hanging safely between her breasts by a ribbon, while Mistress Ashley, ever the nurse, removed Elizabeth's boots and rubbed her feet to warm them.

Laughing, the queen thrust a cold foot at Dudley and, after undoing his doublet and shirt, he took the slender foot in his hands, braced it against his hairy chest and rubbed vigorously, one hand straying on alternate strokes above her ankles. These were the acts of lovers who thought to disguise lust with play, or who were beyond caring what others thought.

Kate didn't have to look to see the reaction from the queen's clustered ladies. Their audible intakes of breath told her of their shock.

Elizabeth leaned back on her elbows, waving faithful Ashley away. The queen's face was marked now with more than high spirits from the day's ride. Kate saw that desire had replaced sport, until Mistress Ashley gave out a loud cough of warning.

Desire was an expression Kate now knew she must banish from her own face, though the sense of Ned filling her was yet upon her and the scent of sandalwood would never leave her.

"Majesty, a swan pie from your privy kitchen," Kate said, her hands losing their steadiness.

Elizabeth laughed and gave a little kick with her captured foot. Dudley fell back as if struck by a thunderbolt, clutching his chest and groaning.

A relieved sigh from several throats echoed through the chamber, and both Elizabeth and Dudley fell to laughing wildly, performing and seeing their own spectacle in each other at the same time.

Kate kept her gaze on the dish she held, wondering how Elizabeth could pull herself back time upon time from the brink of desire. Kate knew she could not retrieve herself from yearning for Ned, had not done so, and now that she knew what desire fulfilled truly meant, she could not suffer being without it.

The queen abandoned her laughter and, looking up, waved her ladies away. "Have you no work, my daughters?"

"Majesty." The word echoed through the chamber from every lady as they curtsied.

"Then to it! My lord Dudley and I are near starved to bone."

Kate heard a rustle of satin and silk behind her, and lowered her meat pie.

"Leave the pie, Lady Grey," the queen said, sipping from a silver wine cup, her amazing eyes commanding Kate from over the rim.

"Yes, Majesty." Kate set the dish before them.

"Tell her, Robin," Elizabeth said, not taking her gaze from Kate's face.

"Should I, Bess?"

"We command you."

"My lady Grey, the Earl of Hertford is to be married." Dudley bowed to Kate from where he sat.

Kate smoothed her gown and stood. She had expected the announcement, but not so soon. Smiling, her face calm—indeed, she suspected, benevolent—she nodded to Dudley. "Please give His Lordship my best wishes for long life and happiness." Though she did not look at Her Majesty, she felt the sharp sting of the queen's malice. Or was it satisfaction?

When Kate did look into the queen's face, she saw something quite different: a sadness, as if Elizabeth regretted her cruel intent. Regret was a rare thing for this queen, and Kate thought she must have mistaken the expression.

"My lady Grey," Elizabeth said quietly, "you seem tired. Rest in your chamber tonight and on the morrow we will walk in the knot garden and laugh together about men and their infidelity."

"Thank you, Majesty," Kate said, forcing a smile as she backed to the chamber door, sensing the queen's royal stare following as she left the room.

In the hall outside the queen's apartments, she leaned against the wall, laughter wanting to escape.

"Do you ail, my lady Grey?" a red-coated yeoman officer said, stopping to offer his arm.

At that, Kate did laugh, a bit helplessly, seeing several people stopping to stare. "I do not ail, sir. I have never known better health." How could she explain an unknowable changeling queen to a man? He bowed. She curtsied and they walked in opposite directions. She kept her hand against her stomacher, hearing the slight crackle of her wedding contract as she pressed.

Smiling as she heard it, Kate saw others passing smiles in return. *They must think me in rare humor,* she thought, which amused her more, though she knew there was something near hysterical about this mad desire to laugh, to cackle, to shriek with mirth.

She took a hall that led her to Jane Seymour's room. When she was announced, Jane came out to greet her and drew her to the fire. "Sister," she whispered, "do not look so happy, or you will surely give all away."

" 'Tis easier to say than to do."

Jane nodded, fortifying herself with a cordial of wine into which she dropped a tincture of poppy.

Kate, needing her head about her, refused a cup. "Dismiss your servants, my lady."

Once they were gone, Kate withdrew her marriage contract, and spoke with serious intent. "Keep this safe for Ned. I dare not have it in my room. I don't doubt Lady Saintloe searches my chests when she can."

Jane Seymour reached for the parchment, but Kate wanted to look at it, memorize it, before giving it up. She stared at the bishop of London's wax signet seal, the signatures, the—

"Jane, where is the priest's name?"

Jane looked over her shoulder. "Perhaps he made a mark. Not all priests can write a fair hand."

"What was his name?" Kate asked, her former good humor completely swept away.

"I know not if I heard it. A priest is a priest," Jane said. Putting a calming hand on Kate's arm, she laughed. "Edward will know it. It is a trifle. There is naught that need alarm you."

"Hide it well," Kate said, handing over the contract, not completely reassured.

Moments later, she hastened from Jane's rooms, coming face-to-face with Robert Dudley in the hall.

"My lady Grey," he said, bowing slightly, his Gypsy eyes alight. "I would not have thought that you would look so . . . so refreshed."

"My lord, I think you would have easily thought it."

His face bore the mark of scarce-hidden high good humor. "Perhaps. But how is it that you find such a ready friend in my lady Jane? Ah," he said, bowing again, more deeply and in a mocking fashion, "I am obviously no judge of women's minds."

Kate turned her back and walked away, speaking in a voice that would carry. "My lord, I could accuse you of much, but not of lacking good judgment of women."

Some distance away, she heard him laughing and pounding on Jane Seymour's door, from whom he would gain every secret in minutes.

CHAPTER FIVE

"It is a natural virtue incident in our sex to be pitiful
of those who are afflicted."

—Elizabeth Regina

St. Augustine's Feast Day
May 26, 1562

A line of carracks and smaller fishing boats beat their way up the Thames River toward London as the queen's barge nudged the Thames seawall and rounded into the quay of the great water gate at Greenwich Palace. When winter had turned to spring, the court had traveled from Hampton Court to Richmond for Eastertide and, since that palace now reeked beyond the power of the best pomanders to sweeten, the court was removing this day to the queen's birthplace.

Seated on the barge immediately behind Her Majesty's, Kate could smell the clean salt air of the channel as she felt the river mist cool her face. She heard the shriek of seagulls and the flap of rigging against taut canvas sails well above the amusing gossip Lady Saintloe retold for the third time in as many days.

Sailors lined the forecastles of passing ships, doffing their caps to the queen with shouted greetings. Obliging, Elizabeth cried her appreciation across the water: "Ho, my good seamen! We bid you find safe harbors."

Kate could see Ned and Dudley ahead on the royal barge's deck, kneeling beside the queen in her great chair as she argued with her councilors, who were uncomfortably seated before her on the first rowers' benches. Attending her were the cautious William Cecil, stroking his beard over his heavy gold chain of office, and the even warier Sir William Paulet, the queen's treasurer. Elizabeth had not chosen reckless men to advise her and usually followed their leanings, unless they leaned too far in the opposite direction of her own desires, as they were this morn.

Kate heard the queen assert her prerogative in a dissenting voice that carried easily between barges. "It is our will that we must delay our meeting at York city with the Scots queen, Mary."

Cecil spoke reasonably, forcing Kate to lean forward to hear. "Majesty, all preparations for this meeting have been made final. Much treasure has been spent. The queen of Scots has assembled her lords for her progress south. And more, Majesty, it is an opportunity to persuade her to forsake her claim to your throne, which would give English Catholics less cause for estrangement from your rule."

Elizabeth glared at him. "Mary, that popish pretender, can wait." Her next words were more restrained and said with a satisfied smile. "Worthy Spirit, we will send our portrait in our stead."

There was no more to say, Kate knew, especially when the queen called her chief councilor by his special name. Cecil was her Spirit, Robin her Eyes, a mark of her special favor. No other person, least of all Kate herself, had such honor.

The queen's voice now rose in command. "Therefore, my lords, we would send our troops to France with all speed to help the Protestants being so cruelly slaughtered by the Catholic de Guise party. The weak Medici queen regent, Catherine, seems helpless to stop their rampages against her dissenter subjects."

"But, Majesty," her treasurer, Paulet, had the courage to respond, "we helped the Protestants in Scotland and in the Hollander provinces. We cannot help all, or we are bankrupt."

Elizabeth, lowering her hood, allowed her hair to blow free about her face, looking more an ancient temple goddess than a modern ruler. She said a single word meant to stop all further discussion: "Pish!"

She rearranged her skirts, displaying her beautiful long fingers heavy with jeweled rings. "As all know, it is in the nature of our womanly sex that we must have care of those who are persecuted in Christ's name."

Kate smiled to herself, knowing that an English army to aid the Protestants had taken on this holy importance once the Huguenots promised to hand over the city of Calais to English troops. The loss of Calais three years earlier, during her sister's reign, still roiled the country, and Elizabeth longed to regain this ancient city, English since Plantagenet rule and the last of England's French possessions.

"Highness," Cecil said in his unhurried, scholarly way, "such a war will be costly. The Huguenots request over three hundred thousand ducats and ten thousand troops. Your treasury will not bear—"

Elizabeth's tone cut him off with a solution only she could offer. "We will sell Crown lands. There is no greater cause for their use." She lowered her voice, but it rang clear. "And know you not that it pleases our English Protestants and shows our love for them?"

Cecil bowed his head, accepting what no wise councilor could debate further.

Then, in a voice that carried easily across the short distance, Kate heard Dudley begging to be allowed to command the French expedition.

"Nay, Robin," the queen answered, her voice no longer a queen's but a woman's, yet all the more unassailable. She thrust her hand out to halt his further entreaties. "I could not bear to be parted from you. Your brother, the Earl of Warwick, will go in your place."

Every courtier knew well the finality of that answer, although Kate thought she saw Cecil shudder within his black robes to hear the queen so boldly declare her need for Lord Dudley's presence. And under Mistress Ashley's always alert, protective glare for her

Elizabeth, no lady of the bedchamber dared look knowing at the queen's words.

Earlier, Her Majesty's ladies had been dispatched hugger-mugger to the following barge, when Elizabeth had announced that strong talk of war was no conversation for women's ears.

Her Majesty could deny her own womanhood by talking war and yet, womanlike, be unable to allow Robin to leave her side, both views declared in the same hour. Though Kate was amused, she had learned as a child that no subject ever laughed before a sovereign laughed. Now, as a woman, Kate also understood how difficult was separation from the man you loved. Bound by blood ties, she and Elizabeth were now as one in their hearts.

As oars were shipped at the quay, and in answer to Kate's silent prayers that she would not have to attend the queen immediately, Elizabeth moved swiftly with her council past a row of kneeling servants and courtiers. She swept through the fountain court with bare acknowledgment and into the council chamber to continue her war plans.

Kate knew that Parliament must authorize further monies for large levies of troops and provisions. Gaining the agreement of Parliament men always necessitated much wily planning.

Slipping quickly away, Kate made a detour to the common jakes, hoping to find herself alone for a few moments. The unusual pressure she'd felt of late had returned. Please God, it was her flux at last.

Commanding a passing usher to guard her privacy, she entered the jakes, yet sweet-smelling with clean rushes and rosemary boughs on the floor. Quickly, she lifted and examined her innermost shift, dropped it and leaned her head against the door, suddenly dizzied. Moments later, she straightened, her expression controlled, and knocked on the door, which the usher opened at once.

Withdrawing a coin from her pocket, she gave it to him and walked with a fixed smile toward the queen's apartments. Three times she had been with her lord husband as his wife. Except for their wedding day, Ned had been very careful to withdraw in time. Was she to be caught out like any foolish village maid after one tumble?

At first, Kate had thought her flux had not come because missing it was nothing unusual; it had ever been so with her. Though it was also well-known that all female problems were righted with the breaking of the hymen.

The second month she had thought her flux absent because she had lost a good stone of weight. Facing Elizabeth Tudor every day, hiding the great secret of her broken oath, had quite taken her appetite. Even lark pie did not tempt her.

But there was no denying that she had now missed her flux thrice. And that required any woman of sense to have quite different thoughts.

Kate clenched her hands under the Flanders lace on her green velvet oversleeves, her senses scrambled with fear. So many women died in childbirth or later of uncontrollable fevers. Would she? But quickly, joy overtook her as she imagined a blond child running free on the greensward of Eltham, Ned waiting on his knees with his arms open. Every step toward the queen's apartment raised another question. If this were truly Ned's babe growing in her, was it destined to be the next Earl of Hertford, or the path of her own and Ned's disaster?

Kate passed through the presence chamber, which was bustling with grooms, ushers and guards arranging the queen's gold cloth of state over her throne. Lesser servants were dusting everywhere, for the presence was well lit and aired from large open windows overlooking the Thames.

As Kate exited around bowing servants, Ned rounded the corner, his face scarcely inches from hers.

He stepped back, bowed, looking hurriedly about to see who might be curious. "I must be with you, sweetheart . . . tonight or I am for Bedlam!"

Quickly scanning every passerby, she curtsied, her smile remaining fixed. "The queen will surely need me unless she is late in council. Ned, I cannot plead my teeth or my belly *now*."

He seemed not to hear what she was trying to tell him.

"My love, tonight, or remember I die," he whispered, his gaze bright on her and scalding with its urgency. He bowed in parting, courteous for all to observe, though his knuckles were white as he gripped his sword and walked on, his heavy boots snapping the rushes beneath his feet.

Directing her steps to the queen's apartments, Kate passed sweating porters with chests of gowns she would need to see aired immediately. The wardrobers were probably waiting for her. She hurried past Elizabeth's precious virginals and lute as they were carried through the doors to be placed in the inner chamber.

Mistress Ashley, Mistress Perry, Lady Saintloe and Mary Sidney— Robin's sister—were all directing the flow of traffic.

"Where have you been, my lady?" Ashley asked.

Kate lifted her brows. Her father, the duke, would have been severe with such questioning from a lower rank, but she knew Ashley was being protective of her lifelong charge, as usual.

Saintloe spoke over Kate's head to Ashley. "Our lady Katherine seems flushed." Then, with more curiosity than sympathy, she asked, "Are you ill again?"

Kate shrugged. "I am but a poor sailor, madam."

"What a pity then that you will not be with the queen's party when she reclaims Calais."

Kate smiled a counterfeit smile, which she made no attempt to improve. "I doubt not that you, madam, will be sailor enough for all Her Majesty's ladies."

Keeping her wits, though they seemed to be flying away faster than she could gather them, would be a problem with Lady Saintloe, who always wanted to play at words to see what she could detect that remained unspoken.

Instinctively, Kate ran her hand across her stomacher, sensing for the first time her belly's slight swelling with what she carried. Aware that Saintloe's eyes were judging her as they always did, Kate smoothed her stomacher again and shook out her skirts. A natural act, after all, and nothing for Saintloe to think on.

Every royal possession was in its place, every picture hung, Her Majesty's gowns and linen unwrinkled and her books at hand when the queen came late from her council, having missed her dinner and not calling for it. For the first time this entire spring, Kate was hungry—indeed, ravenous. Now she must feed her child, but not grow conspicuously. Not yet. Ned must have more time to gain the support of Cecil and other powerful lords at court, perhaps even Dudley. If anyone could sway Elizabeth, it would be her sweet Robin. Who could plead the case of frustrated love better? Though he still seemed unable to advance his own case to completion.

Kate breathed in deeply and cautioned herself against finding a *no* for every *yes* she thought, pulling her mind about willy-nilly until all was certain, then all was doubt. She must ever be happy and trust that God would sustain her in the right. Without that trust, the devil could enter her heart and touch her babe with evil.

She'd grown skilled at keeping a calm face before the queen, though calm was more difficult as time passed. All Ned's attempts to reach Cecil had been turned away by the press of official business, and Lord Dudley had dodged every effort to commit to aiding them. Why? He had helped them wed. What was his game now?

"Come!" Elizabeth said to Kate, throwing off her cloak and opening the full parapet windows her father had installed for her mother, Anne Boleyn. Above, carved in stone, was Anne's motto: *Semper Eadem.* "Always the Same." Elizabeth had taken it for one of her own in the first year of her reign. Kate wondered if that was Elizabeth's quiet attempt to honor the woman who had been called the Great Whore and accused of sleeping with five men, one her own brother. Her young, beautiful mother whose head had been taken off on her father's orders to make way for another wife mere days later.

"Look down there," Elizabeth said, taking Kate's arm and guiding her attention to a place in the courtyard below. "There my mother stood below my father's windows, holding me up for him to see and begging for her life . . . to stay with me." Her voice was a private one, soft and sad, as Kate had never heard it.

"Do you recall that time, Majesty?" Kate asked, shocked and saddened at such an awful memory.

"I was not three years. I remember, or was told of it. I don't know, except that it is in my head." The queen shrugged the moment away as if it did not matter, but Kate thought it did, more than the queen would ever say, more, perhaps, than she knew.

As Kate stepped away from the balcony, the motto "Always the Same" took on a more ominous meaning: *All traitors die.* She forced herself to shake off such worry, allowing the salty, chill wind blowing from the great estuary to cleanse her mind, as it refreshed the chamber beyond the ability of sprinkled attar of roses.

"We are tired with this business of state," the queen announced, regal again after breathing in deeply, her eyes closed. Clapping her hands, she rushed to her painted virginals and sat before it. "Let us sing."

It was a command, but one Kate and the other ladies eagerly followed. As Elizabeth was a skilled musician, she was quick to take offense at a wrong note sung, but she was also happiest at her music, lifting her sweet voice above all for the space of a song without the weight of royal care.

"What shall it be?" She was laughing, her fingers running nimbly up and down the keyboard.

"Let us sing the song that begins, 'Fain would I sing, but fury makes me fret,'" called out Mistress Ashley.

"Much too slow and dismal, Nurse," the queen announced.

She did not choose new music, but an old country song Kate thought more fit for milkmaids than highborn ladies, two with the royal Tudor blood flowing in their veins and, in one instance, in her babe's. Kate brought herself back from such reverie as the queen began to play and sing.

" 'So to the wood went I . . .' "

Her attending ladies joined her in their parts, Kate taking the lower voicing: " 'With love to live and lie . . .' " They sang the many verses of an argument between fortune and love until the last note died away.

The queen did not remove her hands from the virginals' keys, and Kate was resigned to sing more. But the queen did not play another song and waved all about her away, not showing her face. The words had moved her, and Kate suspected Her Majesty thought of the hunting lodge and the carefree hours of the picnic in the glen after, and of her Robin, who had made winter into spring for his Bess. Surely Elizabeth had heart enough to understand—

No, no! Kate shook herself from that false reverie. *Never think it,* she commanded herself, dodging again the trap of believing that the queen's heart was like any woman's. Elizabeth's heart would bleed tears for Dudley, yet when she could have him by one nod of her head, she protected her single rule as reigning queen. She was Henry VIII's daughter, not the longed-for son for whom he'd divorced his queen and thrown down an ancient Church, but yet and all, she was a lion's cub. She would bestride this kingdom alone, as Henry had. Yet she would keep Dudley near, trying to have it all.

Kate's head told her that despite all the queen's strength and knowledge there would come no understanding for another woman of the blood royal who could not put England's throne or its queen before her love for a man.

Ned *must* reach Cecil or Dudley. And soon, before the child quickening under her breast could not be denied before the whole court.

Ned. She must see him. This was all too much to bear alone, though bear it she did for interminable hours of service to Her Majesty until she could make her way to her chamber, thankfully no longer shared with Lady Saintloe, and then swiftly through the rush-lit halls to Jane's apartment, where he waited.

"Ned!" She collapsed in his arms, nearly sobbing with relief. But instead of taking her to bed, where she could reveal her secret inside the circle of his strong, warm arms and thrill to the knowledge of his son and heir, he seated her at a small table by the fire. A sparse supper was laid; a pot of syllabub nestling close to the flames simmered, filling the room with its spiced scents.

He knelt before her. "The greatest news, sweetheart!" he said in a burst of words.

A sheen of health and sweat shone on his face, as if he had been late at sword practice. And indeed, he wore neither ruff nor doublet, his sleeves rolled above his elbows, his light brown beard glistening, his hair damp and tightly curled, springing alive under her fingers.

She leaned away and stared into his face, taking in his eyes flashing excitement. Had he guessed she was with child . . . his child? Did it show on her face? He was unlike other men, who were always surprised, as if they'd had no part in making a child. Yet his next words proved his mind was elsewhere.

One word tumbling against the next, Ned spoke. "My lord Dudley is indeed our friend, Kate, though I know you doubt him. He has approached the queen for me."

"What?" Kate came instantly erect. These were the words she'd been hoping for. She could not doubt him, but she had just come from the queen, who'd said by no word or glance—

"Yes, sweetheart, I am to raise a thousand men from Hertfordshire and take them into France." Ned was near breathless as he looked for her response.

Kate, her mind refusing to make such a complete retreat from what she'd first thought he meant, spoke haltingly. "Ned, I don't—"

But he was too excited to be long interrupted, his hands pressing her shoulders. "Robert has promised me that his brother, Warwick, will give me command of the men who take Calais!" He searched her face, his expression telling her that he expected her delighted surprise, even wonderment.

The food was untouched, the syllabub gradually simmering away, a thick, milky skin forming atop the pot. She was speechless.

Ned frowned. "Sweetheart, don't you know what this means to us?"

"No," she replied dully, as unwell as if she stood outside in the unhealthy night air.

"Say you so, Kate?" he replied, impatient with her for the first time. "It means I, Edward, Earl of Hertford, will hand Elizabeth the keys to Calais. I, Edward, will wipe away the disgrace of Calais's loss." He shook with determination. "Then *I* will be her hero of the day. She might not want to grant us marriage, but think you she could refuse me anything when all England sings my name?"

Kate was struck dumb. His face was lit with the fever of war and glory. She'd seen this expression before on other men. It was the warrior call a man could not deny and retain that which made him a man to himself.

He filled a plate with meat nestled in fine manchet bread, dipped under the milk skin on the pot for a cup of syllabub and placed it beside her. His excitement grew as he talked on, his face lit with visions of coming triumphs. All their problems would vanish, he said in a dozen ways, painting such pictures of success, scattered with such kisses on her nose and eyes and cheeks that she believed he saw victories in his mind. He was so winningly a boy with his first sword that she was at last won to his words, and believed them true. There seemed no other way to bring swift acceptance from Elizabeth. And swift it must be.

"How long would you be in France?"

Ned leapt to his feet, pacing the room, moving in and out of the firelight's reach, his shadow twice that of mortal man. "Two months and possibly less. The men of Hertfordshire will flock to my banner within the week. Our English troops are in every way better than the frogs', Kate." He dropped down beside her again. "Think, sweetheart. In two months, we will declare ourselves openly to the queen and the country. She must accept our marriage. And then we will to Eltham and to our life." His face glowed at the thought of home.

"Is our parting the only way, Ned?" she said, and, leaving the food uneaten, clung to his sword arm with both hands.

"It is the surest and fastest, sweeting, to bring us together forever. Trust me, and trust Dudley. He knows her best."

Kate could not stand against Ned or force him to stay by her side with the words, *I am with child.* She could offer no better way to win Her Majesty's consent. Though she doubted Dudley, or anyone, knew the queen as well as they thought. Elizabeth could always surprise. *But not this time, please God*, Kate prayed, *not this time.*

She must allow Ned his great possibility. It was a risk they both must take. Any other way and all could be too easily lost upon a queen's whim. If the queen could be blocked by glory, then it must be done. A traitorous marriage might be worth her head, but never Ned's, never her babe's. She sat straighter and resolved against further questioning. "My love, when do you leave?"

"Early on the morrow," he said, stroking her hair, smiling at her firelit face until his smile was swallowed by desire.

He carried her to a small truckle bed and laid her gently on the silk coverlet and fitted his long legs in beside her.

As he stoked the flames between them with his mouth, she held her need to tell him what great thing was happening to her, to them both. And it took all her will.

Even in the heat of the flash of fire he sent through her, she did not speak of what she knew, though it filled her throat.

Later, after the satisfaction of desire as he held her lazily in his arms, he whispered his whole love in her ear, and still she did not tell him.

Two months and all would be resolved. Two months. She could withstand anything for two months.

When she slipped away to her own chamber, leaving her sleeping lord with a soft kiss on his lips, the sea coal in the hearth had lost its last glimmer and turned to ashes.

August 1562

Elizabeth took a fever in August as the courtiers, gentlemen, yeomen, scullery maids and all removed to Hampton Court, Cardinal Wolsey's hasty gift to the queen's father for daring to build a palace greater than Henry's own.

To Kate's mind, Hampton Court held the most charming inner courtyards of all the royal palaces. The queen's apartments overlooked the ordered knot and herb gardens and tree-lined cinder paths, but Elizabeth had not enjoyed them as she usually would. She'd taken to her bed even as she ordered additional troops to France.

Kate tended Her Majesty for many hours each day, spooning broth into her reluctant mouth and cooling her with rose-water compresses. The privy bedchamber was hot and steaming. The doctors refused to allow outside air to circulate lest it carry plague or the sweating sickness. They dosed her thrice daily with a decoction of feverfew laced with honey to take away the taste of the bitter root, until the queen rebelled and would take no more.

Every day Kate followed the dispatches from France, as the queen heard them. Kate showed no interest in Cecil's reports, but she listened to every word while busy about her duties, ever hoping for news of Ned. Though she knew from his letters to his sister, he could not chance writing to her beyond, *Remember me to my friends and the ladies of the bedchamber and tell them I am well*; nonetheless she looked for her own letter with every courier.

The news from France was endlessly bad. A full civil war had begun, with atrocities first by Catholics, then by Protestants, with English forces occasionally drawing fire from both sides. While she prayed nightly for Ned's safe return, her prayers now included his *swift* return. She was near seven months gone and no longer able to hide her swollen body, except under the most elaborate farthingales. She now blessed the awkward devices, because they had hidden her swollen belly, though she could not hide her expanding waistline. She had hired a seamstress to let out her gowns, sworn her to secrecy with a gold crown, and warned her of dire consequences if she carried any word of what she knew to others.

One morning as Kate was staring down at linen she had dropped on the floor and dreading having to bend down to retrieve it, Mistress Ashley announced, "My lady Grey, you have grown fleshy and lazy."

"Lady Katherine is overfond of sweets and lark pie with honey," Lady Saintloe observed with a wry smile and calculating eye.

She knows! Kate was sure of it. And if that lady knew, most assuredly some of the others had whispered amongst themselves. Someone would tell the queen as soon as she recovered.

Ashley moved into the queen's bedchamber to hover about her bed. Kate followed Saintloe to confront her. What could she offer? Money on Ned's return? Her mother's emerald necklace, much admired by Saintloe?

Before Kate could make any offer, Lady Saintloe rounded on her and widened her eyes in alarm. "I see nothing, my lady, and will ever say it is so."

Kate drew needed breath. "Why? You are no friend to me."

Saintloe's low voice went lower still. "You will lose your head, my lady, and so will your defiler—my lord of Hertford, isn't it?—and I would not be the one who brings on such royal angers. To be near the block is to be besplattered with blood."

Kate's hand leapt to her throat. "You are cruel, lady. My lord and I are married. Yet I thank you for your silence and—"

Saintloe raised her hand to stop a flood of gratitude, her voice grating against Kate's ears. "Harlot or wife, you are named by Henry's will as heir to the throne of England. Marriage without the queen's permission is treason. Think you well, lady! Which is worse in Elizabeth's mind . . . a whore or a fertile heir?"

Kate's throat closed against any vain defense she could have offered.

"No, my lady of Hertford, I want no thanks from you. I want nothing but to be a world away when the queen discovers your betrayal. Her anger will fall on all in her service, and for that I curse you, as will all the ladies. If there is sympathy in any corner of this court, Lady Katherine, be assured it will be silent."

There was nothing to do but walk away past the guards and into the hall. Kate thought to walk to Jane's chambers, as she was the only person she could call friend, but it was agony to talk about Ned when she knew nothing more than that he had been assaulting one French-fortified town after another all summer.

Nevertheless, she turned toward Jane's rooms. Frightened by the green venom in Saintloe's face, Kate suddenly was unable to bear her secret alone. She must confide in someone who could get word to Ned. He must return; *he must!*

Jane had said nothing of her thickening middle; indeed, Kate thought her too witless to notice. She could prattle of nothing but her new position as a lady of honor who walked out with the queen to take the air. And Robert Dudley. Always Jane talked of Dudley.

Alvarez de Quadra de Avila, the Spanish ambassador and a bishop, followed by his dark dons, some she suspected of being Jesuits in courtiers' clothing, stopped and bowed as she neared Jane's rooms. They were quite alone at this hour, when all were at their supper.

Kate curtsied and sought to pass.

"My lady," de Quadra said in his accented lisping English, "I have long wanted an audience."

Audience? "My lord ambassador, Sir William Cecil will most gladly arrange an audience with the queen when she is recovered."

He smiled at her deliberate misunderstanding. "How goes the queen's health, my lady Katherine?"

"A slight summer fever, but she will soon mend."

"God's will be done."

"As it will."

He nodded. "I was speaking, my lady, of an audience with you as heir to a sickly monarch."

Tread softly, Kate thought, the words swimming through her head. "Sir, do not think me a dolt. It is known that Spain favors Mary, queen of Scots, or one of their own for the succession."

He smiled and bowed slightly. "What is known can be unknown, my lady Grey."

She would not respond. It would be treason to speak of such matters with the Spanish, or even the meanest scullery maid.

He lowered his voice to a whisper, so that his retinue moved forward en masse to hear. "If you would consent to form a union with a Spanish prince, perhaps our King Philip's son, Don Carlos—"

Kate almost laughed, and she was sure de Quadra saw it lurking behind her mouth. Don Carlos was a notorious whore chaser who liked to whip his whores to death when he finished with them. A madman. She was sure the ambassador saw the revulsion that now flooded her face. She meant him to see it.

"—or another prince of the blood," he continued. "And, of course, as infanta you would embrace the true faith. It is my belief that you are not a strong dissenter."

For want of a fan, Kate used her hand to cool her face, uncertain whether she should walk past the man or call a yeoman guard.

But de Quadra wasn't finished. "The might of Spain with its fleet and armies would support you"—he leaned closer—"and the son you carry by the Earl of Hertford."

"Your spies are everywhere," Kate said, almost beyond shock, yet struggling to find her tongue.

"They are diligent, madam, as needs be in this hostile court."

"Not diligent enough, sir, or they would know that although I am everything you say I am and think of me, I am more than that; I am English, and Protestant enough never to make a bargain with the devil."

She swept her skirts away from touching him and strode on, head high, straining to keep her back straight, though her belly wanted to bend her forward. The Spaniards' angry murmurs followed her, but Kate was not worried. She wore Elizabeth's miniature portrait. Was that why she could queen it before Philip's men? Or was it her own true Tudor blood and Tudor courage speaking?

Though her body was heavy with Ned's babe, she felt lighter than she had in months, believing herself worthy to confront any Spanish trick.

CHAPTER SIX

*"The name of a successor is like unto the tolling
of my own death-bell."*
—Elizabeth Regina

*Michaelmas
September 29, 1562*

Edward opened his eyes in a thundery forenoon to pain, fever and chills, seeing a dull gray sky with a cold September rain falling hard outside his tent flap. Beyond, in the campgrounds, his good Hertfordshire men huddled around smoking fires of green wood.

James, his squire, advanced toward Edward's camp bed to place on his thigh a hot compress, which had been prescribed to draw out poisonous humors.

Edward steeled himself not to cry out when the steaming linen settled on the torn flesh that had taken a barbed enemy arrow before the walls of Le Havre and later been pulled out inexpertly by an English medico. Unhorsed, he had scarce known which hurt the worse, his leg or his arse when he hit the ground.

Today, he knew. He clamped his teeth together until he feared breaking one as the searing wet cloth settled on his open wound, roiling torments through him. He knew that he was falling into the dark again, though he clung to a rope of golden-red hair that broke his descent. Kate's image, as he remembered her on his pillow that last evening, buoyed him up somewhere between his tent and bottomless darkness. He saw her as she had been before the hearth fire in Jane's apartment. Her sweet face came floating before him, and he reached out to touch her. She said nothing, quiet as she had been that last evening.

He had been so proud of her. She had sent him to his duty showing the courage of a true warrior's wife, with no tears and no recriminations. He had adored and honored her with his name before that night. Afterward, he worshiped her.

"My lord," Edward's squire was saying, his face swimming above his master's cot. "You must take this strong poppy drink. The doctors have ordered it."

"Why?" He knew, but had to ask, fearful they planned to amputate.

"They must cut the bad flesh from your leg, and it will be . . . ah, most painful."

Edward reared up on one elbow, pushing the cup away. "Nay, I'll not have those bloody butchers with their dull knives, bloodletting and purges touch me."

"But, my lord of Hertford, the wound is suppurated and—"

Edward squeezed his eyes tight against the pain he'd inflicted on himself by his sudden upward movement. "Send for the French doctor, the one we captured before Saint Quentin. I hear he is not so eager to take off a man's leg. Quickly now, James!"

His squire bowed and left hastily to do his duty.

Edward lowered himself carefully to his pallet. He must not faint or the English doctors would be upon him. Instead he dreamed. Every day for so long a time he had ached to write his love and longing to Kate, but had dared not. Cecil, a friend to Kate's succession rights, would keep her safe, though she had no ambition for ruling, and the Lord Secretary knew that. He faithfully acted as Elizabeth's spymaster and opened all communications from the Continent and kept nothing from the queen . . . or almost nothing. He did keep to himself the scurrilous stories rampant in the French court regarding Elizabeth and

Dudley. Edward was sure she demanded to see all army dispatches. Veiled words to his sister were all that he had succeeded in sending from this endless bog of battle. The French adventure, begun with such high hope of retrieving Calais, had been impossible almost from the first day, though Warwick did not see it yet . . . or would not see it, when each victory was followed by a loss, or some desecration that turned the peasantry against them and their cause. Years of this grinding struggle faced them; Edward had no doubt of it. Elizabeth would not give it up unless a Protestant took the throne of France.

"The frog surgeon, my lord," James announced, holding the tent flap open for the Frenchman, a tiny man whose gown of office was comically too long for him, the dragging hem frayed beyond mending. "He speaks no English," the squire announced.

"He needs none," Edward said gruffly, spacing out the words to cover his pain.

The little doctor advanced and bowed. "Phillippe Bellon, *monsieur.*"

"Monsieur le docteur," Edward gritted, giving the man's expertise the benefit of many doubts. "Aw—ye!" He groaned through clamped teeth as the man removed the compress, bringing forth a gush of blood and foul pus. All physicks were fools, but he hoped this fool was better than the London quacks who had come over with his troops carrying their magical elixirs and star charts. And there had been good reports in plenty of Bellon's work with other wounded Englishmen. Better to risk French treatment than his own doctors', when they had shaken their heads and muttered amongst themselves. Ned knew what that meant.

As the Frenchman bent to examine his wound, Edward rasped out a polite, scarce-remembered phrase from the schoolroom. *"Tout ce que vous pouvez faire."*

"Monsieur," the doctor said, agreeing with a little bow to do all he could. Bending over the wound, he shook his head at what he observed, making a very skeptical Gallic face.

Edward performed a frantic sawing motion with his hand, shaking his head and shouting, *"Non! Non!"*

The doctor raised an eyebrow and bent to his instruments and herbs, pills and potions that had been rolled in a small carpet now spread on the wooden floor of the tent.

Edward felt dizzy and weak. What would he do if the Frenchman removed his bone saw? He could not return to Kate less than a whole man, yet he had never wanted to live more than at that moment.

Bellon picked up clamps to hold open the wound and a slender curving knife, gleaming and honed. He took the lantern from the bedside and handed it to James, motioning him to hold it close over his master's thigh. *"Un peu,"* he said, and Edward understood he needed to cut away a little corrupted flesh.

Next the little man held a vial to his mouth, and Edward recognized the odor of poppy syrup. He swallowed the numbing liquid, gratefully this time, though even poppy would not block out all the pain of the knife as it entered his wound.

Edward bit the leather strap James thrust into his mouth, and the Frenchman was quick with his scalpel. He could say that much for him.

He gripped the sides of his cot until he felt his arm muscles bulge with the effort. Then his mouth opened involuntarily to scream as the knife went deeper into the corruption. Yet he had sense enough to bless the poppy, which took away his speech, keeping him from disgrace before his servant. On the second cut, Kate seemed to reach out to pull him to her, and he whirled once again with her into a soft void.

He awoke hours later during the night, the rain gone and several braziers lit to chase the chill and keep the tent lit. Bellon dozed on a stool by his bed, James on his pallet.

When Edward moved, the doctor rose to look in his eyes and feel his forehead. He nodded, looking satisfied, but if he spoke Edward did not hear, drifting away again into blessed sleep.

He awoke the next morning, reaching for his leg and finding it where it always had been. He called down blessings on the Frenchman and then, ravenous, summoned James for food, and quickly.

Bellon smiled, but shook his head. *"Ne pas . . . pain,"* he said, pointing to his stomach, as if broken French were more understandable when forbidding bread. He gave a bowl to James, indicating hot broth by pointing to the brazier and pretending to drink.

When James returned with a bowl of good English beef broth, Edward drank it all, feeling strength flow into him. He sought to sit up, but Bellon said, *"Non,"* again.

The doctor bent to search his carpet roll and brought up some herbs mixed with pork fat, from the smell of it. "Betony," he said in English.

"A sovereign cure for wounds, my lord," James said.

Edward nodded. "I have heard so."

The doctor replaced the lint packing from the wound and looked satisfied. He spread the betony salve on a thick bandage and wrapped it tight about Edward's thigh, indicating that he should stay prone.

Pointing to the hourglass and raising four fingers, he left.

Edward watched Bellon go, the man's shoulders rounded with fatigue. "When I am on my feet, James, take the good doctor to our lines and see he has safe passage to his own."

He slept and ate again, this time—bedamn the doctor—of bread and good English cheese. Although his wound yet throbbed, it became less and less hurtful as the day advanced.

Bellon appeared twice more, each time changing his bandage and each time finding less heat in the wound. He seemed pleased and smiled.

Although the doctor had not allowed it, Edward tried to take a step or two, but fell back to his cot, having set his wound to throbbing like all the drums in the queen's processions. He tightened his jaw, which pulsed with the effort. Tomorrow, he would walk inside the tent. The following day he would show himself amongst the men to prove he was well enough to lead them. God's blood, but he would!

As dusk settled over the campsite and the shouts of men-at-arms at their duties grew fewer and dimmer, two days' dispatches awaited his attention.

Sitting on his camp stool, his bandaged leg stretched in front of him as more braziers were lighted, he saw the usual victory claims in copies of dispatches from Warwick for Cecil to report to the queen. Finally, at the bottom waited that for which he searched. A letter from Jane. He tore away the wax seal and saw its date. Only five days from her hand!

Edward stood, leaning heavily on a staff, and took halting steps to a brazier burning high, holding the heavy parchment letter to the light. Jane had avoided Cecil's couriers and sent it by an English ship's captain, probably with good coin for his trouble.

> *My most beloved lord brother, Edward,*
>
> *I have news of great Import, which will gladden your Heart and speed your Return.*
>
> *Your lady wife, Katherine, is with Child. And, I hasten to add, far gone with your Child, which she and the Astrologers are certain will be your Son and Heir. She cannot escape Her Majesty the Queen's eyes much longer. I beseech you, for family's sake, complete your Victory and return with greatest haste.*
>
> *Lord Robert remains our friend. He does not whisper to me about my lady Kate, but he may suspect. Not much escapes his eyes. My lord Dudley, even more than ever in the queen's favor, has been most attentive and of Service to . . .*
>
> *Your Loving Sister, Jane Seymour*

A son! To his almost instant shame those were the first words that rang through Edward's head.

Then his hand containing the letter dropped to his side, almost as numb as his wounded leg. *Sweet blessed Christ!* Kate was alone and in mortal danger. What could he do? Nor would he escape Elizabeth's revenge. Only Calais would have saved them sure, and the surrender of Calais would require a God-sent miracle. And a quick one.

Edward stumbled to his cot to lie breathless, his hand over his bandaged thigh to contain its throbbing.

He must act. But how?

It would be some time before he could travel without breaking open his wound and making himself more useless.

He lay long in his cot, his eyes clenched tight in order to think more clearly without the many distractions of a camping army. How could he leave his men in this foreign place, this quagmire of mud and blood?

Yet he was to have a son! And Kate? His stomach twisted in agony, her face rising before him as if she were no more than inches away. She needed him more than ever. It was his highest duty to be at her side when their son was born. And after. Whatever "after" would bring.

Finally, he came to the only plan that made even the smallest amount of sense. "James, attend me!"

The squire appeared instantly from outside the tent, where he'd been cooking a stew of pigeons and parsnips, from the smell of it. "Aye, my lord."

"Pen and paper and my writing board."

The board was laid carefully across his lap, ink in the little pot, with paper and freshly sharpened pens.

"Prepare yourself for a trip, James."

"Aye, my lord, to what destination?"

"London."

"My lord of Hertford, I will find another man to serve you during my absence."

Edward could see that James just barely held back a smile at the thought of going home, immediately donning his cloak and beginning to place essentials into a blanket and tie it in a leather saddle roll. He left the tent to take his savory stew from the fire and find his substitute from amongst the lesser servants.

Edward was brief:

> *Dearest Lady Sister,*
> *I have been Wounded. Do not tell Kate, as she will be too much Concerned for my sake. It is a minor Scratch, but will keep me from Horseback for a fortnight.*

Edward's pen paused in midair. He hoped that Jane did not know that being unable to sit a saddle for two weeks meant more than a minor wound. He dipped his pen.

> *Sister, I beg you to help Kate retire to my house in Westminster at once on any pretext she chooses. The Bearer of this letter will assist my lady in all ways.*
> *Then ask my lord Dudley to gain from the Queen my release from Duty without delay, since I am unfit for further Command.*
> *Know that with or without Consent, in two weeks' time, I travel to the one to whom you must present my everlasting Love and Honor.*
> *Edward, Earl of Hertford*

His squire heated the wax and dripped it on the folded paper. Edward quickly pressed his signet ring into it while the wax remained soft, pushing hard enough to make sure there could be no mistaking that this seal was truly by his hand.

"Godspeed, James. My lady Jane will give you instructions to aid my wife until I can join you. This is the greatest service you can ever do for me and one I will never forget."

"My lord, do not concern yourself. It is done," his squire said, placing the letter inside his liveried doublet, bowing, then pushing the tent flap aside. He galloped away on the horse always kept saddled and waiting.

Edward hobbled to the opening to see his squire riding for the nearest port. Pray God he would not have to wait for an English ship making for London. Edward watched long after the rider carrying his precious letter disappeared from view. He counted the days on one hand: a day to the port, another to take ship, a swift crossing, with another day to beat up the Thames with the incoming tide and then to Hampton Court.

Four days. Five. A week at most.

A clumsy servant helped him to his bed. His dreams that night were of a beautiful boy with Kate's Tudor hair and eyes and the Seymour height and strength. A boy named Edward, an heir to the earldom, the next to succeed as master of Eltham and Hertfordshire. He prayed silently that it was not a foolish dream, but a foretelling.

At Hampton Court, it was the hottest October in memory, the sun's heat shimmering across the inner gardens, turning the edges of green leaves to brown, forcing the queen and courtiers into the woods for some relief. At night the full moon shone bright as day, so that guards at the gate needed fewer candles for their lanterns.

As Kate walked through numberless halls from Jane's rooms, past high mullioned windows, the harvest sun seemed to follow her like a faithful old dog.

Poor, poor Jane. She was taken hard with the small pocks and was on her way by coach to Westminster. Kate had hoped to find a letter in Jane's apartment from Edward, but she was denied entrance until the rooms had been washed clean with strong vinegar.

The heat of summer and now of autumn always brought plague with it and the digging of lime pits for the dead. All who could removed themselves from London and court until snow and the freezing over of the Thames refreshed the noisome air that carried death with its every stirring. She would pray for Jane, since her sister-in-law was now in God's hands, the final physician.

As was most certainly the secret Countess of Hertfordshire, Kate had to admit. If the queen had not been ailing from an intermittent fever that her doctors could not cure, and the dispatches from France were not so full of demands for more troops and gold to occupy Elizabeth's attention, Kate knew she would have been discovered by now. Every day, as she approached Her Majesty to kneel with her dinner, she saved her breath to deny that her clumsiness was what it was . . . a babe growing large in her belly. Yet the queen—dining these days with her sober chief counselor, Cecil; elderly treasurer, Paulet; her cousin Sir Francis Knowles; and Robert Dudley . . . always her Robin—seemed not to notice the thickening mistress of the wardrobe through the thicker veil of dispatches from France.

Kate hurried into the privy chamber to her duties. All the queen's ladies were breathlessly waiting for Kate's discovery by Elizabeth and ready to pretend shock and deny any knowledge. Thus the dinner ceremony had taken on added interest for all of them. Each kept their pomanders close to her nose now that the pocks were in the court.

Elizabeth would remove again as soon as she was well enough to travel by a coach that rattled bones and sometimes broke them. Until that day, her fireplaces roared with fires to burn away all ill humors.

The sound of four viols and the queen's boy choristers' sweet voices singing "Rejoice Unto the Lord" floated through from the outer hall as Kate knelt before the queen and her councilors with a platter containing a peacock with its beautifully colored feathers elaborately wedged under and arranged on the carcass as in life.

The queen lowered a dispatch and took notice.

"Majesty, baked peacock."

"Eat to please your stomachs, good sirs," Elizabeth said, waving food away from her own silver plate, taking a little watered wine, but scarce aware of Kate.

"My queen, you should eat something," Dudley said, leaning

over her chair to reach her ear. "If you eat the meat, I will dine on the feathers."

Elizabeth smiled, but it was a pale response in contrast to her usual appreciation of Robert's wit.

"We have no hunger when we read of these new demands for gold and men . . . always more, Robin. Is my purse bottomless?" she asked, and his attempt to jolly her was wholly dismissed.

The carver stepped forward to take the platter from Kate. Finding steel in her legs and back, she stood up with as much determined ease as a very pregnant woman could manage. Her babe gave her a sharp kick of complaint, while Kate all the while damned the look of anticipation on Saintloe's long, disagreeable face. How had such a woman come up from nothing to be one of the queen's ladies, when Elizabeth demanded beauty in her servants? Kate hid a smile. Of course, the queen meant to keep an eye on the wealthy, thrice-married schemer, who gained a little better title and more property with each wedding. Lucky for Saintloe that she was married and had children before she became Elizabeth's lady.

Kate backed to the chamber door and waited, resting her aching spine against the tapestry wall. She could hear Saintloe and the others exhale, somewhat piqued by the lack of drama they'd anticipated if Kate had been unable to rise from her knees after serving the queen. At the same time, they were relieved not to have the queen's fury fall on all within her sight just yet.

Elizabeth bent over the table, tracing her finger along a map of the French coast, always hesitating over the port of Calais, while Dudley hovered near. A moment later, she slumped in her chair, her face paler than its natural pallor, her cheeks flushed.

"Majesty," said Cecil, standing, his dinner unfinished, "you are so recently recovered from your fevers that—"

"Yes, good Sir William," Elizabeth said, sinking deeper into the upholstery. "Later this afternoon we will continue. Remain ready."

The councilors bowed and left, Dudley last. "Bess," he whispered.

She shook her head, one hand squeezing it. "Return, my lord, before the others, when my head does not ache so."

He bowed, his hand covering his heart, worry on his face.

Mistress Ashley was immediately hovering over Elizabeth, her ample bosom ready to mother. "I will prepare your bed, sweet girl. Even in youth you were prey to megrims, fevers and dropsical swellings when so much was demanded."

The queen shook her head slowly. "This unusual heat, Nurse . . . A cool bath will set me to rights. Prepare my bathing room."

Ashley looked alarmed. "But you have taken one bath previously this month. It is dangerous to—"

As her ladies muttered agreement, Her Majesty shook her head, her complexion now ashen. "As I command."

"It is done, Majesty," Blanche Parry said, always ready to step to the fore.

The queen nodded. "Parry, before my lords return, you must give me my true complexion."

"Majesty, my carmine pots are always ready," a pleased Parry responded.

Later, the queen returned from her bathing room, announcing she was refreshed, as she had expected. Kate, Blanche and Mistress Ashley dressed her in clean linen and a silver-and-gold silk brocade gown fit for receiving her councilors when they returned.

"Now leave us to study these dispatches," Her Majesty commanded.

As the other ladies backed away to an outer chamber, Kate carried the queen's wet, discarded bathing gown into a closet to place in a wooden tub with the other linen for the mistress of the body to give to the royal washerwomen on the morrow.

Longing for her bed to rest in, Kate was almost at the threshold of the privy bedchamber when she heard the door open, followed by Dudley's voice. Something in the softness and intimacy of his tone caused her to step back and hold her breath.

"Bess, you force yourself too greatly to your duty," he said, concern and caring almost smothering his words. "Would that I—"

"Robin, I am queen," Elizabeth said in a tone that said no one could take on her burdens.

It was all she needed to say, and in the following silence, Kate thought to slip away. But one step outside the closet and she hastily drew back again to hide herself.

The queen was standing before her windows, her head on Dudley's shoulder, his arm tight about her.

"Sweet lady," he murmured. "Most dearest heart."

"Robin." The queen breathed his name. "Kiss me, sweetheart. Your mouth is my heart's ease."

Kate heard Dudley's next words tumbling from his mouth. "Here is one for your eyelid. Now the other, each in turn . . . a hundred times."

Elizabeth sighed.

"And here. And here. And lastly here, sweetest."

Kate held her breath.

"Don't leave me ever, Robin," Elizabeth whispered, and the whisper carried to Kate.

Her heart broke in the silence that followed. She could feel their hunger nearly swamp the room and she understood it, felt it with Elizabeth, ached with it for her. The queen loved him, yet denied herself loving. This queen who could command anything on this island could not command her own happiness. As Kate couldn't. They were like sisters in that. Sisters.

"Bess, you're burning hot! The fever is back. Ashley was right: You shouldn't have gone to your bath."

"Robin."

Kate heard a noise and stepped from the closet in alarm to see Elizabeth slumped to the floor.

Dudley lifted her slender body into his arms and carried her to her great bed. He looked up, his eyes wild, and spied Kate. "Stay with her. Do not leave her on your life!"

He rushed from the privy chamber, calling for the queen's ladies and the queen's physicians.

Mary Sidney was first to reach Kate's side as she knelt by the bed. "Call Mistress Ashley, Mary. Bring rose water and linen," Kate next ordered Saintloe, who had not approached closer than midroom, keeping her pomander to her nose.

"Too much ado," Elizabeth murmured, trying to rise.

"Majesty, quiet yourself," Kate said, gently pushing Elizabeth's shoulders to her pillows. "Lord Dudley has gone for your doctors."

"We want him . . . here. Only Ro . . . bin," the queen said, not in her usual commanding voice, but as a plaintive plea.

"He will come soon and will not leave you," Kate said close to Elizabeth's ear. "Rest now, Majesty. He loves you and all will be well."

Elizabeth opened her eyes, her face now flushed red. "Don't leave me, cousin."

"Never," Kate said, and meant it with all her heart. They were one now, two women of the same blood who loved in silence, each unable to openly have the man they desired, both keeping their longing buried deep from other eyes . . . for different reasons, but with the same hurtful consequences.

The queen's fever raged for several days, but the pocks did not come. For it was the small pocks, Kate knew long before the doctors dared to say it. She also knew that if the pocks did not come, it was a sure sign of a severe case. The queen would surely die. She heard these words whispered from the antechamber and felt the mantle of despair settle about them.

Kate snatched what sleep she could at Elizabeth's bedside, and on the evening of the third day, the queen came to herself after hours of senselessness.

Cecil and her councilors hovered near the outer door of the stifling chamber, vinegar cloths tied about their noses and mouths. "Majesty," Cecil's muffled voice begged, "you must name your heir."

Elizabeth turned eyes bright with fever on Kate, kneeling exhausted by her bed. "You get your wish, cousin," the queen whispered through her swollen throat. "You will see me dead."

Kate was horrified, the more so because in anger she had once wished Elizabeth dead, but not now, not like this. She leaned close to the queen's ear, tears falling hot down her cheeks, her life and her babe's life already at risk. "No, Majesty, I do not wish it. On my hope for heaven, I do not."

It was the expected response, but also true. Suppressing her own needs, even to risking her own life, was the ancient fealty a subject owed the monarch, and it was a part of her, in her blood, fixed at the moment of her birth. While her head held her fear that Cecil and the council might force her onto the throne, her heart fled from the thought that Elizabeth must die.

"Majesty, name an heir for England and for your people," Cecil repeated urgently. "Your doctors can do nothing more."

But the queen had lost her power of speech.

A commotion at the outer door caused all to turn as Robert Dudley broke through the crowd of councilors. "By Christ's blood, she will not die! I have brought a German physician who has cured many close to death." Dudley pulled a robed doctor, carrying a bundle, into the room. "Save her, Burcot, or you're a dead man this day. By my sword you are!"

Kate and Mary Sidney stood aside while the doctor examined the queen's body for the pocks, then wrapped her in red flannel and carried her to the hearth, laying her on pillows before a roaring fire.

For two hours Elizabeth lay, eyes closed, mute; then she regained her speech.

Cecil was relentless in his duty. "Majesty, assure the succession! None of your council wants the Scots queen, though some do favor Lady Katherine Grey, according to your father's will. Tell us your wishes."

Kate waited, her chest tight at the thought of what might come next. Elizabeth would not have named her in life, but now there was no choice for the queen, or for her mistress of the wardrobe. She bowed her head. If it must be, then it was surely God's will, and she could not fight that.

"Lord Dudley," the queen croaked between cracked lips, "Robin will be regent of England with a pension of twenty thousand pounds . . . nay, fifty thousand." Elizabeth took a gasping breath. "And his faithful body servant, Tamworth, will receive five hundred pounds per annum for life."

Kate knew her face must reflect the shock she saw in others'. Dudley to rule? And so princely a sum to Dudley's manservant must be meant to buy his silence of all he knew. What else could be thought?

Immediately, the councilors spoke as one: "But, Majesty—"

Elizabeth, her chest heaving with the effort, cried out, "Although I love and have loved Lord Robert, upon my faith, nothing improper has passed between us."

Kate knew the queen left her beloved Robin the realm, her most precious possession, and by her very act branded Robert Dudley her lover. And with the legacy to the servant who slept each night at his door, who would now believe Robert was named regent over all the peers of England for any other reason?

Locked on Cecil's face, Elizabeth's eyes shouted, if she could have given them voice, *Believe me! Believe me!*

Dudley had the intelligence to say nothing even after loud, angry protests rose from the councilors.

Kate moved to a chair, needing to sink into it, perhaps never to rise. She was tired unto death and fearful for her babe.

"Look, my lords," the doctor said in his thick German accent, bending near the queen, "the red spots! They appear on her face and arms. She *vill* live."

"Will she lose her youthful beauty?" Dudley murmured low, for only the doctor to hear. "That would be a kind of death for Bess."

Burcot shrugged. "We vill soon know, my lord. Beauty is give by Gott and may be take by Him."

Kate felt her head falling forward.

Dudley took her arm and lifted her from her chair. "Come, my lady, you can do no more." He lowered his voice. "We have both won and lost a throne today, and that is a day's work for anyone." He spoke aloud next. "You must rest. She will need your care later." He led Kate from the privy chamber. "Sir William," he said to Cecil, "I will return as soon as I have escorted Lady Katherine to her chamber." With a twist of a smile, Dudley added, "Do not fear, my Lord Chancellor; I will not steal the domed throne in the presence chamber while I am gone."

Cecil nodded, his mouth drawn into a grim line. Kate knew he was still dismayed at the queen's startling bequests and none too happy at Dudley's jesting about it.

Kate wondered what else Robert could do but jest. They had both smelled the crown this day. But she was too relieved and too tired to wonder what he felt. Sleep was the only thing she wanted— indeed, must have.

The halls were full of clusters of courtiers calling to Dudley: "How goes it with the queen?" "Does Her Majesty yet live?"

They left much rejoicing that the queen lived behind them.

"I'm pained to report it," Robert whispered in her ear, "but word has come that our friend Lady Jane is dead of the pocks."

Kate sagged in his arms, her head lolling against his shoulder, almost too weary to replace exhaustion with regret for Edward's sister, but quite aware their only friend was gone. The small pocks took young and old, peasant and queen. There was nothing she could do, not even for herself. She stared at her own skin through weepy eyes, expecting the red spots to appear as she gazed. She didn't know for whom she wept, perhaps for all—queen, Jane and the countless others on their last journey by torchlight to the lime pits.

Dudley delivered Kate to her nurse. "Give her a sleeping draft," he said to Sybil.

Kate started to express her thanks for his care, but he was already racing back down the halls to Elizabeth's apartments. She waved away the draft, thinking not to need it.

"Oh, lady," said Sybil, "I be sorry in my heart to hear the dreadful news from France."

"What news?" Kate asked, sitting on her bed, now suddenly more alert than she'd been for hours.

"Why, about the Earl of Hertford, your—" She stopped, knowing not to say the word *husband* aloud.

Kate fell back onto the bed, grabbing at Sybil's arm. "What about Ned, Sybil? Not dead! Please God, not that! Tell me at once!"

"He is wounded, my love, in a bad way, they say, and—"

"No! Jesu, please . . . This is too much to bear."

Sybil cradled Kate in her arms. "Hush now, my babe. All will be well."

But Kate was no longer listening, the pain in her belly following her into a soft, dark place empty of dreams.

"Quiet yerself," Sybil was saying over and over when Kate woke with a cry, memory flooding in. The thick candles around her bed burned low.

"Ned," she groaned.

"There be no more news for ye from France."

"My child?" Kate murmured her next question, her hand searching for her belly under the thick coverlet, and finding the familiar mound under her shift.

"The babe did not come, lady," Sybil whispered softly, as if her words would fly to the queen's apartments. "I be stoppin' a small bleeding. Ye be fine with sleep and food. But the babe be not far off. Ye must get away."

Kate closed her eyes again, a murmured prayer on her lips, then struggled to sit up. "But the queen?"

"My lord Dudley sends to tell ye that Her Majesty improves with the hours and does not ask for ye."

Kate nodded. Elizabeth could no longer pretend that Katherine Grey, niece of Henry VIII, daughter of the Duke of Suffolk, was in line to succeed her. Twice the queen had used her, once to the Scots ambassador and again at the council meeting. But on her deathbed, she had named Dudley. The game was over. Elizabeth could not think to use Kate again to thwart demands for a royal marriage. Jesu be thanked. No more pretense now. The queen must let Kate and Ned go.

That happy thought did not last for the space of a minute. With the prospect of Dudley looming over them, the council and Parliament might try to force Henry's will on Elizabeth.

Escape! Kate knew she must flee Hampton Court to Ned's house in Westminster until the babe came, then to France. If birth was imminent, she could wait no longer. But how to leave the palace? She must have help to get away . . . a barge, a carriage. But she had no friends. Only one name came to her mind.

Robert Dudley. He had his motives, but he had been kind in his way, and now that Jane was dead, he was her only help. And he was her brother-in-law. He must find a way out for her.

Sybil warmed mutton broth over a brazier and spooned it into Kate, who slowly regained some energy. The nurse constantly felt Kate's skin for fever and examined her body for spots. Finally, on the second day, she smiled. "No pocks, my lady, though I hear Lady Sidney, Lord Robert's sister, be hard taken and greatly disfigured."

"Mary Sidney? I will pray for her."

"The good Lord be watchin' over ye, lady, for yer little babe's sake."

Every word of the queen for the next days was of swift recovery, and Sybil brought news that the entire court was celebrating and praising God, seeing the queen's escape as the hand of God protecting His anointed, His face smiling on England.

"It be said, lady, that Lord Dudley does not move from Her Majesty's chambers except to sleep on a straw pallet in her antechamber, for she has the doors open and calls him to her at all hours."

Kate listened, taking more manchet white bread dipped in good broth. "Tell me immediately, Sybil, when he leaves the queen's side to sleep in his own chambers."

"Aye, lady. It be also said that the queen is not so much scarred, though she be wearin' a veil before her face."

Kate smiled. Perhaps Robin's Bess would not lose her beauty and he would have queen, beauty and all, though neither she suspected. He must know that Elizabeth would make him ruler if she died, but not while she lived. Except, did any man ever truly believe a woman could withstand her own heart? He would hope still; he would hope forever.

"And she be meetin' with her council," Sybil went on, breathless with the court news.

Kate nodded. Though the queen would give all thanks to God, she would believe herself saved because she was indestructible. Kate could not help but wonder if the queen thought herself God's servant or He hers.

"Oh, my lady," Sybil said, "to see yer smile again be answer to my prayers."

"You are good, Nurse. When I am with Lord Edward at Eltham, you will remain servant to my body with ten marks a year . . . for your life long, Nurse." It was a handsome sum, but loyalty and devotion were priceless.

Sybil bowed her head. "I thank ye, Kate. I would be with ye always."

Kate felt Sybil take the bowl from her hands as she drifted into a dream of Ned holding her to him, both astride his horse and flying across the countryside of Hertfordshire before all others.

She had received no summons from the queen. Had she been discovered? Saintloe had told Her Majesty after all. It was worse to wait than to know.

The next day she was up from bed and dressing in a gown grown once again too tight for her, though she'd had little to eat these last days. Desperate to speak to Dudley, she went to the queen's apartments, the gentlemen ushers opening the doors, only to be stopped by Saintloe.

"On your life, do not enter. There is further disaster come from France. If the queen discovers your . . ." Her eyebrows said the rest.

"Is my lord Dudley with her?" Kate asked, wishing for once to be a man with a sword, or a Medici with poison in her ring, to be rid of this damnable lady.

"Nay, she has sent him to his bed and—" Saintloe answered, shutting the door on her own words.

Kate stood for a moment, rage filling her. She forced her anger to leave her. Resentment always caused her babe to kick, and now he had moved lower. She was sure of it. The babe was dropping. Birth was near. *Oh, God, help me!* She moved quickly along the hall toward Lord Robert's rooms nearby.

Now a full moon followed her through the high mullioned windows of Hampton Court. Was the heavenly light sent to guide her, or to rebuke her? She came to Robert's rooms and knocked before she could puzzle an answer.

Tamworth, the poorer by five hundred pounds, answered. "My lady Katherine, our lord is sleeping, faint with exhaustion."

Two of his other servants tried to block her way, but she knew how to deal with servants. She rushed past them and opened Robert's bedchamber door and shut it softly, approaching his bed, lanterns and candles guttering low.

"My lord," she whispered. He did not move, snoring softly, his chest scarcely rising.

She knelt beside the bed, not wishing to startle him when he woke to see a woman in a wide farthingale casting a huge shadow over him. "Robert," she said again, and gently shook his arm.

He sat up suddenly and reached for the sword that he was not wearing.

"Who—"

"Robert, it's me, Katherine. I need your help. You must take me away from here for Edward's sake. You know we are married and I am with child."

"Kate! What in the name of all good sense are you doing here?" He jumped from his bed and hastily pulled on breeches and doublet, though not hose, since she could plainly see the dark hair on his legs. "If the queen finds you here, you'll need the devil's own help to save you. You must leave!" He jerked away from her. "If she hears of this, as she hears of everything, she may believe we are lovers and that the babe you carry is mine."

"But, brother . . ." On her knees, she looked up at him, her hands clasped, praying harder than she had ever prayed before the cross.

"Stop it! Kinship won't save me or you." He grabbed her by the arm and forced her to her feet, moving her quickly toward his outer door. "I must think what to do."

CHAPTER SEVEN

"The strength to harm is perilous in the hand
of an ambitious head."
—*Elizabeth Regina*

St. Crispin's Day
October 25, 1562

After leaving Dudley's apartment, heedless of the obvious stares and whispers from courtiers and servants alike, Kate rushed through Hampton Court's halls and connecting grand rooms toward her chamber, holding hard to her kirtle especially, which was necessary, since the strings were now loosened as much as she dared.

As Kate burst through the door, Sybil started up from the chest where she was placing the last of the summer lavender. "Lady?"

"Quickly, Nurse," Kate said, her mind settling on the one option that seemed to hold any hope. "I want you to find a sheep barge, a pig boat . . . any floating thing to get us to London in all haste."

Alarmed, Sybil seemed frozen where she stood. "But, my dear, I be not knowin' how to—"

Kate, hardly aware of her own actions, grabbed her nurse's arm. "If I am arrested, you will be on the streets of London with no bread and only your body to sell for it. Is that what you want?" Immediately Kate regretted her harsh words. She sat down, unable to stand any longer. "Sorry . . . so sorry."

"My babe, you are overwrought," Sybil said, hugging Kate's head to her breast. "How will I find a boat and men to row it?"

"Ask one of the fowlers in the privy kitchens. They will know. Pay them for their silence." Kate unlocked her jewelry box at her bedside and withdrew several shillings, thrusting them into Sybil's hand, trying hard to calm herself. "Now," she said, forcing her nearly hysterical voice lower by an octave, "I know you will do this for me and all will be well." She watched as Sybil left swiftly with one backward glance of her loving face.

There was little time remaining. She had seen alarm in Robert's eyes and a tightening about his mouth. Would he betray her?

Kate firmly locked her door against Saintloe, who would surely come to snoop or gloat. Donning her own cloak, Kate knelt to wait at her *prie-deux*. Prayer was all that was left to her. Surely God, having saved Elizabeth from death and disfigurement, could spare a thought for Katherine, Countess of Hertford, lawfully married by His priest and ordinance.

Waiting to be exposed was the hardest of all trials. She could not imagine the Tower would be worse, though her sister, Lady Jane Grey, could probably have told her that waiting for the ax was far worse.

Would Her Majesty dare to imprison her, to treat her ill so soon after her own near death when her council had thought to name Katherine Grey heir to the throne? Perhaps for that very reason. Elizabeth would never believe she had no desire to rule. The queen had no knack for such a belief.

Kate clasped her face in her hands as she bent over her *prie-deux*. Instead of prayer, her mind swung between the surety that the queen would not dare to deal harshly with a kinswoman, who had cared for her night and day through the pocks, and the certain knowledge that Elizabeth feared all possible claimants as much as death. Hers was a terror born of the fearful plots and accusations that had landed her in the Tower and too near the headsman during her sister Mary's reign.

Marrying Edward and carrying his babe had made Kate's claim

too strong to be ignored. And Elizabeth was not a queen to ignore a threat to a throne she'd waited her life long to claim.

Ned had thought Elizabeth would have no alternative once they were joined in God's eyes, but a ruler always had an alternative.

Kate's head sank lower, the candle guttering before her, and Sybil still did not return. Though she'd thought to pray for her own rescue, to remind God in heaven that she was in need of His intercession, Kate found herself praying instead for Ned, thinking before she could stop the blasphemous thought that the sensation of his arms about her and the babe in her belly were what she needed before God's attentions. And needed at once.

"I must speak with Her Majesty," Robert Dudley announced to the gentleman usher in the outer chamber, having been admitted without question to the queen's apartments.

"Her Grace is with her councilors, my lord."

"How does she fare this morn?"

"The doctor is most pleased with her progress."

"Has the queen seen other than her councilors and doctor?"

"My lord?"

Robert nodded. The man said nothing but by order. And yet he hoped no guard had seen a woman leave his rooms in the dark of night and rushed to tell it. Since his mind could not settle to prayer, he crossed his thumb and forefinger in the sign of the cross and began to pace from one wall to the other. He ignored the giant Holbein portrait of Elizabeth's father that she carted in its own conveyance from one castle to another. He had always understood her need to wave her royal claim under everyone's nose. Yet he often thought there might be more to this need of hers. Was she forcing her father, a man of vast girth and charm and even vaster cruelty, to take heed of her? In life, Henry had ignored and coddled in turn, and more than once declared her a bastard. Yet today she was more the old king's daughter than her older sister, Mary, had ever been, and, yes, more his son than poor, sickly Edward VI.

Robert was certain Bess still hated Henry VIII for all his malice, the chiefest among them keeping a mother's love from her forever. Yet Robert had seen Elizabeth from her childhood in that same hand-on-hip, haughty, commanding-the-world stance that Holbein had captured so well in the painting. But when was his Bess not all contradiction? Perhaps he faced the greatest one now: Though she could love intensely, and he felt that love deep in his soul, could she forgive such love in others, love that could compel them to defy her and England's law, risking life and freedom?

He stopped before the usher. "You'll announce me when the council is gone?"

"Aye, my lord, immediately."

Robert sat on a velvety chair for a moment, but found it too soft to suit his mood. He needed steel to sit upon, to harden his spine. And his heart.

He closed his eyes, lost in some childhood place with the young Bess, her hair like fire shining on gold tumbled about her sweet face, her skin flushed with the heat of their game of Duck, Duck, Goose. He had been the goose she'd never tired of capturing, and her merry laughter had pealed throughout the courtyard at Greenwich and rang still in his heart. Had he loved her since that day when they were both but eight years from the cradle? Or had he been born with his love, a part of his heart already hers at his first sight: so small, so pretty, but with the regal look of a true princess in Henry's mad court, and ever after the princess of his heart? Had she been plain Elizabeth, would he have loved her? How could he know? He knew only what tore at him night and day.

The doors to the privy chamber opened and he rose to bow as the councilors, led by Lord Secretary Cecil, a stack of signed documents under his arm, hurried away, Elizabeth's distinctive, circling signature still shining damp on the topmost charter.

"My lord, the queen commands your attendance," the usher announced in a loud voice, as if he were half the court away.

Robert strode inside, sweeping his hat to the floor. She stood before the hearth, dressed simply in dark velvet robes with long oversleeves and a small lace ruff. An embroidered white cap sat snug to her head to cover the hair she'd lost during the pocks, her face showing only faint pink marks now that the scabbing had fallen away. God be praised, she had escaped the deep pitting that had destroyed his sister Mary Sidney's face so that she must hide it forever under a thick black veil even from her poet husband, Sir Philip.

Dudley knelt before the queen.

"Robin, rise, rise, sweetheart," she said, and gave him her hand to raise him up.

"Majesty," he said, standing, wanting to take her in his arms, but as ever careful to show her every respect in private until her words and body unquestionably invited more. "I pray God always favors you as He has surely done these last weeks."

"And why should He not?" she asked teasingly, a tinkle of mirth breaking forth at her own audacity.

She came close to him, and he smelled the Tudor rose scent she wore, heated now to high summer's warmth by the fire. He could have had her in his arms, but he did not, knowing that it would go the worse for him if she didn't believe he was innocent of what he must be the first to tell her.

"Madam, please seat yourself, for it is my duty to report unpleasant information."

Elizabeth, seeming to stand a foot taller, swept past him to the center of the room and spun back toward him. "We need not sit like some fainting dame. Let us hear this news. More of the pocks at our court? The French Catholics have won another battle against your brother, Warwick?"

"Nay, Bess." He came close and said it outright before he choked on it. "Katherine Grey, your mistress of the wardrobe, is pregnant."

Had it been a cannon in one of her warships, the queen's face would have spewed black powder smoke, fire and ball at that moment. She struck out in all directions, flailing wildly, blindly. Robert took the hurts as they came, saying nothing, doing nothing to protect himself.

Spent after using energy she had only recently regained, Elizabeth sank into a high-backed chair. Her hoarse whisper enveloped him. "Is it yours?"

He fell to his knees before her and took her lovely hands in his own, holding them against his pounding heart. "Before my God, no, sweetheart. Never mine. On our love, never mine."

Her breathing quieted and he saw a tear of relief quickly blinked away. "Who has dared defile her?"

"Edward, the Earl of Hertford, Bess."

Her hands turned to ice under his touch. "The false rogue! Pretending to woo another. I'll have his head for taking a virgin of the blood royal."

Robert turned her hands over and kissed each rigid palm. "There is worse, Bess."

She slumped forward and he caught her, cradling her head on his shoulder.

"Worse? There is no worse."

"They are married, Bess."

He felt her shake and feared she'd faint. "They are plotting for the throne," she gasped. "She has been seen talking with the Spanish ambassador, de Quadra. They plot, or why would Edward want such a dull-witted, flat-arsed ninny?"

He held her hard, but as her fear mounted, she escaped him, bursting out of her chair. "Guards! Guards!"

A yeoman officer and three men appeared instantly, kneeling. "Captain," she shouted, "take my lady Katherine Grey to the Tower at once under guard! She may not come to us, nor send us her begging scribbles." Elizabeth took a much-needed breath. "And send to Cecil that the Earl of Hertford is to be recalled from France in chains . . . *in chains!* . . . and taken to the Tower."

"Majesty," Robert ventured, "the earl is wounded."

"Bring him on a litter!" Her furious response was final. "Send also to the Lord Lieutenant of the Tower with these our instructions that the two traitors are to be ever separated . . . *completely!*"

The captain rose and bowed. "It is done as you command, Your Grace."

Elizabeth whirled about to face Dudley. "Robin, don't you dare plead for them."

Robert thought it best to say nothing, lest she suspect him again. She was in a mood that allowed her no hearing, but what her own fearful mind conjured.

He watched her pacing back and forth in the privy chamber, her fists clenched by her side, stirring clouds of dried herbs strewn on the floor. "Hertford and his whore are guilty of high treason by my father's will, and all know the king named it treason for an heir to marry without their sovereign's consent."

Elizabeth gave a bitter laugh. "But she has damned herself in higher eyes. She swore an oath to God on her soul that she would ever serve me and never marry." The queen's face reddened so that her faint pock scars became bright spots on her cheeks. "She is a lying, hell-bound slut, and so she is proved for all time!"

"Bess," Robert said quietly, but soon realized that she would not hear him. Her hands were on her ears, shutting out all she could not bear to hear.

"Mistress Ashley," he called loudly enough to reach to the anteroom, "tend the queen."

"Robin," Elizabeth said, sagging against him, "they must lose their heads, though she pleads her belly."

"Bess," he whispered, feeling her fear shake her.

"They have left me no choice. No choice at all."

Ashley rushed in, gathering Elizabeth into her arms and guiding her toward the bed, cooing as to a child.

Robert bowed himself out, walking through the outer chambers and out into the great hall, as Cecil rushed toward him.

"My lord, is it so?" Cecil asked, catching his breath.

"Yes," Dudley said softly. "The queen has taken to her bed. Come later, Sir William, but delay any death warrants, if you can, until Her Majesty has time to think again upon what she does."

"The council—nay, Parliament itself—will petition to save Lady Katherine," Cecil replied, obviously worried.

"That will only assure her that there is a plot. You might relieve her mind that she faces nothing more than foolish youth led by the heat of their loins."

Cecil eyed him, and Robert saw a smile playing just inside the councilor's mouth.

From the direction of Kate's room, Robert heard the sound of a battering ram smashing against solid oaken doors.

Cecil looked saddened. "Ah, the lady Grey will soon be taken." He bowed and hurried away toward his rooms.

Dudley walked in the opposite direction. There was little he could do for her, or could ever have done. The young fools! As all lovers, they had been determined to believe what they wanted to be true: that their love could overcome all obstacles.

Shutting his ears to the sound of wood splintering, he wondered how different he was from Kate and Edward. He had recognized the source of Cecil's amusement.

Robert smoothed his wrinkled doublet, then put one hand on his sword hilt to halt its tripping movement and walked toward the soothing sounds of a consort playing in the presence chamber and the dancing master calling the figures.

His legs longed to sit astride a horse, heedlessly riding down red deer over fields and into woods with Bess at his side, as they had done so often, and not to think about youthful fools who had the same hopeless dream as he himself and now must surely pay. He shrugged. He saw no other course open for them. Their marriage, combining Tudor and Seymour blood, had sealed their fate. Unless . . . ?

Unless there had been no marriage.

Kate nearly lost her footing on the slimy stone steps of the Traitor's Gate, the huge iron grate crashing down behind her. She had no more tears, having lost the last of them midway on the Thames between Hampton Court and the Tower. Her feet and hands were numb as from winter cold, though unseasonable summer heat still shimmered over London.

The Lord Lieutenant stood on the small green before the Church of St. Peter in Chains, the last buds of hot October drooping around its blood-soaked sward, fed with the lifeblood of the queen's mother, Anne Boleyn, Kate's own sister, Jane Grey, her father and others without count . . . and perhaps soon her own blood. A troop of yeoman warders stood behind her. So many for just one small woman? She gestured toward them with a faint smile. "My Lord Lieutenant, I am but one maid and you have need of no such great protection from me." There, at least she still had a noble voice.

He bowed, his gentleman's face blushing at her words. "My lady Grey—" he began.

"Countess of Hertford," she corrected. Now that she was exposed, she would claim all that was hers by her marriage right.

He bowed again. "Please you to follow me."

"It pleases me little, my lord, but I will not be the first woman to be unjustly lodged here. It would give me pleasure to be received in the Bell Tower, where Her Majesty was kept when her sister, Queen Mary, sent her here for the same unfounded treason."

Kate did not know what had given her such a strong spine, braving it like a rogue on the scaffold to win one last laugh from the hanging's revelers. Perhaps the babe, heavy in her belly, increased her courage. She also knew that every word of hers would be reported to others. She meant them to bring her credit. She shivered, knowing also that she might need to borrow from that store of strength at some future date.

"I am sorry, my lady, but my orders are to lodge you in the Beauchamp tower."

So, no decent quarters. "I am ready, my lord," she said, her head rigid in case a tremble escaped from inside her body and gave her fright away, making her guilty in the eyes of all who kept close watch.

"It is my duty," the miserable man explained.

"Come then," she said, taking his outstretched arm, pretending to gaiety, "since it is also my duty to bear the queen's anger for love of my lord of Hertford, we will do our duty together and with good heart."

As they ascended the narrow winding stone steps up to the tower, Kate prayed to be alone within minutes. She would be able to keep this brave pretense for no longer. But she had to know one thing. "My lord of Hertford, is he to be arrested and dragged from his bed, wounded though he is in the queen's service?"

"I am at liberty to tell you nothing, madam." He coughed. "Forgive me, but I received word of your coming only a short time ago. I will have a fire laid and food brought. Your maids—"

"Must be sent for, good my lord. I'll want Sybil from Hampton Court and two more from my husband's Westminster house, as is due my rank." *Now go*, she wanted to scream at him.

He left immediately, but not before making a pitiable face at the door, placing his hand on his heart. He had no liking for this duty. But was he a friend? Would he send a message of warning to Ned in France? As she asked herself the question, she knew the answer. He had a tender heart, but it was treason to go against the queen's orders.

Kate sat before the cold fireplace, scarcely knowing where she was as the day waned, shadows growing outside the narrow, barred window on the opposite curving wall. Had the queen known of her babe despite the farthingale that had hidden others before her? No. Elizabeth would have acted immediately upon such knowledge. Who had exposed her? She had to think.

Saintloe? No, that lady would not risk imparting such knowledge, waiting rather to take what advantage she could of Kate's exposure.

Dudley! He was the only one who knew and feared having such knowledge. But she wasn't at all sure. Though she was certain that half the court was in on the secret. Jane could keep nothing to herself. God blast her bones! Kate's heart pounded in her chest. She had thought ill of the dead, but it could hardly worsen her condition. Then, too, surely her own belly in the last month must have raised questions from those at court who always watched and whispered. Only the queen's ill health for two months past had saved her for so long.

Now Ned must be warned. But how, and was it too late by hours, a fast ship already in the channel making for France with the queen's arrest orders? She feared for him, as she longed for him. At least, if he was quickly brought to stand trial with her, they could be together for their son's birth. It was Ned's right, and hers.

So, deep in endless circling thought, Kate scarce knew when the coal fire was laid and lit, but as dark night fell she was glad for it. The cold of five hundred winters seeped from the stone walls, penetrating to her very marrow, and set her to shaking, unable to eat the hot dinner that the Lord Lieutenant's wife delivered with her own hands.

Robert Dudley pleaded London business the next day and the queen gave him leave to tend to it, begging him to hurry his return. The business was true enough. He wouldn't lie to Bess. But he had not been ordered to refrain from the Tower while in the city.

He concluded his business with his tailor and booter, then rode the winding streets of Cheapside, stopping at several merchants, buying a fruit tart on Thames Street and then on to St. Paul's. Paul's Walk was crowded with easy slatterns, vendors hawking everything a large port city of nearly seventy thousand souls had to sell, a city now recovering from a hard summer of pocks, plague and the sweating sickness, so that some doors and windows were already thrown open to air and a few shops were busy again. As the cold nights came on to halt sickness, the court would remove to Whitehall across the river for Christmas celebrations.

He stopped at a jeweler's stall, looking for a Twelfth Night present for Bess, but the man had only small and inferior jewels, nothing suitable for his queen.

He rode on to the Tower's western gate and presented himself to the Lord Lieutenant. "I would see Lady Katherine," he said.

The man bowed. "My lord, I have sent for the lady's servants, but I have no instructions regarding visitors."

"I am come from court, and this lady is my sister-in-law."

The man looked pained and uncertain.

Robert thought he needed but a slight jostle against his conscience. "I've come to offer the poor lady what comfort I can."

The man blinked and swallowed. "A short visit then, my lord, since I have no instructions against visitors save for my lord of Hertford."

Dudley bowed. "I am grateful, sir."

The man stiffened. "I but do a hard duty, my lord, no more, nor less."

Robert followed him silently up the familiar stairs. He could say much the same, though it meant the lives of three people.

He must save Bess from the consequence of her own deep-held suspicions. He knew she could not live with herself if she took these young lives in a fit of fear, and he did not want his Bess hardened forever by regret she could not undo.

Also, he had to save the lives of two young and very stupid idiots. He accepted some blame. He should have warned them more, stopped them, rather than standing by, amused. He'd had some faint idea that another's love and marriage might bring Bess to . . .

Kate, wrapped in her cloak, was warming herself by the fire, her belly thrust before her, freed of its farthingale and kirtle. "My lady," he said quietly, closing the heavy door.

"Have you come to glory at your handiwork?"

He had never seen her so outspokenly bitter, and he could not blame her. "I have come to offer you a way to save your head and Edward's, too."

At that, Kate looked at him, her face already thinner and shadowed with sleeplessness and pain. "Ned . . . The queen has arrested him?"

Dudley nodded. "He should be here within a fortnight."

Her head tipped back and she closed her eyes. "Jesu, Robert, how could she?"

"Kate," he said, wondering still at her willful ignorance, "it is treason to take the virginity of a lady of the blood royal."

"Then look to your own head, Robert."

He had never seen her like this. His timid, dutiful, pale sister-in-law now seemed to have grown as large with courage as with child. He swallowed some anger at the accusation, but would not be detracted from his purpose. "Kate," he said, sitting on the settle beside her, without touching her, "I have come to help you, if you allow it. Have you so many friends here that you can turn one away?"

Her mouth flew open, but he shushed her. "Think before you answer, Kate. The queen feels betrayed by your broken oath and threatened by a plot she thinks you and Edward have to take her throne."

Kate sat up, her face hot with exasperation.

"Stop!" he shouted. "Do not plead love. That is no balance

against the laws of treason and broken oaths to a sovereign . . . to *this* sovereign, who spent all her miserable youth dodging the snarls of treasonous plots."

He saw her chin go up. Good. Defiance would keep her in spirits while he did his work. "Kate, hear me, you will receive no other offers of friendship."

Her lips quivered. "The Parliament will not allow this. After all, I am in Henry's will. Surely that will save us. You know I do not want the throne, indeed dread it."

He lifted her cold hands with his and held them tight against his doublet. "Listen to me; listen to someone who wants only your good." He said that truth so that he wouldn't choke on the coming lie. "The queen thinks that you are not truly married. If you cannot prove it, it means you stay here for your life and Edward's head rolls on the green below before a cheering mob."

She shivered at the image, and he damned himself for such necessary cruelty.

"You know we are married, Robert," she said, her eyes pleading the truth of her words. "You helped us."

"By what priest?" he demanded.

"I don't know."

He did not show his relief at that information, but made his words as terse as his heart would allow. "There is no proof of my aid except for the word of two desperate people in the Tower facing a trial for treason."

"Ned's old servants know."

"Who do you think the queen will believe . . . a traitor's loyal servants, or her own fears? She sees only your ambition in this, and that alarms her past forgiving."

Kate's shoulders sagged. "You would not testify for us." It was not a question.

"I could not, but . . ." He grabbed at her hands slipping from his. "It need not come to a trial. Don't you see, Kate? If you tell me where you have the marriage contract, I can prove you are lawfully married and save Edward's life."

"I beseech you, Robert, for charity, save Ned and my babe. I care not what happens to me."

Dudley nodded, able to offer nothing more.

She raised her head. "Would Her Majesty not allow us to retire to Hertfordshire?"

Despite her hopeless words, he saw hope in her eyes, and, God help him, he fed it, damning himself for a fraud as he spoke. "I'm sure of it, Kate. Just let me prove you are not defiled unlawfully and perhaps she will soften and consent to your union."

She did not think further, but answered him immediately, rash as ever, but he blessed her for it. "As you will, Robert. Jane had our marriage proof put away for safekeeping, since I feared Lady Saintloe would spy and discover it. The witnessed contract must still be in her rooms, if they are now free of the pocks' vapors."

He took a deep, relieved breath, looked around the room, noted the garderobe with its familiar stinking closestool, and changed the subject. "I was over a year in this very cell, Kate, and my father, John Dudley, before me." He pointed above her head and she looked up with him. "See there, high over the mantel, my father's name and mine carved under the bear and double ragged staff. When you despair, look at my name and think that I am doing all in my power to save you and Edward, and have full knowledge of what you suffer."

Dudley loosed his hold on her and stood. He bent and kissed her cold cheek, then quickly left.

He claimed his horse from a stable boy below and rode hard through London and onto the Windsor wagon road, galloping past Richmond for Hampton Court in the quickly gathering dusk. He would keep his promise to Kate to do all in his power. He had not lied in that, although there was no way the queen could let their marriage stand, which would save them from beheading or burning, both punishments for treason. Kate, perhaps due to her advanced pregnancy or just the shock of her fall from favor, did not seem to comprehend what she faced. His horse pounded on through the night, Dudley's head spinning at what he must do. Rather to be a named whore with a head, he thought, than a countess without one. Surely Kate wouldn't choose the block to life, even life without Edward. He wasn't certain, but he had set this course and now he must follow it.

Above all else, he would save his Bess from the folly of taking the lives of two foolish young lovers. This one act could take from her the love of her people, alienate some in the council she relied on, and shock her Parliament, which was already at odds with her over her reluctance to marry and to produce an heir. Not to mention the need for more and more subsidies and levies for France.

Kate and Edward would pay for their ill choice, but not with death, if he could stop it. And perhaps, just perhaps, when all danger was past, Bess would relent and allow them their freedom.

The rutted road was dangerous in the dark. Rather than risk a broken leg for his horse, Robert stopped at the sign of the Great Heron, waking the innkeeper and his wife, who gave him a cold supper and enough ale to warm his jittery insides, which were sadly in need of heat.

With his horse rested, Robert reached Hampton Court two hours after dawn, knowing that Elizabeth, always an early riser, was already sending for him. After stopping by his rooms to hastily change from his dusty travel clothes, he raced upstairs and down halls to Jane Seymour's former apartment, drawing out the key she'd given him to open the unguarded door. He smiled at the memory of her shy hopefulness as she had pressed the key on him. She had been such an unlikely and most tongue-tied seductress, he had kissed her from mercy.

Searching through her possessions packed in chests to be taken to Westminster or offered to the high palace servants, he was nearly frantic, his hand slipping easily through the gowns and sleeves without touching parchment. He was kneeling in front of the last crate of kirtles, hoods and shoes when he found the contract, stuffed in a pair of green embroidered slippers to shape them.

Well and good! Her maids could not read to know its importance. He sat back on his heels, relieved, spreading the contract on the floor. He pressed at the wrinkles until the heavy parchment lay flat.

"Robin, at last you are come."

"Majesty," he said, kneeling. "I beg leave to speak to you ... alone."

Elizabeth smiled and waved her ladies into the anteroom. Sour-faced Saintloe looked suspicious and Mistress Ashley worried, but they were accustomed to obedience, or pretended to it.

"Rise, Robin, and tell me how it is in London."

"Unusually hot days for October, Bess."

Still smiling, she took his hand and held it to her cheek. "Do I cool you, my lord?"

"No, Bess, London is all snow and ice compared to the heat your hand rouses in me." He wanted to take her in his arms. She wanted it, too, but he retrieved his hand and stepped back from the heady scent of roses that enveloped her.

Parry had not as yet been at her pots of color, so Elizabeth's lashes and eyebrows were still pale, giving her that somewhat amazed look he had seen in her child's face. He kissed the inside of her wrist for the memory.

"What do you have for me?" she asked, looking about his person for a present, her face as alive as he remembered it when she had captured her Goose in the courtyards at Greenwich.

"Only myself, Bess. Nothing in London suited you, but I have put the best jewelers in fear of their lives unless they find the most perfect pearl to hang on the ear of the most perfect queen of my heart."

He kissed her hand again, and each of her long, slender white fingers. She was vain about her hands and had the right to be, seldom covering them with gloves and always keeping them in full view.

As he bent, the parchment in his doublet crackled, reminding him of his duty. He pulled the document out and presented it, knowing better now than to suggest she sit to prepare for a shock.

"What is this?" she said, frowning, squinting a bit from nearsightedness.

"It is the marriage contract of my lord of Hertford and my lady Katherine Grey."

Elizabeth dropped it onto the tiled floor and stepped away as if it were a foul thing. "No!" she said. "It's a forgery." She whirled away, then back again. "How came you by this?"

Robert saw that her suspicions, always near the surface when it concerned her throne, now showed plainly. He knelt again. "Majesty, I went to the Tower and Lady Katherine told me of the marriage contract and where it lay, thinking to save Hertford's life. I found it and brought it to you."

"If it is real, then they are both doomed out of their own mouths. To be in my father's will of succession and marry without my consent is treason, and treason is . . ." She turned away and stared into the hearth, her shoulders heaving. "They have left a queen with no choice but to obey her father's law."

The gentleman usher knocked and opened the door. "Your Grace, the Lord Lieutenant of the Tower with urgent news."

Dudley rose and waited behind the queen.

Elizabeth reddened, her rage building. "God's precious broken body! What more for us this morn? Admit him."

The lieutenant entered, bowed to Robert, murmuring his name, and fell on his knees before the queen.

"What say you, sir?" the queen demanded.

"Majesty, the lady Katherine has been delivered in the night of a fine son. My own wife attended her."

"A son!"

"A bonny son, Your Grace."

She was shaking, and Dudley stepped to the Lord Lieutenant. "Leave us now, sir. Your duty is done."

He bowed himself out and was probably still bowed down when he reached London.

Robert brought himself close to Elizabeth. If she wanted his arms, she would reach for them.

She fell against his chest and he held her. He could not tell if she was shaking with rage or anguish.

"Bess, there is a way out."

"Where? How?" She lifted her head and breathed deeply.

"If there is no contract, there is no provable marriage; therefore the son is illegitimate and no male heir to the throne to bedevil your years."

"Disinherited?"

"Yes, therefore not a male in line of succession."

"I could show mercy . . . Kate and Edward?"

"Leaving their sin to God's judgment."

"But, Robin, there is still the matter of Edward's defiling the blood royal."

"Who's to say, Bess, that Kate, once bedded, did not many nights go from bed to bed, with countless lovers? That is what the people always believe of an unmarried woman."

"Think you she'd rather be a whore than . . ."

Robert walked to the hearth and without hesitation held the contract to the fire, setting it firmly ablaze before throwing the blackening parchment into the center of the flames. "I always preferred my head to my reputation."

Elizabeth laughed nervously. "Let them stay in the Tower, then."

"If it is what you must do, Majesty."

Elizabeth nodded and moved toward him. "Kneel, Robin."

Hesitating only a moment, Robert Dudley knelt.

She tapped his shoulder. "For your gracious goodness and good service, we do pronounce you Baron Denbigh and Earl of Leicester, granting you the ancient castle of Kenilworth in Warwickshire with all rents—"

Robert bent far forward and kissed her foot. "Bess . . ."

She laughed, reaching down to lift his chin. "Your investiture will be at Westminster Abbey, but I wanted you to hear the words from my lips."

It was an invitation, and Robert accepted, standing to take her lips with his own, thinking over and over that he was noble now. Was he noble enough to share the throne with Elizabeth of England? Was that what she intended?

A fortnight later on a foggy, rainy November morn, Edward, Earl of Hertford, wrapped in his heavy campaign cloak, limped in chains onto Tower Green near the church. He thought he heard his name on the wind, but he could see no face in the Beauchamp Tower windows.

"Follow me, my lord earl," the Lord Lieutenant commanded.

Edward fell into step behind him, taking two to the commandant's one. The Tower warders crowded behind with their pikes at the ready, whether in salute or menace he could not tell.

Edward knew the Tower grounds from visiting his father as a boy before the Duke of Somerset's death on this very green. So it was to be the Bell Tower, he thought, and he was to be separated from Kate, the queen making good on her threat. "Sir, allow me one sight of my wife and son," he said to the man's back.

"I cannot, my lord," the man said, turning toward Edward. "The queen has ordered you to be kept each from the other."

"You would deny a man sight of his own son?" Edward did not have to pretend to be stunned. "To keep a man from his family is against God's higher laws, sir."

The Lord Lieutenant, who had resumed his march, stopped again to face the Earl of Hertford, his hands gripped together as if in prayer. The warders close behind nearly piled into both men. "My lord, surely you know I have my orders."

"Sir, your orders are to keep us apart?" Edward tried to make his voice reasonable. "Surely, sir, the laws forbid a peer of my rank from being put to the torture."

The Lord Lieutenant worked his mouth, but only a mumbled, "Aye," escaped.

"Think you not," Edward said, his voice trembling beyond his ability to control, "that never seeing my beloved and my first son and heir is not torture worse than the rack? Rather would I have my arms and this leg wounded in Her Majesty's service torn from their sockets than live one more day without sight of them . . ." His voice trailed away. "When they are so close."

The Lord Lieutenant blinked hard, looking at his men, all leaning forward on their pikes, a good few of them with new tears on their weathered cheeks. "Dismissed," he ordered, regaining command of them.

They scattered, eager to be out of the rain, though some looked back.

Edward saw, too, and thought it a good sign that men hardened to the sight of the ax and heads rolling could show charity.

The commander of the Tower spoke low. "I will follow my orders, my lord earl, and will not allow you to approach, but I cannot in the Son of God's name keep you from all sight of them." He bent and unlocked the chains. "Nor would I have your wife see you in chains within a month of her birthing."

Edward took the stairs of Beauchamp Tower two at a time, despite his wound throbbing like all the drums of hell.

The Lord Lieutenant grabbed his arm to hold him back. "You must follow my instructions, my lord. You may stand outside the door, but may not go inside the room, nor attempt to . . . to touch."

Edward nodded, swallowing hard. The chief officer had a kind soul, but he did not know what agony he commanded of a man.

Edward reached the top room in the tower, a rushlight grabbed at the bottom of the stairs held before him.

"My lord, move no closer." The Lord Lieutenant bent and unlocked the door. It swung open.

Kate sat by the fire beside Sybil, her nurse. His wife wore no hood, her Tudor hair glowing. She turned slowly toward him, the babe at her breast.

Without thinking, Edward took a step across the high lintel, his arms raised.

"Stop, my lord. Remember your promise."

"Kate," Edward said, barely more than a murmur.

"My lady, do not approach. I would exceed the queen's orders to allow you . . ."

Kate was not moving. But Edward could see her legs trembling under her thin shift as she raised her babe from her breast. The child gave a lusty red-faced cry at the loss of his nipple. She thrust him forward for Edward's inspection. "My own love, his name is Edward and he is your true, legitimate son and heir."

"A handsome lad, Kate. You did well." He was surprised at his own words, though what he yearned to say was for a private time.

Edward saw that her face was thinner, but her eyes glowed with the joy of motherhood, the crying babe quickly returned and tugging at her lovely breast. His feet did not move, but his wounded leg told him he was leaning toward her and the child. "I would say so much more, Kate," he said, almost choking on the words. "Surely the good Lord Lieutenant will allow us to write."

But the good Lord Lieutenant closed the door, leaving her alone save for Sybil and the crackle of the fire. "Come, my lord," he said, gently tugging on Edward's arm. "I can do no more."

Edward followed him slowly down the stairs and across the green to the Bell Tower. He tried hard to swallow his anguish, appalled to hear the sound of a sob issue from his soldier's throat. He climbed up to the stone-lined room and saw that he had been expected. Fresh straw littered the floor, and a merry fire burned. A table was laid with a trencher full of porridge and a tankard of strong ale to drink. He sat and stretched his sore leg to the fire. "I thank you, sir, for your compassion. I will not forget it, nor fail to repay your kindness when I am free."

The man bowed and closed the door, locking it.

Before the day was out, pen, ink and paper were delivered, and Edward poured the words in his heart onto the pages in such haste that scarce one page did not suffer from heavy ink blots.

My dearest Desire,

Katherine, forgive me for not being near when our Son was born. The Channel seas were high, delaying our departure from France. My leg heals well. I beg you, do not worry yourself. I swear on our Love that we will all be together soon. We have friends in Parliament and at Court who work for our release. They doubt Her Majesty will bring us to trial for treason. Even Elizabeth's power cannot sunder God's ordinance. Have faith.

My Sweetest wife, I found a Stone projecting under my window and, with my good leg, I raised myself to see the Tower across the green where you and little Edward wait for me. When the bells ring for prayer, wave a hand outside your window and I will reach mine toward you. I think often that I can hear our son's cry . . . and your voice calling me. You must know how sore in body and mind I have been all these months away from you.

Look in your Heart and you will surely find mine,

Ned

For want of wax, he sent it unsealed that very day and the next morning was delivered a letter from Kate with food to break his fast.

Edward was reading Kate's hasty letter for the second time, longing nearly choking him. His uneaten porridge had congealed by the time the Lord Lieutenant entered his cell, bidding his yeoman guards wait on the landing.

"My lord earl," he said, obviously troubled, "I will send a doctor to make certain your leg is healing well."

Edward nodded, not trusting his voice.

The commandant paced to the fire, then back several times, though Edward was half-unaware, his mind filled with Kate's tear-splashed pleas and distress. "My wife?" he asked, looking up.

"The lady Katherine is . . . well. My own wife has tried to tempt her to eat more, lest her milk dry up. We cannot find a suitable country girl to wet-nurse the babe. I'm sorry, my lord."

Edward, holding his head in his hands, shook it slowly. "This will kill her, sir. Don't you have a conscience?"

The Lord Lieutenant walked to the door, but did not open it. Without turning, he mumbled, "It is against God's law to keep a man from his wife and babe. By His precious memory . . . I cannot keep you from your family. I will pray on it, my lord."

CHAPTER EIGHT

"I grieve yet dare not show my discontent.
I love and yet am forced to seem to hate."
—*A love poem by Elizabeth Regina*

Accession Day
November 1562

Kate had fallen into a fitful sleep after her babe's last nursing. She woke after midnight and slipped from her narrow rope bed to bend over her son's cradle, breathing in the warm, milky air above him, listening to make certain her precious child was alive and resting well. Reassured, she tucked tight his sable blanket, a gift from Lord Dudley, swaddling him against the seeping cold of the tower. Still, she could not leave off hovering above her babe, watching his sweet, round face, the long lashes that cast candlelit shadows against his cheeks, the sucking sounds he made with his tiny mouth. Soon young Edward would wake for feeding and she would feel his tug at her breast, his strong little legs kicking against her. She could scarcely bear to put him back in his cradle, forever cooing over him.

Whenever his small, warm body was in her arms, she planned his life. Little Edward would be loved every minute. He would have all the love that had been withheld from her as a child, know the affectionate comfort of being embraced when ill, or frightened by bad dreams. Her son would live where laughter would not be shushed and where he ran to his mother and not away.

She cupped her hand about his little head and whispered a promise: "When your father is with us, we will both know more love than ever imagined in this world."

A milk bubble appeared as he breathed, and she smiled. Surely, if wellborn women knew a moment of what passed between Kate and her babe, they would never allow their children to be sent off to wet nurses until they were weaned, or hand them to tutors later, seeing them only to chastise, as her mother had.

For an anguished moment, Kate was overcome by the fear of being parted from young Edward. *Jesu Christo!* She gripped the cradle; then her hands flew to her mouth, covering the sudden dread that filled her.

To quiet herself, she took one of Ned's letters from under her pillow. He promised that they would be together forever in the green deer park, shady woods and grassy meadows of Eltham, describing its sunlit rooms and gardens until Kate had endless mind pictures of what her life could be.

Not wishing to wake Sybil, who slept on a pallet in the corner, Kate bent to add more fuel to the fire and watched it leap to warmer life from the cushioned bench. Her mother, Frances Grey, Duchess of Suffolk, had gained the queen's permission to bring the cradle and other furniture and hangings from her manor of Bradgate. They made the Tower cell almost livable, Kate had to admit. Her head rested against the back of the settle, looking up at the firelit stone arches of her cell and remembering what else her mother had brought: her bitter disappointment, blame and deep anger.

Kate saw her yet, standing rooted in the middle of the room this past Lord's day, wearing the Spanish hood from King Henry's court that she would not give up, since it represented the time of her greatest power.

"Wait outside, but listen for my call," she'd ordered the ladies and ushers in her procession, after they had installed the furniture and wall hangings to her satisfaction.

Kate had stood watching her mother reorder her daughter's prison, her lusty son on her hip, a living son that her mother had never been able to produce. Young Edward was Kate's triumph, but she had only a short moment of satisfaction.

The duchess sat, arranging her gown, and ordered Kate to remain standing.

"I have been to see my niece, the queen," she said, staring at her daughter with cold eyes. "What your father did not complete for this family with his disgrace, you seem to have finished with your bastard . . . banished from court, our lands yet attainted, our name without its rightful reverence and your right to the throne overturned."

Shaking with rage that she'd repressed for a lifetime, Kate held little Edward up for her mother to see. "My lady mother, *this* is what I have accomplished. Your grandson, Edward Seymour, my child from a lawful union with the Earl of Hertford."

"There is no proof of any such marriage."

"Lord Dudley will find it."

Her mother's bitter laugh pierced Kate's heart. "You were always an empty head. First with young Seymour, then with Lord Pembroke, your husband, and now with *this!*" she said, pointing at young Edward. "Gone . . . all is gone." She turned her face away from the baby. "Take the child from my sight."

Kate continued standing, opening her shift and giving young Edward her breast.

Frances Grey's mouth twisted as if she'd tasted bile. "And now you make of yourself a common country wet nurse." Her mouth was set in contempt. "I will remedy that at once."

Kate did not raise her voice, but it was filled with determination. "No, you will not, madam. I will care for my son, feed him, change him when he is soiled and hold him when he cries. . . . I will be all the nurse he needs."

Her mother stood, opening her hand to punish such unheard-of insolence, but for the first time, she let the chastising hand fall to her side. Shoulders drooping, the duchess looked bewildered. "All my dreams vanished, when they were so close, thrown away by an ungrateful child."

"They were always your dreams, madam, never mine." Kate's voice rang with the courage of truth. She would never fear her mother again.

The duchess walked to the door and, without turning, said, "I lowered myself to beg the queen to allow you to come to me at Bradgate."

Kate shuddered. "What did she say?"

"She was unyielding. You stay in the Tower for your offense."

Kate drew in a deep breath of relief and her babe lost the nipple, crying out.

The duchess walked through the door to the tower stairs. "I think she means to take your head and Seymour's, our name further besmirched in every London alley and alehouse."

The door closed on those last choked words. There was no further good-bye.

Days later, deep in the night, Kate sat before her fire remembering every word with no sense of loss. Her mother had always predicted the direst punishment for her daughter's failings. Once, those prophecies had left her with no choice but to obey. Now, even in this prison, she was free. She had her babe and Ned, her lord and love in his cell across the Tower grounds, and was no longer subject to her mother's will.

Hugging the blanket about her, Kate allowed her mind to seek out ever more optimism, as important in the Tower as any food. Every word from a guard, every positive change was a possible sign. If Elizabeth allowed her the comforts her mother had brought, then surely Her Majesty's heart was softening, as Dudley had said it would, although it was certain the queen would banish them. She would need to be seen to punish harshly, and all nobility would think there was no worse punishment than to be denied the court, the very center of life in the realm.

Kate smiled to herself. Who would believe that she and Ned would welcome a life in the quiet country? There had been no trial, and even if there were, Elizabeth was known to waver, ever reluctant to sign death warrants.

Exhausted from reliving her mother's visit, her mind leaping at every possibility, Kate decided to wait in her bed for young Edward's feeding.

She closed her eyes and quickly became drowsy.

The sound of her door creaking open on its rusty hinges sent Kate lurching up in her bed. In the dim light, she saw a man's outline and opened her mouth to scream as his shadow moved quickly toward her.

"Hush, my love."

It was a voice she heard nightly in her dreams, the voice she'd longed for when so terribly alone, fearing a sovereign's wrath could fall on her neck at any moment. "Ned, my love," she murmured, and held out her arms to him.

"My sweet, my dearest, my blessed wife." His voice came closer and closer. Then he was sitting beside her, his arms holding her, one hand on the back of her head, which she buried against his doublet, inhaling the remembered scent of him, which set her to trembling.

"Sweetheart," he breathed against her ear. "I have longed for this moment, though I thought to hold you in front of the queen and the court, as the hero of Calais, triumphant. . . ."

She shook her head, planting kisses against his unshaven cheek. "Calais was not to be, husband. Our son is our triumph now."

His arms tightened. "Does the queen know of our marriage? The Lord Lieutenant is slow, telling me nothing, taking two weeks to decide if we should be allowed together as man and wife."

"The queen knows, Ned, though she would never have believed it until I told Dudley the whereabouts of our contract."

"You—"

"Yes, dearest. It proves our son's legitimacy."

His body went rigid under her hands. "But can we trust him?"

"I had to, or your life was surely forfeit. . . ."

"Ah, the blood-royal virgin," he added. "Since I pay the price, I'll have the pleasure, wife. All this past month since I left France I have thought of nothing but you next to me." He raised her blanket and she felt his warm and well-remembered body slide into the narrow bed beside her.

Her breath came quickly. "Ah, my sweet lord, will the Lord Lieutenant allow us to live together, as God commands?"

"Nay, he cannot go further than an hour or two in the late night, and he risks himself doing this much. Yet he promises more meetings like this."

"Did you bribe him?"

Edward shrugged. "I didn't have to. The queen made a mistake in her Lord Lieutenant of the Tower. He has a soft, romantic heart." Edward shifted his injured leg. "Although he has no such soft bed."

She laughed, her face buried against his chest, surprised at the sound, not having heard her own laughter since he left for France. "But your wound, Ned . . ."

"Your touch has healed it more completely than my French doctor," he whispered. "Your maid sleeps sound?"

"Sybil sleeps like one dead," Kate answered. "Can you not hear her snore?"

"I thought it thunder."

Now they were both laughing, trying to make it inaudible against each other's body. And she thought them quite possibly lunatic: laughing and loving, for she hoped that was soon to follow, in the Tower of London, where they might be waiting to die. No one but a Bedlamite could achieve such folly.

It was too cold to disrobe, so she opened her nursing shift to him, not needing to guide his hands to caress her full breasts. When he touched her nipples she flinched away, and he lowered his head to lick at the trickle of her milk.

"Nay, sweeting," he said when she started. "I should not take what will break my son's fast."

"They were yours first," she whispered, pulling his head back to her breasts, surprised at her own daring bed sport. She had thought to feel shy as a wife after so many months, but she felt only mounting desire.

"You are only a little more than a month from birthing, Kate. I will take great care," he said, his breath coming fast and hot, his need shaking him, shaking them both. "I must not get a babe on you."

She twisted under him until she could put her legs around his back, inviting him to enter her, indeed, the pressure of her legs demanding it. "Husband, we have done right according to God's ordinance. Our souls are safe in His hands. Besides, if we are to die for one child, we cannot die twice for two." The words were clipped short and even, like a formal privet hedge, until broken by a sharp intake of her breath as she felt him dip into the center of her.

"At this moment, my dearest love, I care not for my life . . . only you." He settled deeper into her with a groan that became words. "Do you have regrets?"

"I love you more this moment than ever I thought I could," Kate said, holding him with all her strength, as they again became one burning flesh. He was as she remembered him and as she had thought of him in all those lonely, buried months of secrecy . . . her beloved.

There was no room to turn on the narrow bed, little more than a straw pallet on ropes slung between poles, but she did not need the luxury of a huge bed with rich tapestry hangings. Ned's body was enough, all taut, smooth velvet and searing, pushing demand. She had wanted him this way, and now, despite her mother and even the queen of England, Kate had him. Such was Katherine, Countess of Hertford's power over a ruler; she was a woman who could give herself, all of herself, to a man's love.

A wondrous agony was building inside her and she lifted herself to meet it, once, twice, thrice . . . until the tempest inside her over-whelmed her counting.

His mouth met hers. "Ahhh." Edward's cry passed her lips and she met his cry with her own.

The snoring across the cell stopped.

"Dearest Kate," he choked out against her ear, "I didn't mean for you to . . . You know a woman can't get a child without pleasure."

Kate realized her fingers were dug into his arms and loosened them. "Oh, my sweetest lord, Ned," she whispered, panting a little for air, "I did never truly believe that old witch's tale."

"But the doctors say—" he began.

"They are men," she answered, almost laughing, but not wanting to offend him with knowledge that only women shared.

Instead, she held him, loving the weight of his long body against hers. They lay joined until the snoring began again across the room and their breathing was slow and even; they lay that way, whispering their dreams without moving, until finally a soft knock announced their time was gone.

He left her, kissing his son, then kissing her hand, holding hard to it. "Kate, hear me. If the Tower cannot separate us, no earthly power, not queen nor man, can keep us apart forever."

"I pray God it is so, husband," she said as the worried face of the Lord Lieutenant appeared in the open door, and her lord was gone.

She lay awake remembering every word Ned had said, sens-ing him still part of her body. She smiled to think that Elizabeth would soon rise to celebrate her Accession Day with a tournament at Whitehall, a reigning queen, but not as full of happiness with her throne and adoring courtiers as a woman locked in the Tower of London.

Then Kate turned to praying for her babe, for Ned and for their future together, until the pale wintry light of day crept through the high tower window and into the hard corners of her cell that had so recently been a stone paradise.

The Queen's Next Birthday
September 7, 1563

Elizabeth sat under the canopied throne in her Whitehall presence chamber, her crowned red hair in a mass of tight curls, Robin noted as he approached. He knelt, kissed his gift and presented her with her favorite jewel, a large teardrop pearl, twice the size of the one he'd given her for last Twelfth Night.

"Oh, Robin," she said, holding the glowing gift in the air for all the courtiers and petitioners to admire. "It is the most perfect pearl—"

"For the most perfect queen of my heart . . . and body," he said, whispering the last two words just for her ears.

She bent toward him and, for a long moment, while he held his breath, he thought she would kiss his mouth in front of all, but at the last moment she pulled back. He could hear feet shuffling in the chamber, as she must have heard. He didn't need to look behind him to know that shocked faces were everywhere, and ambassadorial letters detailing the queen's brazen behavior would be flying to courts of the Continent by the first couriers.

The consort's flutes and citterns were playing a French country dance, which the young Robin and Bess had sung at play.

" 'I saw the wolf, the fox, the hare,' " he sang, nodding in time to the lively tune and looking up into her face.

Laughing, she sang the next line: " 'Saw how the wolf and fox did dance.' "

He joined her sweet voice with his best baritone and they sang the last line together: " 'And I myself yet spun them around.' "

She handed the pearl to him. "Place it here on my crown so that it hangs—"

His gift was dangling over her fair forehead before she finished asking for it. He always knew what she wanted, and was about to whisper an invitation in her ear when she gave him a warning glance, a rare heeding of what others thought, gaily lifting the small silvered mirror tied about her waist to admire his gift.

Cecil, the Lord Secretary, approached, his face somber, his eyes steady. "Your Grace," he said as if Dudley weren't there, "the Austrian ambassador has presented a marriage contract from the grand duke, and your councilors wait to hear your wishes."

A little angry, Elizabeth took a deep breath. "Anon, my good Lord Secretary, the business of our people must be attended before the Austrian can be heard."

Dudley watched the Austrian ambassador flush, bow briefly and leave the chamber without permission. Cecil remained stoic at the queen's side while she listened to two petitioners.

Dudley's mind held a dozen questions. Did she mean to reject the grand duke? Was this a public encouragement for him to press his case? Was it true that she had made him Earl of Leicester to marry him, as everyone hinted? Yet marriage was the one thing on which he could not know her changeable mind. This was a woman who loved to be endlessly courted, but had recoiled from marriage.

The queen waved away the rest of the petitions and, with her retinue trailing after her, she left the presence chamber on Dudley's arm. Cecil walked before them with his white staff of office. "Marriage, marriage!" she complained, and Robin was certain she meant Cecil to hear her displeasure so loudly voiced. "Is that the sum of the business of my realm? I tell you, Robin, I am sicker of the word than the pocks ever made me."

"They say the Archduke Charles is a Catholic."

"We hear not a strong, unreasonable one, Robin," she replied, now teasing.

"He is said to have a very large, misshapen head. A monster head!" Robert bent and whispered in her ear. "He would need two pillows in your bed, Bess."

She laughed softly. "His ambassador says that such a tale is but their enemy France's rumor put about to work against our union."

"The ambassador could say nothing less, my queen, so you must set your fowlers to plucking your largest, softest swans, and at once. Would you have me tend to it?"

He could feel her shake with mirth. He put his hand over her hand where it rested on his arm. "Bess, would you rid yourself of the marriage problem for all time?" He had bent close again to her ear, certain that he had sensed an invitation in her complaints. Her every action today pointed to it. His heart knew it; the warmth of his surety spread through him.

"My lord of Leicester, I would knight the man who—"

"No need, Bess. The better man, an earl, walks by your side, where he would ever be. Marry me, Bess, and end your torment . . . and my own."

He felt her arm stiffen and she wrenched it away, leaving him behind.

She moved swiftly to Cecil's side, and when Robin heard her harsh words spoken so all could hear, his heart almost stopped its beating.

"My lord Cecil, do you think me so unlike myself and unmindful of my royal majesty that I would prefer for husband my servant, whom I myself have raised high?"

"Majesty, I pray not."

Cecil and Elizabeth swept into the council chamber, and Robin walked in after, his steps firm and of the same length, taking his customary seat, his face numb from the effort to show nothing of his sinking emotions. *Fool! Idiot! Right time, wrong place. You gave her what she needed to convince the court gossips that she would consider the Austrian marriage, consider any foreign prince rather than the Earl of Leicester, suspected yet of his wife's death.* Or did she truly mean those hurtful words? Did she think an earldom enough when he would have her love for his lifetime and . . . her body? He held his hands tight together under the council table, one thought repeating: *The first to laugh at Robert Dudley is a dead man!*

When the Austrian contract was passed around the council table, he looked at it dutifully, his eyes sweeping to and fro as if he read the words. But he saw and remembered nothing.

Cecil was deep in the problem of the Catholic grand duke's desire for a private Mass in Protestant England when the yeoman officer of the guard knocked and entered. "Majesty, the Lord Lieutenant of the Tower craves urgent audience on an important matter."

Elizabeth was annoyed. "Welladay, then, as a fair sovereign we must give the Lord Lieutenant what he craves," she said with a shrug.

Robin breathed easier. He knew what would be reported and also that this event would take precedence with the gossips over the queen's snub of him.

The man, his eyes bulging, knelt three times when approaching the queen's chair and would have thrown himself prostrate had Elizabeth not motioned him to stand and bade him speak.

"Your Grace . . . Majesty . . . my queen . . ."

"God's sacred son! Speak your urgency, man."

Dudley saw the terrified man dribble from his mouth and swipe it away with his sleeve, to Elizabeth's disgust. She turned her face away from him.

"Lady Katherine, Majesty . . . has been delivered of another son."

"A son. Another son!" Elizabeth leapt from her chair. "God is a supreme jester to make that traitorous whore so fertile!"

The man crumpled before the rising color in Elizabeth's face. She looked at Dudley. "Did you know of this?" The words were spat.

"Nay, Your Grace." He had long ago learned the art of telling an unblinking lie.

Elizabeth towered over the cringing man, the matter of her marriage to the grand duke of Austria quite forgotten. She did not rage as yet, her voice even and dead of emotion, which Robin knew was all the more frightening to those in attendance. "My Lord Lieutenant, take you to the Tower at once and send the Earl of Hertford under guard with his two illegitimate sons to his manor of Eltham, there to stay until I give him leave." The queen took a much-needed breath, though her breast had been heaving from the first word. "Then, sir, Lady Katherine is to be taken under guard and lodged with her mother's cousin, Sir William Rogers, in Somersetshire, with instruction that she is never again to see the earl or her bastards. Let her be gone forever from our sight and hearing!"

Even Cecil looked pained at this vindictive sentence.

"It is done at once, Your Grace," the Lord Lieutenant said, finding his voice.

"And then, sir, you are to remove my badge from your doublet, place yourself under arrest and lodge in that same lady's cell, awaiting my further pleasure."

"Majesty, I beg you—"

"Have a care, sir. I will decide later whether you lose only your office, or be the shorter by a *head!*"

"But, Your Grace, for pity, they . . . Edward and Katherine . . . are so much in love, so much in love. Their letters—"

"Love. Love!" Her fair face turned as red as her formal wig, her eyes wide. "Love does not rule in my realm. . . ."

Dudley watched as Elizabeth's rage broke over the man's head, first in the form of the flung Austrian marriage contract and then a sound pounding about his ears, with curses few stable hands could better on so short a notice. He smiled to himself, as satisfied as when his brothers had been punished and he'd escaped. He wasn't the only fool for love in the room. The Lord Lieutenant had lost his position and the young idiots in the Tower had lost each other. The second son had doomed them. Elizabeth could not take their heads for fear of rousing Londoners who were buying penny ballads on street corners about the doomed lovers in the Tower. People wondered out loud over their drink if the true male heirs of the Tudor line slept behind those forbidding walls. One overloud ale maid, Hannah Barnes, had been hauled before a magistrate for saying so and suffered a tongue slitting.

Still, Elizabeth could not stop her people's sympathy for Edward and Kate. She must be satisfied with taking their young love forever.

The Lord Lieutenant and his wife came to Kate's cell early the next morning, as she was feeding her newborn, Thomas William, with her wobbly firstborn, Edward, clinging at her knee, fussing to be fed with a steady cry of, "Mama, mama, ma-ma . . ."

The cell's heavy door swung open on rusty hinges, and the Lord Lieutenant entered. Kate wondered at this early visit, then smiled a greeting. He and his wife had been most kind for more than a year, making her imprisonment in the Tower as gentle as possible. Seeing yeoman guards crowd in behind him, Kate felt her smile waver. Was this the day of her trial? Why had she not been told to prepare, been allowed a priest? Elizabeth would not be so cruel.

But with her babe so warm at her breast, she could not hold such horror for long. Perhaps she and her boys were to be moved to Ned's quarters . . . or, Jesu be more blessed, allowed to retire together to Eltham. Both of these possibilities traveled quickly from her heart to her mind, like brightly colored paintings, clearly drawn so that for a moment they were real.

"Lady . . . Katherine," the Lord Lieutenant began haltingly, "the queen has ordered that you be sent to your mother's distant kin in Somerset . . . you alone."

"Alone!" Kate jerked erect, her newborn losing his nipple and complaining robustly for a two-day-old babe. "You cannot do this. What is my wrong?" she said, knowing in her heart that her fault was being everything that Elizabeth was not. "Am I not to have a trial? Be judged by my peers?" she asked, seeking some different answer, any different answer. "And what of Ned?"

"He is to go to Eltham . . . with his two sons."

The bright picture in her imagination faded to gray. The heartless verdict threw her to her knees, clutching at both her babes. "Noooo! I beg you . . . for mercy. . . ." Her scream was ripped from a heart unloved for so long, a heart that had finally come to know every kind of love a woman could know, a heart that could not bear the thought of a return to cold emptiness.

"The queen has judged you," the Lord Lieutenant said, his face as impassive as the stone walls. "Indeed, I have lost my commission and must lodge in this cell after you with all my family. We will pay a high price for disobeying Her Majesty's law."

"I am most heartily sorry, my lord, but . . ."

Sybil came forward and took the frightened young Edward into her arms, cooing softly into his ear while he reached his arms back for his mother.

Kate clung to the settle and dragged herself to her feet, finding steel in flesh and bone, her newborn again trying to find her nipple. Her voice shaking, her body jerking as if she had the falling sickness, she grasped at reason and sought any delay. "I will write to Her Majesty. I am but two days from the birthing stool, and I cannot believe she would take my nursing babes. Jesu, no sin is worth such punishment. Elizabeth is a woman. . . . She cannot . . ."

The Lord Lieutenant motioned the guards forward and a young woman appeared from behind them.

"No . . . no, I will not let you have them!" Kate howled the words until they filled the cavernous chamber, her hands clasped tight about Thomas William.

But the Lord Lieutenant's wife came on grimly with the guards at her side and they pried Kate's newborn from her desperate arms, handing him to the wet nurse.

Kate's legs buckled under her and she fell to her knees, putting her hands together in prayer, willing her heart to continue its beating.

Scarcely breathing, she raised her white face to the Lord Lieutenant. "You cannot . . . You are a father. . . . The queen is no mother—"

"I warn you, do not speak treason, my lady. You have your life."

"My life! What life?" she choked, her lips unwieldy, barely forming intelligible sounds. "Let me go to my husband . . . please, my lord."

The Lord Lieutenant motioned two guards forward and they pinned Kate's arms to her side, then lifted her up, holding her sagging body.

The Lord Lieutenant's face softened. "I beg your forgiveness for these harsh measures, my lady," he said, and added, "Have courage." He motioned to the guards' captain, who ordered the yeomen to take her out. They half carried the struggling Kate to the stairs. She screamed, near madness, reaching back to the hated prison cell, now a haven from a far worse terror. She tried to plead further, but her throat closed against the words. At the bottom of the staircase, regaining speech, she shrieked again: "Ned, help! They are taking me. . . ." Her voice rang through Beauchamp Tower and was absorbed by the unyielding stones.

Sybil's words reached her from above. "Kate . . . I will care for your babes, then come to you."

A carriage waited below, torches lit front and back. Heavy black clouds hung above her, rain blowing slantwise into her face. Her gown and cloak were quickly sodden.

She clung to the carriage door, moaning incoherently. Two guards pried her hands free and threw her inside, sitting opposite to hold the doors against escape.

She managed to grab the strap keeping the carriage window up and tore it free. "Ned!" she screamed as it dropped open, lifting her face toward the tower that held him. She heard no answering call over the wind, driving rain and horses' hooves striking the cobbles of London's streets, heading west. She collapsed into a corner, staring without seeing, her arms crossed in front of her as if they yet held a child.

Elizabeth sent for Lord Dudley the next night, very late. He had dressed with extra care for that invitation, which he had known all the day would come, when she could wait no longer to assure herself that she still owned his heart. He entered the secret passage behind his room, which opened into her linen closet, stepping out into her bedchamber, kneeling three times before he reached her standing alone by the hearth.

His irony was not lost on her.

"Rise, my lord earl," she said softly.

"Your little dog is unable to rise even at your command, Majesty."

"Stop it!" she said, kneeling before him, the fire backlighting her hair, which he was certain her ladies had brushed one thousand times to give her such a shining halo.

"Then how would you have me, Bess?" He kept his voice very light, without any shade of meaning or feeling. "Shall I roll over and play dead for you?" He began to twist his body.

"Stop it!" The words were strangled. "What do you want of me; what must I say, Robin, to stop this mockery?"

"Nothing." He had not known he could so drain a word of caring.

"Please . . ." She kissed his lips, which grew more firm against her soft, trembling pressure.

But he would not yield to please her. He could not. She had cut his heart into unfeeling pieces. "Let me go, Bess. Let me marry another and live a man's full life."

"I cannot . . . I will not marry the grand duke, nor the prince of Denmark, nor a French prince, nor yet a Spanish king. England is my husband and its people my children, Robin. I can marry no man, but I can love . . . I can love you."

She kissed him again. And again her salt tears touched his lips.

Now he was struggling against himself. *Firm*, he thought. *Stay firm.* How could his manhood give in to a few kisses after what Bess had done to humiliate him before all?

She took his hands in hers and pressed them against her damp cheeks. To Robin, her hands were warm, alive, strong.

"Know you this, sweet Robin: If I were free to marry, I would marry you, only you . . . but I am not free."

"Bess, then I must be liberated."

"No, my love," she whispered, and he saw the torment in her face, "you will never be free of me, as I will never be free of you."

He took her kiss then, holding her slender, shaking body against his fiercely, knowing he was trapped in his desire as much as ever Edward or Kate, maybe a hundred times more. He would not be removed from sight and sound of Elizabeth, but must each day of his life live with her close and forever not his.

Part Two

LAST LOVES

CHAPTER NINE

*"To be a king and wear a crown is a thing more glorious
to them that see it, than it is pleasant to them that bear it."*
—Elizabeth Regina

*Twelfth Night
January 6, 1599*

$\mathcal{M}$ary Rogers wanted to push aside the enormous ermine-trimmed hat on the courtier in front of her. No matter how she moved her head, he blocked her clear view of Elizabeth, the queen Mary had waited all her life to see. Her hand was half raised when she remembered Lady Katherine Grey's repeated warning: "Child, the queen prefers her ladies docile as well as decorative. You are quite pretty enough, but that impatience of yours will not gain you a place with Her Majesty's ladies. Learn to wait . . . as I have." Mary could even hear her sad, sweet voice add for this occasion, "Mary, it won't do to begin your first day in court showing a temper in the Royal Chapel."

Mary lowered her right hand and held it tight with her left hand. She had dreamed since she was a child of being one of the queen's ladies, and she would not spoil the slight chance she might have now with one hasty act. Her rank and connection were too unimposing to gain automatic admittance to royal service, though any connection was better than none. Her family had cared for Lady Grey until her death, but the queen had never shown gratitude for their service, and Mary's grandfather had warned her against expecting any. Service to the Crown was counted an honor, though sometimes a costly one, as the queen was not known for paying her bills.

Mary congratulated herself on thinking twice before acting, an unusual sequence for her, she had to admit, and a comfort. She was learning. She leaned close to her grandfather's ear. "Sir, please . . . may we move closer so that I can better see the queen?"

Her grandfather took a deep breath. "Mary, it cost me a gold mark to bribe the usher for this standing room in the Royal Chapel. Now quiet yourself, I beg you. You will see Her Majesty closer at the audience to follow." He lowered his voice, but she thought he said, "You will soon see more than you may want."

Mary drew back. Her grandfather Sir William Rogers had been making similar veiled warnings since they left Somersetshire. At first she had thought it his usual rough kindness, since her hopes of serving the queen were impossibly high. Still, since reaching Whitehall she had thought his tone sharp. "Surely, sir," she whispered, though whispering, too, was not a part of her nature, "Elizabeth is high in God's favor to have been queen of this isle for over forty years." The man in front of her was jostled by others and moved aside so that Mary was able to gaze full on the glittering sovereign. "Why, sir," Mary continued, keeping her excited voice low, "she is older than you in years and yet so young." Having blurted the words, she bit her lower lip, silently admitting she needed more diplomatic skills.

Sir William Rogers shrugged. "Mary, Her Majesty will put on years as you approach her."

She smiled to herself. Her grandfather was jealous of the queen's ageless beauty, a queen just as Lady Katherine had described her to a very young child long ago standing at her knee, eyes wide. When Lady Katherine was not in chapel at her prayers, sitting up with a sick cottager or helping the village midwife with a difficult delivery, Mary had begged to hear that lady tell one of her countless stories of the magical court with its masques and plays and grand tournaments. The child had heard of all the thrilling palaces and intrigues, and knew all the ladies of the bedchamber's duties by heart.

And now this same faerie queen was in front of her, a dazzling crown atop her red-gold hair, her gown heavy with jewels, her long-fingered white hands held before her in devout prayer. A queen over all queens, without flaw and above doubt.

Mary's eyes misted as she remembered how Lady Katherine's memories had flowed to a child at her knee for all her first ten years, and how that lady had insisted on her love for the queen, though the queen had banished Katherine for life from court, husband and sons. Mary would remember always how Katherine toiled late into the night by candlelight, her red hair streaked with white, writing . . . begging the queen to allow her to return to her husband, the earl. Word had finally come from William Cecil, Lord Burleigh, that the queen refused to read a word and that Sir William was commanded to cease forwarding the letters of a traitor on pain of arrest.

With the brutal honesty of a child, Mary had reported to that lady, "I heard Grandfather say the queen will never have you back."

Tears had flowed from Katherine's dark blue eyes, and Mary had regretted her words, as if she had told a lie. "We love you. Stay with us, my lady," she'd begged, urgently plucking at Kate's sleeve. "Are you not content here? Why do you want to leave?"

"Mary," Kate had said softly, always showing Mary great patience, "to be without my Ned and babes, though they are older boys now, is a kind of living death. Someday Her Majesty will forgive me. She must." Katherine's shaking hands had tightened until the knuckles turned white on her black gown. She always wore black in perpetual mourning.

"Lady, my grandfather said you were banished because you wanted to be heir to the queen?"

Katherine had shaken her head, her still lovely face angry for the first time. Mary had begun to cry, and the lady had swept her into her arms, comforting her, though Mary struggled at ten years, no longer a babe. Perhaps being an heir was a secret she was too young to know, or the poor old lady had forgotten.

Each evening Lady Katherine fell again to writing about her day to the man she called her husband, though Grandfather returned her letters the next day unopened on orders from the queen's council. Still, she wrote again the next night.

Despite all, Lady Katherine had spoken often and loudly of her love for Elizabeth. Maybe Katherine's words were truth, or, having barely escaped a traitor's death, she dared not speak treason even to a loving child, lest someone hear.

Forcing her thoughts away from Lady Katherine back to the present spectacle in the Royal Chapel, Mary feasted on her view of the sovereign. She sat bejeweled and sparkling like the summer sun, though a winter storm blew outside Whitehall, battering the old palace, its gardens and bare orchard. Her Majesty's back was as straight as a yeoman guard's, and she was as tall seated on her throne chair as some men standing. No, this queen could never be old. There was time yet to serve her, to be close to the greatest ruler on God's earth, a heady thought for a motherless girl.

If Mary's slippered feet had not been freezing from the cold stones of the chapel apse, she could scarce have believed she was here in the queen's . . . well, if not exactly in her company, near it . . . her long-held dream come wonderfully true. Almost.

After two hours of sermons and carols, Mary, her temper tried well past its former limits, groaned and shifted her feet, now sore as well as cold. She looked high into the chapel arches to search for the Garter Knight banner of her father, who had met a hero's death fighting the Spanish, leaving her an orphan. She found the banner hanging in the pale winter light near a stained-glass window depicting England's glorious victory over the armada. Her family had a rightful place at this court, paid for with her father's life. She would give no less to honor his memory and name.

Mary's starched ruff itched, but people pressed in so close she dared not raise her hand to scratch her neck, lest it come in contact with some embarrassing body part not her own. She must get used to such finery. At home they had dressed plainly. But in the court any evidence of Puritan leanings would draw the wrath of a queen who clung to her father's high church and insisted on the compliance of her subjects. Though Elizabeth had said she did not make windows into men's souls, she did demand they mirror her beliefs. That knowledge had given Mary her first hope: She could pretend to be submissive and unassuming, while remaining herself. Such behavior would not be easy. This church service had already shown her how vigilant she must be.

She sagged on her grandfather's arm. Would the Epiphany sermon never end? Her ears were numb from the preacher's drone, and she felt ready to protest as he suddenly switched from Matthew to Old Testament prophecy. But there was no need.

The queen stood, shaking her fist toward the altar. "Stick to your text, sir, stick to your text!"

The sermon ended abruptly with the shortest prayer Mary had ever heard. She beamed. She herself might have only diluted Tudor blood, but she had a queen's temper and took delight in Elizabeth, who could be wholly herself. It was endearing.

Her Majesty descended to the altar, leaving there traditional gifts of gold, frankincense and myrrh. The sweet voices of boy choristers caroled. The queen departed and the chapel emptied of courtiers, trailing in a long train after their sovereign, who set a quick pace.

Mary and her grandfather fell into their place in procession among the other visiting knights behind the queen's ladies, her council and the peers of the realm. Mary murmured her latest tidbit of royal gossip. "She still rides to the hunt, you know."

"So I hear." Her grandfather took her arm. "My dear girl, I think me that you are doomed to great disappointment if you continue in this dream of yours. You must aim lower than the queen's privy chamber. Since Mistress Ashley, her childhood nurse, died, the queen's attendants have had higher station than a much-removed cousin, the granddaughter of a country knight."

"And the daughter of a Garter Knight hero against Spain's armada," she corrected, adding, "*And* she chose you, Grandfather, to guard the lady Grey when she was released from the Tower. Surely Her Majesty remembers your great service to her, since she invited us here for Christmas."

"Not enough to pay my costs. I believe Her Majesty may think that an invitation to court is reward enough."

Her grandfather smiled—at least, Mary thought it was a smile—and they walked on, emerging into the grand presence chamber, which was draped with fresh boughs of fragrant pine, the walls painted and gilded where they were not covered with rich-colored tapestries.

A throng of courtiers crowded nearer the queen, who sat on her throne under a golden dome, watching from behind her fan.

Mary had never seen so many perfumed gentry dressed in cloth and colors new to her, all in the latest fashions from France and, she suspected, some of their own devising. The grand ladies in their glittering white-and-silver gowns and jewels did not outshine the gentlemen, who wore exaggerated wide-shouldered doublets and overstuffed breeches to their knees, each meant to provide the appearance of a spectacularly muscled body that God had never actually given them. Some had dyed their beribboned beards red and yellow and wore diamond earrings and jeweled swords, adding to their general gaudiness. Some had ruffs so high they could not turn their heads. It looked for all the world like a tournament of clothes where each had to best the others.

Mary snapped her mouth shut lest she laugh at these strutting peacocks, or look shocked by each new parading gentleman more outrageous than the last. And above all this fantastic court sat Elizabeth, more alive than all these preening cocks, her eyes fierce, fathomless and challenging.

Mary pulled her grandfather forward to be nearer that great radiance before noticing those closest to the queen. "Who are they, Grandfather?" she asked, nodding toward two gentlemen kneeling on cushions before the throne.

"The one in embroidered black velvet is the stepson of the Earl of Leicester, Robert Devereaux, the Earl of Essex and the queen's high young favorite . . . until he o'ersteps himself again and is sent packing from court."

"And the other, the dark young man, who is smiling? Oh!" she said as the queen slapped the smiling man with her fan.

The punished man removed his hat, kissed his fingers and gallantly touched the cheek that bore a red mark. She knew him . . . from somewhere.

"He's the queen's impertinent godson, Sir John Harington, a notorious scoundrel and writer of things you should not read, indeed I forbid you to read. His translation of *Ariosto* is shocking. Stay well away from him, my girl."

Mary laughed, and to her own ears her laugh was strained. "Don't worry, Grandfather. He won't even notice me. I remember we met at a masque near Taunton once and he paid me no attention."

Her grandfather's face sobered. "You were not a woman then, Mary. Don't let well-learned modesty blind you to present danger. I do assure you that your fresh beauty will bring you more attention than you know in this court where innocence is a challenge . . . most especially for John Harington."

"Why him, Grandfather?"

"I would not soil your ears with the tales I've heard."

"Tales?" She longed to know more court gossip, since all she knew from Lady Katherine was a decade old just before she died.

"Harington's a seducer, child. Your virgin's perfume would draw him like . . . Never you mind." Sir William set his mouth to say no more.

Mary hugged his arm. "You are a good and gentle knight, sir, but you need not worry. I am not come to court to find a husband, less a lover." She drew closer to his comforting bulk to stop a little shiver, for the thought of a handsome husband was not strictly abhorrent. The air laced with musky perfume, the courtiers splendid in gems and silks were suddenly nearly overwhelming her senses. Her hands crossed over her breasts as if to hide her gown. "Even my best is all tatters in this court."

At that moment her fears were confirmed. "Who is that creature new come to court?" The woman dressed in much silver lace nearby was looking at Mary.

"My lady Warwick," her companion answered, "she is nobody, naught but some country mouse."

Mary could sense the heat rising to her face and opened her mouth to answer but thought better, since the Countess of Warwick was the queen's chief lady.

Her grandfather tightened his grip on her arm. "I will ask permission to leave if you are to be insulted."

"No, Grandfather, you must be paid what is owed you and recover the properties you had to mortgage to pay for Lady Grey and her attendants' care." She left unsaid her own precious purpose, which was to gain a place in the queen's service. No insult would deny her this one chance. She put on her brightest smile and curtsied to Lady Warwick. "My lady, my name is Mary Rogers, and I make it my duty to bring the look of a plain Somersetshire woman to Her Majesty's court . . . for instructive purpose only." She curtsied humbly to take away any sting.

Warwick glanced at her, nodded, and then walked on toward the throne.

"Guard your tongue, child." Her grandfather pulled her forward on his arm.

"I'm trying, Grandfather," she replied, resolving to try harder, since her most recent effort had not been completely successful.

The closer Mary came to the queen, the more she was forced to admit that Elizabeth was no longer the youthful, beautiful queen of the portrait hanging in her grandfather's great hall. It was true, then, what she'd heard and for so long rejected: The queen no longer sat for her likeness, but a pattern of her face from earlier times was used, turned first one way and later, for another portrait, turned the other.

Though outlined in kohl, Elizabeth's eyes were sunken into her thin face, her cheekbones sharp and the softness of a youthful jaw become as slack as the skin of her neck. No paste of alum, ass's milk and egg white could glaze over what great age and great cares had made of her features and bosom. The closer Mary came, the more she saw that the layer of added complexion covering the wrinkled skin had cracked on her cheeks to expose what the paste was meant to hide.

And yet, in spite of all the destruction, Mary thought the queen a commanding, even handsome woman, her still-luminous eyes and her sharp ears missing nothing. She had probably seen the little scene with Lady Warwick, had perhaps heard what passed. Mary knew she must, *must* regain every appearance of docility.

The queen motioned her grandfather forward. He knelt on one knee and swept his hat sideways in a slightly unpracticed bow. "Majesty," he said.

Mary, almost numb with excitement, knelt next to him, daring to glance up only hastily.

Elizabeth motioned for them to rise. "Who is this?" the queen asked sharply, pointing toward them.

A gentleman usher in his red-and-black uniform bent to the queen. "Sir William Rogers, come to petition Your Grace for the return of expenses for the care of a certain lady."

The corner of the queen's mouth lifted. "Ah," she said, and Mary thought she had known full well who her grandfather was. "Sir," the queen said, dropping her fan again, "is this pretty young maid the wife and bed comfort of your elder years?"

Essex, standing closest to the queen, laughed heartily. "Fie, sir! If you old fellows take all the pretty girls, what will we young men do for amusement?" He elbowed Harington in jest, who turned about and stared at Mary with curiosity.

Mary felt her grandfather's arm muscle tense even more.

"Majesty," he said, standing and leading Mary two steps forward, "my granddaughter, Mistress Mary Rogers."

The queen raised a hand to silence Essex, who frowned his dislike of being silenced.

Mary thought that a kind gesture, and confusing after the queen's earlier pointed jest. Did a queen ever regret her words?

"You may come closer, Mistress Rogers."

Mary advanced almost to the throne, amazed that she felt a sudden inner calm. She thought she saw some interest in the queen's face.

"You wear our portrait," the queen said, pointing to the brooch tied by a ribbon at Mary's waist. "Advance to us."

Mary rose up the last step, aware that the two men beside her were straining to see the portrait.

The queen frowned. "How came you by this?"

"Majesty, this picture brooch was a gift from the lady Katherine Grey when I was a child and greatly admired it. I treasure it still."

The queen's eyes narrowed. "That is no name to speak in our court."

"I beg forgiveness, Majesty," Mary said, surprised that her voice was steady. "I but answered truthfully."

"You are truly new at court. Truth for a sovereign is what we would hear, Mary Rogers."

The presence chamber was utterly still.

Elizabeth raised her fan again to rest below her eyes. "And do we still resemble our portrait of long ago?" The queen watched her closely.

Mary could sense courtiers leaning forward to hear how she

would answer, though she was in no doubt of her reply. "No, Majesty," she said softly, and didn't stop for the warning gesture from John Harington. "You were new come to the throne when this was painted and had not grown in magnificence and the dignity of many battles won, as I see you today." It was truth that flattered and not flattery that held but little truth, which the queen had no doubt expected, heard many times and dismissed. Mary curtsied and bowed her head for whatever was to come, though if she had guessed wrong, she would run straight to the near-frozen Thames and leap into it, hoping not to come up.

Elizabeth motioned to Harington. "What think you, Boy Jack? Should we listen to the words of a maid schooled by that traitor Lady Grey? Perhaps she, too, learned traitorous ways."

John mounted a step and stopped very close to Mary. He brought a finger under her chin and turned her face to him. She was so startled that she did not resist. "Godmother, in this instance I see no treason in this fair face, for true treason never held so much beauty. If it did, then none dare call it treason."

The queen laughed but knocked his hand away from Mary with her fan. "Though I have known beauteous traitors, I think me this is another of your epigrams, sir, and in this case holds some truth."

Harington bowed as Elizabeth stood suddenly. Mary gathered her skirt and carefully backed down the steps until she was again on the arm of her grandfather. Had she gone too far, said the inexcusable, been too clever, misjudged this queen who had heard everything in her long life?

As the queen moved past them with Essex at her side, she commanded, "Sir William, bring your granddaughter to us after Twelfth Night revels."

With no further word, the queen swept from the room, a long line of courtiers rushing to follow in the procession.

John Harington stopped briefly and bowed. "Sir William, your granddaughter is a credit to you."

"Sir John," Mary, near the end of her unaccustomed serenity, answered for her grandfather, "I thank you, but our Lord God made me as I am."

Harington grinned. "And a fine job the Lord has made of you, Mary Rogers, and continues to do since we last met."

Mary kept her mouth from falling open. He remembered her.

Her grandfather's voice trembled with anger. "Sir, I have warned her about you."

The courtier laughed aloud, winking at Mary. "Have no fear, sir. I seek a wealthy and widowed countess. But you were wise to warn her, sir . . . very wise. She has face and form . . . and wit enough to make me forget all my ambition." He bowed again and, with one last glance at Mary—and still highly amused—he rejoined the queen's procession.

Her grandfather sputtered angrily into the nearly empty presence chamber: "The arrogant whelp presumes!"

Mary watched the queen's godson to see if he turned to look back at her. He didn't. "Grandfather, don't you think he was gallant to come to my aid before the throne? He hides it well, but perhaps there is some good in him."

"Mary, my dear, this is not a court for the guileless. Give up this dream of serving the queen and return with me to the west country. I would keep you as you are."

Mary smiled. "Surely not, sir, with all my tempers. And Her Majesty commanded my presence. I must have pleased her."

Sir William huffed. "Her Majesty's pleasure is often as short-lived as her memory of debt."

She held tight to his arm as they moved toward the sound of trumpets and drums that always preceded the queen. She did not blame him for his vexation. He had gone nearly bankrupt tending Lady Grey, her ladies and her nurse. To his great credit he still provided for Nurse Sybil, who wished to remain near her dead mistress. Every bill to the Lord Treasurer had been ignored. Now, desperate for money, he had come to try in person to collect what was long overdue, and Mary was determined to help him.

It was near midnight when Sir William and Mary Rogers were announced by one of the queen's gentlemen ushers.

"Sir William," the queen said with a dismissive wave, "you must petition Robert Cecil, our Lord Secretary of State. We have no business with you."

He bowed himself back into the antechamber and the door closed.

Remembering protocol, Mary knelt three times as she approached the queen sitting near a fireplace in a heavy satin robe of black and white, her crown removed, her chin in her hand.

An unsheathed sword hung from the arm of Elizabeth's chair. With some unease Mary, watching the light glint from its blade, sank to her knees again.

Elizabeth turned a weary head to follow her gaze. "You need not fear, girl. My sword is not for you, but for those who would have done with my rule and come upon me to seek my life."

The queen returned to her study of the fire, staring fixedly into the flames. A long moment later, she said, "We spared Lady Katherine when we did not spare the queen of Scots. A crown is a difficult burden to those who bear it, Mary Rogers."

"Yes, Majesty."

"Yet you think us cruel."

Mary bent to kiss the hem of the royal gown. "It is not for me to judge your royal actions," she said softly, sensing the queen's fragile mood, and suddenly filled with sympathy. One day, Mary thought, she herself would look in her own mirror and see another face no longer youthful and flushed with health, one she scarce recognized and was reluctant to own.

The queen twisted her neck about. Some of her white complexion paste cracked off and fell on her black gown. "So you do not judge your sovereign. Another of your country truths, Mary Rogers?"

"Majesty, I beg forgiveness. I am new come to court and do not know its ways. Country truth is the only truth I know." Her head bowed, Mary scarcely dared to look in that ravaged face for fear of showing her compassion, surely unwanted by this proud monarch.

Elizabeth gazed past Mary for a long moment before she spoke in a voice that had none of the commanding quality Mary had heard in the presence chamber. "So, mistress, how did Kate die?"

Mary was surprised, knowing that her grandfather had sent much correspondence about Katherine Grey to the queen's council at the time of that lady's death, these ten years past. "Of consumption, Majesty. My grandfather provided every physick and care. She died in the faith with her chaplain at her side, blessing you and begging forgiveness for her sins." Lady Katherine had also died in a pool of her own blood with Lord Edward's name the last word from her lips, crying out that having been denied him in this world, she would be with him and her babes in the next. But Mary withheld that knowledge, hoping an untold truth was not a lie. Would Elizabeth recognize such a lie no matter how well hidden?

The queen nodded, then seemed to forget Mary was there, giving her time to look about, noticing what she had been too nervous to see before. The queen's huge, high bed was covered with gilding, carved animals and ostrich plumes. A virginals made of heavy glass stood in one corner, and from a partially open door, Mary heard the sounds of ladies in low voices talking and laughing, waiting to help the queen into her bed, if the queen decided to sleep. It was known that she slept poorly, often bending to her state papers until first light, when she did not spend the night at cards with her favorite, Essex.

Mary also saw what was not in the room. There were no mirrors or reflecting surfaces anywhere, not on walls nor tapestry-covered tables. Even the table that held pots of paint and kohl had no gazing glass.

She knelt until she was not certain she could stand.

"You are come to ask for money," the queen said, rousing herself.

"Not for myself, Your Grace, but to save my good grandsire the loss of his mortgaged properties. He yet cares for one of Lady Grey's servants." She swallowed hard, knowing how much too far she had already gone. "As for me, Majesty, I seek only to serve you in any way you choose."

"Ah, a profitable position so that you can wring gold from the lords of our court for putting their words in our ears."

"Only if their words serve Your Majesty." Mary was not surprised to have her purpose doubted. Elizabeth was hounded for positions.

"Pish! You search out a rich husband and think your distant blood ensures we will find you a highborn one."

Mary shook her head, true tears welling, which she tried to blink away. "Majesty, may I make so bold as to ask you a question?"

"Ah, a brave country mouse to challenge her sovereign."

Her tone told Mary the queen was now disbelieving. Yet what more could Mary say but what she thought? "It is true that I am not trained for court, Your Grace. Forgive me if I cannot understand why England's greatest queen would not believe that a true English woman of good family would desire to serve her for herself alone."

Elizabeth's head jerked toward her, her visage haunted and angry. "We have believed such before! Yet many of our ladies—our beloved daughters—have betrayed us. And our good servants"— and here her voice caught on the name—"Leicester . . . Burleigh, Walsingham . . ." Her memory trailed away to bitterness. "You would leave us as they all did."

Elizabeth blamed Leicester for dying? Did she yet love him so and keep his stepson Essex as a substitute for her long love?

But Mary felt the queen's deep loneliness in her bitter words, and it emboldened her. She had not desired to quiet a heart so much since Lady Katherine died. Lifting her hands palm upward in supplication, Mary said, "We cannot know when God will call us to Him, Your Majesty."

Elizabeth jerked upright in her chair. "As governor of the Church of England, I remind you that you need not instruct us in theology!"

Mary bowed her head and whispered, "I meant only to comfort, Majesty."

"We are the queen of England and need no comfort from you, Mary Rogers. Go back to your country manor. There is no place for such a lamb in our court."

Desperate, Mary blurted, "Majesty, you would find me no lamb in your service, but a lion as Your Majesty was with your troops at Tilbury before the armada."

"We see you are too clever for us to trust. Now leave us." Elizabeth angrily waved her away.

Her throat aching with regret, and feeling close to tears at her clumsy tongue, Mary rose and backed toward the door, her head bowed. She dared not look at the queen again, lest she burst into sobs, in truth, and completely disgrace herself.

In the anteroom, her grandfather rose to greet her. With one look at her face, he put his arms about her.

"She could not hear me," Mary said, swallowing sobs. "I could not find the right words to make her believe me."

"We will leave for home on the morrow. Cecil has my petition. That is all I can do here. Her Majesty does not wish to remember the service she asked of me. To stay longer would tax my purse the more for clothes and bribes. Come, Mary."

From the queen's privy chamber, they heard the queen calling irritably to her ladies. "Where is my lord Essex . . . that silly boy? Send again to tell him we cannot sleep and require his presence at once!"

"Majesty," the usher answered, "word comes that His Lordship is gone from the palace to his manor in Wanstead."

"By Christ's pierced body! Send guards to find him! Drag him back in chains if you must, for he has disobeyed my express command. Meantime bring me Sir John."

The usher bowed and rushed to carry out the queen's shouted commands, followed by yeoman guards at the double, trailing halberds.

Mary glanced a question at her grandfather, who shrugged and walked her quickly along the hall, speaking in a low voice. "It is said the Earl of Essex is too handsome, too ambitious, too filled with his own consequence . . . but she calls him her Wild Horse and dotes on him. She is all contradiction, punishing impertinence and yet attracted by it." Sir William waited until a group of drunken revelers staggered past and they were once again alone in the hall. "He flatters her, entertains her and awakens the feelings of her youth . . . an old woman's last infatuation. I think half her court and many foreign ambassadors joke about it, though not to her face. And they fear the earl's power, for though she always first denies him appointments for his friends, fearing he will gain too much power, at times she relents when he leaves her suddenly. As with Robert Dudley, she cannot bear to be without him for any time."

As they walked to their small assigned rooms, Mary, though saddened by what she'd heard, better understood the emotions she had seen in the queen's features and behind her words. How could the queen, England's Gloriana, facing the end alone, not rail against the loss of everything and every man whose adoration had made her fabled virgin life bearable?

After a fitful night of dreams and waking with the better words she could have said on her tongue, Mary sadly directed her maid to pack their belongings and joined her grandfather to break their fast with a simple meal of porridge and small ale in the great hall, where all at court ate who did not have the rank to have their food delivered from the palace kitchens to their rooms. Thinking of the days-long, bone-jarring carriage ride over wintry roads she must soon endure, Mary avoided many richer honeyed meat dishes and puddings.

As they ate, those about them talked of nothing but how often the queen had danced like a young girl with Essex at Twelfth Night revels the night before. There was no laughter, only amazement.

Sir John Harington appeared from nowhere, still dressed for festivities as she had seen him in the presence chamber, and wearily bowed, settling himself on a bench across the table from her.

"Good morrow, Sir William, Mistress Mary," he said politely, and called a serving man for bread and ale.

"Sir," her grandfather said without rising, his tone not at all welcoming.

"And I am exceeding joyful to see *you* again, Sir William," Harington said, smiling. "But I have not come to rouse your choler. I come bearing news of import for your granddaughter. The queen's chief lady, the Countess of Warwick, has sent for Mistress Mary. I think there might be a post among the queen's ladies for her."

Her grandfather looked astounded, then sputtered, "Is this your doing, sir?"

Harington smiled, and Mary knew the answer, though he put his hand over his heart in mock horror. "I beg you, sir, have some pity. Accuse me of a kindness and you damage my exceeding hard-won reputation! But I fear that you do not rate your granddaughter as she deserves. The queen, though she thinks the girl brash, came to her decision with only a trifle added from me."

Mary's heart pounded with excitement. She had given up all hope and now the door to the queen was ajar, opened by this man. "I do not think kindness is a trifle, sir, and I thank you most heartily. If you desire it, I will never mention your consideration where it can be despised, though I will remember it always."

Harington looked at her, his eyes sweeping her face, and though she couldn't be certain, she thought she saw him struggle not to believe her. Finally, he shrugged, tossed back his ale and rose, holding out a hand to her with exaggerated courtesy just short of mockery. But whom was he mocking? Sometimes she thought it was himself.

"Sir William, I will bring Mistress Mary to her audience and promise on the honor of a fellow Somersetshire man to be a faultless escort."

Mary's grandfather stood, bowed briefly, just short of insult and, with a warning look at her, said, "Mary, I will wait for you in our rooms."

She placed her fingers on John Harington's outstretched hand, walking with him in silence through the labyrinth of halls toward the queen's apartments. For several minutes he did not speak, and she could not think of a suitable topic to open conversation, or rather she thought of too many. To thank him again would be to grovel. To talk of their former meeting years ago would be to take notice of his remembering. Finally, unable to endure the sound of their wooden heels clicking against marble, she said, "Sir, I believe you are godson to Her Majesty."

"Yes, I am so honored. My father was first married to one of Henry VIII's bastard daughters, though I am the son of his second wife. Both my parents were in the Tower when the queen's sister imprisoned Her Majesty, and she remembers their loyalty. You will find many such tangled relations in this court, mistress. You have a thin stream of Tudor blood yourself."

"That is so, sir, though the Duchess of Suffolk did not think it so thin."

"Aye, for all the good it did her family, everyone dead or banished."

Mary knew he was half laughing at her, but she showed no such knowledge. Hers was a country pride, but every bit as important to her as Harington's to him.

They turned into the gilded presence chamber, walking past small groups of courtiers who stared with interest, whispering among themselves, but gave him no greeting. "Ah, Mistress Mary, I see that I will need to explain myself to all my friends."

Was he laughing at her or again at himself? She could not tell, but she had tired of being the quiet country mouse the court expected. "And what will you say to your friends, Sir John . . . that you have helped plain Mary Rogers to a position of importance?"

"I may say that, Mistress Mary, if you are determined to have the court think me a saint." His eyes sparkled with roguish mischief. "That motive will not be believed by any in Whitehall."

"Your friends may not see you as I do, sir. I do not see a convincing rogue."

He looked down at her, his dark brows drawn straight together, whether from temper or surprise that she had challenged him, she could only guess until he responded: "Mary Rogers, you have the spirit of a petulant angel . . . irritating and delightful in turn. I am entirely captivated."

For once she had no response . . . petulant angel, indeed. Was he making fun of her? Somehow, she did not think it. "Thank you, Sir John."

"Do not be so trusting, mistress. Not of me, not of any in this court." He resumed his silence until they paused at the queen's apartments, waiting for the gentleman usher to admit them. "You are something of a little Puritan," he said, "so be wary, especially of me." He smiled down at her to soften his words.

She saw by the lantern that his eyes were not dark, but green as the sea on a misty day. That made defying his charm much more difficult.

"The queen's often angry," he continued, "stabbing her tapestries with her sword and, in a breath"—he bent and blew gently against her cheek—"changeable to deep melancholy. Never think it your doing, Mary, or she will crush that spirit of yours."

"I thank you for your warning, and I promise to behave with great care, Sir John. You will have no reason to regret your support."

"No, I don't think I will have any regrets about you, Mistress Rogers."

She was very much aware of his lascivious tone, but also how warm his velvet gloved hand was on hers.

The door to the anteroom opened to them and she heard her name announced. They stepped forward. "Perhaps," she whispered, "you are not as wicked as they say."

He laughed and the charming moment was gone. "Oh, but I am exactly as they speak of me, young mistress. There are two sides of the John Harington coin . . . both, happily, for the same purpose."

She glanced up at him. "Then I will remain on my guard, sir." She certainly would not allow him to mock her further, dizzily pushing her from him, then pulling her to his side.

At last they walked into an anteroom filled with ladies busy at doing little. All pretended to ignore her, although she doubted they missed a move by John Harington.

Sir John stopped before the haughty lady from the presence chamber dressed in a new pearl-seeded silver gown. He bowed. "My lady Anne, Countess of Warwick, I present Mistress Mary Rogers of Somerset, as I promised. You will find her eager for her work." He gave Mary a little shove on her back, and she stumbled forward to dip into a curtsy. When she turned to frown at his presumption, he was disappearing out the door.

"So, I see . . . The little country mouse with spirit," Lady Anne said, but her smile was welcoming. "Sir John is a handsome, appealing scoundrel, but do not invite his attentions," the countess said, watching after him with a wry smile. "He has broken half the hearts in this room . . . and is working to break the other half."

From the harsh looks being cast in Mary's direction, she did not doubt Lady Anne.

"I fear, my lady," Mary replied before she could stop her mouth, "Sir John needs little invitation."

"Indeed, you have a decidedly pert tongue for a country mouse. Remember that Her Majesty needs no response to her words unless your opinion is invited . . . which it won't be."

Mary assumed a meek pose, or what she supposed to be meek, realizing she needed more practice.

Satisfied, Lady Anne continued: "Now, mistress, what do you bring to the queen's work?"

"A desire to serve Her Majesty, my lady, that I have nurtured since a child."

Lady Anne nodded, her face stern, but not unkindly. "You are willing to do any task? We are all servants of the body here."

"Any task that pleases Her Majesty." Mary gathered her courage. "Lady Anne, may I ask why the queen changed her mind about me?"

"You may never ask that. The queen's mind does not change; her needs change."

Mary tucked this information away for sure use later as the Countess of Warwick gave an impatient tug at her silver gown. Mary bowed her head again in acknowledgment, determined now to keep to submission, as she knew a good servant must.

"Welladay, my dear, I will hope for all our good that the queen finds you docile enough. You are surely decorous—one of the qualities wanted in Her Majesty's young serving ladies." The countess stared about her at the other ladies, who had stopped all pretense of bustle to listen and giggle. "Not loud and flighty, as too many are." She returned her attention to Mary. "You are to be mistress of the stool at thirty marks per annum. It is the lowest post of the ladies of the bedchamber, but do not think it mean. Many of higher rank would fight for the job and will not take it kindly that they were passed over for one of so much less rank, though a minor kin to Her Majesty."

The words were out of Mary's mouth before she could stop them: "I have not heard of this position, my lady."

"Nor would you. It is new created. Her Majesty detests foul odors in her chambers and in the persons who serve her. Her grooms of the stool do not know how to please her. No doubt the queen saw something in you . . . a fresh and honest eagerness. Do not disappoint."

"I will not, my lady," Mary said, trying to remember that she had been willing to take any service, though in her own household this had been the work of the lowliest menials.

"Good," Lady Anne said, her hands folded. "You will have three grooms to assist you. They await you through that door." She pointed past the gathered ladies, who were listening to every word. "When you have seen to your duties, return to me. Lady Margaret, the queen's mistress of the wardrobe, must determine what we can do about your gowns . . . if that gown is any example. No lady may outshine Her Majesty, but neither must she be disgraced by a style not seen in this court for ten years or more."

Mary curtsied again, resisting the proud reply on the tip of her tongue that her apparel was highly regarded in the west country. Instead, she moved quickly toward the rear door, which was opened for her. She gladly left behind giggles and whispers, which was particularly demanding of her determined docility.

Three men waited in the hall, one stepping forward. "Mistress, my name is Thomas Wright," he announced with a bow. "*I* am master of the grooms of the closestool."

"And *I* am the queen's new mistress of the closestool. You may call me Mistress Rogers, Master Wright. If it please you, show me to my place of service."

He preceded her into and through the queen's soaring vaulted bath, more a small cathedral than a bath, and to the closet that held the royal closestool. No longer able to hide his displeasure, he blurted, "Mistress Rogers, there has never before been one appointed over me."

"As you see, Master Wright, it is the queen's will to appoint me now. Do you disagree with Her Majesty's choice?"

He bowed hastily. "Nay, it is not my place to do so."

"Exactly, Master Wright." Once servants were allowed to question their orders, there was no controlling them. She motioned for him to open the door, which, after only the slightest hesitation, he did, bowing her in.

Although she'd been prepared with her pomander to her nose, knowing how even the best jakes usually stank, she thought the queen very ill-served by this one. There were no fresh rushes, no masking scents, and the tank needed to be emptied . . . badly. Even in her grandfather's country manor the jakes was better kept. She was relieved. This had not been a make-work position, after all. The queen needed a woman to govern the careless men who kept her closestool. She was surprised they had not landed in the Tower dungeons earlier.

"When was the tank last emptied, Master Wright?"

"The tank is always emptied by long custom when the court comes to Whitehall, Mistress Mary."

Weeks, it had been. "Now the custom will be that the tank is emptied each day."

The grooms looked at one another, one smirking, the others astounded, by the look of their open mouths and wide eyes.

"Every day, Master Wright, and quicklime added each morning . . . all to be well-done before the queen rises." She looked about her, walking the length and width. "The rushes are to be changed today and each week hereafter. The walls and floors will be washed with vinegar and fresh lemon . . . and there must be flowers, boughs of them in season, fresh herbs at other times."

The youngest groom, a beardless boy, giggled.

It was time to show these lax servants her authority or she would never be their mistress. "Master Wright, if you cannot control the behavior of your undergrooms, then discharge them immediately for servants who will take seriously their duties for the queen's good. I will return in two hours to see that all my orders have been followed . . . to perfection, Master Wright." She swung about, waited for a scrambling groom to open the door and walked out, not wanting to give them time to think that her voice might not have been as strong as it needed to be.

Mary returned swiftly to the ladies' anteroom to see a pile of gowns all of white or pale silver laid out everywhere on chairs and chests.

Lady Margaret, a woman past her prime, for she was at least nearing thirty, was alone save for two serving maids. "My lady Warwick and the others attend the queen in procession to her council," she announced, and began unlacing Mary's gown, which dropped to the floor. "The smock and petticoat will do, but not the bodice."

"Lady Margaret, these gowns are of the same color. I prefer yellow or blue."

The lady's mouth set in a firm line. "No lady of bedchamber wears color but Her Majesty. Is that understood?"

So the queen's ladies laughed at country mice, but were palace mice themselves, meant to creep about in the background, being decorative, but not too decorative.

The maids swarmed about to help Mary into bodice, skirt, kirtle and then a gown and puffed sleeves, adding to these a collar, cuffs, stomacher and ruff.

The mistress of the wardrobe eyed the fit. "You are not as thin as the queen when she wore this gown, not having lost the flesh of youth, but it suits you well."

"I am several months past twenty years, my lady," Mary said as Lady Margaret led her to a large mirror.

Uninterested in that news, Lady Margaret stood behind her. "These will do. Later, the queen's glover and shoemaker will take your measure. If you wish, you may attach your pomander, watch or fan to a black ribbon about your waist. Take my advice, mistress, and do not wear the queen's portrait until she gives you leave, for that is a high favor at court and may be granted only by Her Majesty. Yet a decent pearl would help, a rope necklace even better. That gown once carried hundreds of hand-sewn seed pearls, which were removed for Her Grace's newer gowns."

"I thank you, my lady," Mary said, looking with astonishment at her changed image from a country knight's granddaughter into a fine court lady. Her hand flew to her throat and she wondered where she could possibly obtain a pearl necklace.

Lady Margaret dropped her too-sober look. "I must say the silver gown sets off your dark eyes and hair most generously, indeed. And the country has not ruined your very fair complexion. Indeed, you have the natural coloring desired in this court. The queen will be pleased."

"I am glad of it, my lady." She curtsied. "May I have an hour to take leave of my grandfather?"

Lady Margaret took her arm. "One further caution, mistress. Do not ever show yourself to the queen fresh-skinned as you are." She lowered her voice. "Remember, Elizabeth does not like to be reminded of . . . well, fresh young skin." She raised her voice again. "When you return—and do not tarry—a cosmetic will be applied. Later, you will receive several other gowns and fittings, after which you will be presented to the queen for her approval."

Mary bowed her head to hide her dismay that she must now wear the itching white paste on her face. But she prayed that the queen, who was rumored to have more than three thousand gowns, would now commend her fashion, since it had once been Her Majesty's own.

Making her way into the presence chamber, Mary strode straight ahead as if already on the queen's business. Sir John Harington stood with Essex in the center of a group of loudly laughing gentlemen. All stopped and looked her way, bowing. Mary walked on, a newly made court beauty who was certain they had taken notice of her. She nodded and smiled at their courtesy. They bowed again, Sir John lower than the rest. The court was a welcoming place in spite of its reputation.

Her grandfather sat in his rooms on a chest before the fire, his fur-lined traveling cloak over his arm. He looked up, his eyes as sad as she had ever seen them. "I see by your gown that you are decided on your course, Mary."

She sat next to him and rested her head against his shoulder. "Grandfather, the queen commands. Surely this is a boon for your business at court and our family."

Sir William lifted a bag of clanking coins. "My bill has been partially paid and I have been wished a fair journey."

"Partially?"

"Yes, the queen withholds thirty marks for your pay."

Mary took his hand, astounded. "Grandfather, I will refuse the queen's offer." Though it broke Mary's heart to say it, she also meant it. "How could Her Majesty?"

Her grandfather laughed. "You do not know her yet. She is well-known to be . . . frugal, even close dealing, where she can, since all costs of her government come from her purse."

"But—"

Sir William shook his head to silence Mary. "She will pay the rest, the Lord Secretary Robet Cecil assured me, when you have proved your worth this coming year. I have quite enough here to stave off my creditors. And I could not deny you what you hold so dear."

Relief raced through her. "She will pay if pleased, and I *will* give her such service that my salary is certain to be returned to you. And with me at court, you need no longer fear for my future."

Her grandfather shook his head. "I fear more and more, Mary. Servants have carried word to me that your name has been talked of in the court . . . in a most shameful way."

Mary stood, her hands shaking beyond her ability to control them. "Who could say aught against me? I have done nothing ill."

"It is not against anything you've done, Mary, but shameful nonetheless. It is said that there is a wager abroad that you will lose your maidenhood within a month."

"Who would make such idle and hurtful speculation?"

"John Harington, I suspect. Be watchful, Mary. He is a man who pretends to care for nothing and so must often prove it."

Her chest tight with anger and disillusion—and perhaps more

she refused to inspect—Mary sank down and took both her grand-father's hands in hers. "Have no fear. He has lost more than a wager, Grandfather. I had thought him a pretend scoundrel. If he has true evil intent toward me, he has lost my regard, and once lost, it can never be recovered."

"A man like that cares nothing for a woman's regard."

She laughed, perhaps a bit too heartily. "As with most seducers, he sees himself as irresistible. He will care greatly when I refuse to give in to him before the entire court." She hugged her grandfather. "Do not underestimate this country mouse."

CHAPTER TEN

"The stone too often recoils on the head of the thrower."
—*Elizabeth Regina*

St. Hilary's Day
January 13, 1599

John Harington stood in front of his mirror. "What manner of man is this?" he asked aloud, turning away from the face staring at him without answering the question, at least not an answer he could fully own. A chill swept through him, for, by tradition, this saint's day was the coldest day of the year. Yet he knew that Saint Hilary was not to blame for his icy distress.

John had tried for a week to absolve himself of fault for the foolish wager he had made, attempting to convince himself that the Earl of Essex had left him no other honorable choice. Devereux had announced in the presence chamber that he would have the queen's new lady, Mary Rogers, on her back inside a month.

John had been angered, and surprised by his anger. "My lord, to take a Puritan maid new come from the west country is beneath your talents."

Essex had laughed. "But not, I think, beneath yours, John, since you are a Somerset man. You but keep her for yourself. When have we not shared like brothers?"

John had kept his irritation close, perhaps because there was too much truth to what Essex said and he was suddenly shamed by that truth. "Beware, my lord. I have felt her tongue and she is not as timid as she first appears."

Their raised voices had drawn a larger crowd of gentlemen. Essex was smoking one of Sir Walter Raleigh's pipes, though he hated the man, who had once had the queen's affection and kept some still. "Then, John, you do fear your manhood would fail in a trial against me." He bowed to the crowd's burst of applause.

"My lord, you insult me to no purpose. My manhood has never failed me." Some of the men applauded him. John braced himself for Essex's anger and to keep his hand from moving to his sword. This was not a new dilemma, though John was a long-forbearing friend, as were all the earl's friends, including the queen. She'd forgiven Essex getting Elizabeth Southwell with child, and his affairs with Lady Mary Howard and Mistress Russell, both ladies of the queen's bedchamber—and his bedchamber, as it happened. Even his marriage to the daughter of the queen's spymaster, Walsingham, had been accepted when Essex, prostrate at the queen's feet, swore that Elizabeth, alone, was the true and only queen of his heart. He kept his wife away from court at his Wanstead manor northeast of London so that he could be many a woman's fair russet-haired boy, but be damned if John would allow Essex to add Mary Rogers to that long list.

John saw his fists clenching in the mirror and surprised himself with his own fervor. He did not usually care whom Essex bedded.

"Then, John," Essex had said, his words loud enough to carry through the presence chamber, "be a man and take my wager. Ten gold marks, sir, that I have the little maid impaled upon my upstanding cock before you." Essex, holding his pipe in front of his breeches and thrusting forward, swaggered a few steps and added most reasonably above the applause of the changeable crowd, "What say you, John? Shall we let the winning cock determine the better man?"

John turned from his reflection and sank into a chair. That intolerable taunt had forced his response. He had heard his agreement to the wager before he'd thought. Ever his problem. Mary Rogers was a girl, barely a woman, who needed gentle wooing, not an Essex frontal assault that amounted to little better than amused and playful rape. What Mary needed was an advance-and-retreat strategy that gradually broke down her resistance. Now there would be no time for such delicate games, because Essex would move fast. If John Harington were to save Mary Rogers from ruin and banishment from court, he would have to outflank Essex.

The thought brought a smile. "You fool!" he said aloud. He had never before thought it necessary to claim keeping a virgin for himself as a charitable act. He must be a little mad. Or had the girl's spirited innocence bewitched him? Was she a sorceress who could change a man?

He groaned. Time was short. Essex would force Mary, if necessary. The wager was the talk of the court, and no doubt the gossip had traveled to the queen's ladies and come to Mary Rogers's ears. Almost daily she passed him on her duties without returning his normal courtesy. In the queen's privy chamber she did not know him. He was now the villain in her eyes.

Essex be damned eternally! Restless, John rose and went again to his mirror. The same man stared back at him. He smiled, not very heartily, but like a sick man pretending to superior health.

"One good thing may yet save your soul, John Harington," he said aloud, straightening his ruff to better show the queen's gift, a valuable pearl earring. "You seem to have some little conscience remaining."

The court theater was decked with every bough and flower that the royal hothouse could force open in deep winter. For once, Mary thought the air at court almost breathable, as she followed the queen in procession to the great hall. She was still not used to living with a thousand people and twice that many servants. Though Whitehall Palace had two thousand rooms, it seemed always teeming, the people moving about in crowds rather than in twos or small groups. She lived and slept in an antechamber next to the queen with the other young ladies, never alone, scarce able to sort her thoughts. Perhaps that was a good thing. Let her thoughts remain unsorted. She did not want to face her disillusionment . . . oh, never with the queen, who was every great thing she'd hoped . . . but with John Harington, who was the cause of her disappointment. She had hoodwinked herself into thinking there was some good in him. Now she knew him for the blackest of blackguards.

They moved into the presence chamber toward the throne, the ladies chattering about the play they would see. Today, Master Shakespeare and the Lord Chamberlain's men were presenting *A Midsomer Night's Dream*, one of Her Majesty's favorites. White plaster columns were in place to serve as the Athenian court, and trees on wheels peeked in from the next hall, ready to become the faerie forest outside Athens. Mary was already familiar with the play, since its tangled love stories had been the talk of the bedchamber for days.

The Earl of Essex escorted the queen to the dais and her throne, turning once to smile at Mary, a smile other women were said to find alarmingly exciting. She had to admit that he was a very handsome man, extremely tall, and he wore his multicolored, gem-covered clothes as if they were his second skin. His hose were very tight, showing every muscle in his fine legs to advantage. Mary doubted that any woman at court missed a single stride of those long legs.

John Harington lounged near the throne, not so finely dressed, indeed attired in plain black with a white ruff. His short dark beard and hair were neatly trimmed, while Essex grew his russet curls long and tumbled. Harington's only ornament was a great pearl drop in one ear. His very simplicity made him stand out from the other courtiers, as he was no doubt well aware. He stepped toward her, but Mary turned her face from him. "Fool," she muttered. There would be no avoiding him forever. He was too much with the queen, and she might be offended if one of her ladies was rude to her favorite godson. Taking a deep breath, Mary turned her head to acknowledge him, but he had engaged Lady Warwick's ear in whispered conversation, which made the countess laugh.

Mary's face flamed beyond her control. *Christ's blood!* Whether or not he was abusing her name, it was time to set him in his place. She left the queen's retinue and curtsied to Lady Warwick, who looked her caution at Mary.

"Sir John," Mary said, gaining control of her voice, indeed making it bright, as if she had not a single care. "I understand your purse may soon be lighter by ten marks, as will my lord Essex's? I suggest hereafter you save your money, for neither earl nor knight will be the richer by me." There! Now the scoundrel would be in no doubt as to her knowledge of his sham of friendship.

She expected him to show some unease, but he was too practiced at hiding what he truly felt. He'd been at court long enough to learn advanced deception. "Mistress Mary, my purse does not contain so great a sum, nor do I wish it."

"Nor will it soon, sir," she said, unable to let the matter rest, though she saw regret on the rogue's face. *Too late for that, Sir John.*

He bowed, as etiquette demanded. "Next time we meet, mistress, I will wear armor against that cutting tongue."

"A wise decision, sir."

Lady Warwick raised her kohled eyebrows in warning. "Docile, Mistress Rogers, docile . . ."

With a curtsy to the countess, Mary swept on, holding her gown away from the possibility of touching him, as if he were a running sewer in the meanest London alley. She looked up to see that Lord Essex had viewed the scene, and his wide smile confirmed his interest. Mary took a deep breath to quiet the heat rising to her face. The palace was full of rascals with their cocks on offer. They would soon learn she could not be cozened out of her virginity by either a witty scoundrel or a fine-turned leg. She had come to serve the queen, and there was no more certain way to end that service than to grow a belly. Mary, her head high, walked toward the throne, but Essex stepped in her way.

"Mistress Mary." He bowed as if paying the new lady of the bedchamber a usual civility. "As you know, I hold Her Majesty's interest high in my heart. I would know you better and hear about your west country people. Are they loyal?" His gaze dropped to her breasts and he smiled. It was a clear invitation.

"My lord, I do not speak for all, but my father was loyal enough to die for the queen during the first coming of the armada, and I am too loyal to abuse her trust." She tried to step past him, but he took her arm.

"Perhaps we could meet later to talk further . . . a little supper in my rooms this evening."

"As does the queen, I eat sparingly, my lord."

"I promise I'll have such a dish to tempt even you."

It was time to put an end to his hopes. "My lord, release me. I am come to court to serve Elizabeth Tudor . . . *and for that purpose only*. Your *dish* will never appeal to me."

He laughed softly. "You are too proud for a country maid without rank. Do not make *purposes* you cannot keep." He bowed, whispering, "I never lose, pretty Mary."

"If the queen hears of this, you are indeed lost, my lord of Essex."

He reddened. "I take no person's threat, man or woman. The queen will believe me, mistress. Beware. You have made of me an enemy."

Before she could answer his unpardonable behavior with words no lady should speak, he went, smiling, to Her Majesty's side.

Shaken by his reckless approach so near the throne, Mary arranged herself in her place at the rear of the ladies, as she had learned on her very first day in the queen's bedchamber. What did Essex plan? If the queen had seen or heard such an exchange, would she have blamed Essex or Mary? Was her Wild Horse forgiven all behavior as boyish excess? Mary determined to stay as far from Lord Essex as from Sir John, admitting that Essex would be the easier task.

Thus far, Her Majesty had paid Mary little attention beyond approving her appearance, although Mary doubted that much escaped Elizabeth, who had learned as a child to observe every shade of court behavior and what it could mean to her.

Nor had much in the queen's quarters escaped Mary's notice. She had learned her duties quickly, but had waited in vain for any praise on the improvements in the queen's closestool, which she had even covered in purple velvet. Her grandfather had spoiled her, praising her for every little effort. In the queen's service, she must become used to excellence being expected and appreciation being rare.

The actors approached the domed dais and knelt before the queen, caps in hand.

"Let the play begin, Master Shakespeare." The queen addressed a balding man of average height but with large, lively eyes. "And let us see more of Bottom and Puck . . . a most amusing Robin Goodfellow."

"I have added to their parts to delight Your Grace," Shakespeare said.

Bowing low, some players disappeared.

Lady Margaret whispered to Mary, "The boys playing women must change to their costumes and wigs."

At last, Master Shakespeare signaled the trumpets for an opening fanfare.

Mary saw from the corner of her eye that John Harington had left the court theater. Now she could enjoy the play without being always aware of where he was and what he was doing . . . wondering what he was planning and waiting for him to turn his eyes toward her. For some reason, she thought him more dangerous in his humor than Essex in his practiced advances. She did regret that she would have no further opportunity to rebuke John Harington this day and wondered why she needed to.

Lady Margaret gasped and nudged Mary's arm, looking toward the throne. Essex was leaning in very close to the queen . . . and she had her long fingers sliding up his neck and through his hair. It was so intimate a move that Mary looked away, embarrassed for Her Majesty, since many in the court saw.

Trumpets sounded and the first act of the play began with Hippolyta, queen of the Amazons, appearing before Elizabeth holding a spear and wearing a polished cuirass and red-crested helmet. Elizabeth was pleased and suddenly pushed Essex away as if he were a naughty boy, applauding this obvious tribute from the playwright. The queen was often called an Amazon in poetry and obviously liked the comparison.

Mary suppressed a smile. How else could Master Shakespeare, or any man, explain a woman like Elizabeth, who for so long had ruled her council, her Parliament and her people through wars and uprisings without a man? Such a queen without a king must be a goddess and no ordinary woman. Otherwise, how could she take care of regal duties which women, being weak-minded, knew nothing about?

Mary knew that most men and many women accepted this natural order of being: God was overall, then kings, nobles, common men and, last of all, women. That Elizabeth had defied this order had emboldened more than one of her female subjects. Mary smiled to herself. If Elizabeth Tudor could confront France and Spain, then Mary Rogers could defy Harington and Essex.

The scene before her shifted to the forest and recaptured her attention. Trees were rolled in to make a bower, and Mary was fascinated to watch as Oberon, the king of faeries, sent Puck to seek the juice of a magic flower and place it on his queen Titania's eyelids while she slept. The magic potion would cause her to madly love the first creature she saw on waking. The ladies around Mary, who had seen the play before, giggled in delight.

In another place in the grove a group of men practiced a play. One of the actors, called Bottom, seemed familiar to Mary. When he turned toward the throne, she saw it was John Harington, dressed in rags. She was not surprised that he had a player's ability, though she was intrigued by yet another talent. Writer, courtier, cavalryman, now an actor. She made up her mind: She would not applaud him.

Bottom was a raucous fellow who wanted to play every part, which Mary thought required little acting skill for the man who wished to bed every woman in the queen's bedchamber. She tried to pay him little attention, but that was impossible.

Puck trickled the magic potion on Titania's eyelids, then, ever the trickster, placed a donkey's head on Bottom, who galloped about, braying loudly. Titania woke and was love-struck at first sight of him. The faerie queen gave chase and Bottom dashed about the stage, trying to hide from her behind trees. Each time he was nearly caught, he somersaulted away.

Mary was surprised that John was so athletic. She had thought he had no great exercise outside his bed.

The courtiers laughed helplessly as John Harington became more and more vigorous and shocking in his broad humor, at last jumping out of his breeches as Titania clung to them.

Mary tried to remain sober-faced, but when John leapt on the faerie queen's back in his donkey head, she could not help herself: She laughed aloud just as Titania bounded near the dais and John shouted to Elizabeth, "Though an ass, yet I guard this queen's honor and will not yield to her magic-made lust."

Elizabeth signed her pleasure at this raucous tribute to her virginity, though Mary wondered if the scene seemed more of John's making than Master Shakespeare's. Bottom rode away on Titania's back, whipping her arse to speed her through the forest. The courtiers roared their approval.

At last Puck lifted the spell, all the lovers were united and the play ended happily and to great applause. John, his breeches restored, approached the throne with the rest of the players and laid the donkey head at Elizabeth's feet. He bowed to the queen's ladies, though Mary saw his gaze search for her. It would be unseemly to ignore him. She applauded politely, while promising herself that small congratulation was as much as she would ever give him. She doubted the other ladies of the bedchamber, appearing weak from laughter to attract his attention, had so firm a resolve.

Her Majesty stood and handed Master Shakespeare a bag of coins. "We thank you, sir, and your players all." She graciously extended her arms to encompass the entire company.

John, kneeling in Bottom's rags, chest and muscled arms exposed, handed the donkey's head to Shakespeare, who retreated with his company into the adjoining hall.

Though Essex tried to move in front of John, the queen waved him off. "Boy Jack, we think you are a better Bottom than a writer."

John stood and bowed, his tone playful. "Godmother, though I am but a poor player, I think me that there is little difference to make an ass upon the stage . . . or an ass upon the page."

Elizabeth raised her fan to hide a smile that would have encouraged him, though some of her ladies laughed aloud until they realized the queen's amusement had faded.

Essex was scowling, and he again stepped in front of Harington. "Not one of John's best epigrams, Majesty. Indeed, he has done no good work of late. Mediocrity should not be encouraged."

John clenched his hands at his sides, obviously controlling his temper.

Elizabeth snapped her fan shut, displeased. "Do you seek to instruct us in poesy, my lord of Essex? Or are you jealous of another's talent which you, yourself, in your present humor, seem to lack?"

Why would Her Majesty goad Essex so? To take that overproud lord down? Or to contradict her own amorous feelings for a man thirty-five years her junior? Mary thought either reason would seem enough for a queen who was also a woman fighting her own emotions, and then wondered if her own goading of Sir John was any less a denial.

At that moment, Essex did the unpardonable: He turned his back on the queen and stalked away from the court theater without her leave, unable, it seemed, to take rebuff at the hands of two women in one afternoon.

The queen stood, swaying, holding to her throne. She pointed her fan toward the retreating Essex. "Return, my lord of Essex," she shouted, stamping her foot. "Beware, sir. The stone often recoils on the head of the thrower."

Essex did not return, and the queen gripped her ivory fan until it began to bend double, her face thunderous.

No one moved. Mary thought some had ceased to breathe, rather than draw the queen's attention at this moment.

Elizabeth, at twice her usual fast pace, set off toward her apartment, her fanlike ruff bouncing in rhythm to her stride. Mary and all the other maids scrambled to keep step. The trumpeters, caught unaware, were hasty with their fanfare and missed notes.

As they neared the door to the privy chambers, Elizabeth shouted ahead to the gentleman usher: "By God and by Christ, and by many parts of His glorified body, and by saints, faith, troth and all things— open at once!"

It was a soaring curse, which Mary had never thought to hear even from the queen.

"Call our Lord Keeper Edgerton to us!" The queen stamped into her inner chamber and arrived limping.

"But the queen has hurt herself," Mary said to Lady Margaret.

Lady Margaret answered behind her hand. "She has a swollen foot, but she dares it to be gout and, by denying, she seeks to cure it."

Mary had no time to marvel at this information except not to doubt it. If this queen could cure gout with her will, she could deny a childish lord his tantrums with one of her own.

Lord Keeper Edgerton, who had been present at the play, was announced.

Elizabeth whirled on him. "Bring my lord Essex to us at once!"

There was no mistaking the urgency of the command, and the Lord Keeper left at a near run.

It took most of an hour for Edgerton to bring Essex to the queen. During that time, Mary saw Elizabeth throw herself into a frenzy of paperwork, change her gown twice, leave it open to show her breasts, then have it tied and pace the floor, her anger seeming to grow hotter by the minute.

Edgerton returned, Essex following, with three yeoman guards behind him. He could have been a prisoner.

Mary began to edge toward the antechamber with the other ladies.

"Our daughters will remain!" It was a regal command that could not be ignored, though Mary doubted any lady wanted to be witness to what might follow.

Essex did not look at the queen, nor kneel as custom demanded. "You do better to be on your knees to your sovereign, my lord," Elizabeth said, her words ringing throughout the chamber, probably through half the immense palace.

Mary saw the queen's body quake and remembered that her anger was such that she often collapsed. Mary, being closest, pushed one foot forward, ready to rush to the queen if she began to swoon.

Essex raised his face, his reddish brown curls tumbled about his face, his stylish doublet half undone. He showed a boyish, pouting defiance, as if a schoolmaster had caught him asleep at his books and meant to rap his knuckles.

The guards forced him to his knees.

The queen walked around him, her hands clasping and unclasping, never still. Essex tried to keep his gaze from following her, but Elizabeth would have his attention, and at last she did completely.

He looked up at her, his eyes glistening with tears.

Elizabeth's face showed him no pity.

Essex crumpled at her feet. "My queen, I beg forgiveness and—"

"You may not beg for anything, my lord. We have given you honors, estates, the tax on sweet wines, commands at sea against Spain. We forgave you last year when you failed to intercept their treasure fleet off the Azores—"

That was too much for Essex's pride, and he lurched to his feet without her hand allowing it. "I have explained that Raleigh was much to blame. He is my enemy and lies—"

"Failed, we said, for you spent our money and returned with nothing gained because you sought personal glory and lost much of that." Elizabeth had spoken with such force that she had to stop to breathe deeply. "We forgave you a hundred times over, and now you show us your back before our court. Here is ours." The queen turned away from him, motioning to the guards. "My lord of Essex is banished from court to await our further pleasure."

"Majesty, you cannot—" Essex began.

"Cannot!" Elizabeth roared, whirling about and stepping quickly to him. She slapped his face with her open palm.

He reached for his sword, grasped the hilt, but the guards were upon him. "I would not have suffered such treatment from your father, the king!" he shouted.

Elizabeth drew back, frightened. "This is treason!"

"What!" Essex said, all his limited caution spent. "Cannot princes make mistakes? Cannot subjects be wronged? I cannot accept that."

"You dare to threaten our life and then question our authority over our subjects!" Elizabeth flared back, shaking with anger. "Be gone and be hanged."

Restrained by the guards, Essex bowed as best he could, though Elizabeth didn't see him. She had walked away, her back rigid, her golden crown glowing in the firelight.

Mary felt her own hands shaking at her sides. "Is it always like this?" she whispered to Lady Margaret.

"This is far worse than I've ever seen. She could have sent him to the Tower, condemned him . . . and yet may."

Mary knew she must keep her thoughts to herself, but it was inescapable that Essex seemed to want the queen's whole attention while she wanted his entire submission, both seeing anything less as utter rejection.

The ladies of the bedchamber were full of gossip and had shared it freely. From all Mary had heard, the queen would flare at Essex. Essex, appearing wounded, would answer in childish haste. Elizabeth would rage and banish him. He would take away his injured feelings, leaving her to spend days and weeks in deep melancholy . . . until one forgave the other and it all began again. Could there possibly be forgiveness this time?

That night Mary was waiting in the antechamber for the queen to command her, though she had called no one to her since Essex was taken away and had sent her supper dishes away untouched.

"Why so pensive, mistress?" Lady Warwick sat down beside her on the chest below her bed at the far corner of the chamber.

"I am sad because Her Majesty is sad."

"Then you will be sad often. It has been thus between the young earl and the queen for a decade . . . since Robert Dudley died." The countess lowered her voice to a bare whisper. "Both Elizabeth and Essex lost the only man who could control their black humors."

"You knew my lord Leicester?"

"Yes, I was a young woman then, but I will never forget that the queen's Robin desired to serve her for herself. He was as ambitious as Essex, yet she came first in his heart and she knew it."

Mary smiled. Lady Warwick was a romantic. "I think I understand," Mary murmured, happy that the countess had trust enough for a rare confidence. "Both Her Majesty and the earl need the complete devotion that only Robert Dudley could give." Oh, she'd gone much too far. "My pardon, Lady Warwick, it is not for me to say."

"It is not," Anne Warwick agreed sternly, and then went on in a softer tone, "But say it you did, and you are right in your conclusion." The countess placed her hand on Mary's sleeve. "You might use that clear-seeing for another man, mistress."

"I must to my duty, my lady, and ensure Her Majesty's closestool is in readiness for the morrow." Mary stood and curtsied, knowing that the countess was about to come to John Harington's aid. She did not want to hear a plea for that rogue.

Before she could walk away, she heard Lady Warwick's further word: "I see that it is not only queens who do not forgive foolish men."

Her Majesty's closestool was in good order. Mary spread more fresh marjoram, the queen's favorite herb, but was not as diligent as she should have been. Her mind filled with what she'd learned . . . and what she hadn't. Was she truly a country mouse, after all? Lady Warwick probably thought her unable to adjust to the sophistication of the court. Was it then so usual for a woman's honor to be the subject of a wager in Whitehall? She would not have thought it, though the queen was often bawdy in her own wit. She sat down on a stone bench near the queen's bath, thankful for the echoing silence of the vast room, and watched the lantern light shimmering on the water.

"Mistress Rogers."

Mary was alarmed at that voice and stood so quickly, backing away, that only John Harington's quick grasp of her arm kept her from a fall into the bath . . . a winter bath at that, against every good doctor's prescription.

"I've startled you. My apologies. I thought to find you here. I have heard you are most diligent at a difficult duty."

She pulled her arm away and began walking toward the door.

"No, wait," he added. "At least do me the courtesy of listening."

"Do I owe you a courtesy, sir?"

He shook his head. "You owe me nothing. It is I who owe you, and I am come to make payment."

"I see," she said, without seeing anything, without wanting to, clinging to her anger and beginning to wonder at her need to keep it hot. "You have decided honeyed words will gain you what ten gold marks would not."

"That could be what you see, but your sight would be clouded by your righteous anger . . . the most blinding kind." He stopped, took a breath, and began again. "I have come to beg your forgiveness"—he put up a hand to stop her objection and knelt—"yes, beg you most humbly, and to tell you this: I have paid the wager in full and admitted before my friends that I am the most utter fool, though some did claim to have prior knowledge." His mouth twisted at the wry jest.

He raised his face to her, and it was illuminated by a nearby torch. It looked almost angelic and not to be believed by any woman with good sense, the kind of woman she had always thought herself.

Though the light shone upon him most favorably, she had never been ruled by handsome features. "Surely this is a miracle," she said, immediately disliking the sarcasm she heard. She struggled to guard her tongue. "Why do you think, Sir John, that I would believe you a changed man in so short a time?"

"Because I no longer wear the head of an ass."

She wanted to smile and realized it wasn't for the first time. She must have shown some amusement, because he rose and with the sweep of his hand motioned her to sit on the bench. To her amazement, she obediently took the seat.

He sat well away from her and rubbed his ear.

Desperate for another subject, she said, "Nor do you wear your pearl drop earring, the queen's gift, I believe."

"I had to pawn it to pay . . . debts."

"I do advise that this is no good time to tell it, sir. Her Majesty is deep in melancholy."

John looked into the marble-lined bath dancing with light. "Someday the queen's patience will break and Essex will not be forgiven. I hope I am not at court when that happens."

Mary looked hard at him. "I hope I am, Sir John. Her Majesty will need a woman's understanding."

He looked at her, his gaze serious with none of the scarce-hidden amusement that she usually saw. "Could you offer Her Grace . . . the knowledge of a woman's forgiveness?"

She did not answer him because she did not know. Why was it easier to forget that Essex was more to blame than John? Why had he so disappointed her? Was she so vain of her own early misjudgment of John Harington that she would be unforgiving when he offered an apology that seemed sincere? Mary knew she would not admire such pride in another.

He bowed, his hand on his heart. "I have sought you tonight, Mistress Mary, for a double purpose."

Standing quickly, she readied herself. "I should have known there was no good in you, sir. My grooms of the closestool are waiting beyond that door." She was lying, but God would forgive her.

His mouth tightened. "You are quick to think the worst of me, Mary. Am I to have no second chance? Even the thief on the cross was forgiven by our Lord."

She stared at him, sensing her face flush. By all the saints, he would quote scripture next. "What is this second purpose, sir?" She watched him narrowly, but he did not move toward her.

"I believe I have invented something that will gain for you Her Majesty's gratitude."

"Why would you do that?"

"To gain your admiration."

"And, incidentally, the queen's," she added.

"Perhaps, since your regard seems even less attainable."

"You had it once and threw it away. Why would you ever wish it now?" She held her breath for fear of having gone too far. She had no skill in coquetry. "You but jest with me. Surely no such grand invention exists." She realized she was being headstrong now just for its own sake.

"I believe it does."

He was forcing her to ask him. She sighed. "What is this miracle invention?"

He grinned. "A jakes fit for a queen . . . one that flushes away foul odors."

In a hundred years she would not have thought John Harington would try to impress her with a new jakes. What manner of man would woo a lady's affection in such a way, but a mad rogue of a man? She could not help herself; she had to laugh. "You are . . . you are mad, sir," she said, though he looked serious. "Can it be?"

"It can if you trust me," he said, reaching for her hand. She moved suddenly toward the door and he added, with his usual humor, "Just a little."

CHAPTER ELEVEN

*"I have had good experience and trial of this world . . .
I have found treason in trust, seen great benefits little regarded."*
—Elizabeth Regina

*St. Gregory the Great's Day
March 12, 1599*

*M*ary climbed the stairs at Richmond Palace immediately behind the queen, who trailed her scent of Tudor rose and musk. The queen's ermine-trimmed silver gown was splendid with a black silk shift pulled through slashed oversleeves. A mass of seed pearls covered every inch, making it so heavy that the queen seemed to have trouble lifting it, but Mary dared not offer help unless it was asked for. She remained surprised to have been singled out alone of all the ladies to follow immediately behind Her Majesty to the council chamber. The queen usually did not leave her apartment without a large and regal retinue and every possible display of her royal dignity.

Outside, Mary heard an early spring storm sweeping in from the west, thunder rattling the sturdy old towers.

"Pish! Pish!"

With a concealed smile, Mary thought a storm about to break under those towers as well. "Majesty?"

The queen didn't answer, but gave sure signs of being displeased about something. Mary thought she knew the source of that anger. Not Essex this time.

After numerous begging but proud letters filled with tributes to the queen's beauty, jeweled gifts and petitions from his friends, he had finally returned to court, although not quite to his former favor with Elizabeth. Mary had heard her mutter after reading one of the earl's letters, "I mean to stand upon my importance as he has stood upon his pride."

She flirted and jested with Essex almost as before, but there was a distance between them, and she often took occasion to chastise him for mischief she would formerly have tolerated as youthful high spirits. All her ladies remarked that the queen no longer called him her Wild Horse. So far, he had been careful not to repeat the disastrous behavior that had propelled him forcibly from court. Lady Warwick thought they were reconciled, but Mary was not so sure, and sensed that the queen watched and waited. Her Majesty had spent a lifetime watching and waiting and knew well how to bide her time.

Elizabeth climbed slowly up the staircase and Mary measured her steps to the queen's, wondering if Elizabeth's current displeasure was caused by John's pamphlet "A New Discourse on a Stale Subject," his novel plan for a better jakes. He had not resisted including jests with double meaning. The pamphlet was thought indecent by the queen, who was careful to monitor the reputation of her court . . . though she had ordered the installation of the clever device next to her privy chamber.

"How does Boy Jack's invention work?" The queen sent the question back over her shoulder. John had explained the device to the queen and shown his drawings to her several times. Was Her Majesty becoming forgetful? "Come up to us," Elizabeth said, impatiently waving Mary forward.

"Your Grace, Sir John is installing a water cistern which flushes the closestool, wherein a stopper prevents foul odors rising from the pit."

"A water closet? He was always a clever boy . . ." Elizabeth said, but her voice swayed with her body and she took Mary's arm to steady herself. "You spend too much time with Boy Jack, mistress."

"Majesty, I must attend to my duties as your mistress of the closestool."

Elizabeth nodded. "Yes, yes. We grant he is a charming rogue, but do not think to marry him."

Mary tensed and the queen sensed it. "When the time comes, daughter, we will provide a better husband for your good service to us. Someone of fortune and good name. An older man, we think, to balance impetuous youth."

"My thanks to Your Majesty." What else could she say when offered what every lady of little rank and small fortune was said to want? And why should such high regard sadden her when any courtier would think her fortunate? The queen had noticed her work, after all. But of what future time was Elizabeth speaking? Her death? She didn't release her ladies easily . . . unless they were pregnant and unwed. Then she drove them away, sometimes with blows, and always in disgrace. Mary took a deep breath. "Your Majesty, I have no desire to wed."

"So you have told us, but we have eyes, mistress."

What had the queen seen? Surely Mary had shown no outward favor toward John. Or had her strict caution been as telling? She could not know. She hardly knew her own mind. John had been much with her these past months, and gradually she had become less guarded with him, finding him . . . well, good company. And, she reluctantly admitted, good to look upon. And thoughtful.

He had sent her a gift of his translation of Ariosto with an inscription: *Books give not wisdom where none was before. But where some is, there reading makes it more.* She thought of those words often, because they were so like him: a bit arrogant, but engaging despite her every effort not to be charmed.

At first, she had kept a good distance, but when he made no ungentlemanly move, she had relaxed. Still he had not approached, until the game reversed almost without her knowing it. She put herself in his way, only to make him more careful. Perhaps he believed she was still angry, though she'd given every indication that she was not. Maybe not *every* indication.

Courtiers bowed on either side of the council antechamber and seemed not to notice the queen's wavering step, though Mary knew they did. The entire court was on a death watch in this, the queen's sixty-fifth year. And the queen knew it, battling age at every turn. When her doctors advised her to stop riding out or walking in her gardens on windy or rainy mornings, she had scoffed: "We have buried six doctors and will live to bury you and all your physicks, plasters and purges!"

Did the queen think herself immortal after all? She had purchased an elixir of perpetual youth from the famous Dutch alchemist Cornelius Lannoy. It was foul to taste and costly, so highly recommended. But as wrinkles were added to Elizabeth's pale cheeks, the man had been sent to the Tower before he could escape the country. Fooling the queen was treason.

Her Majesty stopped before her council's high doors, waiting for them to be opened, which they were immediately. "Attend us, Mistress Mouse."

Mary moved forward, bearing some of the queen's weight on her arm. Lady Katherine Grey had told Mary of attending the queen in council. A lady's job was to pretend to hear nothing of council business and to speak not a word of it later, no matter who asked or offered expensive gifts.

The council rose. Young Robert Cecil, the son of William Cecil, Elizabeth's late well-beloved adviser, stood from his father's seat opposite Elizabeth. Now the Secretary of State, he was short and crook-backed, with a bland expression that revealed nothing of his clever brain. A large pile of state papers lay before him on the tapestry-laden table.

Mary knew that Elizabeth called him her Pygmy. Such nicknames were a sign of her favor, so everyone had said. Mary doubted Robert Cecil liked his favor much more than she liked Mouse, though she was the only woman to have been honored with a special name. Why? Was it jest or endearment?

The queen's older councilors, along with Sir Walter Raleigh, sat on one side of the long carved table. Essex, the Earl of Southampton and other younger council members sat across from them, spoiling for war. Essex acknowledged Mary with a frown.

"Sir Walter," the queen said, wrinkling her nose, "you have been at the pipe again. We like not your weed."

Raleigh bowed, his hand upon his heart. "My humble pardon, Majesty."

Impatient, Elizabeth sat and the council was seated, scraping their chairs forward. "That other isle is always troubling," the queen announced, squinting hard at the map on the opposite wall. She refused to use the perspective glass her doctors had provided. "That traitorous villain the Earl of Tyrone has risen again in Ireland, destroyed our army, and is now scheming with the Spanish to send another armada against us. Ireland is England's back door; we cannot allow it. We are minded to dispatch Lord Mountjoy as our Lord Lieutenant with a new army."

Mary moved a step to one side of the queen's high-backed chair to better watch the discussion. Essex was clearly angered by the appointment. Robert Cecil showed nothing, but Mary was convinced he weighed every word.

Essex spoke and for once kept good control of his tongue. "Your Grace, this expedition needs a military man of vast experience, a noble who has commanded an army in battle."

Cecil spoke softly. "My lord, that description points to you. Do you propose yourself?"

Ignoring Cecil, Essex bowed to the queen where he sat. "Trust me, Majesty. I will hand to you an Ireland on its knees."

Contemplating her hand, holding a quill to sign the warrant, the queen muttered, "We have seen treason in trust."

Mary saw red rise up Essex's neck to his cheeks, deepening the color of his russet beard.

The queen shrugged. "Yet let it be so ordered." She signed the warrant with her elaborate swirling signature more quickly than usual.

Surprised at Elizabeth's quick change of mind, Mary wondered if the wily old queen had maneuvered Essex into a trap where he could either redeem himself or lose her favor and the people's adoration forever. Did Elizabeth know in advance that he could never allow another man to have the honor of leading an English army, needing military glory as most men needed breath? Putting together what Katherine Grey had taught her about the queen with what she had learned in the past two months, she wondered if Elizabeth had indeed been devious. But why would she be so, when she so obviously loved him? Was this one time when the queen did not know her own mind, or was this a test where Essex could redeem or sink himself and she would bear no blame?

As Mary watched, she saw triumph rise in Essex, quickly followed by doubt. Ireland had been the sinkhole of more than one courtier's career, trapping English armies for centuries in its impenetrable bogs. But Essex must know he could not refuse without losing what status he'd regained. She saw triumph on more than one face at the council table. Robert Devereaux, the Earl of Essex, was a man whose pride and scheming had made him many enemies, even among those who could have been his friends.

He quickly regained his composure. He smiled at Elizabeth, his tousled hair and unlined face looking younger than his more than thirty years. "Majesty, I would have my lord of Southampton at my side and . . . Sir John Harington as my master of horse." He glanced at Mary.

Mary was startled. Why had Essex insisted on John to accompany him? The two men had not regained their old friendship, since John was seen by most in the court to have behaved more honorably, if surprisingly. Did Essex seek to keep John close as someone who might gain in influence while he was gone, or was he simply the best man and Essex knew it? Mary had many questions and no answers.

The queen stood, signaling an end to her patience and the meeting. "You may have Boy Jack when he has completed his work for us."

"Majesty," Essex said, also standing, "surely this great venture has more importance—"

"We yet rule here, my lord Essex, and we decide where importance lies. It will be as we will it."

The queen swept from the chamber, everyone bowing behind her except Essex, whose youthful face was dark with anger. His friend Southampton had a grip on his straining shoulders.

Trumpeters, drummers, yeomen guards and some courtiers were assembled outside to escort the queen to her presence chamber, where she would hold an audience for petitioners.

As soon as the queen was seated under her domed throne, Polish ambassadors approached in long black velvet robes and presented petitions in Latin from their king. The Polish king demanded that the English queen stop interfering with his shipping trade. Drake, Hawkins and Frobisher, the queen's sea dogs, roved the sea-lanes, while the queen looked the other way . . . and accepted a third of their captured treasure.

Elizabeth heard the ambassadors out, her eyes flashing and dark with anger, then stood and spoke her mind in the elegant Latin of diplomacy. Mary knew the queen's Latin was graceful, though she caught only a phrase here and there. The arrogant ambassadors dropped to their knees in rapt astonishment before the royal onslaught.

Finally, smiling with satisfaction as Cecil stepped forward to offer his hand, the queen announced, "We are well pleased, my Lord Secretary, that we have this occasion to use our rusty Latin."

Mary bit her lip to keep from laughing aloud. The queen studied her Latin every day and had since she was a girl. It was about as rusty as her crown. At that moment, Mary lost the last of her fear of the irascible old queen. From childhood, Mary had admired this ruler, who had taken the small island nation her father left her and made it a world power. Who would not long to serve her in her brilliant court, at the center of all England? Now Mary felt something much more than pride of position. She could not help but love Elizabeth. It was a love not unlike Mary's love for her grandfather, indebted and tender. And wholly accepting.

One afternoon, while the queen met with her councilors in the royal apartment's inner chamber, objecting loudly to the costs they projected for the Irish venture, Mary went to inspect the progress on John's new water closet. The workers were at their supper, and John was not there or in the old closetool chamber.

Aimlessly, she walked back to the ladies' antechamber.

"Mary, the queen is having only a little watered wine for her supper today. If you would dine," Lady Warwick offered, "the great hall will provide."

With a curtsy, Mary left to join the other ladies. The passages were emptier than usual, or contained straggling cooks carrying sugar plates and other confections. She was very late for the meat dishes and bread, which would be cold from the icy drafts sweeping through the old palace, though Richmond was considered the warmest of all the queen's residences. Since Mary had no taste for a sweet meal, she turned down another hall to circle back to the queen's apartments.

A door opened and a liveried servant stepped into her path. She backed away, but an unseen man who followed behind him caught her arm. She was trapped.

"My lord of Essex requests you attend him, mistress," said one, not bothering to hide a leer.

"Give His Lordship my regrets, but I am on a duty for the queen."

"His Lordship will not require much time," one servant said as they each gripped an arm.

She was inside the apartment and being propelled toward a back chamber before she could scream. And who would hear her loudest protests? Outside, the wind howled and the rain pounded against windows, with rolling thunderclaps intermingled.

Mary was pushed through the doorway, the thick doors closing behind her. She heard a heavy lock click into place.

The room was lit from a large fireplace roaring its defiance to the storm. She straightened her shoulders and stiffened her back. This lord, so much in disfavor, would be mad to molest one of the queen's ladies who was unwilling to suffer his attentions. This would be a great disrespect to the queen's authority and he must know it, unless he was a little mad. Perhaps more than a little mad.

She determined to keep her calm, pretend that a mistake had been made. She would not be a frightened child. She suspected that would only please Essex, embolden him, since she marked him as a noble bully.

Essex appeared from an inner closet in shirt and breeches, his feet bare, the better to feel his plush Persian carpets, she was sure. "Ah, you have accepted our invitation at last, Mistress Mary."

She opened her mouth to protest, but he turned away to punch at the fire. Without his padded court clothes, he was slender as well as very tall, taller even than the queen's father, who had been considered a giant in his time. It was no wonder that he had so many women begging for his attention, even if she would not be one of them.

"My lord earl, what means this? Surely, your servants took me for another." Her voice was haughty, and she recognized some of Elizabeth's tone, which would have made her smile at any other time.

He did not turn to her, or answer. Perhaps he only wanted to frighten her, thinking he could, not knowing her at all.

His bed was hung with tapestries and the room held every evidence of royal favor, including the queen's coronation portrait. Her soft, pretty young face stared out from under her crown. Her lovely hands, pushing from under her robes, held the orb and scepter of England. Mary had heard these rooms had once been Robert Dudley's, who had loved the queen at the moment the artist had put his brush to paint. Essex had proved a poor replacement for Dudley in every way. From all Mary knew about the queen's first love, Robin would never have needed to waylay a woman to win her.

The earl edged toward her and mistook her look of wonder and observation. "Gaze your fill upon me, mistress, and count your good fortune that I am not your enemy . . . though I am near to it, unless you choose to make me a . . . friend."

Mary curtsied, determined to keep to stiff formalities. "I am happy to hear it, my lord . . . yet I think you are in error if you do not allow me to continue on the queen's business. As you know, Her Majesty does not abide waiting."

He laughed. "You aren't very clever, after all. Don't you see how it is with the old queen? She won't admit to it, but she is miserable when I'm away and happy to have me back."

Mary stared at him, thinking his overconfidence almost unbelievable. In all his years at court, he did not know Elizabeth as well as he thought.

"Nonetheless, mistress, I must say that many have sought to turn her affections from me. Robert Cecil and Raleigh and perhaps even your Boy Jack. Oh, yes, I have seen how he dreams over you." He almost spit. "But I will win over all, Elizabeth and you, mistress. Watch my triumph when I return with Tyrone on the point of my sword."

Now Mary was astounded, for she saw into him as she had never seen before. He blamed himself for nothing and twisted his mind from suspicion to certainty to grandiosity. She realized that he was self-deluding, far worse than mad. That thought took away her fragile composure and she moved toward the door. "All that may well be true, but I will take my leave now. Unlock the door, my lord."

He looked puzzled.

"Remember, I am under Her Majesty's protection." She neared the door, but he reached it earlier and barred her way. "My lord Essex," she said, her voice shaking with anger under which she hid her alarm, "Sir John is more gentleman than you."

His laughing scorn was high-pitched, and the strange sound chilled her. "What does it matter?" he asked, untying the top of his shirt. "I will take him to Ireland with me and put him in the front rank."

Mary was truly frightened now. This lord would see John killed for righting his mistake and gaining in honor. When she turned to look for another door, Essex stepped very close.

She could not keep the contempt from her low, withering tone. "What you cannot win by wager, you would take by force. That is unworthy of your rank and the queen's trust."

His face reddened. "You dare to question my right? I have had four of the queen's ladies, and all of higher rank than you."

Four? She had heard only three.

Essex's voice grated against her ear. "You have insulted me, mistress, before the court. You must pay for that with the only coin you possess."

She opened her mouth to scream, but as she drew breath, he laughed. "Scream if you will. No one will come against me."

One long arm snaked around her shoulder; his other hand fumbled at her breast, his fingers trying to rip away her shift. More terrified than she had ever been in her life, she shoved him with all her strength and he crashed back against the outer door.

He regained his footing, but his face twisted into an angry mask.

Mary shrank back, certain that she was lost. His next words and actions confirmed her worst dread.

"You will be quiet and giving to me," he announced, his softened voice even more alarming. His hand pulled at his breeches and he exposed his upstanding cock. "If you say a word of the prize I am about to take, I will say that I came upon you and John . . . that you had bewitched him. Would you like to burn, Mistress Mary of the closestool?"

He moved toward her, pushing her toward the bed in short, disdainful thrusts. At his final shove, she caught her heel on a carpet and was thrown on her back into silk sheets that allowed her no easy grip for escape.

She pleaded, desperate and hoping to engage his mind. "Why, my lord, when so many are willing?"

He laughed. "You are a stupid little flirt. What true man does not want what he cannot have . . . and takes it?" He was on her, breathing hard, as if in a fight for his life.

The stale odor of wine enveloped her, and her shaking body no longer obeyed the commands of her head. His weight bore down on her as he fumbled with her skirts. Frantically, she twisted beneath him; clenching her legs together, she beat upon his back, but he was too strong and knelt upon her shoulders, pinning her to silk, his cock dangling over her face. She wanted to weep for frustration, but her hot tears dried before they fell. She wanted to scream, but her throat closed on the strangled sound. She knew that she was ruined; even John would see her as damaged, and she groaned, a desperate sound rising from her very soul.

Dimly, she heard shouts in the outer chamber. Sounds of sword against sword.

The door flew open, crashing back against the paneled wall. John ran in, sword drawn. *Praise God!* He stopped, seeing Essex atop Mary. Doubt replaced anger. "Mistress, are you here of your free will?" His voice was choked with regret.

"John! Help me!" It was a wail.

He started forward. "My lord, I suggest you take your exercise upon the tennis court." He smiled as if it were all a jest.

Essex had twisted about for a better view. For a moment he hesitated, then spoke, attempting his old casual manner. "Come join in, John. I was always a man to share with my friends."

"Please, John!" It was a rising cry, breathless and frantic.

"Release her, my lord."

Essex growled. "Away, sir. I'll have no interference here." But as John moved forward, Essex scrambled up, allowing Mary to pull down her gown and roll out of his bed, swaying, stumbling, trembling, but determined not to give in to tears of relief beyond measure.

Essex laughed. "John, the little whore came to me . . . begged me to take her, I swear."

"It's a monstrous lie." Mary breathed deeply again and ran to John. "As I know you have regard for your honor, take me from this place."

John sheathed his sword. "How came you here, mistress?"

He was suspicious of *her*, and that was infuriating. "Unwillingly!" She shrieked the word at him. "His servants dragged me into his chamber when I was returning to the queen's rooms."

Essex pretended to laugh and dismissed her words with a disdainful shrug. "John, you know I can have better fare than this. Whom do you believe . . . the man who bestowed your knighthood upon you, or this upstart?"

John bowed, but his arm went about Mary's waist. "Whatever the right of it, my lord earl, the lady is now unwilling."

"What difference? Women are easily persuaded every day." Though Essex tried to continue his casual sham, he soon shrugged and waved them away. "Take her and welcome. She is too changeable and unbiddable for me . . . for any true man."

John smiled, refusing to be goaded. "My lord of Essex," he said very formally, bowing and guiding Mary rapidly to the hall door, which was opened by two servants who did not look at them.

Once they were in the hall, John led her quickly into an adjacent anteroom. She was shaking now, unable to stop. "Sit down," he said firmly, but not unkindly, escorting her to a fireside bench. "Straighten your gown and ruff." His hand gently brushed the hair from her face.

She forced herself to stop her hands jerking like those of one with ague. John waited while a question nagged at her, and she had to assure herself that John had not known what Essex planned. "How came you to look for me in Essex's chambers?"

"You were not with the queen, not in the dining hall where Lady Warwick told me to look for you." He glanced away, then back and full into her eyes. "Long experience told me where next to look."

She believed him, but she had to know one last thing. "You don't believe that I—"

"No, I don't believe Essex. Since his quarrel with Her Majesty, he is unlike himself."

"In that you are wrong, John," she said, drawing in a deep, shuddering breath. "He sees the world as he wishes it to be. He threatened to put you in the forward line in Ireland."

"Do you care so much for my life, Mary?"

She avoided an answer. "How could Her Majesty love such a man as Essex?"

John's eyes grew sad. "She never did love the Essex we just left. He is much changed since he lost some of the queen's favor and with it his chance for even more advancement. He cannot tolerate losing."

"It's the wager, John. He will see you dead. He can never forgive you for besting him in front of all."

"He is wrong in that. I did not best him. . . . I bested myself alone. I will make him understand that." John moved closer, bent and searched her face, his next words much softer. "Though I cannot make you understand."

Mary gave him her trust. It settled in her upturned face and stopped her quivering hands. Awaking from her own misery, Mary saw that Lady Margaret and one of the queen's gentleman ushers were passing by and stopped to stare at them with interest.

Rising, Mary excused herself. "Sir John, I thank you most heartily for your rescue of me," she said formally, curtsied, nodded to Lady Margaret and walked swiftly toward the queen's apartments. Her mind was in great confusion, and she dared not look back at the man who had created the most turmoil. Not until she could think of what more to say. Or not to say.

Some days later a splendidly dressed Essex, backed by his lieutenants, took leave of the queen and the palace to gather his army of sixteen thousand troops and take ship for Ireland. As he left the presence chamber, he seemed to have eyes only for the queen, and Mary was relieved that he had not glanced her way. He probably thought she was too intimidated by his grandeur, and, since she had kept her silence about his assault, he gave her no more thought. True or not, it was a relief to think so.

Mary was in a position to watch the queen's face as she wished Essex and his troops well with one admonition: "My lord, too much of our treasure and troops have been wasted in raids about the Irish countryside, where they ambush us at every turn. We bid you march directly to the enemy and crush him in his northern lair. Bring us triumph once and for all time."

Essex laid his fist over his heart and bowed low. "Majesty, I will bring you that triumph and more . . . an end to the Irish troubles."

Mary stared at his face for any sign of his often arrogant disdain for a woman's generalship, but saw none. She remembered something that John had said: "Ireland is his last chance." Mary did not wish the lord Essex ill, nor well; she didn't want to think of him at all.

Later that day, word of his triumphant exit from the city reached the queen. Crowds, chanting his name, had lined the road for miles out of London, throwing flowers under his horse's hooves.

For a moment Mary thought she saw displeasure flit across Elizabeth's face. In the ladies' antechamber she mentioned what she'd observed to Lady Warwick.

"You see far too much, mistress," Anne chided, though she smiled to soften the words. "Londoners have always belonged to Her Majesty since her first Accession Day. She dislikes their adoration of a handsome young lord who has so recently challenged her in a way her father would never have allowed. Indeed, Henry would have had his head on a pike above London Bridge within a day and his quartered, treasonous body hanging on the city gates."

Mary shuddered. She didn't wish that fate on her worst enemy, though she realized that Essex was probably just that. He would not forget her rejection. She had denied his manhood, questioned his famous appeal to women and gone from him willingly with another man. And she would do it again.

As was her duty, Mary inspected the queen's private jakes early every morning after she broke her fast with bread and a little of the queen's favorite tart ale. The new water closet adjacent to the old closestool closet was almost finished.

Torches flared in the bathing chamber, lighting John, his shirtsleeves rolled high, as he directed a crew of workmen, his plans spread on a tool-laden table.

Curious, she bent to see the neat drawings. He was an accomplished draftsman. While she was engrossed he walked to her side, reaching with a finger to point as he explained. She was aware that his hands were dirty and also that they looked the stronger for it.

"See, mistress, here is the cistern of water that releases into the jakes below. This is the scallop shell to cover the pipe from the jakes into the vault when not in use."

Mary looked up and smiled at him. "It is a most ingenious plan,

John, especially when the queen does so hate terrible odors. With all the herbs in England, I cannot rid the closestool of its foulness."

He moved closer until his warm breath reached her. "Always remember to have the grooms empty the vault at noon and night and leave it half a foot deep in freshwater." His face was very close to hers now. "This being well done, Her Majesty's water closet will be as sweet as her bedchamber. And you will seem to my godmother the more lovable for it . . . as you seem to me now."

Mary looked up at him as his voice became smoother and softer. She was not alarmed and realized at once that she now trusted him above any man. It had been a gradual change, resolved completely by his rescue of her and added to each day since.

He was too close, his voice too intense. She tried to move away, but her feet did not obey her head. She searched for another subject. "Your water closet is truly a marvelous invention, Sir John," she said, motioning to the draft plans. "You will surely be famous." She saw he was pleased.

"Aye, every manor of consequence will have a John Harington jakes."

She smiled slyly. "Much too long a name for a convenience."

He joined in the game. "What then? A John?"

She blushed. "Perhaps."

John's mouth twisted in amusement. " 'Tis a strange subject, indeed, for a man who wishes to court a maid."

She drew her hand away because he had laid his over hers. "There is no path to courtship for us."

"There are many paths, Mary, and I will find the right one for us. Believe me." He sobered. "Come to the privet maze before supper so that we may make our farewells."

"Farewell?"

"I leave tomorrow at first light . . . for Ireland."

"But, John—"

"The maze . . . in the hour before supper," he repeated, and stepped away to talk with his workmen, who had only pretended not to listen.

At four of the afternoon, with sunlight slanting in low from the west, Mary, wrapped in her cloak, walked along the garden path toward the tall ancient yew maze . . . to tell John why she couldn't meet him. The stone benches at the entrance were empty. He was nowhere to be seen.

As she reached the opening to the green maze topped with quickly melting snow, a long arm reached out and pulled her against a male chest. A man's mouth under a neat mustache met her lips and kissed her gently.

It was their first kiss that she'd dreamed of when she'd lost her senses so far as to dream of it. His mouth was warm. As his pressure increased, her mouth opened and she felt what she hadn't known to feel as a dreamer: heat rushing into her body, a melting weakness in her legs, a longing to come impossibly close.

John broke free first, though his arms held her fast. "After our first victory against Tyrone, I will write to the queen for her consent; then I will write to your grandfather."

Mary shook her head helplessly. "I cannot leave the queen." She shivered. "Her Majesty has said she will find a husband for me in her good time."

He held her closer. "She will offer you to one of her doddering old Howard or Carey cousins." He withdrew his arms and paced away, then back again, scuffing the withered sod.

She missed the warmth of his lips and the weight of his arms, leaning in to retrieve them. They were soon returned to her.

"Do you love me, Mary?"

"John, this cannot be. I will not taunt a good man."

"Too late. I am a better man by your example. . . . Your loyalty and courage . . . And your beauty taunts me every day. There is no other lady—"

She had to stop him before she was lost in what he said, in his face, in the curve of his mouth. "Sir John, that news will distress so many ladies in this court."

He did not smile. "I no longer deserve my former reputation. You may be the last woman in the court to know I am a new man . . . your man."

Repentance overwhelmed her. "Forgive me, John; you do not deserve any further censure from me. . . ." She tried to harden her resolve and step away. "I must go. I have forgotten what the queen demands of me. Speak no more of marriage. It cannot be."

Footsteps crunched on the path outside the maze.

He pulled her into his arms again, close against his rough military clothes, covering her completely with his cloak. "But if it could be," he whispered.

The footsteps paused at the maze entrance and then receded into the distance.

"John . . ." She tried not to say more, but the words insisted. "Dearest John, I must return to the queen's chambers before I am missed or we are discovered." Yet her feet refused to move away from his warm shelter.

He laughed softly. "I could tell them that I found you freezing and revived you."

"Do I look revived?" she asked, feeling the warmth in her flaming cheeks. Where did her coquetry come from? she wondered. She had thought herself unpracticed, but with John she had words that meant more than they said.

"You look as I will remember you, Mary, Mary, quite contrary, when I am in Ireland, beautiful and very much alive." He grinned. "But not quite so vigorous as I am . . . deep in a part."

He lifted her against his body and she clutched at his arms, enough heat surging through her to melt snow. Mary was so close to sin she shook with it, and dared not cling to him longer. And he knew it, his body matching hers for warmth.

With her last strength, she broke away and ran back through the garden now darkening with early-winter night, then slowed herself to stroll into the palace as if she had been casually taking the air without other intent. She dared not turn around to see if he followed. If he did, there was no earthly way she would not run back to him to tell of her discovery, a secret she *must* keep for now and perhaps for all time.

Yes, yes, she thought, her lips moving with the words. *I love him, adore him, want him forever.* She tried to bring her feet solidly to the marble floor to feel again the reality of a world where Queen Elizabeth ruled, Gloriana, a woman who had long denied love and had forgotten . . . *must* have forgotten how wounding it was for mortal woman to live without a man like John Harington.

When she reached the queen's apartments, Mary was outwardly the same as when she had left and quickly took up her duties, but she was in truth much changed. When she walked into the queen's bath to check the water closet John had made for Elizabeth, Mary saw him at his workbench, though it was no longer there. She looked away and still she saw him. His image was captured for all time inside her head.

About midnight, she went to her bed, blew out her candle and slipped beneath the coverlet, her eyes wide. She slept little that night, and as early light crept into the room, she heard the clatter of horses in the courtyard outside. John was leaving. She held her breath and waited, almost hoping to hear him shout that he had changed his mind and could not leave. But all she heard was receding hoofbeats. She covered her ears lest the sound set her to howling.

Dear God, keep him safe, she prayed again and again until she rose to her duties, the cold days stretching ahead without end.

CHAPTER TWELVE

At the court of Greenwich from Her Majesty to the Earl of Essex:

*". . . if you compare the time that is run on and the
excessive charges that are spent with the effects of anything
wrought by this voyage . . . (we) can little please ourself
with what has been effected."*

—*Elizabeth Regina*

*Lammas Day
August 1, 1599*

*J*ohn Harington sat in his Dublin quarters, his windows open
to a full moon and night breezes, his shirt damp and unlaced to his
breeches, writing by candlelight. *My sweetest girl,* he began, then
scratched it out, making a large blot of the effort. He crumpled the
sheet and pulled another to him. He would be himself and not some
love-sick lad mooning after the village beauty. He dipped his quill
into the lampblack.

Mary, Mary, quite contrary, he began again, and then grinned at
the inky words from the child's rhyme that were so fitting, though
he didn't wish Mary, queen of Scots' final fate on his own Mistress
Mary. He hoped the greeting would raise her temper enough to
scold him by return dispatch far sooner than any sugary words.
Even at this distance, across the Irish Sea and a good three days'
hard ride beyond to London, he felt her presence in the room. It

was the sense of her upturned, lovely young face and dark eyes all about him that he had carried through the Irish campaign. After Essex had led them on three months of fruitless marching about the countryside subduing minor lords, who surrendered easily and then re-formed their troops behind the English, they had arrived back in Dublin. Half their army had been left behind to garrison small outposts, or as casualties of skirmishes, sickness and desertion. They had failed.

John knew that the queen must be wildly unhappy, because Essex raged after reading each one of her long letters. The earl paced his headquarters, railing at her woman's lack of understanding military matters, but in truth, John knew, Essex could no longer see the main purpose that had been the queen's command. Subduing Tyrone with depleted forces was now almost impossible without a miracle, and there were damned few miracles to be found in Ireland.

John pulled the candle closer, it being near eleven and full dark at last. Pleased again by his greeting on the page before him, he began to write:

> *I have received no recent word from you, though I expected to see a letter waiting for me on my return to Dublin. Now I eagerly await each London pouch, sweetheart. I dare call you that because I'm a soldier and familiar with bold advances, though not in this campaign.*
>
> *There is no need to tell you of our lack of success, as I'm certain the queen has made our situation clear in very many loud, hard words heard by all. What you have not heard, because none can see into my heart, is how much I long to see you, to make my petition to the queen and to your grandfather. Do I presume your assent? Am I right that you return my feelings? That last day in the maze your kiss and concern for my safety told me all I needed to know. Perhaps not all, but the rest awaits another day . . . or another dream.*

Though my cavalry led the charge into every skirmish, I have ridden through half of Ireland without injury, yet I carried a bursting heart over every field and hedge.

He looked up from the letter and out the window. A horse and rider had clattered to a stop at his door. He knew he must hurry if he were to add this letter to the next dispatches for London.

You wrote that, despite your grandfather's prohibition, you were reading my translation of Orlando Furioso *and did like it quite well and, better, did not pick apart my words. That pleases any author.*

Readers like my books.
Yet other writers cannot them digest.
But what care I for when I make a feast,
I would my guests should praise me, not the cooks.

Yes, another of my epigrams, though one made just for your eyes.

Essex tells me with some pleasure that the queen will offer you to one of her Howard cousins. I cannot believe my godmother would force you to marry. She often has hidden purposes for her promises and as often changes her mind. When I return, I will plead with her. That leaves your grandfather, Sir William. There I take heart. If you disobey your grandsire by reading my Orlando, *I can hope you will disobey again and consent to marry me. I have found in you the qualities of mind and spirit that I would have by my side for a lifetime. Only with you am I become the man I always hoped to be and, I hope, the man you want me to be. . . .*

He heard a heavy tread upon the stairs and loud knocking, happy for the interruption before his letter took a loftier, even begging tone that would embarrass him as soon as it was in the dispatch pouch and beyond recall.

The messenger knocked again. "Sir John, my lord of Essex requires your attendance at his headquarters. At once, sir."

He thought of several true endings to his letter . . . how his last thought of the day was of her and how he saw her in every dark-haired proud Irish beauty. He wrote neither, hastily signing the letter:

John Harington, Knight

He dripped hot wax on the folded sheet. Pressing into it his signet ring, he sealed it from other eyes and slipped it into his doublet.

A fast ride through narrow Dublin streets brought him to Essex on the outskirts. His Lordship paced the great hall of the manor he'd commandeered, alternately depressed and loudly outraged. As John waited to hear why he had been summoned, Essex dismissed his officers in the room, except for the Earl of Southampton.

"This is insupportable!"

Southampton, a man with the body of a stripling and a round lady-face, nodded sympathetically. "You bear the burden of too many slurs, Robert."

Essex slammed a dispatch into John's hand. "Read this and you will see what my enemies in the council—especially that God bedamned Raleigh and Cecil—have done to my reputation while I am on Her Majesty's business, at risk of my health and very life."

John immediately recognized the queen's beautiful, flowing script in the close-written lines. Reading quickly, he saw in a minute that the queen's sarcasm and fury were on full display. Her Majesty said plainly that Essex had accomplished little and at great cost, without taking one major rebel prisoner. It was clear that she blamed him and accepted none of his many reasons or excuses. She ordered him to march north and attack Tyrone at once and not to return until it was done. *We do charge you, as you tender our plea-*

*sure, that you adventure not to come out of that kingdom without
our warrant.*

"Do you see," Essex yelled loud enough to be heard in adjoining
rooms, "how petticoat generals have little understanding of war and
no care for my health?"

John remained silent. Essex didn't expect an answer to his question. He assumed agreement. All the queen wrote was true, but
Essex was livid because she would not agree to his many reasons for
inaction and his desire to come back to court. He certainly did not
call it failure, or blame himself.

Despite long acquaintance, John was a little shocked by the earl's
recklessness. Surely the queen had her private correspondents in
this camp, and if she didn't, Robert Cecil surely had. Was Essex so
certain that he was still protected by the queen's love? Was he so
blinded by pride that he couldn't see he'd whittled away at her affection by using her forgiveness too many times? Perhaps Mary had
been right and Essex was a little mad. His next words confirmed
Mary's opinion.

"By heaven, I'll take the army and march across England to the
queen. I'll remove my enemies Cecil and his friends to the Tower.
Then the queen will act as I wish!"

John bowed and went to the door before he heard too much. It
was treason to listen to treason, and someone surely was listening
at this moment. Yet he had to try to reach Essex's rational mind for
one last time. "I beg you, my lord, think long before you take troops
against the queen or say such aloud. That means you lead a civil war
against the state and Her Majesty's rule." With no hesitation, though
John knew that he made a firm enemy with the words, he added, "I
can never join in such a scheme."

Essex glared at him, then seemed to gain some control and veer
away from rashness. "We will march into Ulster against Tyrone,"
he shouted at Southampton. "If I am killed, she will be satisfied at
last!"

Later that night, Essex, sleepless and distraught, walked among his snoring troops by torchlight. On his command, John followed behind him, fearing his mood. A man who thought himself conspired against was capable of any rash action.

It was near dawn before action came. Essex ordered a select force to set out as a diversion to draw forces away from Tyrone.

"Send me to lead them, my lord," John begged, preferring battle where he could face a real enemy than to watch this lord slowly lose his senses to inner demons.

"No, John, despite your opposition to my will, there are few men I can trust as I can trust you. I want you beside me."

"My lord," John said, bowing, amazed that Essex, who forgave no slight, had granted him so quick a pardon. Did Essex merely want to witness the death of the man who had taken a desired woman and refused to follow him into England? Essex had ever been impetuous, but not murderous. Though past behavior might not predict the future with this man who grew more reckless by the day.

At Nonsuch, the queen's fairy-tale castle her father had built south of London, Mary had withdrawn to the antechamber with the other ladies. She busied herself with folding and refolding her gowns, which now numbered a dozen, trying to ignore the raised voice she heard from inside the queen's privy chamber.

"One thousand pounds a day?" Elizabeth shouted. "God's wounds! One thousand!"

Lady Warwick shepherded several whispering ladies away from the door, but not before everyone heard the queen's words.

"Pygmy, does the Earl of Essex seek to go on a leisure trip through Ireland? He will bankrupt our treasury."

"Majesty, it appears so," said Raleigh, also with the queen and always ready to criticize his enemy when the queen was agreeable.

Though Essex was Robert Cecil's open adversary and had been

since they were boys together, Cecil spoke in his usual moderate voice. "Indeed, Majesty, there are great problems with this venture." He paused. "Now the earl seeks two thousand additional troops. It seems that the diversionary force of horse he sent into Connaught was caught crossing a bog and slaughtered to a man."

Mary's hand went to her mouth to stifle the cry that had risen to her throat. *Oh, sweet Lord,* she begged, *not John. Tell me it wasn't John.*

Cecil spoke. "I'm sorry to say that reports of Sir Conyers Clifford's death accompany the news."

"A good and loyal man," Raleigh added.

Mary stumbled back to sit upon her bed, dizzy with relief and for the first time made aware that her feelings for John had not been buried as deep as she hoped, nor had she hidden them from Lady Anne, who was staring at her.

The queen, in her inner chamber, exploded. "Good men and goodly treasure! And for what?"

"It seems that Ireland has defeated us again, Majesty," Cecil said, though in a tentative voice.

"Never," Elizabeth answered, and Mary could hear Her Majesty's feet stamping about her privy chamber and imagined her with her sword in hand.

"Your Grace, there is some good news." It was Cecil again. "My correspondents do tell me that His Lordship the earl makes preparations for an immediate march against Tyrone."

"At last we take the field, Your Grace," Raleigh echoed.

The queen was silent; then, in a lower voice but one all could hear, she said, "Cecil, tell him his queen orders him to take all care for his life."

"At once, Majesty."

Mary could easily imagine the thoughts behind Cecil's calm face and Raleigh's jealous one. The queen was pulled in two ways, one by her desire to conquer an unruly part of her realm, the other by her remaining fondness for a wild boy bequeathed to her by her Robin.

How long could she overlook that the boy was now a powerful and dangerous man with an army behind him?

Lady Warwick answered a knock on the outer chamber door and accepted a letter from a courier. She looked at it, turned it over to observe the seal and frowned. Mary stepped forward without planning to do so.

"From Dublin for you, mistress," Warwick said, holding the folded letter out to her.

Lady Margaret and the other ladies gathered round, but Mary slipped it into her kirtle, to their murmured dismay. When her duties were finished, she would go alone to a quiet place to read it unobserved, not here, where too many curious eyes watched.

Shortly, with all pomp, pounding kettledrums and trumpets, the queen marched through her palace to the presence chamber to hear the day's petitioners. Mary walked at the rear of the ladies, having the lowest position among them, though courtiers were bowing as she passed, followed by red-coated yeomen guards. As she moved forward to take her place behind the throne, she felt John's letter caressing her breast.

The presence chamber was filled with baskets of gilded fruit and draped with garlands of fresh flowers woven on cedar bark to mask the aroma of a summer palace crowded with people. Nonetheless, Elizabeth often raised her pomander.

Cecil announced the first petitioner. "Majesty, Edward Seymour, the Earl of Hertford, craves audience."

After some hesitation, the queen raised her hand in assent. "My lord, the peers of our realm are always welcome in our court."

Mary shifted to see him better. Lady Katherine's husband. The brave and handsome man who had kept her heart for a lifetime, whose name, not her hope for heaven, was the last word to pass her lips before a gush of blood from her corrupted lungs ended her breath and earthly troubles.

The now elderly earl approached slowly, using a stick to steady himself, and knelt, wincing when his bad leg settled on the unyielding marble floor.

"Your wounded leg should not rest on the cold floor. Rise, my lord."

"My thanks for your kindness, Majesty," Lord Edward said, standing.

His face was lined but still fine-featured, his gray beard streaked with the lighter color it had once been, and, with obvious effort, he kept his back straight.

Mary moved again to better see the queen. Hertford was part of an unattractive episode of Elizabeth's reign, a reminder that she had separated her close cousin, Lady Katherine Grey, from her husband and sons until her death. The aged earl also was a reminder, and perhaps the worst one, of what her magnificent gown and jewels could not veil. Her own youth was now as much a memory as the earl's young love.

"We always have a care for our old soldiers, my lord earl," the queen said, raising her black silk-and-ivory fan.

Mary appreciated the way it matched Her Majesty's black-and-white gown and tall crowned hat brimmed in the latest fashion. Chains of alternating black and white pearls wound round her neck, waist and wrists. No one could mistake the symbolism, for the colors were the universal symbol of virginity.

Edward opened a velvet-lined box containing a large and most perfect rare black pearl that shone from its core like a ripe grape penetrated by sunlight. He held it up to her, his head bowed. "This poor gift is the twin of the one I presented to Your Majesty on my first night in court. It is my hope, Your Grace, that you will accept this as a token of my love and obedience." He looked up as the queen removed the box from his hand.

"We thank you, my lord earl." She said nothing more, handing the box to Lady Warwick. Hertford looked disappointed, though she gave him a gracious nod of appreciation.

He shifted, leaning into his cane. "Your Grace, I have come to petition for my sons, Edward and William, both men now with sons of their own. I beg you to grant them legitimacy." He attempted to hand her a written petition, but Elizabeth motioned for Cecil to receive it.

"My lord of Hertford, we will study your petition when it is accompanied by the marriage contract which proves your sons' legitimacy. It is God's ordinance that makes sons legitimate and not among our earthly powers. You petitioned us not five years ago and, long before that, spent some time in the Tower for that impertinence. Do not think that your age saves you from another visit."

Hertford sagged on his stick, and Mary was afraid he would collapse. A gentleman usher stepped forward to add support and began to lead Hertford away. But the earl, with courage to spare, spoke again. "As Your Majesty wishes, but I beg you to grant me one request. I would remove Kate's body for burial at my manor of Eltham . . . for my boys' sakes."

There was no pity on the queen's face that Mary could see as she motioned the usher to lead the earl away. Elizabeth's fear of conspiring claimants to her throne was stronger as she approached her end than it had been long years ago, when she had sent Kate and Edward to the Tower.

Elizabeth stood, signaling that she would hear no more petitions that day, and they all returned to the queen's privy chamber, where Cecil's secretary waited with fresh news from Ireland.

"Is the battle won?" the queen asked, her body sagging with a fatigue she would not acknowledge.

Cecil scanned the dispatch and handed it to Elizabeth without a word. In seconds, the queen exploded in anger. "A truce until May! What accomplished? All my treasure and good English blood gone for naught! Tyrone has walked away from a dozen such truces." Her face as red as her lips, the queen seemed to weaken and sat suddenly at her writing table.

"A little wine for Her Majesty," Cecil called, and Mary responded quickly, presenting the glass on her knees.

Elizabeth took it with a hand she'd made steady with her great will, and sipped, hiding her face.

She lowered the glass. "My Lord Secretary," the queen said, holding up the dispatch, "we will discuss this further with you in the council chamber at three of the clock, but we do not mean to ignore this disobedience by Lord Essex; indeed, we dare not."

Cecil and his messenger bowed and backed away.

Lady Warwick motioned the ladies to withdraw and they all walked quickly into the antechamber, leaving the door slightly ajar to listen for the queen's call.

Mary looked back and saw that Her Majesty had closed her eyes and rested her head against the high back of her upholstered chair, nothing to be read in her expression. She had long ago learned to hide her thoughts from her face.

Mary hoped she had showed a tenth part of Elizabeth's skill later, when she asked Lady Warwick if she might take the air in the courtyard garden and made her way toward that exit. It had rained earlier and swept clean the rough-cobbled palace courtyards. She turned away from the smooth gravel garden paths laid in geometric patterns, drawn out into the open by the fresh scent of rolling fields and woods. She swung out through one of the four-story gates into the north pasture, which was filled with tents and frolicking dogs. Nonsuch was not as large as Whitehall or Richmond, and many lesser courtiers had to live as they could. She took the carriage road toward the wooded hills, where she might find solitude and read John's letter without raising questions.

"Mistress Rogers."

She looked up to see the Earl of Hertford approaching slowly. She curtsied. "My lord."

"A word, if you please, Mistress Rogers. You were with my Kate for many years."

"As a very young child, my lord."

"Was her death"—he breathed deeply—"an easy one?"

"Very peaceful, my lord earl," she lied.

His mouth relaxed, though she suspected he would question her answer later, since everyone knew that the bloody coughing death was never easy.

He bowed and walked away.

"My lord," she called softly.

He stopped, but did not turn back to her.

"*Ned* was the word on her last breath before she saw heaven's gate open to her."

Hertford grasped his stick tighter and walked on slowly, though Mary heard him mutter, still defiant, "I will soon be with her where God rules."

Wondering if she had said the right words, and if they would bring future solace or hurt, Mary moved toward the woods to be alone, to hear no command, no entreaty, no sly hint . . . the daily currency of the court. She stepped well into leafy shade and shafts of light under an old oak, kissed John's signet seal on her letter, then broke it and slowly read the single sheet. Every word was so like him, she heard his voice speaking. She lifted the paper to her nose, trying to catch his scent, but there was only leather from the pouch and the salt of the Irish Sea. Distance had shed what there had been of him, except his words. She leaned against the rough bark and slid down, not thinking about her gown, and sat in leaves to read the letter again. And again.

Michaelmas Eve
September 28, 1599

Early in the morning, just after sunrise, John, exhausted and covered with the dust of hard travel from Dublin, arrived at the ferry to Lambeth with Essex and a half dozen of his handpicked friends. John was certain he had been included in the party because His Lordship thought the queen's liking for her godson would soften her anger at his return from Ireland against her express orders, nearly a treasonous action in itself. John wasn't so sure he could help Essex or wanted to. He was also not at all satisfied that Essex and the eager lords around him were not prompted to rebellion, or some bold act against the queen's person. Their speech was rash and, if overheard, surely would be counted treason. They talked of killing Robert Cecil and reducing Elizabeth to a puppet queen with Essex as the real power.

John knew he had to reach the queen first or be suspect himself.

At Lambeth, Essex seized fresh horses and headed for Nonsuch, ten miles south of London. A rider, whom John recognized as Lord Grey of Wilton, passed them at a gallop, refusing Essex's shouted orders to stop.

"Let me go after him," Sir Christopher St. Lawrence begged. "I will kill him and afterward Cecil."

"I forbid it," Essex said, and John saw that Essex was suddenly aware that such an act would be unforgivable and had stepped back from the brink. But Essex was half-crazed and might change his mind in the next minute.

"My lord," John shouted, "I have the best horse. I will follow Grey and command him in your name not to speak of your arrival at court."

"Go, John, and block Grey's way to Cecil."

Eager to escape the escalating madness, John spurred his horse toward the dust cloud, though he knew he would never overtake Lord Grey of Cecil's party, who now smelled trouble and was whipping his horse to a furious gallop.

Reaching the main entrance towers at Nonsuch, with its enormous stucco wall painting of Henry VIII as Zeus on his throne, John clattered into the cobbled courtyard. He turned right toward the stables, throwing his reins to a groom and running on stiff legs toward Cecil's office. The secretary was eating breakfast with one hand and writing one of his endless papers with the other.

"Sir John," he said, half standing as John burst upon him.

"Essex is hard by the gate, Cecil, and his mood is such that you should warn the queen." John collapsed into a chair to take needed breath.

"Lord Grey has been and gone in haste and reported as much." Cecil seated himself, but made no further move.

"My Lord Secretary," John pleaded, "did you not hear what I said?"

"Yes, Sir John, I have had communications from Ireland since he arrived. I know what was done and not done and what was said in his closest councils. I have been ready for the earl since he left Ireland, and was troubled to hear you were among his men." He shrugged. "The guard has already been doubled around the queen, though I didn't alarm her by making it obvious."

John was not surprised, but he was upset to have his loyalty doubted. "I have served my godmother always, my Lord Secretary."

Cecil nodded and dipped his pen into the ink. "I know that as well."

John clambered up, swaying with fatigue. "Stop Essex and the hotheaded scoundrels around him, or you send him to his doom."

"He sends himself, Sir John. No one can save Essex from Essex. It was always going to end this way."

Cecil sat as straight as his crooked back would allow and smiled.

John summoned energy he thought had fled and flung himself away, running down endless halls, through the presence chamber and into the queen's antechamber. He meant to warn the queen, to protect Mary from desperate men . . . to do something, anything to interfere with events that were now cascading beyond control.

The queen's antechamber doors stood open, the guards stationed near the presence chamber down the hall. They should be nearer.

Surely Cecil would not endanger the queen to trap Essex. Or would he?

John walked into the antechamber, knocking on the inner privy chamber door, his hand on his sword, ready to draw if necessary. "Majesty, my lord Essex swiftly approaches," he called.

Inside the Queen's bedchamber Mary heard John's voice with relief. He was here. She would see him, touch him. Then she saw Elizabeth's eyes grow wide, wounded, her hand jerking to her face. The queen touched what Mary saw, what everyone saw, felt what she had not been able to look at since banning all mirrors: her puffy eyes in her sagging face.

Elizabeth clutched at her brilliant blue embroidered silk morning robe, open and showing her ashen neck. Wisps of gray hair straggled from under her nightcap. Elizabeth was abruptly more distraught woman than queen.

Essex, his rough clothes covered with dust, his face exhausted, but still impossibly handsome and boyish, opened the privy chamber door without knocking and rushed in, his men crowding close behind him.

John, held by Sir Christopher in the antechamber, twisted out of his grip and slipped inside, standing to one side of Essex's men, separating himself, his hand on the hilt of his weapon, alert to any sudden moves.

The earl knelt and began to swear his love and duty in a choked voice. "Your Grace, I must speak."

The queen gripped the table before her. "Say on," she said, her voice unlike Mary had ever heard it.

"Majesty, it is beyond the strength of any man to be absent from your beauty for so long. I have gained for you an end to the Irish rebellion, as you commanded, led men to their death for your honor. Now I find I cannot breathe without the sun of your person shining on me. I am more yours at this moment than any man."

Mary's hands were frozen in midair, holding the queen's curled wig, her eyes on John's face to see if he was well, unwounded. Then the queen's hand jerked to her breast to cover her heart. Elizabeth was in fear for her life.

Lady Warwick, obviously stunned by this astonishing intrusion at such an hour and into the center of the queen's privacy, moved to protect the queen with her own body, but as suddenly as fear had descended on them, it lifted.

The queen's face softened with a slightly tremulous but fond smile. "My lord, I see you as you are. You see me as I am. Now go and refresh yourself while I finish my toilet. Return later and we will talk much of the Irish adventure."

Essex, pouring out more words of longing, his shoulders slumping with what Mary thought must be relief at this reception, rose and backed from the chamber. He looked at John with an air of triumph and, before the doors to the antechamber closed, Mary saw that John looked a warning to her . . . or a question . . . or more she could not read, but hoped she could guess. She must see him alone. He had been so close, across a room, and yet as far as he had been for months.

"Boy Jack," the queen called, regaining her full voice and courage. "I believe you innocent of any foul intention."

"Godmother, never in my life have I acted or had a thought to act against your royal person."

Elizabeth nodded. "Follow my lord Essex and see that he goes to his quarters, then quietly send Cecil to me *at once*."

"At once, Majesty," John said, bowing, and left, though Mary could see that his body sagged with fatigue. She longed to speak to him, to be pulled into the warmth of his arms. Soon, pray God, soon.

"Lock the doors," the queen shouted at the gentlemen ushers and yeoman guards whom Essex and his followers had bypassed, probably by coming through the servants' hall.

Mary, the wig in her hands, stood behind Elizabeth and saw that the queen's counterfeit welcoming smile had been replaced by taut relief. Mary saw no affection for Essex there.

"He saw me like *this*?" The words, sad and wondering, violated, trailed away. The queen took one deep breath. "Dress us quickly," she said, and it was her regal dignity that spoke, swallowing the betrayed woman's voice.

Two hours later, when Essex returned alone, the queen waited in her apartment, wearing a gown of true silver threads and a pendant necklace of three huge emeralds. She graciously gave him her hand and allowed him to sit opposite her, while Anne Warwick, Lady Margaret, Mary and the other ladies were arrayed behind the queen's chair. Silently, yeomen guards with long pikes stationed themselves inside both privy chamber doors, their eyes never leaving the earl.

Her Majesty spoke for some time with Essex as he explained his troubles with the Irish and personal fevers and sundry ailments, obviously delighted with his now cordial reception, flirting with Elizabeth and her ladies in turn.

"Majesty," Essex said as he knelt to depart, "after the many storms of battle in Ireland, your loving soldier is happy to find such sweet calm in you again."

But Mary knew he would find neither sweetness nor calm. She'd heard Elizabeth give orders to Cecil to put him under doubled guard and call him before the council that afternoon to give account of his actions in Ireland, especially his disregard of the queen's orders. For hours, it was reported later, he had only excuses, admitting to no fault of his own, blaming others, including John Harington. The council listened and voted against him. This handsome favorite had at last gone too far and fallen. Even his friends would not speak for him.

Essex was commanded to keep to his chambers. And the queen, always fearful, ordered Cecil to watch for any suspicious troop movements in London. No one yet knew if all or part of Essex's army was loyal to him and followed close behind him. His falseness raised fears in a queen who had been weaned and raised on lies and fear, a queen who knew how an ambitious and impatient man's mind worked.

The next morning, after reports from the west and in the city assured the queen that no such contingent loyal to Essex was abroad, she ordered Lord Keeper Edgerton to take Essex a prisoner to York House in the Strand. She refused to see him or read his letters of love and submission. "We have read and heard all his words before," she said aloud to no one in particular, "once finding them delightful and moving, but now knowing them to be empty."

As Mary backed away, she heard the queen murmur again and again as if commanding her heart, "Strike or be stricken. Strike or be stricken." Essex would not be pardoned this time.

Later that day, in answer to a passing whispered invitation, Mary managed to slip into the woods near Nonsuch to meet John. He was waiting in the grove where she had read his last letter, leaning against an oak tree.

"Come," he said, lifting his arms to enclose her. "The shade is cool, but I am warm."

She laughed and ran into his embrace. He lifted her, swinging her about, careless of who might see, holding her so tight she could scarce draw breath.

"John, oh, John, have a care that we are not seen."

"I cannot, with you so close at last."

She caught her breath. "You didn't find the Irish maids pretty?" It was a jest, but an answer she needed.

"I didn't look."

She laughed, not believing him and wanting to believe him together.

A party of courtiers came strolling on the carriage road near the woods.

He pulled her deeper into the shade, kissing her face, her hands, and taking her lips again in a searing kiss. He stopped and loosed her a little to let her breathe. "Earlier when I saw you—"

"John, I wanted so much to run to you when you came to warn the queen."

"Sweetheart, I feared for you, as well as Her Majesty, knowing Essex was half-mad with worry and hating you above all women. He knew that too many reports of his conduct had come to the queen." He kissed her again and they forgot Essex for as long as they could.

"Essex is finished," she said against his lips, not wishing to be even the slightest distance from him.

They stood in silence to let another group of strollers pass, but one man stopped to look inside the glade.

"Soon, my love," John promised, and strode quickly to the carriage road. "Ho, Sir Josiah," he said, drawing the group away.

As she tended to her duties in the palace, Mary saw everyone wondering and wagering how many days or weeks it would take the queen to forgive Essex this time. When Mary returned to the ladies' chamber, Anne Warwick motioned for her to come close.

"The queen wishes to speak to you at once . . . and alone."

My sweet Lord! She had been observed. But at Mary's indrawn breath, the countess reassured her: "Nothing to worry you, my dear."

After a quick tug on her kirtle and a glance in the ladies' mirror to see that no leaves clung to her gown and her ruff was straight, she entered the bedchamber as quietly as possible. The queen often forgot that she had called for a lady and was displeased to be disturbed. But this evening she sat close to her fire as she had during their first meeting. Mary approached and knelt.

Elizabeth looked up, distracted. "Mouse?" she asked, not completely focused. Mary had no doubt what had occupied the queen's mind to bring such sadness to her face, and she remembered seeing it before. It was the face of lasting loss that only a death, or something as permanent as death, could bring. She had seen it before on her grandfather's face when her father was killed and when Lady Katherine Grey wrote to her Ned.

"Your Grace," Mary said.

"You are an unaffected, sweet-tempered maid, Mary Rogers, and we are well pleased with you. Lady Warwick has high regard for your diligence."

"Majesty, to serve you well is my happiness." It was not a lie, but not the whole truth, either.

The queen smiled ironically and took a deep breath. "If you wish to serve us well, give up all notion of Boy Jack."

Mary did not raise her head because the queen would see everything confirmed in her face. Of course, Cecil opened all the dispatches and reported their content to the queen.

"Do not mistake us. We love the rogue dearly, but we would be a natural mother to you and warn you from unsuitable men . . . although we grant you have had a settling effect on Jack. We would see you rewarded as you deserve for your caring of us. We have in mind for you our distant cousin Lord Matthew Howard, a lesser member of that family, but good advancement for you, in our eyes."

Before showing her face to the queen, Mary made an effort to compose it. "Majesty, is it true that Lady Howard yet lives?"

"That unfortunate lady has a growth in her belly that has not proved to be a babe at her years. You will be mistress of a great northern manor. His Lordship has already spoken of you with me."

Mary felt her clasped hands tighten at her waist. Such a lord, who looked for a replacement before his current wife had suffered to her end, was not a good man, to her mind. A graybeard, he must be approaching fifty years.

The queen smiled, rightly reading her thoughts. "Men of any age do not like to be without a bedmate."

As if Mary's life were now completely written, the queen added, "We are promoting you from mistress of the stool to mistress of the sweet herbs. You will have care of our body linen, a great responsibility. And one final duty . . . the care of our ivory treasure chest." She motioned to her bedside table to the small carved box that she always kept near her in the same place in every palace. No one knew what was in it, but everyone guessed it to be precious.

Mary forced a smile. "I thank you, Majesty, for this honor, but who will care for your closestool?"

"The grooms, having been taught well by you, will have their post again. We intend Sir John to install his water closets in all our palaces, and it is more fitting that a groom should travel and work with him." The queen looked away and into the fire, a signal that she had no more to say.

Mary stood, curtsied, and backed out of the chamber. Before she could quietly close the door, Elizabeth spoke again: "You may now wear our miniature, Mouse."

Warwick waited just inside the ladies' antechamber. "Congratulations, mistress of the sweet herbs, and when you wear her portrait brooch all will know how the queen loves you." The countess looked closer. "But why so gloomy? You've been promoted to the queen's third lady of the bedchamber and promised a titled, landed lord who will have the salt tax when he takes you." Anne lifted Mary's chin. "And here I read nothing but misery on your pretty face."

"No, my lady—"

"But yes, mistress," Warwick said, lightly mocking. "Yours is a very old story. Think you that you are the first to form an unsuitable attachment that the queen must save you from in her greater wisdom?"

Mary looked at her with new understanding. "You, Lady Anne?"

Warwick shrugged. "Long ago and all for the best. Leicester's brother, the Earl of Warwick, was a good man and good husband to me, though we were not blessed with children."

"Who was this unsuitable man, my lady?"

"I have forgotten," she said, and turned away.

Mary sensed rather than heard that the countess had lied to herself for so long that she had passed into believing the lie. Mary wondered if that always happened and hoped that the countess was proof that it did and that it would be so for her. Unless there was a way to deny the queen's good care of her, and she couldn't think of any.

The new mistress of the sweet herbs was not sure of anything later that night. Passing by John's rooms on an errand for Lady Margaret, Mary was unable to stop herself from looking inside when she found the door open. Her gaze had turned there without any command from her head.

He was standing by his narrow bed in an open shirt, breeches and bare feet, smiling at her, appearing as she wanted ever to remember him. He bowed.

She curtsied.

He motioned her inside, and in spite of the danger of being seen and reported for entering his apartment, she obeyed as if on a leash. "I didn't have time to ask you earlier, but did you get my last letter from Dublin, Mary, Mary, quite contrary?"

"Yes, John." And she laughed in spite of her apprehension.

"Were you going to answer it?"

"All dispatches are read by Cecil," she said.

"Shut the door," he ordered.

"No, John."

He grinned. "'Yes, John, no, John.' Are you afraid of what I'll do?" he asked, moving rapidly toward her, his arms outstretched.

"Of what I'll do, and it cannot be, John. It cannot," she repeated, and fled, half hoping that he would follow, though it was only her own feet she heard echoing in the marble hall.

CHAPTER THIRTEEN

"Affection? Affection's false!"
—*Elizabeth Regina*

Accession Day
November 17, 1599
Whitehall Palace

$\mathcal{M}$ary managed her side-skittering white mare as the Tower cannon saluted the queen's entourage entering the city's crowded streets across London Bridge from Southwark. Citizens lined their way, calling, "God save Your Majesty." In return, Elizabeth waved on each side and up to the highest windows, shouting, "God bless you all, my good people." Mary knew that the queen's greeting was her heart's truth. She loved her people, the richly dressed nobles waving from their grand gilt-painted town houses, the shopkeepers by their ware benches and the ragged beggars kneeling on the broken cobbles, loved them as if they were all the children she'd denied herself.

The forty-first anniversary of the queen's accession to the throne was a holiday for all the people. The queen continued to smile and wave to her subjects past St. Paul's and down Cheapside toward Ludgate. She sat her prancing black hunter superbly as flowers were thrown under its hooves, forming a fragrant carpet to be crushed atop the refuse running in the gutter midstreet. The scent of roses masked even the rank odor of the tanneries near the Fleet River.

Passing York House on the Strand, the queen turned her head away and called out no greeting. Mary did not see Essex's face in a window, but knew the queen thought he might be lurking out of sight. He was said to be ailing, but no one knew from what cause, other than his total loss of the queen's favor. He had always been disposed to unknown illness when, after a quarrel, he was sent from court, and Elizabeth, knowing this, tried to keep her heart from being engaged by his yearning young face.

Everyone held their breath as to what would come next between angry sovereign and a disgraced former favorite, though the queen seemed in no hurry to decide, unable to settle for very long between melancholy and fury. Fortunes had already been wagered on the possibilities, with the most money bet on her forgiveness and the earl's reinstatement to all his former high positions, as had always previously happened. This time, Mary was not so sure. She had sensed Elizabeth's heart slowly hardening these past two months.

Cecil remained reserved, waiting for the queen's decision. Mary overheard the Lord Secretary remark that advice to Her Majesty often brought trouble to the adviser, and she observed the truth of those words in what followed.

Raleigh and Francis Bacon did not heed Cecil, each for his own reason. Raleigh, obviously the earl's enemy and unable to hide it, strongly advised the queen at every turn to prosecute. The queen was often angry with Sir Walter, because his judgment was frequently faulty and he would invariably criticize Essex when the queen was in her downhearted mood, forcing her to the earl's defense, which annoyed her greatly.

Bacon, once an Essex follower, was more subtle, and used lawyerly argument, keeping the queen's interest. "Your Grace," he reasoned, "His Lordship has clearly gone very far this time, and tried your forbearance to the limit."

"Quite so," the queen said, pleased to be understood, though Mary knew a courtier's understanding wasn't essential to Elizabeth.

"On the other hand, Majesty," Bacon reasoned, "his prosecution without clear proof of treason could anger the more unruly citizens of London, who are always ready to erupt in riot. The public temper, Your Grace, ever seeks expression."

All this Mary saw and heard, while knowing Bacon's arguments for and against prosecution echoed the queen's own indecision and encouraged her to weigh his opinions as much a match for her own. And, without doubt, caused her to consider him for a position on her council, which all the court knew he sought. Though he had influence, Mary determined she would never seek Bacon's opinion about John, since he gave answers to please, not always the best advice for queen or subject. She already had too many such reactions swirling in her own mind when she was with John. And when she wasn't. How could she defy the queen, a woman anointed by God whose will was law, making all defiance treasonous? Mary's grandfather might give his consent to John in time. But how much time did she have? Back and forth. Back and forth. Her tangled thoughts allowed her no rest.

As the long royal train rumbled into King Street and through the Holbein Gate into Whitehall, the ladies left the grooms and gentlemen ushers to place all the queen's furnishings. After decades of moving from palace to palace, each man, many of them the sons of her first grooms, knew his duties. Mary quickly followed Elizabeth and her other ladies to the long stone gallery overlooking the tiltyard, where the queen and her ladies traditionally watched all tournaments below.

The moment Her Majesty appeared in the window, trumpets heralded her coming and a knight in full polished armor on a richly caparisoned horse rode up the gallery steps to proclaim the day:

> *"In honor of our queen's holiday*
> *A gracious sport, fitting this golden time*
> *The day, the birthday of our happiness,*
> *The blooming time, the spring of England's peace."*

The queen waved, thanked the knight and motioned Londoners in the bleachers to sit. At once trumpets proclaimed the entry of pairs of knights and their squires, most on horses, but one lord sitting astride a float built like a dragon who entered to great applause.

The tilt began and the weather stayed coldly crisp and clear.

Mary waited, her heartbeat mounting noticeably as John, his armor burnished to bright silver, took the field on a large dappled gray. His lance was tied round with black and white handkerchiefs, the symbol of virginity. Was it a tribute to the virgin queen or to Mary Rogers, or to all the court ladies who remained virgins or appeared to do so? Clever rogue! Each woman could think as she liked and only John would know. Mary suppressed a smile when she saw Elizabeth look pleased and nod. How could Mary's woman-heart not adore such a man? Indeed, it was apparently impossible, since her hands were trembling, moist and warm.

On the first pass down the S-shaped barrier, John and his opponent's lances both missed. At the turn, John took up another lance, lowered his visor and, following the trumpet's sound, spurred his horse to a full gallop. Mary felt her nails bite into her palms. John's lance shattered on his challenger's shield and, without thought of her own risk in doing so, Mary rushed forward toward the open window, her legs having a will of their own. Such a sharp blow was dangerous to both men.

John reined in and rode around the barrier to the other knight, who had dropped his lance and swayed in the saddle. John valiantly held his opponent upright as they rode from the lists to applause from all the people who had paid their shilling to sit in the bleachers.

Lady Anne was at Mary's back, whispering urgently, "Return to your place at once, mistress."

Mary obeyed, stepping back behind the queen, who did not look at her, though she knew that the queen was probably aware of which knight had drawn her forward. Mary glanced up at the brilliant painting of Moses on the ceiling. Would that she had such wisdom.

Could Elizabeth understand that Mary, too, was torn between love for a man and her duty to the sovereign? Surely the queen could see how alike women were, no matter what their station.

It was five of the clock when the tilt ended and those knights not too bruised or injured retired to the great hall for a feast with the court, the queen and her ladies. A fool with a belled cap led a monkey dressed in a gown and ruff from table to table, introducing the animal as the Duchess of Egypt, to the general merriment.

Her Majesty, as usual, was seated on the dais, taking a little of the many dishes offered, then eating only a bite or two of each. Drinking her watered wine in small sips, she graciously received each knight in turn. When John approached, his gaze on Mary, the queen greeted him fondly: "My gallant Boy Jack."

"Majesty," he said, kneeling.

"We congratulate you on your victory today, Sir Knight, but do think your talents wasted in the tiltyard. Your future fortune surely lies in the jakes." Laughter swept down the hall.

John grinned and seemed to grow taller, though he knelt. "It's not every day, Your Grace, that a poor knight can lay claim to more gaiety than a fool with a monkey."

The queen raised her hand for silence. "Boy Jack, do not mistake us. We are well pleased with your water closet and bid you build one in each of our palaces of Windsor and Greenwich. When you have finished, you may return to us." The queen had spoken loudly enough for all to hear, and again with barely suppressed amusement.

John stood and bowed with great flair. "Most well-loved godmother, I thank you with all my heart. Dame Fortune, men say, gives too much to many, but never gives enough to any."

Mary gripped her chair. Oh, sweet Lord, another epigram, this one aimed at Elizabeth. And maybe Essex? How did he dare? He could be banished permanently.

But John had not mistaken Elizabeth. Clever impudence engaged her humor always. She smiled, then covered it with her fan, dismissing him with a wave of her hand. When John turned his head from the queen to glare at the diners lining the tables, the laughter ceased.

But the queen would have the final word. She called to Cecil before John had taken a seat at a lower table. "My Lord Secretary, send word that we desire the Lord Howard to attend us next month for Advent festivities and before Twelfth Night. I would have him meet a certain lady."

Those in the court who did not know the gossip beyond John's giving up his wager with Essex for the first bedding of Mary Rogers knew more now when they heard the queen and looked from John to Mary.

There was a buzz of whispers around the tables.

The next morning John left again on the queen's service. Mary watched him adjust his bridle and stirrups from a shadowed seat overlooking the stable yard, and although he looked back toward the palace, he could not see her. She leaned heavily against the stone wall, needing support as he rode out, the dust and strewn hay he stirred quickly settling. Another month or even two without him. And what more? Would Lady Howard die and Mary Rogers's betrothal be announced during Christmastide, when that lord was at court? Or would her marriage be celebrated? It was a great honor for the queen to attend a lady's wedding, since she disliked them so. Others would be envious.

Mary looked far down the Thames, thinking to see the Tower, understanding at the thought of such a marriage what it was to be a prisoner for life.

On November twenty-eighth, late in the afternoon before the supper ceremony, the queen called Cecil to her. Mary labored with the queen's personal and bed linen in the closet, folding clothes just delivered by the queen's washerwomen. Placing them in the press, an ingenious machine that lowered one plate on a screw to rest tight against another plate, flattening all the wrinkles, she then separated the personal from the bed linen and laid them in their separate chests with small cloth bags of dried rose petals and violets between the layers. Lavender would have been sweetest, but the queen could no longer abide the heavy scent.

"Majesty," Cecil said, his long, narrow face purposeful as always, "I have brought several documents for signing."

Mary heard him clearly through the open doors to the queen's antechamber.

"Not now, Pygmy. We have decided to see for ourselves if my lord Essex is truly too ill to answer the charges we will bring against him in Star Chamber, with or without his presence."

Cecil hesitated, and Mary could sense him carefully choosing his words. "Your Grace, the people might be better satisfied if he were allowed to openly answer."

Following a long silence, the queen, unable to keep all bitterness from her tone, asked, "Is he yet so much their hero?"

"Your Grace, they remember him from the heroic attack on Cádiz harbor and the taking of that town."

Elizabeth replied impatiently, and Mary wondered if the queen were advancing on the chair where her sword customarily hung. Did she use it as a symbol of her power, as when the sword of state was carried before her in procession? Or was it the only way an old queen could express serious anger without fear of fainting?

But the queen was speaking, her tone ever more fierce. ". . .and do they not remember his more recent great failures off the Azores, when he missed the Spanish fleet because he sought personal glory over following his sovereign's orders, and again, of late, in Ireland for the same reason? This much-too-mighty lord will be tamed, sir! I rule here!"

Cecil hesitated again, and Mary sensed that great intellect atop the twisted body working on a careful response. "Majesty, the people need their faith in heroes, someone to lift them out of their daily miseries and offer them purpose. When their hearts are invested in such a man, it is difficult for them to give him up, no matter what his exposed failures. They simply dismiss them."

Mary held an embroidered silk night shift in midair, expecting to hear the queen fly into a jealous rage. She was relieved by a thoughtful answer.

"You are wise, Pygmy. We made no mistake in you, or our worthy Spirit, your father. Yet we must see for ourselves if he is truly ill, for he *will* answer the flaunting of his sovereign's orders. And to my face!"

"Majesty, your doctor reported him near death."

"Doctors are fools. We will judge, and will require Lord Worcester to attend us with two of our ladies. Tell him to meet us at our barge."

"As you will, Majesty."

Mary heard the doors close behind him. Finished with the linen chests, she rose and silently entered the room where Elizabeth sat.

"Mouse, you and Lady Warwick will accompany us. Cloak yourselves."

"Yes, Your Grace." Mary curtsied and stepped quietly into the ladies' antechamber, where the Countess of Warwick was already donning a suede rain cloak.

They traveled by the queen's barge, the bargemen fighting the outgoing tide running fast, and at dusk ascended the river stairs at York House. Mary looked up at Essex House next door, facing the Strand with a garden running to the Thames. A woman in black mourning stood in a rear window, watching. Mary looked a question to Lady Anne, who nodded and mouthed, *His wife*. The queen seemed to pay no notice. Why would she? She had ordered Essex to be held in York House, next to his own Essex House, but not to allow visitors of any kind, least of all his wife.

For a moment, Mary's heart ached for Lady Essex, so near her husband. Her Majesty was still firm in keeping them apart, allowing no loving comfort or extra support by his friends to the man who had betrayed her own love and friendship. Mary imagined herself standing in some northern manor window, looking out, remembering, regretting, and drew her cloak tighter about her body against the chill.

Lord Keeper Edgerton rushed from a rear door with a lantern and knelt. "Majesty, I did not know you were coming, or I would—"

The queen barely acknowledged him. "Take us to Lord Essex."

Edgerton bowed the queen through numerous halls and doors to an upper floor. "He rests here, Majesty. I have provided him with the best physicians in London—"

"Yes. Yes. We do not doubt it. Is there a side door, where we may see without being seen?"

"This way, Your Grace," Edgerton replied, bobbing nervously up and down.

Mary and Lady Anne followed Elizabeth as she was ushered into a large paneled room, a merry fire burning in an open fireplace. The queen threw off her cloak, which Mary caught, and motioned for the side door to be opened. "A little only," she commanded in a tone much softer than her usual one of command.

Her Majesty looked inside the bedchamber, holding to the silver door latch. Mary could just catch a glimpse of the Earl of Essex's head on stacked pillows, his face as white as the fine Flemish lace behind the flowing russet curls. His beard had been shaved, giving him an even more impossible youth than usual, though he approached thirty and two.

Essex turned his head slowly toward Elizabeth, and his feverish huge eyes pulled the queen toward him. She opened the door wide to allow for her skirts, walked in and shut it softly.

Lord Worcester and Edgerton retreated to a small table across the room near to the fire to sit uneasily at a card game of primera, ready to leap up at the queen's summons.

Lady Anne took Mary's arm and led her to a window looking out on the Strand, which was busy with the cries of the last of the day's fish sellers, the peddlers with hearth brooms and old shoes and the first of the roistering tavern crowds. At the corner, apprentices on late errands for their masters loitered to watch a man juggling three torches, which cast bouncing light on the scene. The two women observed all below in silence for a few minutes.

Lady Warwick sagged and leaned her forehead against the cold, thick leaded diamond panes, one hand squeezing high on her left arm.

"My lady," Mary said, alarmed, "are you ill? May I call for a chair or a little mulled wine?"

"No, my dear, just a passing pain. I am coming on old age," she explained with a faint smile. "I beg you, do not trouble yourself."

But Mary *was* troubled. Lady Anne's face had gone quite pale, so the pain must have been sharp. Before Mary could think to stop herself from such a liberty, she had taken Anne's hand in both of hers and gently chafed it.

The countess lifted her head, her lips trembling slightly. "You are a good girl, despite your misplaced desire for that charming scoundrel John Harington." Her strength returning, she gripped Mary's hand. "Promise me that you will always stand by her."

Mary knew Lady Anne meant the queen. "Is Her Grace—"

"No, no, but betrayal of her affection by anyone has always sent her into a deep sadness. Betrayal is the same as death to her. She still weeps for Leicester, William Cecil and Kat Ashley, her nurse, all of whom served her so well, but"—Lady Anne's eyes sparkled with mischief—"died without royal consent when she would have had them serve her forever." The countess was suddenly serious again. "Promise me you will not deny her wishes. I ask this only of you, not the other ladies, because I know you love her, too. She sleeps not, eats little and declines alarmingly."

Mary had observed these things in the queen, but before she

could think fully what that promise would mean, she whispered, "I do promise to serve Her Majesty faithfully as she needs me, my lady."

Lady Anne closed her eyes to rest for a moment, obviously relieved.

The door to Essex's bedchamber swung slowly open and they all moved quickly to attend the queen.

But the door had not been securely latched. Elizabeth remained bent over the earl's bed, her hand in his.

Anne Warwick barred the way inside and Lord Worcester and Edgerton returned to their card table. Both Mary and Anne looked away from the intimate inner scene, though Mary knew that she would carry a clear picture in her mind. She doubted she would ever forget the shadowy, candlelit room, the queen's sad face matching the earl's for pallor . . . his hand in hers, or hers in his. She could not know who had reached out to the other first.

And who ailed more here? Mary wondered. She had seen no tears on any cheek. Perhaps both Essex and Elizabeth were beyond tears, each thinking of the other's perfidy and yearning for a return to earlier times, when both had been headstrong without paying so great a price.

Moments later, they followed Elizabeth through the halls and down the lantern-lit stairs. The queen spoke in a soft voice to Edgerton as they approached her barge. "My lord, we grant Lady Essex the right to visit her husband during daylight hours."

Lady Anne glanced at Mary with the silent message, *Her heart has softened.*

Yet could even those closest to her really know the queen's heart?

In her barge, Elizabeth sat very straight in her high-backed chair, facing the cold, whipping wind off the wintry river not yet frozen, seabirds hovering under the lanterns on the prow, their heads under their wings, waves pounding against the oars as the bargemen pulled to the Whitehall water stairs. The queen held her sable cloak trimmed in ermine tight about her slight figure laden with jewels and lace. Resting her feet on a beautifully dyed Persian carpet, she stared into the middle distance toward the approaching shore, her face set as hard as veined marble. Then all heard her voice, above the wind, commanding, rasping out the words: "My lord Worcester, summon Cecil and Bacon to us on our return to the palace. Tomorrow, we will have our council read out in Star Chamber an account of my lord of Essex's failures to fulfill his duties, his shameful treaty with Tyrone and his defiance of our commands. We would have our people know of his delinquencies and the cause of our just anger."

In the days that followed, all that the queen charged was made public and accepted by the lords and lawyers of Star Chamber. Essex stood trembling and white faced to answer and deny each charge in turn.

Citizens were invited to attend, and the queen later checked the list of those who had witnessed the proceedings and noted those who had not, afterward counting those who refused to attend enemies of hers and friends of Essex.

By mid-December, Lady Warwick became too ill to continue her duties, though the queen kept her in a near apartment and visited her daily. The doctors had prescribed bleeding and purging, braziers for extra heat and no unwholesome fresh air, but Anne grew weaker. She could no longer walk and her mouth drooped to one side.

Elizabeth often spoon-fed the countess the broth she refused from other hands, and brought her green bottles of the Queen's Own Physick, which Anne swore gave her greater ease than any other.

Mary often accompanied the queen, heartsick to see both great ladies in such a sad state, Anne dying and the queen trying to intervene with God by willing her trusted friend back to health.

"Majesty," Anne whispered, "do not disturb yourself."

"Pish! This is nothing, Anne."

When Lady Warwick could swallow no longer and seemed to sleep, the queen rose and Mary followed her to the door.

Lady Anne roused herself enough to speak scarcely understandable words. "Mary Rogers, remember your promise to me."

"I will remember, my lady," Mary answered just loud enough for Lady Anne, who heard and fell back on her pillow, her eyes closed.

Elizabeth gathered her skirts as the door was opened on her approach. "What promise, Mouse?"

Mary blushed. "To always care for you, Your Grace."

"And your answer?"

"That I would ever faithfully serve you."

The queen walked on, her head bowed, Mary suspected to hide unbidden tears.

In the week following, a newcomer to the queen's service, Lady Fitton, daughter of an earl, joined the queen's ladies who walked out with Her Majesty of a morning and served her in the presence chamber. Lady Margaret had taken Lady Warwick's place as mistress of the wardrobe, though no lady could take Anne's place in the queen's heart.

Mary was content with her promotion to mistress of the sweet herbs. What could be better than dealing in herbs and silks and the finest Bruges lace? She thought it the best job of all. No one served the queen's body closer than Mary Rogers.

Lady Fitton was the image of Her Majesty's preference in the women who attended her, young and beautifully decorative, though perhaps not as submissive as the queen first thought. It was obvious to Mary that Lady Fitton was more of a brilliant flirt than Elizabeth realized.

Mary tried to warn the new lady that she played a dangerous game, but Lady Fitton's mind was so intent upon finding a grand husband that she laughed at Mary, who did not press her concerns further. How could she, when John had urged her to meet him at the Bell's Inn on Grace Church Street, hard by Candlewick Alley, during Christmas celebrations on December twenty-ninth? He would be riding from Greenwich to Windsor to start another water closet, as the queen had ordered, and would stay in London for one day only.

His letter, sent by private courier, was full of his love and loneliness.

> *My sweet Mary,*
>   *We are quickly coming to the year of our Lord 1600. I will not wait until a new century to see you, nor can I storm Whitehall, or risk the queen losing her temper as I have surely lost my heart to a certain lady within those walls. I will wait for you all the day and night of the twenty-ninth of December.*

At once, she stopped reading. She could not meet him. The trip from the palace into the city, though not long, would be dangerous for a richly dressed woman alone, even in full daylight. And if she bribed a yeoman to go with her, no coin would be large enough to keep him from telling such intriguing news to his comrades, news that would wend its way to the queen's ears. How could a faithful servant seek to heap more troubles on Her Majesty when ther queen's heart was so heavy? But how could she deny John? Or her own heart's need?

Mary hastened to his postscript.

> *There will be a trusted friend waiting for you at the Holbein Gate. I cannot betray the name of this friend for fear this letter might fall into other hands. He will be identified by a cockade in his cap of former fashion.*
>   *Impatiently, John*

Mary flattened the letter against her breast, holding it as close as possible. If the queen had meant for time apart to do its job, time had utterly failed. John did not sound changed, and Mary Rogers knew with all her heart that she would never change. She longed to see him, if only to tell him why it was so impossible. But if she did see him, look into his face, how could she speak any words but her love and yearning? But if she spoke them, she would be denying the queen's express wishes. She must deny either her heart or her loyalty. God help her, she could do neither.

Advent, 1599

December twenty-ninth dawned with a westerly ice storm sweeping into London, rattling Whitehall's windows and bending low the bare, pruned fruit trees in the queen's orchard. That alone would not have kept Mary from venturing into the city. But Lord Howard had arrived the morning of the day before, and her grandfather that same evening. It would seem that God, the queen's choice for a husband and Mary's own family were all conspiring to keep her from John. She had even considered faking illness, but had discarded that notion, which would be a great untruth and forever shame her in her own eyes.

Mary kept a tight hold on her anxiety, lest it show. Once that day, Lady Fitton had caught her with swimming eyes and drawn her own conclusions, taking her arm and pulling her into the hall outside the ladies' anteroom.

"Mistress, you are troubled at the thought of meeting your intended," she guessed with a giggle. "I saw him arriving and think you have no worry on that score. He has belly enough, but"—she brightened—"is richly attired and yet maintains an old-fashioned codpiece." She tried unsuccessfully to stop her amusement. "But you would have a title and a grand manor."

"I'm not at all troubled at meeting Lord Howard," Mary insisted, not much liking this too forward maid, who had shown herself to be a gossip almost immediately upon entering the queen's service and was not to be trusted.

Lady Fitton smirked. "Our ugly old queen is too jealous to find us handsome young lords. She would keep them all for herself as tribute to her departed beauty, but I will find a lord without her."

Mary was shocked. "How dare you speak so of your sovereign! She is beloved of all England and—"

"Surely not all Englishmen." The lady giggled again. "There must be one left for me, now that you have yours. What a silly old mouse you truly are."

Mary broke away from Lady Fitton's grasp. "You do not know Her Majesty's burdens, or that I have sworn to serve her to death if that is her wish. Have a care how you speak of her in my presence."

Fitton looked puzzled. "Many in the court are laughing at her back."

Mary was shaking with rage. "Never speak to me of this again. If Lady Warwick were here, she'd have you birched and sent home in disgrace."

"Another old one on her deathbed. A new generation is coming to power, Mistress Rogers. When James of Scotland takes the throne, you will be left behind. Don't you know half the courtiers are already writing to him for places in his government and sending him gifts? You will have no place with the new king, and I will."

"It is treason to speak of or forecast the queen's death," Mary said angrily. "I will not abide it."

Fitton laughed nervously and swung on down the hall, drawing all passing male attention.

Late that afternoon, Mary prepared the linen the queen would wear at the grand party that night and then rushed to the dining hall to have supper with her grandfather. With storm winds rattling every window in the long gallery, she looked out, despairing of any possible way to get a message to John's friend waiting at the Holbein Gate. What would John think when she did not come? That her love had been so pitiful it had failed her in his absence; that she had thought better and accepted a rich old lord after all? She grasped the window-sill. Would he take a tavern maid to his bed? She groaned loud enough to draw attention as she hurried on to the great dining hall.

She caught Sir William's eye where he sat at table and rushed to him, bowing her head for his blessing, needing some comfort.

"Mary! Child, there is no need for tears," he said, granting his blessing with his palm on her head and a kiss for her cheek. He looked upon her face as she sat down beside him.

"You look well, Grandfather."

"You are older."

"By nearly a year. I have learned much, Grandfather."

"And yet you are sad. Why is that so, when you have gained the queen's great affection? I was wrong to think you reached too high. You were a Somerset girl when I left you. Now you are a great lady and hold the queen's confidence." He stuck his knife into a lamb shank and put it into his bread bowl, spooning in broth, carrots and leeks to make a meat pie, and fell to with great appetite.

"My affection for Her Majesty is not feigned, Grandfather."

"Nor is hers for you, my child. She has written to me, calling you 'her beloved daughter' and informing me that she has chosen her second cousin Lord Howard for you . . . once you are both free to marry. I have, of course, given my consent." He looked up from his supper and frowned. "But you never mentioned His Lordship in your letters, and I can see in your face now that you are not pleased at the honor Her Majesty has done you and our family."

Mary dared look into her grandfather's eyes, not in the least humbled. "As you love me, do not force him on me. I do not love him. Please speak against this marriage to the queen."

"Are you mad? Her Majesty chooses him for you, and I choose him. Can't you see we are privileged? What of love? Love always comes after marriage, not before." He glanced up and down the tables in the great hall. "That rogue John Harington is not in attendance, though the queen mentioned that you had formed an . . . attachment. Surely Her Grace is wrong in this. The man wagered for your honor in open court. You could never . . . ."

Since her grandfather could read her so well, she turned from him to take a little bread and soften it in a cup of ale.

"Mary?"

"Grandfather, you do not know John." Her voice trembled. "*I* did not know him. I was so wrong, so very wrong. The wager was Essex's idea, and John repudiated it at great cost to his fortune. Later, the earl sought to ruin me by kidnap to his bed . . . but John—"

Her grandfather put his hand on his sword. "Essex did what!"

"Grandfather, the earl is in disgrace and perhaps dying. He no longer matters. It's John who means everything to me. I cannot marry Lord Howard when his wife dies. But the queen thinks it best and . . . ." She buried her face in her ale cup, hoping it would catch her tears.

Sir William looked troubled. "We must talk more, Mary, but not in this place at this time. There are too many eyes and ears. Come to me tonight, after you have attended the queen at the entertainments and have met Lord Howard. Your mind will surely be altered on this subject. Come, Mary," he said, putting his wrinkled brown hand on her smooth young one. "I am lodged in my old rooms, child."

"Yes, Grandfather," she agreed, bending to kiss his hand atop hers. "Now I must return to my duties."

"But, child, you have scarce eaten a bite. . . ."

She heard, but quickened her step, unable to swallow more food or talk of Lord Howard.

That night, the storm still howling outside, Whitehall was alight with lanterns and torches as Mary followed Elizabeth with all her ladies and yeomen into the great hall, which was covered with wreaths of holly and sweet-smelling fir boughs. Tinkling bells on the fools and dogs made a merry hall. Musicians gathered on the balcony played the less solemn music of William Byrd, the queen's favorite composer. As Mary glanced about at the richly dressed courtiers, lords of both England and of Europe who'd come to bring gifts to the queen, it seemed that all the world recognized Elizabeth as their sovereign. How could she defy such a queen?

As Mary glanced about the great hall, she could not help but try to determine which older lord fit the description of Lord Howard, but she could not. The room was full of country lords who came only to Christmas court, and all too many had bellies and had refused to give up their codpieces, no matter the change in fashion. Soon enough she would know her intended. She tried to keep her face bright, but her smile felt like a painted mask.

Elizabeth sat on her domed throne in a beautiful black damask gown cut very low on the withered skin of her breasts, indeed almost to the edge of her rosy nipples, causing a general whisper to surge through the courtiers. Mary heard no laughter, but her heart ached for the once beautiful queen who, despite her great age, needed to show she was still so much a woman. Perhaps that need was all that remained of her youth, now that Essex and his love had proved false.

The queen motioned for the dancing to begin. "We would have our ladies choose a virtue and dance for us," she said in her carrying voice when the orchestra began a saraband.

Mary curtsied in her turn before the throne and repeated the virtue she represented. "Steadfastness, Majesty, in honor of your motto: 'Always the Same.'"

The queen smiled, pleased.

Lady Fitton curtsied to the queen. "Majesty, will you dance with us?"

"And what virtue do you represent, my lady?"

"Affection," the lady replied, obviously thinking herself clever.

"Affection? Affection's false!" The queen's words, laced with scorn, pulsed through the great hall and were not absorbed by the beautiful Arras tapestries hanging from every wall. Now everyone knew she had not forgiven the Earl of Essex, though it was said he slowly recovered his health.

The queen rose to dance, and Mary could almost see the courtiers at that moment deciding to abandon again any friendship or allegiance with Essex. And to make no further wagers in his favor.

Later, a man of middling years, wearing a short cloak slung in old fashion over his left shoulder, and a doublet that did not completely hide his rounding figure, approached the throne and knelt. He added a small silver chest to the many gifts that were gathered about the queen's feet, and she smiled her thanks.

"Lord Howard, we welcome you to our court and hope you left your lady in better health."

"Alas, no, Your Grace. The doctors do not give me much hope."

"Doctors never give hope, cousin, because there is no immediate fee in it."

"So true, Majesty, though the grace and beauty of your ladies do give a man still in the prime of life . . . more than hope."

"Mistress Mary Rogers is such a one, my lord, and tonight she calls herself Steadfast. We can confirm that she has this virtue in abundance, being as dutiful as she is beautiful."

Mary stepped forward and held her hand out to Lord Howard. Now was no time to refuse.

The dance was a slow pavanne, yet his lordship soon begged to sit down. "I would have you know that I am not weary, but seek to speak to you privately." He led Mary to a window alcove and she sat on the cushioned seat, looking out on the dance floor and its swirling colors and flashing jewels, until he moved to stand in front of her, deliberately drawing her gaze to himself.

She took him for an avid hunter, which would explain his lined face, hard used by outdoor life. He had been a handsome youth and retained his noble features, though he had grown somber with his years.

"My lord, I am most sorry to hear your lady is not improving in health." Mary thought those words would tell him how she felt, but they did not. He took them for womanly kindness.

"I thank you, Mistress Rogers. It is only a matter of time now. I have no hope of her recovery."

Mary took a deep breath and looked down at her hands twisting in her lap, searching her mind for an answer that would not insult the queen's choice, yet would give him knowledge of her feelings.

Lord Howard bent down, his face closer to hers, and she saw he had hard eyes. He would not give up the queen's promised portion of the salt tax easily.

"When that unhappy day arrives, mistress, I will come for you, though I would tell you now that your firstborn son will not gain the title. Have no illusions of that, since I have five sons living. I will, of course, make ample provision for ours."

Mary leapt up, nearly knocking into him. "Lord Howard, I beg you . . . I cannot possibly discuss such matters while your wife yet lives."

Angry, Lord Howard blocked her way, his face florid. Though he opened his mouth to speak, Mary didn't hear what he would have said.

She dodged past him, thinking of nothing more than heedless escape from the great hall and from the promise she was being forced to make. She pushed her way among courtiers watching the dancing, receiving no permission to leave, but fled out the open doors into the hall, running pell-mell to her grandfather's rooms.

John Harington stepped from the shadows and she fell into his icy arms. "At last. I had to come; I could wait no longer. But, sweetest girl, have you seen a ghost?"

"No, John, a husband I cannot bear!" Mary cried, and sobbed

against his chest, for a moment not caring who saw and reported her conduct. "How came you here? The queen will be furious."

Minutes later, as he held her trembling body against his growing warmth, she noticed that John was wearing a cockade in a frosty cap of former fashion.

As Mary's body folded into his, John shook more with desire than with the freezing cold he'd endured waiting through the day's hours at the Holbein Gate on King Street. Happily, those at court who did not have the rank to be invited to attend the queen's masque hid in their apartments, so no person of any consequence saw the queen's godson cradling one of her ladies in a palace hall. Nor did they see him kiss her hair and cheeks, her eyes and lips in the shadowy corner. Or her hands clutch tight to his fast-defrosting doublet.

At last, he reluctantly let her slide down his body until her toes touched the marble floor, though he bent forward to retain his hungry pressure on her lips.

She broke free and panted for breath against his shoulder. "John, dearest . . . I cannot *endure* this," she said, her voice so constricted by a lump of emotion he scarcely recognized the throaty sound as hers.

"By God, you will not marry Howard."

"How can I not? The queen commands. And my grandfather . . . What woman is free to choose?"

"Or what man? How many times did my own father lecture me on the responsibilities that I have, to come to court and marry a title, wealth and property?"

"And why did you not, when you could have many times over . . . and it was what you wanted?" She tried hard not to show how much she yearned to know that answer.

"True," John said, smiling, "though I think all that long time I was waiting for you." He released his tight hold so that he could look at her and memorize this passing moment; poignant though it was, it was yet precious because of what was revealed in her face. She loved him and suffered from separation, suffering equal to his own. It was writ plain.

"What you say is that it is impossible for you as well," she said. "You cannot defy your family and queen, no more than I can deny my oath to serve her as long as she needs me."

He put a finger to her lips. "Shhh, sweetheart. Least said, soonest mended. We will find a way."

Mary clutched him hard to her body, her head aching with the mystery of what that way might be.

Sir William opened his door and saw them in the hall. Scowling, he abruptly motioned them inside, and they had no choice but to obey, as several yeoman guards swung around the corner on their rounds.

A fire warmed one side of the small anteroom, throwing flickering light onto the paneled walls and oiled wood floors. A yawning servant poured wine and bowed himself back into a bedchamber, shutting the door soundlessly.

Sir William took Mary's free hand and led her to a chair. John did not release the hand he held, though he earned another frown from Mary's grandfather, who then occupied the only other chair.

Mary spoke first. "Grandfather, it is no fault of John's—"

John could not allow her to speak for him. "Yes, the fault is mine, Sir William. I will not deny that I have done all that is honorable to draw her love to me."

Sir William sniffed. "Sir John, it is dishonorable on its face to court a lady against the wishes of her family and her sovereign."

"Then it is a dishonor I share with countless men and maids through time, sir, as written so well by Master Shakespeare in his *Romeo and Juliet*."

Sir William looked even more impatient. "I do not frequent low playhouses filled with masterless men and pick-a-pockets."

John smiled. "My real hope, sir, is that the amendment I have wrought to my own character will bring both you and Her Majesty to change your minds and grant Mary and me the happiness—"

Impatiently, Mary's grandfather stood, confronting John. "That is always the futile hope of the young, though when you are older you will know true happiness comes from following right courses as well thought by wiser heads." He finished his wine in a gulp, though it made his eyes tear. "Do you think I can possibly give you consent when Her Majesty has flattered our family with her generous attention?" He pointed a finger at John. "If you continue this illicit courtship, you, sir, will end in the Tower and take my granddaughter with you. Is that your selfish wish?"

John stood straighter, well over a head taller than Sir William. "No, sir, my one wish is for her happiness . . . and, I won't deny it, the only hope I have for my own."

"If you wish her true happiness, leave her to the better future Her Majesty and I have planned for her. For sweet Christ's sake, sir, she is offered a noble name and rank. Do you offer more?"

"Yes, Sir William."

"Love again," he said, almost spitting out the words, his face showing that he had long forgotten a time when he had felt that uniquely breathless urge. "You are no beardless youth, no poet despite your ambitions. You should know much better, or, not knowing, heed the counsel of those who do."

"Grandfather!" Mary stood, still clinging to John's hand. "As you love me . . ."

Sir William stepped quickly to the door, wrenched it open and shouted, "Guards!"

John saw that the man was now so angry he could not hear. Bowing to Sir William, John kissed Mary's hand, taking it to his heart and pressing hard. "We will be together," he whispered. "I am not without resources." Then he walked quickly out the door and down the hall, this time without her body clinging to his, though he felt the curves and hollows of her still.

He made his way down the long stone gallery and out to where his hired carriage waited. Though the howling tempest had somewhat abated, he did not hear his name being called behind him, nor see Mary run from the shelter of the huge door and down the steps, her hair loosened from its gold netting, swirling wildly about her face.

CHAPTER FOURTEEN

A LETTER TO JAMES OF SCOTLAND

*"Now to confess my kind taking of all your
loving offers and vows that naught shall be concealed
from me . . . Let others promise, and I will do as
much with truth as others with wiles."*
—Elizabeth Regina

February 14, 1600
Whitehall Palace

For weeks the queen had maintained an unnerving silence about Mary's flight from the great hall and from Lord Howard, so that Mary had some understanding sympathy for Essex, waiting daily for a word of forgiveness, a word that the queen seemed in no hurry to send. Mary thought that waiting for the queen's wrath to fall was far worse than having that anger fully expressed.

Lady Fitton, now firmly installed as the premier court flirt, could scarcely contain her pleasure at the gossip surrounding Mary's behavior. Speaking aloud in the presence chamber, that lady remarked in the queen's hearing: "Today, being St. Valentine's and the day when birds choose their mates, I ask you: What manner of lady is this Mary Rogers? I for one would fear for my sanity if I refused a great lord, and my family would certainly disown me for a Bedlamite."

The queen had ignored that silly, gossiping minx. But she also ignored Mary.

Mary's comfort lay in John's letters, loving, exciting and full of his special humor. In the peace of the royal linen closet, she reread or touched them tucked beneath her stomacher. He called himself Lord of the Jakes, and made her laugh with stories of his battles with Windsor Palace grooms who were suspicious and even afraid they would fall into his invention and be swept into the cesspit and thence into the Thames, the largest cesspit of all. Yet each letter was followed by Mary's own greater turmoil. Could she ever bring herself to betray the queen's wishes, even for John? Could she? All her young life, she had yearned for this place at court that the queen had given her. Was she so ungrateful? Was she, after all, just like Lady Katherine, and would she pay the same terrible price?

One morning in late February, as she was pressing body linen, lowering the press and turning it as tight as she could, the queen entered the closet. Mary curtsied almost to the floor, pulling her hands inside her full oversleeves to keep them from visibly shaking. In all these months of her service, the queen had never appeared in her own linen room.

"We have heard from Lord Howard," Her Majesty said in a soft voice.

"Yes, Your Grace." Did the queen's composure mean that she was no longer angry?

"He is a most understanding lord, Mouse, and now we do see your behavior for what it was," Her Majesty said, looking at the neat piles of linen ready to be stored away in their chests. "You serve us well, knowing our need before we do, as if you had been tutored in how to please us."

Mary kept her head bowed, sending her prayerful thanks to Lady Kate in heaven.

"Indeed, daughter," the queen said tenderly, "we do never want another lady save you to care for our body linen."

Daughter? My sweet Jesus! Mary realized that Elizabeth really believed in her own motherhood, and she was deeply touched. This great queen who controlled powerful men, and had defeated every armada sent against her by Spain, must fill her empty womb with pretend daughters.

Mary remained humble, although the queen had paid her a high compliment, while seeming to lose her thoughts between Lord Howard and the linen.

"Oh, yes," the queen said, as if waking, "Howard thinks you a tender virgin who was distressed by his forward speaking . . . while his wife yet lived. He has the right of this, we think?"

Mary sought an answer that would not be a lie. "Your Grace, I will not deny that I was very troubled by talk of marriage and children with a man whose wife lay so ill."

Elizabeth held out her beautiful, long-fingered white hand to be kissed, one finger containing her coronation ring, and Mary put her lips to that finger, though the creased skin was cold under her lips. "Majesty, may I fetch gloves for you?"

The queen smiled. "Yes, bring us the red Spanish leather gloves. Not perfumed, mind you. Our morning porridge was disagreeable."

Mary rushed to the chest that held the queen's gloves and took them to her. The queen nodded, and Mary backed to the ladies' bedchamber, where she found Lady Fitton crying, in obvious distress.

"What has happened?" Mary asked, thinking some bad news had arrived, and fearing that it was dire if it had upset this pert maid.

The lady seemed not to be able to control her sobs. "He . . . he . . . won't . . ." She threw herself on her bed and into a pillow so hard that swan feathers floated up and settled back into her hair.

"Who are you talking of?" Was it Essex? Surely not John. Mary shook the girl. "Who? What man? Name him!"

"The Earl of . . . Pembroke," Lady Fitton said.

Mary was startled by the name. "The same earl who once married Lady Katherine Grey . . . surely his son."

"Grandson," Lady Fitton answered, and again sobbed and swallowed convulsively. "The queen has sent him to prison in the Tower."

"Why?"

The girl answered in a voice so soft that Mary had to bend to hear. "I am with child. His *child!*" The last word rose to a tremulous wail.

"Calm yourself. The queen will insist on a marriage. Her Majesty cannot endure public censure of her ladies. It reflects on her. She forced Raleigh to marry Lady Throckmorton and Southampton to marry the—"

The distraught girl sobbed convulsively. "He . . . he refused . . . preferring the Tower to *meee.*" The lady gulped back more tears, her voice fading to a whisper. "He told the queen that I was unfit to be his countess."

"What!"

Lady Fitton handed Mary a crumpled, tearstained note, signed with the earl's signet.

> *For if with one, with thousands you turn whore,*
> *Break ice in one place and it cracks the more.*

Mary shuddered for her. The girl had sought a rich husband in the wrong way and had played the flirt, going much too far, it appeared. Yet Mary had heard nothing quite so cruel as this man's reply, though it was common enough thinking.

"What will you do?"

"What can I do?" Lady Fitton said, raising her blotched and swollen face. "The queen has sent for me. I am afraid—"

"Her Grace is kindness itself today," Mary said, unable to think of other words to soothe the girl.

Lady Margaret appeared in the door and her voice brought no comfort, nor did the look on her face. "The queen will see you immediately, Lady Fitton. Gain control of your weeping. Her Majesty cannot abide such."

Mary looked a question at Lady Margaret, who nodded.

Smoothing her gown and removing a swan feather lodged in a ribbon, Mary followed the pair. Lady Margaret gripped Fitton's arm and pushed her into the queen's presence.

Her Majesty stood near the large fireplace, her features now as distorted with anger as they had been gently arranged earlier in the linen closet.

Lady Fitton fell to her knees. "Forgive me, Majesty, for I am not at fault. He promised to marry me, or I would never—"

The queen began to stomp about, clearly in an escalating rage. "Strumpet! Whore! Slut! A man's cock always crows loudest when aroused. We treated you as a daughter, and by Christ's blessed nails and wounds, you have disgraced us and our court. Be gone from our sight and at once." The queen advanced on Lady Fitton with a raised fist.

The girl covered her face, but the regal blow fell harder on her hands than Mary could have imagined the old queen's strength to be, even with righteous wrath so great.

Lady Fitton cried out pitiably as the blows found their target. She scrambled away from Elizabeth on her hands and knees like a whipped cur, one finger already swelling and twisted, obviously broken.

Short of death, Her Majesty had every right to chastise an undutiful servant or, as a mother, an unfaithful and willful daughter. Mercy was a royal prerogative, Mary saw clearly, but not forgiveness. Queens could not afford to forgive, lest it give encouragement to defiance.

Mary guided the stumbling girl to her bed in the ladies' anteroom, where they were alone. From the gusts of excited chatter in the hall, the other ladies of the bedchamber wanted to be nowhere near a disgraced lady, or the queen's temper. There would be no comfort for Lady Fitton from that quarter. She had not made herself popular with women.

Hearing the sound of smashing pottery as the queen's rage continued, Mary quickly tied a tight bandage around Lady Fitton's hand to hold the broken finger straight and grabbed up her cloak, placing it about the lady's shoulders. "Leave at once, to save yourself from worse . . . perhaps even the Tower, where Pembroke will fare better than you. I promise your belongings will be sent after you."

"Mary Rogers, I know you have no cause to help me, but I beg you . . . The earl, my father, will beat me and send me off to some country village. No man of honor will ever want me. Wherever I go, whispers will follow. I am not yet nineteen years and I am ruined."

Mary was truly sorry for the distraught girl, but there was little that she could say or do, for all the young fool spoke was truth. She had trusted in promises spoken in hot, dark haste and now she must pay, as women did who gave themselves to the wrong man.

For the first time, Mary knew herself fortunate that John was not at court. She doubted she would have the strength to continue to deny him what they both wanted. The memory of being in his arms told her of her own woman's weakness, as had night upon night of struggle to ease the restless, hot ache that filled her.

April and May came that year, days alternating the warmth and chill of early spring. Sudden showers of rain and fruit tree blossoms fell as the queen walked swiftly, seemingly tirelessly, through her privy gardens, Mary at her side.

Everyone marveled that a woman now nearing her sixty-seventh birthday could maintain such a pace, and Elizabeth laughed to read and quote to Mary the intercepted and decoded messages from foreign ambassadors writing to their monarchs about the amazing English queen's endless energy. Elizabeth liked this report even more than the French ambassador De Baise's message to Henri IV praising her white skin and her grasp of world affairs, which could put any man to shame. And certainly more than the French noble who wrote that the queen was still beautiful "from a distance." That phrase had banished the foreign lord to a distance from the queen forever.

Though Mary did not disagree with De Baise, only she knew that on occasion, when the queen seemed to stop and admire a bed of spring violets, a leafing eglantine or a pot of clove-scented carnations, Her Majesty leaned heavily on Mary's arm, and for a few minutes her face would grow even whiter under the cherry-tinted cheeks.

One morning, while walking with the queen in the gardens near good shelter, should the clouds sweeping in decide to empty their wet burden, Mary was given the news that Lady Howard miraculously lived on. "It is God's will, Majesty," she answered appropriately, not mentioning that she'd had something to do with it, praying for that lady's recovery every night at chapel. She dreaded the minute Lady Howard breathed her last, for it would send her grieving husband galloping to the queen and the warrant that would grant him Mary Rogers. And the salt tax, which would mean a thousand pounds a year, doubling that lord's annual income.

When she sent John this news, he vowed to work day and night and return quickly after finishing the Greenwich Palace royal water closet, frustrated that his workmen were so slow and the money he needed as grudgingly supplied by the queen. He wrote: *Although my invention may soon be installed in the least tradesman's house and sweeten the whole air of England beyond any flower or fruit, I wish I had never conceived the scheme, for it keeps me from you. I come soon to appeal to my godmother to change her mind for our happiness.*

Mary answered: *Dearest Knight of my Heart, if Lady Howard dies, the queen will hold me to my vow to serve her until her end time comes, not allowing me to leave her as long as she lives and, Praise God, looks to live on.*

In May, the queen quietly released Essex, now well and hearty, from Lord Keeper Edgerton's custody, but the earl was allowed only the freedom of his own Essex House. The queen was further gracious. She now allowed him any visitor he wished. At court the wagering on Essex's restoration to favor began again. Her Majesty was certain to return him to her presence soon. Everyone saw the queen's periods of melancholy and her frolics and reckless riding in the hunt as substitutes for the handsome company she denied herself.

In early June, John Harington, having finished his work at Windsor, made his way to Oatlands, where the court was staying until the inevitable summer plague in London subsided. He stopped, reluctantly accepting Essex's urgent invitation to wait upon him at Essex House before continuing his journey.

John found the earl writing his woes to King James of Scotland, even asking him to send troops to restore him to his rightful place and bring down Cecil and Raleigh, offering to support James's right to the throne in return. The earl was proud enough of the letter to show it to John.

"My lord earl, you tread on exceeding dangerous ground here," John said, alarmed at what he read. Here was Essex assuming James was heir to the English throne before the queen had named him heir, seeking his patronage while the queen lived. Such a communication in Cecil's hands could be seen as treasonous, and that wily councilor would wait for just the right time to put it before Elizabeth, when she had swung from melancholy to anger as she surely would.

Essex scowled. "What more could she do to me? I am beggared, kept from her council and the court . . . even my own rightful place as a peer of this realm."

"You could lose your head."

"She wouldn't dare arrest me. The people of London would rise up."

"And what, my lord? Make you king?"

Even Essex knew he had gone too far, and in an instant his mind swiveled. "Do you go to court, John?" he said in a pleading tone, gripping John's arm. "Tell her that I have loved her more than any man ever living. Tell her that until I may see her, the sun is dead and the world all night to me."

"My lord, have you written this to her?"

"Yes. Yes, a dozen times and in a dozen ways, though I do not know if she reads my letters or, indeed, is in right enough emotion to understand them. Perhaps Cecil keeps them from her. He poisons her mind against me." He began to walk up and down frantically, changing direction without thought, a dripping pen clasped in his hand, heedless of the black ink blotting the clinging hose on those celebrated legs. His face first showed sorrow, then anger and back to sadness again, until finally his long, loping stride nearly ran him into a wall. "Cursed woman! Poor copy of a king!"

"My lord, as a loyal subject, I cannot suffer such talk in my hearing." John hastily sought an exit without leave. It was clear to him who was not in his right mind. Elizabeth's Wild Horse had now gone completely feral.

Essex put out a placating hand. "Stay, John, yet awhile. We have been comrades for years. I have great need of you to bring the queen to right thinking of who serves her best."

John feared to confirm any such friendship with this heedless lord, a friendship that was now long gone and had, in truth, not existed since Essex had tried to take Mary by force. "My lord, according to my communications, Her Majesty's mind is very active, and the court is full of frolic."

The earl clenched his fists, and fury shook him. "She laughs and dances while I am denied all aid and my debts mount. Everyone speaks against me. Cecil and Raleigh work for my disgrace; indeed, I think them the true traitors, for they love Spain and are plotting with the Spaniards."

"Surely, my lord, you are mistaken. You accuse the queen's ministers of loving our enemies."

Essex opened his mouth to say more, but gained control, since at some level of rationale he must know that what he said was false delusion. "I take it that these communications you speak of are from a lady close to the queen." He looked at John, controlling the smirk obviously longing to twist his mouth.

"Yes, my lord." John put his hand on his sword and reached the door.

"Give my fondest greetings to Mistress Mary." He did smirk at that, and John left the room before he knocked His Lordship to the floor and trod on his face. Such an act would bring shame to him, since it was obvious that Essex had lost what little sense he ever had, blaming everyone but himself, unable to hide his most destructive, even treasonous feelings. He wore them on his face without even the knowledge that he did so.

John rode on through an afternoon shower, his mind a jumble of Mary, the queen and Essex, his heart dark with a sense of ominous events in motion that he could not know or protect against. He pushed on into the dusk along the Thames a few miles upstream from Hampton Court toward Oatlands, the smallest of the queen's residences, forcing many courtiers to abide in nearby inns and country houses. He heard the noisy rooks in the elm trees before he saw the jutting towers and redbrick chimneys of the queen's hunting lodge. He rode at last through the tower gate with the Tudor arms carved above and the queen's flag flying to show she was in residence, threw his reins to a sleepy stable groom and made his way to one of the cottages around the central quadrangle, which the chamberlain had said was his.

He liked this place. It was more a village than the impersonal stone heaps he had been attempting to sweeten with his water closets. As he threw himself full-clothed on the straw pallet laid atop a bed of crossed ropes, he wrapped his arms about his chest and slept, imagining that Mary was pressing against him.

❖

"Walk with me, godson."

"With delight, Majesty," John replied the next morn, shaved, trimmed and brushed, wearing a clean ruff newly starched and pleated. He was very aware that Mary, even under the cosmetic mask demanded of court ladies, looked so fresh and beautiful that it took all his will not to stare at her. She followed a few paces behind the queen with several ladies of the presence chamber. He had not spoken with her privately, but her eyes told him that she would soon find a way.

John pretended to be fully exercised by Elizabeth's vigorous stride, knowing she delighted in besting young men with her vitality and learned old men with her knowledge. Before they reached the middle fountain of her privy garden, John told her the humorous tale of the guard's captain at Windsor Castle, who would not go near Her Majesty's new water closet for fear of falling in. He did not turn to Mary to see if she'd noticed he had promoted the groom who had actually feared the invention. Any jest could be made more humorous by a little embellishment, as Will Shakespeare proved most afternoons at the Globe Theatre on the Bankside. And what was this if not the theater of the court, and he, Mary and the queen all players? They said their lines, acted their roles, danced and postured through days and nights. Not for the first time, he knew that it was a life he did not want to live forever. And he did not want Mary to live it, though she had grown up longing for court life.

Elizabeth, her cheeks more sunken than he remembered, made a face at his story. "It seems we must show our brave yeoman captain the way of a water closet."

John bowed, appreciating without laughing. Sometimes the queen was given to scandalous jest, but until he was sure . . .

Her jeweled gown flashing in the morning light, her high white ruff waving behind her bright red wig, the queen bent a little to smell a rose newly opened, dew gathered on its open petals.

John stepped forward, snapped it off and, drawing his dirk, removed all the thorns. No royal blood would water this soil.

He knelt and presented the flower to her, his eyes shining with humor. "A first rose of summer for England's great Tudor rose, Majesty, from your humble subject John Harington."

The queen held it to her nose and looked into the distance. He did not know how far she saw until she spoke.

"My father called my cousin Catherine Howard his 'rose without a thorn.' You honor her memory, sir."

John bowed his head and made no reply. No one dared speak of Henry VIII except Elizabeth herself. Sixteen years old, Catherine Howard had been the king's fifth wife, whom he'd beheaded because she did have a thorn . . . in the form of several lovers. Though Henry was probably impotent at the time, he thought this behavior in his young, beauteous wife deserving an ax on the Tower block. How Elizabeth must have feared him, beheading her mother and her cousin, divorcing or otherwise ridding himself of women who displeased him. She had inherited his steel and his temper without his cruelty . . . John hoped, though she guarded her kingdom as fiercely as a bear her cub. He took a deep breath and determined on a course, the only one open to him.

The queen suddenly returned from her reverie to the present and gave him her hand to rise. "We release you from your duties to give attention to your properties in Somersetshire, which you have long neglected for our sake."

"Your Grace, I confess, having been so long from court in your service, I long to stay with you for a time."

The queen surged ahead down the path toward a far brick wall espaliered with Spanish orange trees in flower, and John rushed to stay at her side. "We will not change our mind about Mary Rogers, Sir John," she said, matter-of-fact. She paused. "Why would you stay at court if it gains you nothing?"

He decided that boldness was always his best foot forward.

"Love, Majesty."

"Don't speak to us of love." Her voice was gruff and flat, almost a growl.

He had no caution left. "Love is all I speak, Majesty. It has become my first language."

"Better you work on your Latin, sir. Love fails, is false and all too soon is consumed in its own fire." She stared at the rose she twirled in her hand. "Or it dies."

"Forgive my disagreement, godmother."

"We do not forgive disagreement."

He fell again to his knees, her bitterness surrounding him, and bowed his head.

The queen of England hit her godson a good stroke over the head with the rose he'd given her. Was it a symbolic beheading? As the petals fell about his face and doublet, he looked up to see her striding from the privy garden, Mary following, her face turned back to John in alarm.

That night, the Danish ambassador was honored by a masque. John attended but did not approach the queen's throne, though Mary stood to one side, until Elizabeth beckoned to him. He walked forward, knelt and on her signal rose, sweeping his hat to the floor.

The flutes, tambours, guitars and drums were playing the Spanish panic, and the queen's foot tapped furiously.

"Majesty, I have need of your instruction in these measures."

"You should take yourself to the dancing master for improvement."

John bowed. He was not forgiven his forward behavior in the privy garden, at least not completely, though there might be a dim sparkle in his godmother's stern eye. As he began to back away, the queen stood and gave him her hand.

"Do not look so whipped, John. It ill becomes a man of your height and closeness to us."

"I cannot smile when you send me from you."

"You need be in no hurry to leave us."

He smiled at her ability to scold and forgive in almost the same breath. With a grand gesture he drew off his cloak and threw it to the floor as if to prepare for strenuous exercise.

"Rascal!" she scolded, but threw back her head and laughed.

She could turn from stern monarch to young coquette on the instant.

Elizabeth danced as she always had, her body very straight, her feet fast enough to show her ankles, and her gestures exaggerated, but no less elegant. He looked toward Mary when he could without discovery and he saw the queen glance at the Danish ambassador several times as they spun with the other dancers, none of the ladies over forty years daring to lift their feet from the floor. He knew that Her Majesty was showing the Danes that the English were ruled by a queen forever young, though he felt the shrunken body under his hands as he raised her through the leaps and gently put her down. She had never had much flesh. Now she was all bone.

"We have invited Lord Howard to court for the hunting," she said as he led her to her throne.

No response was required from him, but he felt his arm muscles tense under her hand.

"Godson," the queen whispered, "look you for another love. We would not have you so unhappy. But when Lord Howard is free— and we are done of this world—he will have her. This lord is one of a very loyal few in the north who does not seek James of Scotland's patronage before we are in our grave. We must keep him close if James grows impatient and comes over the border before it is his time. There are those we once loved who urge that course." She meant, of course, Essex. She removed her fan from its ribbon and tapped it against John's chest for emphasis.

John realized there was nothing about Essex that she did not know. If Cecil had not told her, then perhaps the Scots king had, currying her favor. And she must have spies in Essex's house, among his closest confidants. "Godmother, I do not long to be at any court that does not have you on its throne." He spoke truth and she knew it.

Elizabeth opened her fan and raised it before her face to hide any emotion that might have surfaced, and he retreated, not looking at Mary, though he knew she had seen most everything and guessed the rest.

After the queen was dressed in fresh linen and abed, Mary came to his cottage that night, knocking softly on the door. Her agitation was apparent. "John, what are you about? The queen will surely send you from court and not allow you to return."

"I have done nothing but give her the honesty she expects."

"She needs only a sudden whim." Mary bit her lip. "At every turn you remind her of all that she denied herself for the sake of her throne."

"The queen has said this?"

"No, she doesn't speak it, but it is always there on her face and in the way she opens her ivory treasure box and sits with it in her hands more often now. There is something precious to her inside. And she struggles with Essex's absence. He did know exactly how to make her feel young and loved again."

John pulled Mary over the threshold and into his arms, kissing her over and over and yet another time, all the hot, searching kisses he had saved for months, the ones he'd dreamed and the ones he'd suppressed to give his body some ease from desire.

He broke away first, leaving Mary panting, her arms dangling by her sides, useless without him to hold. "I thought you would never return," she said, catching her breath. "When I saw you in the privy garden this morning, I—"

"You what, sweetest?"

He had set her to aching in a most dangerous way. But Lady Fitton's fate swiftly came to her mind. "John, we must take great care," she whispered, hoping to borrow strength from wisdom.

He retreated to stoke the sea coal fire in the small fireplace. "That is what I am doing," he said, his voice steadier than his hands, which he hoped were well hidden from her.

She choked out the next words. "Then you must double the care you take, for I am no longer able to . . ." She stopped, her body leaning toward his of its own will. "Oh, John, these past months have seemed a long, moonless night."

He came to her and led her to the only chair before the fire, then sat on the straw-matted floor, the fire lighting his face, yet not so near that they could touch. Touching held too many obvious dangers.

He looked up, his face holding that same roguish smile that at first had angered her, but now thrilled her. "We could take ship to the Sugar Islands, where we would always be warm," he said, watching to see her reaction.

"Warmer than we are now?" she said boldly.

He grinned. "That might not be possible."

"John, you have no wanderlust and I have no stomach for voyaging," she said, smiling to show she did not take the idea seriously.

A rueful expression crossed his face as he turned to Mary, his elbows on his knees, his chin cupped in his hand. "You are too wise for your youth."

"Not so wise, John, or I wouldn't be here, tempting—"

"Me?"

"Myself."

"West country honesty again."

She sighed. "I have no other."

John stood in one movement. "Then it is home to my manor of Kelston in Somerset for us."

"I pray so . . . if that time ever comes." She looked down to her hands twisting in her lap.

John lifted her from the chair and held her head gently against his shoulder.

"He is coming soon . . . Lord Howard," Mary said finally.

John retreated to arm's length and looked into her eyes. "Yes, for the hunting. The queen told me. You will give the man no encouragement."

"He needs none."

"Your indifference might discourage him."

"The thought of the salt revenues will hearten him."

John closed the space between them and took her in his arms again. "Mary, the queen has always used marriages to cement alliances. She sees him as her ally against the northern lords who long for a king. He longs for one, too, but is wise enough not to put his wishes on paper, where Cecil can read them." A bit of sea coal rolled from the grate and flared on the hearth. He left her and kicked it back where it belonged

She held out her arms, begging for his return. He obeyed.

"You know that I must attend my estate soon," he said. "I have been too long gone from those duties. The queen is right about that."

Mary was silent for a time, watching the renewed fire as it filled the tiny cottage with warmth and flickering light.

John whispered against her cheek, "Do not despair. God is not so cruel as to grant us this feeling, only to take it away."

"That is my fear. God will leave us with this emotion and no way . . ." A dull pain filled Mary's chest. "Never forget Elizabeth rules here, John."

His hands swept up her back, gripping her hard. "She rules the kingdom, but not our hearts. She will change her mind. She must. I will find a way. Trust me," he said, pressing her closer, and she raised her lips, holding fast to him for a moment to keep from falling; then she fled back across the quadrangle and into the hunting lodge.

❖

Lord Howard arrived in late June with an impressive entourage of one hundred twenty knights and men-at-arms, bringing presents of furs and jewels that the queen loved, especially an exquisite ivory brooch carved with the likeness of Diana, the Greek goddess of the hunt, surrounded by perfect rubies. "Majesty," he said, kneeling, his hand on his heart, "I bring you these loyal men to show you how I am able to protect your northern interests."

"We thank you, my lord Howard," she answered, obviously pleased. "You must hunt with us on the morrow. But tell us, how rests your good lady?"

He bowed his head. "Feebly, Majesty. She does not recognize her own children most days."

"Pray God she is soon easier, my lord."

"Amen," said Lord Howard, raising his eyes devoutly, though they swept across Mary's breasts on their way to heaven.

The next day dawned dry, but with a ground fog that rapidly became swirling wisps as the sun rose. The hunting party was off early, Lord Howard in an honored place at the queen's side. Mary and the queen's ladies who could ride well enough to stay with the queen followed. John rode to one side of the queen on his best hunter, following the beaters.

By midmorning the queen had shot at a doe with her bow and arrow, but, only wounded, the doe escaped, putting the queen in a sour mood.

Toward eleven of the morning, as they grew close to an open meadow where dinner was being laid on trestles, they came upon a magnificent stag of a most rare thirty points, a true horned tree atop its head. It looked like a king standing on a slight rise at the edge of the forest. The queen gasped in admiration. "We must have that stag."

Mary watched as John drew his horse in closer. What was he doing? He dared not shoot first.

Elizabeth signaled for her crossbow, which reached her hands with a loaded quarrel. She cocked the weapon and, taking aim, she shot, her eyes for hunting undimmed. The deer staggered from the impact, blood showing on its chest, but it did not go down. Instead, it shook its huge head as if—like Elizabeth herself—to deny any hurt and leapt to escape into the open.

Elizabeth's anguished cry rang out. "My noble beast!"

"What a pity, Majesty," Lord Howard called.

Mary could not believe what happened next. John dug in his spurs and raced after the stag now thundering into the open meadow. He drew alongside, his horse matching the stag stride for stride. Was he trying to run it to death? "Take care, John!" she shouted before she thought.

John heard her as he wound his reins about his saddle horn and kicked out of his stirrups, tensing his thigh muscles for the leap. He landed not as square as he would have liked, but, grabbing the stag's rack, he righted himself and wrenched the beast's head gradually about, sensing that great heart was heaving. A mist of blood and sweat flowed back over him as he turned the huge deer, his weight slowing its speed.

John's arms were numb with wrestling that giant bone rack while trying not to be stabbed by one of its far-arching points. His knees ached from their strong pressure to stay on the bounding back not made for riding.

The animal staggered as it approached the queen's party arrayed in a line across the field, the beaters frantically waving and shouting. Mary had dismounted to stand by the queen's side.

John hauled back on the horns with all his strength, the air whistling through the stag's flared nostrils as it gave up life unwillingly. With one last, long shudder, the beast stumbled and dropped dead not a man's length from an astonished Elizabeth, the light leaving its eyes as she stared into them.

At the last second, as the stag reeled, John leapt from its back. He dropped to his knees in utter exhaustion before the queen. Reaching for a cap that was no longer on his head, he said, "Your stag, Majesty."

At that moment, Lord Howard rushed now to the queen's side, pushing Mary away. "Majesty, my horse stumbled, or I would have been here by—"

If the queen heard him, she gave no notice. She raised John, bloodying her own hands. "Sir Knight, we name you henceforth Queen's Champion."

Mary wrenched her gaze away from John, covered with blood, but glorious in his near collapse, to the astonished faces in the crowd. Essex had been champion. She knew the appointment honored John and would keep him much at court, but it would bring him the Earl of Essex and his friends' enmity . . . not to mention Lord Howard's.

And now, oh, how could the queen deny her champion's dearest wish?

The next day, amidst the fast-spreading, excited talk of John's riding the huge stag, heard in the court and in all London, the glorious thirty-point rack was mounted in Her Majesty's privy chamber. She was not so grateful to her champion as to give up her prize.

CHAPTER FIFTEEN

"Those who touch the scepters of princes deserve no pity."
—Elizabeth Regina

Michaelmas
September 29, 1600

John Harington cantered up to Essex House on a bright fall morning, crushing the fallen leaves between the cobbles. He found the courtyard and anterooms filled with as many disgruntled men as could crowd within them.

He dismounted and shouldered his way through the throng, seeing severe Puritans in their black garb who did not think Elizabeth had taken the Church of England far enough from Catholicism. They stood chockablock with Catholics openly wearing their gold crosses, who longed for a return of their ancient religion. Roughly dressed, heavily armed members of the earl's Irish army completed the throng, loyal captains and sergeants who thought their leader ill-treated and hoped to gain by their loyalty.

Essex sat on a dais in a large chamber looking like a king holding court, with the Earl of Southampton and Sir Christopher Blount in fawning attendance.

John tensed, determined to watch his back. He did not bring good news from the queen. "My lord," John said, bowing, "I would speak to you in private."

"Ah, the queen's new champion. What say you, champion? We

are all of a mind and dear friends here. What does the queen send to tell her most faithful subject?" There was laughter at that, and John gripped the hilt of his French thrusting sword, lighter than his old slashing weapon and made for closer fighting.

"My lord Earl of Essex," he said formally, "the queen has decided in council not to renew your monopoly on sweet wines at this time. She will return those revenues to the Crown." There, it was out in the open. He steeled himself for the anger that was certain to follow.

John sensed from the instant hush that everyone waited for the earl to react. He waited, too, although he had spared Essex the rest of what the queen had said, but he had no doubt that it would eventually reach him: "An unruly beast must have his resources stopped," she had announced to Cecil and Raleigh, shocking words that soon echoed throughout the palace, since many of the lords relied on the queen's generosity to pay the debts they incurred serving her.

Essex did not speak. Did not move. His face was unreadable, although the blue vein at his temple throbbed. The crowd's voice behind John slowly rose from a hum to a roar, and treasonous shouts urging the earl to rebellion erupted about him. Men drew their swords half from their scabbards, and John saw that a few even wore breastplates. This was a group bent on rebellion.

Essex raised his hand for quiet. "You lie, champion." He chopped his words into harsh syllables. "The queen never removed my monopoly on sweet wines. It is all Cecil and Raleigh's doing. They are planning to beggar me . . . then murder me!"

At that, Essex's men cried out, some now waving their swords aloft.

The earl stared at John, his eyes haunted by doubt, defeat and self-delusion, as he fought on. "I will not believe such an insult unless I hear the words from Her Majesty's mouth. I will go to her at once."

"My lord," John said, more alarmed than he wished known, "you are allowed abroad from this place, but denied the palace." He raised his voice. "On my honor, the queen removed the monopoly of her own will. It is hers to give or take, and her word is now law."

Essex, losing any caution he had remaining, rose, towering over everyone. He choked out angry words that seemed to ring around the room: "Denied the palace! The monopoly on wine seized! If she would beggar me, then her laws are as crooked as her carcass!"

John knew that unforgivable slur would echo across the Thames and into Whitehall to the foot of the throne, perhaps before he could return to soften the blow, if such were possible.

"I take leave of you for the last time, my lord." John turned and pushed through to the door and to his horse, sweat beading on his forehead despite the cool breeze. The air was charged with panic and insurrection, and their weight bore down on him.

At Whitehall, Mary waited for him to dismount in the privy gardens near the royal mews, pretending to search out a bouquet. They had not met alone since his recent return from his western estate and her return from attending the queen on her summer progress.

"John . . . dearest," Mary said when he approached. She stretched a trembling hand to him, wanting to touch him and make him real. But when he reached for her, she warned, "Have a care." She nodded toward the gallery windows overlooking the garden.

"You ask too much," he said, kissing her hand. "If I cannot hold you . . ."

She had to stop him and herself from open disobedience to the queen's will. "I love you, John."

"Love is a word," he said, bowing his head, lest she see his face unmanned. "Mark me, sweetest, my need is greater than ever."

"And mine, John." She wanted to take the two small steps that would bring her to rest inside his arms, but she could not, so she moved away and bent to pick a flower. His face was tanned from a summer in the sun. "You look well, Sir Knight."

Regaining his humor, he answered, "I am now."

She smiled. "You haven't changed." She straightened and grew serious. "When I heard you were sent to Essex, I was so worried for you. They say he is a mad mixture of sweet regret and frantic rebellion."

John bowed again. "I saw nothing sweet this day," he said. "Essex gravely insulted the queen."

"Sweet Jesus! What did he say?"

When John repeated the ugly words, Mary was astonished. "If all his adoring letters are false, the ones she has kept and reads again by her fire at night, she will truly never forgive him."

"I should have challenged him on the spot."

"You couldn't challenge a mob!"

"As Queen's Champion, it was my duty—"

"—to return to her whole . . . and to me, John." The last words were whispered.

They were standing too close now, fueling court gossip, but he could not help but bend toward her. He was using all his strength to keep even a small distance from her lips. "When can we be alone? Tonight?"

"The queen has commanded me to sleep in her chamber tonight. Tomorrow, John. I will come to you as soon as I can."

"I saw your grandfather on my way back to London."

He had surprised her.

"Why? What did—"

He grinned. "As you said, Mistress Mary, we must both wait until tomorrow to gain what we want now." She looked so disappointed that his humor softened. "Have hope," he said.

"Hope falters."

He came so close his breath warmed her cheek. "But it always returns, sweetheart."

He was right. Sometimes she tried to shake it off, yet hope crept back into her heart unbidden. Encouraged, she said, "I will attempt to take my supper in the great hall today."

He winked. "But I am hungry now."

She curtsied, unable to hide her delight in him, which she feared shone like a beacon for all to see. Though she did not look up at the palace windows behind her, she suspected they held eyes that saw and mouths that would gabble all they suspected. John walked on toward the entrance to the stone gallery, and she stopped to pick another small bunch of yellow tansies, proving this was the errand she had always intended.

Mary was delayed in the royal kitchens below, ordering the light dinner of broth, bread and marzipan fruit the queen preferred. When she reached the royal apartment, Her Majesty was playing her lute and her ladies were singing. Mary knew the tune and words were the queen's own and sung when melancholy was heavy on her. Had hurtful news of Essex's personal insult flown to her faster than a high tide?

As a child, Mary had overheard Katherine Grey say that Elizabeth needed the constant flattering adoration of young and handsome men, who declared her the beauty of their hearts as well as of the realm. Mary had not understood the import of those words, but now remembered and understood. At this time of the queen's old age, although she had banished mirrors for two decades, Mary knew the queen could not bear to suspect that those treasured words were now false, or had ever been.

Mary sat in the circle around Her Majesty and joined her naturally vibrato voice to the song. The queen looked up and nodded, no recognizable emotion showing in her kohl-rimmed eyes.

> *"When I was fair and young,*
> *Then favor graced me. . . ."*

The queen's fingers plucked the strings as if she had no pain in them, though Mary knew she did most mornings. And Her Majesty sang no more with her ladies, since her voice was now hoarse and cracking.

"How many weeping eyes I made to pine in woe.
How many sighing hearts, yet I the prouder grow . . ."

Mary looked down and saw that she had twisted the tansy stems, and their petals had begun to wilt in her hands.

As the queen started the chorus, without announcement or warning, the doors to the privy chamber burst open and Essex rushed in. Lady Margaret squealed, her hand flying to her throat. Lady Anne Russell, who had taken Lady Fitton's place, turned white and slumped in a chair.

The earl, looking the gallant young lord in shining black velvet, starched white ruff and flowing curls, threw himself at the queen's feet and grasped the hem of her gown, kissing it as if to devour lace, pearls and all.

"Most beloved queen of my heart—" His voice rumbled low and intense, filling the chamber with masculine passion.

He got no further. The queen snatched her gown from his hands and leapt to her feet, her lute landing on the carpeted floor. She backed away from his desperate effort to clutch at her, saying no word, nor calling for her guard. The cold scorn on her face would have frozen any sensible man.

The earl, though off balance, stood upright. Frightened for the queen, Mary came as close to Elizabeth as she dared. If Essex drew his sword to deliver a blow, she would take the thrust.

But it wasn't Elizabeth who faced danger. The queen did not flinch and advanced on Essex. He held his arms up for her to walk into, but she knocked them wide, pushing her fists against his chest until he stumbled backward.

The earl was obviously astonished. "Majesty! I beg you . . . speak to me. . . . Listen to my sorrow. I have been desolate these eleven months without your love to guide me away from the mistakes of youth and crazed ardor. In truth, Your Grace—"

The queen advanced again, no sound coming from her, no

softening of her cold stare. She showed no hot anger, only hard contempt in every gesture and every line of her face, her corded neck thrust forward. She pushed him again. And again, he stumbled backward, his mouth working, but now no intelligible words exiting. He had obviously relied on the nearness of his person to melt her to forgiveness as it always had.

With one final thrust that must have taken all her strength, she pushed him into the antechamber and slammed the doors in his still unbelieving face.

Mary approached Elizabeth's back, worried that she might be near collapse from her exertions. "Majesty, may I ease you with a little wine?"

The queen whirled about, her face triumphant. "This crooked carcass needs no food or drink to best such foolish men. He thinks I need him, that I cannot let him go . . . that he is the stronger," she said, scarcely above a whisper, and then in full voice: "Pish!"

Only Mary heard all the words and understood their meaning, knowing that they were the best part of the queen's victory over Essex and her own heart.

Elizabeth crossed to the lute on the floor, picked it up and struck a solid chord, croaking, " '. . . and I the prouder grow.' "

For the rest of the afternoon she sat alone before her fire, admitting no one, though Cecil, Raleigh and others of her privy council sought audience. Her usually straight posture showed every sign of exhaustion, and Mary stayed near and busy, plying her embroidery needle on a piece of pillow linen.

Later in the great dining hall, Mary sat next to John, sipped apple wine and dipped a salad radish in the salt, repeating all that had happened. "John, Her Majesty said no word to Essex. It was most strange, even frightening. But after he was gone she repeated what he said of her at Essex House." Mary shivered. "She loved him and gave him everything and now he shows that he was false. I may never forget the terrible look on her face. I have never seen such before."

"Quiet yourself, Mary," John said softly. He broke bread for her plate and, using a hooked knife, speared a piece of meat from a large pork pie in its trencher, ladling its meaty pudding and spicy broth on top. "I think it means that Essex is now completely lost to the queen's affection."

"What will he do?"

"If he takes good council, he will leave for the country and not return."

"Will he take good council?"

"No."

They ate in silence for a few minutes, although Mary felt the pressure of his thigh against hers and returned it until, too heated for the heavy food, she shifted her leg away. She dared not look at him, but pushed her pudding aside, having no appetite left. "The queen needs me more than ever, John." Her voice trembled.

He did not look at her. "I am a man, Mary. Waiting for you is an agony."

Her eyes made tears, but she would not allow them to slide to her cheek. "I am a woman, John. Misery is not yours alone."

The pressure of John's knee returned, warmer than before.

Bowing his head, John whispered, "I humbly beg pardon, mistress." He struggled to regain calm. "All is not lost. The longer she withholds the warrant for the salt tax from Lord Howard, the more time we have to plead our cause." He raised his pewter tankard. "Here's to his lady's health."

She drew a deep, trembling breath, and glimpsed what John must have seen, her breasts pushing against her gown as if they would escape into his hands. She reddened and gathered her courage. "What did you say to my grandfather? And he to you?"

Mary hoped anyone observing them would not know that they spoke words between chewing their food. They had tried to feed gossip through the court that John's absence had cooled their interest.

He speared a piece of fish. "I took him a prize ram, which he thought to refuse, but could not bring himself to do." John smiled. "He is not a stupid man to refuse a gift that would better his flock and his purse."

"But he is proud and would not accept your gift if he had not changed his heart in some way. Did he say anything about Lord Howard?"

"In truth, he did not mention him, or you, nor did I. We talked of his better prospects for the next lambing season, though you were in our minds, sweetheart."

She was amazed and a tad angered, her words tinged with sharp humor. "Am I then the prize dam?"

"My sweet," he said, not bothering to hide his amusement, "it might have been put into his thoughts that he would prefer his grandchildren in Somerset near Bath rather than in the north with Lord Howard." He cocked his head and looked at her, his eyes crinkling. "It cannot be wrong to encourage such desire in a halting old man without a male heir."

"I did not think you so devious."

"Old habits, Mistress Mary, but used now to greater good."

She stood and curtsied, a tremor of a smile she couldn't stop reaching her lips. "There is still some rogue in you."

He bowed where he sat, spooning up some pudding. "You will be glad of it someday."

She laughed now, unable to hold her amusement inside. "Soon?"

He licked his spoon. "If almighty God is good."

Or almighty queen. She could not utter such traitorous blasphemy aloud, but God help her, she thought it.

"Tomorrow night, then," he said in a low voice. "We need to talk more, to plan without every eye on us."

"But it's not wise . . . to be alone, John," she said, but was unable to say the word *no*, which should have made her more cautious.

"Meeting perhaps lacks a certain good judgment, but is absolutely necessary," he said, his voice even softer, but at no less an urgent pitch, "or I do assure you, Mary, Mary, if I cannot hold you, I will run quite spectacularly wild through all of Whitehall."

All that fall and winter, while John, as Queen's Champion, was sent on one and another mission, Mary continued to hope against her reason that all would be well with them at the end, that this was God's test for true lovers. Although her grandfather's letters were more affectionate than ever they had been and even called John generous, there was no bending in him. So she was left with the daily round of duties for the queen, and with her hope—perhaps all that she would ever have of John in this life. But the second she thought it, she rejected the idea. And what was that but more hope? John had told her so and now she knew it.

In January of 1601, Lady Howard breathed her last, but as Mary prayed almost hourly for rain, the swollen rivers and streams overflowed in flood, and roads from the north became impassible for horse or carriage. She began to believe that God was not in favor of her union with the northern lord. It had to be the almighty. He was the only one who could defy Elizabeth Tudor.

By February, news reached the queen's council that Essex House was seething with plots, and these plans had reached a crescendo. The queen called Robert Cecil to her.

"Lord Secretary, there is much churning of people and wild talk about my lord Essex."

"Yes, Majesty. There is an urgent rumor that he plans to surprise the court and take your person captive. I am aware and have spies in his midst."

"He would kill a queen!"

"No, Majesty, though he would force you to call Parliament and alter the government."

"Alter!" The queen was outraged at the top of her voice. "Does he seek to make me a figurehead in my father's kingdom?"

Cecil's answer was tongue-in-cheek, but no less true. "He sees the need, Majesty, for you to accept his advice in all things. Chiefly, Your Grace, to have all his enemies arrested and tried."

"You, Pygmy?" Her voice was soft and the nickname used lovingly.

Cecil nodded. "Me most of all, madam. And many others not loyal to him."

"This is treason!"

"If he tries to accomplish his aims . . . yes. But the proof must be stark for all the people to see."

Mary saw the sting of those words in the queen's hands as they clutched her gown.

"Your Grace, there is more."

"Christ's nails and chains! What more could there be?"

"He has sent one of his men with bribing gold to have *Richard II* played in the Globe this day."

Elizabeth leapt up and began pacing and thinking aloud: "So that our people of London will think to help him depose me as Bolingbroke deposed Richard."

"Tempted, I would say, Majesty. But I have sent a herald through London streets proclaiming Essex and his followers traitors."

"Call him before the council to explain himself."

"Your Grace, as chief councilor, I have already summoned him. He replied that he was too ill and refused a physician."

"Then send my Lord Keeper Edgerton and the Lord Chief Justice to arrest him . . . on a litter if necessary."

"Majesty, Sir John, your champion, returned to court this morning."

"They were once friends." She hesitated. "Send Sir John, as well. Perhaps their old friendship will work to quiet the earl's hot head." She added grimly, "Before it is too late."

Cecil made his limping way to her writing table and laid several parchments upon it. "These are arrest warrants, Your Grace. In addition, I have taken the precaution of doubling the palace guard. Essex has upward of three hundred men under arms."

The queen rushed to sign all necessary orders, which flew from her hand to Cecil's.

Mary hastened to John's rooms and into his bedchamber. He had thrown his dusty travel cloak on the reed floor matting and was warming himself with mulled wine before the fire.

He stood on sight of her, his arms wide. "Did anyone see you?"

She resisted stepping into his welcoming embrace. "John, listen. The palace is seething with news of Essex—"

"What? What has he done?"

"The queen sends for you to help with his arrest."

"Arrest! It has finally come to that?"

"Arrest will surely follow his appearance before the council."

They both heard a loud knocking at his antechamber door and a voice announcing John's summons. "Sir John, you must attend my lord Cecil at once."

John grabbed up his thigh-high boots warming by the fire.

"Have a care, John." Mary spoke softly as she watched him grab up his heavy cloak and sword. She stood close and knotted the ties about his neck. "Essex is planning to take the governance of the realm into his hands." She quickly repeated all that she had heard of Cecil's news.

John shook his head in disbelief. "He has gone too far. The queen will suffer words against her person, but as he touches her scepter, he is a dead man."

"He believes all London will rise against Her Majesty if he calls them to it."

"He was ever overconfident of his own charms."

She could not help herself. "That is a failing of many men, my love."

He tilted her chin. "But not true of me," he whispered, his lips nearly touching hers. "I have charms as yet unused and ready."

She laughed. With his kiss on her lips, he left, though she thought herself quite impossibly foolish, sending him away to danger with merriment. Yet she knew that was how John wished it.

At the Whitehall Palace water stairs, John joined Lord Keeper Edgerton, the Earl of Worcester and Sir William Knollys, kin to Essex's mother, in Edgerton's boat. They were rowed across the Thames to Essex House, the river now unfrozen where a month earlier a frost fair had had half of London gliding about on their bone skates. Even so, jagged ice occasionally swept past as the rowers pulled hard against the incoming tide.

Clutching his heavy cloak about him, John spoke aloud his thoughts. "My lords, we go to a lion's den. Why could we not bring a heavy guard?"

"Why warn him of an impending arrest when he may come peaceably to answer the council?" Edgerton asked.

John thought there was little chance of that. Were they bait to push Essex into full, flaming rebellion?

John, his heart pounding, stepped from the boat onto the earl's riverside pier. Essex and his allies, the Earl of Southampton, Sir Christopher Blount and a rabble of followers at his back, came out upon the pier, their swords, primed pistols and dirks drawn. One soldier even pissed his disdain, arching the stream in their direction.

Edgerton, planting his staff of office, said in a very commanding voice, "My lord, lay down your weapons and come at once to the council at court. The queen commands you to obey."

Knollys added in a choking voice, "Robert, I swear you will be honorably treated."

John saw a flash of understanding cross the earl's face as he realized that any resistance put him beyond the aid of either kinsman or friends. Yet it was not in Essex's nature to hold a sensible thought for very long, especially one that challenged his idea of his own destiny.

With men eager to fight pushing behind him, the earl's eyes swept the queen's men and fixed on John. *"Et tu, Brute?"*

At that moment John knew that Essex thought himself a Caesar and others the traitors. There was no hope for him.

"Take them," Essex said, and his men swarmed about Edgerton, John, Worcester and Knollys, taking their weapons and tossing them to the ground.

"Kill them," someone yelled.

"No!" Essex ordered. "We may have need of hostages. Lock them in the library upstairs."

John, his hands tied with his own cloak, was relieved of his purse by a leering ruffian, then shoved past Essex, who put a hand to his shoulder. "You could have been part of this and had a glorious future in my service."

John could not answer. How could he respond to a fantasy growing in a man's mind like a malignant tumor that took away all space for reality? Rough hands pushing him, John stumbled up the stairs and heard the key turn in the lock. He stalked to the window and looked down on the seething mass of men below.

Essex's voice carried to the upper floor. "Now we go to free England from those scheming traitors Cecil and Raleigh!" He rushed forward, men crowding behind him.

Edgerton, his face choleric, pushed John aside, uselessly shaking his head at the rabble. "They are madmen."

"My lord," John said, "we must get word to the queen that Essex is loose in the streets with a mob at his back, bent on rebellion."

"We are imprisoned, man."

John rushed to the door and put his shoulder to it, joined by Knollys, but the heavy oaken planks did not give. John turned his back to Knollys. "Untie me."

Within minutes he was free, freeing Knollys, who untied the others. He began to fasten their cloaks together to make a rope.

"What is your purpose, Sir John?" Edgerton asked, frowning.

"To stop Essex and warn the queen." He heaved a chair through the window, shattering the glass, then tied the bulky rope to a heavy table and pushed it against the wall beneath the window.

"The rope's not long enough," Knollys announced, catching hold of John's arm.

John paid no attention, but, standing on the jutting stone sill, tested the rope against his weight, then finally began to lower himself. His feet felt for toeholds on the rough stone, but in the end he jumped well over his own height to the cobbled courtyard below. He felt the sharp pain of his ankle giving way and scraped his knee, but the triumph of being free lessened the hurt.

He hobbled to the pier, but the Lord Keeper's boat had been cut free and was floating toward London Bridge. He grabbed up his sword and dirk, fortunately left behind on the courtyard stones, and, steeling himself to his ankle pain, moved rapidly toward the Strand. He arrived just in time to see Lady Essex leaving in her carriage, calling from the window, "Good citizens, as you love my lord Essex, rise up and protect him!"

Lady Essex had not waited for footmen, so John leapt to their standing place at the rear of the carriage and rode there, trying to ignore the jarring ache in his leg until they neared the mob. "To St. Paul's churchyard," he heard them yell.

Windows and doors were shutting as they passed. The streets were empty, though this was Sunday and all Englishmen must be churched on this day or pay a fine. The royal heralds warning the city had done their job well.

A beadle stood in the deep shadow of a goldsmith's shop, having no appetite to try to control such a rowdy, armed mob.

The coach stopped and John dismounted, grabbing the beadle's arm and drawing him from his hiding place. "I am Sir John Harington, Queen's Champion, and I command you to warn Whitehall that my lord Essex is at the head of a rabble in open rebellion!"

The beadle's mouth gaped and stayed that way.

John pointed toward King Street, leading to the palace. "Quickly, man! With all speed! Move, or you'll sleep in the Tower this night!"

Without waiting for him to obey, John drew his sword and hurried on after Essex, detouring up Ludgate Hill, hoping to head him off. He must stop him! He could feel his ankle swelling against the hard leather of his boots, but he ignored the pain. Running down alleys, he heard Essex's voice yelling above the curious quiet of the city: "For the queen! Rally to me! Cecil plans to kill me and sell England to Spain—"

Doors and windows all along his way were tight shut, and citizens caught on the streets were running away from him. John saw Lady Essex draw up in her carriage and call out an alderman, who came from his house, got into her carriage and went immediately out the other door as fast as he could go.

John's heart swelled with admiration. There would be no uprising in the city. Londoners were loyal to Elizabeth.

To catch his breath and cease the throbbing of his ankle, John leaned against a half-timbered house. He caught sight of Essex rushing back from St. Paul's. Though now a cold wind and fog blew from the Thames, the earl's shirt and hair dripped with sweat and he turned in a circle like a blind man, demented. "Back! Back to Essex House," he yelled, his voice a wretched screech.

Grasping tight hold of his sword, John stepped into the earl's path. "My lord, surrender now, while you yet may throw yourself upon the queen's mercy."

"John, you've joined me after all." He wiped sweat from his eyes. "No," he said, his eyes at last recognizing what his ears had missed, "you're with them. You think those traitors Cecil and Raleigh should—"

"I think, my lord, it is over and you must know it."

Essex lowered his sword, his next words pushed through tightened lips. "You Judas."

John spoke softly, as all around Essex's men began to melt away into the dark alleys. "My lord, surrender now and play the man."

Essex lunged, but John's sword met his, sliding up to the hilt. They had bought these new French thrusting swords together and practiced in Ireland for many hours. The sour smell of defeat covered Essex, but he was driven by his demons. He stepped back and lunged again. "You'll die before me, John."

John parried, favoring his sore ankle and saw that the more they exchanged blows, the more the earl's men thought better of their lives and ran away. The army had become a mere company.

Sir Christopher Blount put his sword between them. "Robert, let him loose. We have a boat waiting to take you to France on the next ebb tide. Haste!"

Essex shook his head, sweat flying in all directions. "We'll see who's champion of England," he yelled, focusing all his frustration and hatred on the enemy at hand.

John met his thrust, twisting his blade over Essex's so that he lost his grip and the sword clattered to the street. He could have thrust at that open chest, once so laden with honors, but he lowered his sword, touching the cobbles, his arm leaden, his heart sick of this useless fight with a man lacking all sense.

For a spent man, Essex moved with insane speed. Snatching up his rapier and sweeping it from the street, he stabbed his sword into John's chest.

A sting like a hundred bees staggered John and he fell to his knees. Strangely, his scraped knee now hurt worse than his ankle.

"Robert! For Christ's pity, he let you live!" Kit Blount pulled Essex away and, dazed, he stumbled after, looking back once. Before John's eyes closed, he recognized regret on the earl's face. A moment of reason, a faded memory of the comrades they had once been. Then John thought no more.

❖

Mary waited with the queen, her other ladies and Robert Cecil as news came to the palace with every hour. At first they heard that all London was in revolt.

"Pish!" Elizabeth said, stopping in her pacing. "First news from a battle is always false."

She took up a breastplate and slid her arms through the armor's leather strapping and, taking up her sword, made for the door. "But if they dare reach my palace, they will face me!"

"Your Grace," Cecil said in great alarm, "I beg you, do not expose yourself."

The queen marched on into the hall, her back as straight as any soldier's. "Do you think Henry Tudor's spawn will hide in her closet from traitorous rabble?"

Cecil, much shorter than Elizabeth, threw himself to his knees in front of her. "I beg you, Majesty, stay within the palace. I've doubled the guard. The London watch surrounds the city. Your enemies are defeated and running away on every side."

Joining her voice to his, Mary knelt and begged, her hands prayerfully folded. "Your Grace, I entreat you, allow your guards to do their duty to their sovereign. We will have all traitors by nightfall."

Elizabeth stopped at that, ever aware, as Mary had known, of a queen's place in the chain of being. She commanded; others fought. Her troops knew she stood with them as she had at Tilbury, when the Spanish armada came against England.

Mary saw all the queen must be thinking. "Majesty, your courage is already a legend to Englishmen."

Elizabeth breathed deeply, anger fading in her deep-set eyes until no emotion showed at all. "Pygmy," she said, bending slightly to raise him, her back less rigid, "tell me at once when my lord of Essex is taken."

"Aye, madam, at once."

To chase away winter's early dusk that heightened her concern for John, Mary was lighting candles in the queen's apartments when word came that Essex was taken. Hopelessly surrounded, he and his close followers released their prisoners, broke their swords and surrendered. They were quickly on their way downriver to the Tower.

"Thank you, my lord," Elizabeth said, a stillness surrounding her.

Cecil nodded, composing his face. "And yet there is sad news, Majesty. Your champion, Sir John, escaped his captors, but was gravely injured when he fought the earl in the streets."

Mary dropped the taper from her hand. "No!"

Cecil ignored Mary. "Sir John was carried to the Lord Mayor's house. Your Grace, I have sent your physicians as I knew you would want. The earl's blade missed Sir John's heart, but—"

Mary ran from the queen's apartments, and did not hear Elizabeth commanding her to return.

All the long afterward, Mary did not remember hiring the coach that took her to the Lord Mayor's house, and had only faint memory of flinging her purse at the coachman, too shaken to count out a single silver shilling.

She bruised her hand banging on the Lord Mayor's door, but was admitted, despite her wild eyes and tearstained face. "I come from the queen," she announced to the startled Lord Mayor wearing his heavy gold chain of office, and rushed past him up to a gallery bedchamber, its open door showing light.

Physicians, in their star-studded black gowns, stood around the canopied bed as Mary pushed through to the bedside. "John," she whispered at sight of the bloody bandage on his chest, his face white and lips slack. Cupped leeches sucked at his chest and swollen ankle.

"Why leech him?"

"Lady, if the blade struck his lungs, they will fill with blood."

Fear squeezed her heart and she could not breathe for her head spinning close to the abyss, where darkness would erase this moment and those she feared would follow. "Oh, dear Jesus in heaven, help him."

A hand came down hard on her shoulder. "This man must not be disturbed. Are you his wife?"

With all her heart, she wanted to say *yes*, but she swallowed and answered truthfully, the words tumbling out: "A friend. A *dear* friend. I serve the queen, and Her Majesty must know his condition."

"We have not yet been able to examine his urine, though we have given him syrup of woundwort to provoke it," the doctor replied gravely. "We will send news."

Another physician bent to her. "Do you know his natal day and hour? The heart is ruled by Leo, the lungs by Gemini. In truth, we must cast his horoscope to make a good diagnosis."

She shook her head, only dimly hearing him. Her ears were tuned to John's shallow breathing, her eyes riveted to his face. "I beg you, sirs, will he live? Speak! Give me hope."

"The blade missed his heart or he would be dead at once, but he is gravely wounded."

"Yet will he live?" She heard her own strangled voice echoing against the paneled walls, but it was the next words she was forced to carry away to echo in her mind.

"Who among us knows? The answer lies in his stars."

Lord Essex's trial was swift, and although he tried to implicate Cecil in treason with Spain, no one, not judges nor Londoners, least of all Elizabeth, believed his ravings.

The queen signed his death warrant a few days later, betrayed by her love and tolerance for a wild horse that now would be tamed in the only way he could be.

Mary packed her belongings while waiting for the carriage that would take her back to Somersetshire. She was sent from court until

Her Majesty chose to reinstate her. Temporary banishment was the mildest of punishments for disobeying the queen, but it was far worse to Mary than any broken finger. She would gladly have given an entire hand to have news of John, to know how he fared. Was he taking food? Sitting up? She had failed him. She had failed the queen.

Her Majesty's physicians reported daily that he survived, but despite their superior physicks, they frowned when Her Majesty asked if he would recover, calling his sun signs troubling.

Elizabeth spoke clearly. "If he lives, I will send my best litter to have him safely taken to his manor of Kelston."

Packing done, Mary sat on her bed, clasping her shaking body, shivering half from winter and more from her fear for the future. Would God give her strength to bear the unbearable?

Through the open door to the anteroom, she could hear the queen playing upon her virginals, a merry tune, which she continued despite the sound of Cecil's voice.

"Your Grace," the Lord Secretary said, and Mary could see him kneeling and straightening his bent back with a grimace of pain. "The Earl of Essex is dead this hour of sixteen February, 1601. His last words were in praise of you."

The music ceased for the space of two ticks of the great case clock. And then the cheery, tinkling tune began again.

When Mary reluctantly arrived home from court in early March of 1601, she found her grandfather sleeping in the great hall before the fire, in such poor health that he had not the strength to climb the stairs. She forced herself to turn her mind from John to Sir William, and had him taken immediately upstairs to his bedchamber.

A dreary March passed slowly, its dark, sweeping storms making most roads impassable. Hearing only the steady *drip, drip* from the eaves, Mary bundled against the cold seeping into the manor, swirling down halls and behind bed hangings. She thought back to Lady

Grey and wondered if she and her Ned had watched and waited through winter storms, hoping for Elizabeth's forgiveness as Mary waited now. Jesu, preserve her and John from that fate.

Finally, Lady Margaret wrote that the queen sometimes forgot and called for her Mouse. At last, welcome word came that John was recovering at his home near Bath, and Mary found some bitter relief in caring for her grandfather, since she could do nothing but worry for John.

As winter passed into spring, she was thankful to keep herself busy supervising the lambing and sat long hours in Sir William's bedchamber, which his doctor had ordered darkened. She administered borage, rosemary and citron pills to hold back invasive melancholy vapors, wondering if she didn't need this physick herself.

"Sir William's heart is overheated," advised another physician from Taunton Town, bleeding him from his right arm and calling for powder of bullock's heart as a strengthening cordial, since a strong bull's heart gave the same strength to a man's. Could this physick help John? She determined to dispatch some with her next letter.

As summer came on, she stood at the front windows watching the Bath road, eager for news of John, praying for good reports from his sister, Lora, who cared for him, but few riders passed, and none bearing the words of hope she longed to hear.

Sir William wasted in strength and appetite until he could not swallow without choking. As hot summer became a smothering August, Mary read aloud from the Bible by flickering candlelight to comfort him and to pass hours in some absorbing occupation that would quiet her fears. The two men she loved in all the world were beyond her help. She implored God often, her days thick with prayer.

Sir William came alert only at the sound of rider or carriage below his window.

"Has the queen recalled you to service?" he asked again one day when she returned from greeting neighbors who had come to inquire and leave favored medicines.

"No, Grandfather."

Another day it was the royal post rider. "A letter from Lady Margaret," Mary told him truthfully, but less truthfully did not add that she had also received a letter from John's elder sister, Lora.

"Read what Lady Margaret says, child." Wearily he turned his wasted face toward her, though he was only dimly focusing.

She quickly scanned the cramped writing on the single page. Her heart beat faster to learn that when Lord Howard had come to court in May the queen had sent him away, saying that she would release his promised lady only when her service to her queen was finished. Bless Her Majesty. She couldn't wait to tell John.

"What does the letter say?" Sir William asked again.

Hastily, Mary read the rest of the page. "Lady Margaret writes that the queen says no one keeps her linen as I did." Mary smiled at the look of pride on her grandfather's face, and read on: "She says that if I write to Her Majesty admitting my error, I would be quickly forgiven."

"Have you not written to the queen earlier?"

"Nay, sir, for I do know how the queen hates supplicating pleas until her anger has cooled."

"Then you must write . . . at once," Sir William said, seeming to sink farther into the pillows that supported him, his face white with the effort to speak.

"I cannot leave you, Grandfather." She hid all her longing for Elizabeth's forgiveness and a quick return to her service by the longer north road passing near John's manor.

"The servants will give me care. . . . I have little time left on this earth. Just as well, child. My life has run its course. My only regret is that I will . . . will not see you married and titled . . . secure with husband and children." He stopped and caught a fleeting and shallow breath. "At least you will not go to Lord Howard as a pauper, for you will bring this manor and the second-largest sheep run in the Somersetshire levels." He waved toward a chest near his bed. "My will . . . in there. And call the priest, child. Tell him to come with all speed." Utterly exhausted, he closed his eyes and immediately and deeply slept.

Mary waited to see if he would wake and need her. Finally, when he did not stir, she called his majordomo. "Send for the parish priest at once, and sit with Sir William until I return," she said. She hastened to her own chamber and, taking a chair next to a window flooded with August sunlight, she opened John's sister's letter with trembling hands.

> *Mistress Rogers—or Mary, Mary, as my brother speaks of you—greetings. John wishes me to write that he mends with every thought of you and even speaks loudly of returning to court as if to deny his hurt, though I hasten to add that like any stubborn man he is not as strong as he chooses to think. He knows that your grandfather ails, but begs you to come to him when Sir William improves. I add my wish to his, since he insists he will take horse and come to you if he cannot see you soon.*
> *Lora Harington-North*

Mary read Lora's letter again, seeing John resisting bed and hearing him protest that he was well recovered. She saw him vividly through the words of the letter. He loved and wanted her, his heart answering hers.

The majordomo called to her from the hall. "Come," she said.

The door opened. "Mistress, I am saddened to tell you that Sir William did not awaken."

"He yet sleeps?" Mary asked, hoping for that answer.

"His soul flies to heaven, mistress."

Shocked back to reality, Mary gathered her skirts and raced past him down the portrait-lined gallery to her grandfather's room. "Grandfather," she murmured, leaning over him. She pulled a feather from a bolster and held it beneath his nose. No breath stirred the feather.

For a moment she wanted to succumb to her grief, but relief was there as well. His suffering was ended. He had lived out his last days in pain and darkness. Enough!

She ran to the windows and threw back the draperies and shutters, opening the room to fresh air. She would speed his way on beams of light.

Mary knelt beside Sir William, praying for his soul. Behind her, silent servants crowded the hall, their heads bowed.

The next fortnight was so full of grief, priests, lawyers and the cares of repairing the drainage canals to prepare for winter flooding, and generally ordering the manor, that Mary was glad of the days passing swiftly until she could go to John. She took a precious hour to sit with Nurse Sybil and talk to her of the court and of seeing the Earl of Hertford.

"Were my lady's sons with him?" the ancient nurse asked, sitting by the fire to heat her cold bones.

"No, but the earl spoke to the queen on their behalf." Mary expected that Sybil would ask what the queen had responded and formed a gentle answer. But the nurse, having reached the great age of near eighty years, had fallen asleep.

Mary's letter of apology to the queen had been graciously received, and Her Majesty's mistress of the sweet herbs was ordered to return to court in all haste once her grandfather's affairs were settled. The answer signed by the queen's own hand filled her with tremendous joy. She was relieved to learn that she had found the right words, having agonized over every sentence, but finally yielding up formal phrases to a simple country truth:

> *Majesty, I am heartily sorry for my offense to your Kindness. I*
> *live for the hour I again may greet you in Health.*
> *Your loving and grateful,*
> *Mouse*

By mid-August at last her chests were packed, and she took carriage for Kelston Manor, a near full day's journey from central Somerset northwest toward the Mendip Hills. All those long hours she imagined John, not as she'd last seen him more than halfway to death in the Lord Mayor's upper chamber, but as he had been on her first day at court, when he had maddened and intrigued her by turn, weaving a web of passion about her that she would never throw off.

Though the sun was low, it was yet full summer light when she arrived at John's manor, half ancient stone, half recent timber, the old moat filled in and planted with a knot garden and fountain. Kelston sat nobly on a hill, where she was greeted by a pack of dogs and John limping toward her down a neat graveled entry path. He was thinner, his hair longer, his face clean shaven but pale from lying abed. He opened her carriage door before the coachman could dismount. She took his hand and stepped down, her body nearly numb from hours of jarring travel over rutted, dusty roads.

"Mary," he shouted, and tossed his crutch into a hedge. He almost fell into her, wrapping her in his arms, her name a breath against her ear: "Mary, Mary."

She clung to him, heedless of his sister or the curious onlooking servants, her heart pounding against his, and for long minutes she said nothing. It was enough to touch him, to sense his life restored, a life she had so lately feared was lost to her.

When they parted, she asked, "John, what happened to your leg?"

"Ankle broken when I leapt from Essex's library window," he answered, but quickly added, "Mended well."

"And your wound," she said, touching his shoulder lightly.

"Practically healed. I have but to regain my strength lost abed these months. My sister is a most diligent nurse." He bent close and she hoped he would kiss her, but his sister approached and they were introduced, exchanging courtesies.

"Mistress Rogers, do not believe his tales of vitality. The wound suppurated and poisoned his body. His doctors have prescribed gold pills for strength, which he refuses to take. Tell him, mistress, that he will need them to be a Queen's Champion." She smiled, and Mary knew Lora did not expect her brother to heed her. John retrieved his crutch and they walked into the manor's great hall.

"I have longed to meet you," Lora said, "since John talks of no one but you until I think there must be no other beautiful lady at court."

"Your brother often exaggerates," Mary said, failing to hide her delight.

"He has been known to do so."

Lora smiled, and Mary saw John's smile in his sister's. "Madam, I thank you for your welcome. Your brother is most fortunate in his nurse."

Impatient with talk, John escorted Mary through the hall, servants on both sides bowing and dipping as if she were the returning mistress of the house. She was embarrassed. "You do me too much honor, John."

"Never too much," he said. "How long can you remain?"

"A few days at best. The queen has recalled me to court."

"I will show Mistress Rogers to her bedchamber," John said, his tone that of master of the manor. Lora excused herself to supervise the supper.

He climbed the stairs, refusing to lean on his crutch or Mary, and opened the door of a large bedchamber, waiting impatiently for servants to deposit her chests. "Send a maid to serve Mistress Rogers . . . in an hour," he ordered, and they bowed themselves into the gallery.

As the door closed he grasped her to him and kissed her hungrily, his mouth as warm against hers as it ever had been, and as demanding.

Breathing rapidly, she leaned away, her gaze never leaving his.

"Your sister is quite wrong, sir. You are obviously once again ready to be a champion."

"Did I startle you? Forgive me, sweetheart. It's been so long," he said, pulling her to him once again. "I think I died and am now just come back to full life."

He swayed when he released her, and she drew him to a chair. "Sit yourself, John. You are not as strong as you want to believe you are."

"I am strong enough to show my love," he said.

"I believe you, sir," she said with a lighter tone. But her teeth were chattering with unspent passion and she drew a step away from his temptation. "I have news, John." She retrieved Lady Margaret's letter from her pocket, worn and creased from many readings, and handed it to him.

He scanned it swiftly, looking up at her before reading it again. "Did the queen change her mind about Lord Howard?" he asked, puzzled. Before Mary could answer he thought again. "Or was all this torment just diplomacy?"

As he bent forward to take her hands in his, Mary answered: "John, dear, I don't think Her Majesty knows herself. She has always refused to be ruled by her heart, would not listen to talk of love. Why would she change now?"

"Because, sweetheart, it is her last chance to show she can."

Mary breathed in, gathering his hope. "John, you are a romantic."

He clasped her hands tighter. "You didn't know?"

A flood of love filled her heart. He had not changed. He'd been badly wounded, they'd spent months apart, and nothing had changed between them.

Three days passed too swiftly. They spent long hours in the knot garden, talking about a future they could only dream of, painting word pictures of their hopes as they wanted them to be. But that was enough when all such dreams had been impossible for so long.

She thought he might come to her one night and waited until she heard the clock strike twelve, but he honored her and himself. Once, unable to sleep, she went to her window and saw him sitting on a garden bench under a bright moon, watching her chamber.

John's manor was larger than her grandfather's. Twice they wound their way by cart about his land. She admired his sheep run, his cow herd supping on lush, warm grass, from whose milk John made Harington sharp cheddar cheese. In his barn as maids stirred the vats of milk with large pierced paddles, he boasted, "The best cheddar in Somerset."

John took her to his cellars where the cheese had aged for twelve months and cut her a piece. Mary agreed it was the best she'd ever eaten, exclaiming happily at every nibble, and thus found herself eating pungent cheddar thrice a day. She loved the way he could not stop himself from pleasing her or herself from pleasing him with every bite. "You are a champion cheese maker, Sir John Harington."

All too soon, it came time for Mary to leave, as she knew how Elizabeth disliked waiting. "How long?" she said, clinging to him after saying her good-bye to his sister.

"You have added to my strength, sweetheart," he said at the carriage door. "I will return to court before the rains make the roads impassable. I could not spend another winter from you."

He kissed her with half his servants looking on. "Godspeed, Mary, Mary."

She had to gather all her strength to leave him, and all her strength was scarce enough. She looked back from the window, waving until John, his manor and the surrounding hills were lost in early-morning haze.

CHAPTER SIXTEEN

"Who else but a king could succeed me?"
—Elizabeth Regina

March 1603
Richmond Palace

"Two years. Two years and another come again," the queen said, deep in melancholy before the great stone fireplace of her bedchamber, her eyes staring, her chin sunk to her chest. A winter cold that had settled there made the words from a sore throat almost unintelligible. Elizabeth had removed the court from Whitehall to Richmond Palace in January, when it was no weather for river travel. But she would have it so, and she did, this lingering, worrisome illness resulting.

Mary did not need to wonder what the queen's cheerless words meant. Elizabeth marked each anniversary of Essex's death in deep melancholy. And at other times, coming suddenly upon her, Mary would find the queen rereading the letter he'd written to her from the Tower the night before his execution.

"Why, daughter? Why could he not bend to me?" the queen asked again, as she had so many times before.

And again Mary knew the queen expected no answer, and Mary had none to give her, or none she could give without increasing Her Majesty's sore heart, which she would never do.

Ambition, blind or otherwise, a thirst for power, a handsome, vain young man's need to dominate an infatuated older woman . . . these were answers enough, yet there were other reasons that few, especially not the queen, could know or accept—faults of her own.

If Elizabeth had only punished him earlier, but she had too often indulged his childish quarrels and demands, forgiven him too much, thinking him still the spoiled boy Robin had left for her comfort so long ago. She was unaware at what point the boy had crossed the line from being irresponsible to a man become a treacherous danger, determined to rule her.

Could such a hurting truth be borne by a faded, aged beauty without a mirror for truth, when handsome young courtiers continued to write sonnets to her enduring loveliness, to call her Diana, the Fairie Queen and Gloriana? True, these verses had become fewer in late days, as courtiers slipped north to pledge their service to James of Scotland. And the sweet words still spoken caused scarcely disguised amusement from some who overheard them.

But it was too cruel to say these thoughts aloud, even though she and John had talked often of them when they could since his return to court, not as recovered as he should have been, but unable to be separated longer.

As Queen's Champion, he had spent much of the past year in Ireland with Lord Mountjoy, who now won battles where Essex had failed, chasing the Irish rebels into hiding. Although John proudly did his duty, he railed in their private letters against a courtship conducted by the pen when he had quite another method in mind. He had finally returned to court a fortnight earlier, determined to beg the queen to change her mind.

Elizabeth coughed, a deep, rasping cough that hastened Mary to her. She made a soothing sound and coaxed Elizabeth to take another spoonful of the doctor's decoction of purslane, white poppies and cinnamon. "Majesty, it is a restorative for coughs." Mary did not add that it was also prescribed for the pining sickness.

The queen roused herself and looked about as if first waking.

"Call my lady Warwick to me." Her voice was childish, fretful, as Mary heard it often of late.

Mary said softly, "Majesty, the Countess of Warwick is dead."

"Dead! Anne?" The queen's chin settled on her chest again. "Yes, these near three years gone . . . dreaming . . . dreaming."

She had been forgetful before, but such periods had been followed by days of walking and riding, her old high wit filling the presence chamber. Last summer she had gone on her progress to Surrey and north, almost the old Elizabeth. But she had been forgetful like this now for days, and lethargic, calling for the trusted dead, her mind soon wandering from the answer.

A gentleman usher advanced and knelt. "Your Grace, Sir John Harington begs audience."

"Admit him," the queen rasped without raising her head.

John swept into the room like a fresh breeze from the queen's garden, though it was yet frost-covered, as were John's beard and mustache, flecked with white hairs before his time. His recovery had been long, and his efforts at haste had caused health to return more slowly, leaving both him and Mary with this reminder of how near he had come to death. She trembled with excitement as he approached. It was the same no matter how many times she saw him in a day, each meeting like the first time.

Mary went to him before he could reach the queen, and although it pained her to tell him to wait for what they both had awaited for too long, she did so: "John, dearest, Her Grace is very weak. Do not worry her with our business now."

He grimaced, and she knew that she asked the impossible.

"Majesty," he said, kneeling, holding out to her a small blue clay pot with a single full-bloomed, golden Holland tulip. "When the flowers heard you were ill, they came out to cheer you."

The queen smiled wanly. "You forced this one by helping it to think it full spring."

"Nay, godmother." He grinned. "I but encouraged it, told it

of your illness, and it came right up and opened to gladden your heart."

"Boy Jack, when you feel creeping time at the gate, fooleries will please you less." But she gave him her hand to kiss and, after, rested it lovingly on his cheek for a moment before she let it fall open to her lap.

Mary held her breath, knowing John saw that the queen was dying and he could wait no longer.

"Godmother," he said softly, "I beg you to grant my dearest wish."

Elizabeth closed her eyes and did not answer.

John looked at Mary and she shook her head in warning, but he did not heed the signal, perhaps could not.

"I love Mary Rogers with all my heart and body and have done since first I saw her. I would make her my honored wife."

Mary held her breath until she grew dizzy and was forced to take in air.

The queen coughed, her eyes opening. "Jack, love is no basis for marriage. We, who have kingdoms, have not . . ." The words trailed away and her eyes closed.

"Majesty, I beg you."

Elizabeth spoke, using all her breath. "We have chosen a more suitable prospect in Lord Howard, as is our duty to our daughter. We sent him away until we no longer needed Mistress Mary's service. No doubt that eager lord is on his way to London on hearing of our illness. If his way is flooded, he will swim to us." She smiled grimly at her own words. "If God allows me more life, I will need all my loyal northern lords." She filled her lungs, emptied with so much talk. "Let us hear no more on the matter, sir. We have given our word." The deliberate smile that had faded returned. "You will live, sir. Love does not kill." Her eyes opened full at hearing her own words. "Unless it betrays," she added.

John, his face drained of hope, looked at Mary, who blinked

thrice. It was their signal that she would come to him later in his rooms.

It was late afternoon before she could escape her duties, but finally the queen's physicians coaxed her to take a draft that helped her to rest, though she refused her bed.

Mary was admitted to John's rooms to find him packing his saddlebags. She had no words of comfort, needing them herself. "John, no. Stop!"

But he didn't stop, stuffing breeches and a clean shirt into the leather bags. When he spoke, his anger poured out. "I've waited these three years. You cannot ask more of me. She cannot ask more of you. You have done your duty. Leave with me now!"

"John, dearest John, all about her, those whom she has raised high are leaving, pleading illness, infirmity or simply gone without excuse," Mary said, her throat swelling with too many emotions. "They have hurt her deeply. I cannot forsake her now. Do not ask it."

He was beyond reasoning, his face betraying only anguish. "Howard could be here any day, and she will sign the marriage warrant. She did not allow herself to marry for love of Robert Dudley, and the years have taken away the memory of that pain."

"My sweet knight, she suffers that pain still."

"I love her as you do and would give up my life for her. But not yours, Mary. Not yours." John's intense gaze held hers. "We must leave tonight. Are you with me?"

"John, it is my dearest wish never to be parted from you, but . . ."

"But what?"

"It is not within me to leave her in her last hours. She clings to me . . . needs me more now than ever."

"She scarce knows who is yet with her. Others will physick her," he said loudly, frustration and anger boiling to the surface.

"But none left to serve her with love."

The large empty wine cup she saw by the bed, whose effect she heard in his headlong speech, answered her. "Her long life is ne'er over. Ours could begin," he said.

"Do not ask me to break my vow." Mary nearly choked on her next words, but she was reaching for any compromise that would hold him. "Lord Howard cannot live long, and then . . ."

John recoiled. "Do not offer me some far-off prospect. I will wait no longer. Do you think I can bear to stand aside and see you handed to that old man?"

"But, John, yours is an impossible choice for me. Lady Katherine Grey left her. All my life, I knew that I would serve her better."

"So this is prideful triumph over a dead woman?"

Mary put her hand on the saddlebags stuffed with his belongings. "I no longer know what comes from my own tongue. Or yours," she whispered, then fell to her knees before him, her head bowed. "Please, John." It was a prayer.

He grabbed her and pulled her roughly up, crushing her against him, his lips overwhelming her words.

Helpless to stop herself, she returned his passion until both were breathing as if nearly drowned, and then he thrust her away.

"When you are in that cold lord's bed, remember that!" He flung himself from the room, saddlebags over his shoulder.

Stunned, she groped behind her for the bed and fell back as her shaking legs gave way. Was this the price loyalty demanded? She had been willing to pay it until the debt was called. Now she wanted to run after him, to soothe his despair with her own body, to relieve her own desire this once. This was how Elizabeth had felt when she thrust from her first Robert Dudley and later Essex. How could Mary Rogers match the courage of a queen when the only realm she wanted was a manor set on a hill in Somerset?

❖

Lord Howard arrived in two days' time, worn from hard travel, without gifts or a large retinue. "Your Grace," he said, kneeling before the queen, but watching Mary standing behind the queen's chair. "I would claim my bride. I am of an age when waiting to marry is folly."

"Waiting to marry is never folly, my lord," Elizabeth said, her eyes bright with fever. "It prevents impatient error."

"In truth, Your Grace."

Mary could see that His Lordship could barely scrape up the courtesy to agree.

"Majesty—"

The queen, weary, interrupted. "Hold! The marriage warrant will be drawn today, my lord. . . . Trouble me no more."

"I thank you. Would Your Majesty allow me a private meeting with my future bride?" He looked at Mary, frowning.

She knew her eyes were puffy and reddened from a night's weeping into an already soggy pillow. She hoped he would reject a maid who had lost her bright eyes and skin.

"Time enough for meeting later, my lord. Time enough . . . for you. We have much need of her now and little time."

Lord Howard bowed himself from the chamber, which allowed him to compose his face to one of obedience, although Mary could see that he did not like the queen's answer. While Mary liked it greatly.

The queen waved away some steaming oxtail broth. "His Lordship is an eager groom," she whispered, though some of her old mockery was there. "And Boy Jack has left the palace for the West. Is he then not so eager?"

"He is proud, Majesty."

"And a man . . . too young to know that disappointment fades. I dandled most of the crowned heads of Europe, or their sons. I could have wed any of them, but I only wanted Robin, and I could not permit myself . . ." She made the familiar *pup! pup!* sound of irritation.

"Men are such sorcerers, but you are young and do not understand that to a queen the safety of her realm must come first."

Mary did not answer. Of course she understood. What woman would not understand love and sacrifice, the two legs on which every woman of worth stood all her life?

Again she offered the rapidly cooling broth.

"Nay, Mouse," Elizabeth said, waving her hand. "You are growing forgetful. We were not so at your age, just beginning our reign."

Mary smiled and kissed Her Majesty's hand with affection, needing no permission.

The queen was sunk in memory that afternoon, finally taking a sip or two of fresh broth and sucking on a sweet comfit until her teeth ached. Somewhat restored, she tried to stand as the big case clock chimed four times, but she could not. Mary brought her stick, and Elizabeth stood, pushing Mary and stick away.

And there she stood for many troubling hours, holding on to life.

Finally her legs could not hold her, and she fell down upon the floor.

The physicians who waited in the anteroom entered at Mary's frantic call. Whispering together, one spoke: "Majesty, we think your health will be restored by your bed."

"Then, good physician, you need a perspective glass if you think a bed will add to my days." Her other ladies had approached to assist in raising her, but the queen waved them off.

"Bring my pillows, Mouse," she said, sending the physicians away, bidding them not to return.

All the merry lace and velvet cushions, rose and marigold, covered with fine knotted embroidery were brought and placed, as the queen commanded, on the floor near the fire. She lay there all that darkening day and night, staring into some far distance, seeing other faces, other days. Finally, she drifted far into the past, suckling her finger as if she were a babe at the breast.

John lingered along the road, bitterly regretting his anger, berating himself as soon as he rode south and west of Richmond on a road that would eventually lead him to Somersetshire and home . . . more than regretting. And within hours he had turned his annoyance against himself. His horse's hooves seemed to tap out a message: *You fool . . . you blind fool . . . you idiot fool!* He had not gone many furlongs when full dark came again and he could not chance the rutted roads, the fog-shrouded woodlands and bands of outlaws surely lying in wait for love-addled knights.

The Blue Boar Inn stood close by the road, a lantern lit to welcome weary travelers. He knew that he would be more fit for travel tomorrow if he had food and rest. And drink, enough to blot the memory of Mary's face, her look of abandonment that would haunt him forever.

He awoke at dawn, on what morning he did not know. His head rested on his arms amidst empty wine cups. "Master Innkeeper, bring my horse around." He stood, swaying for a moment, and threw coins on the table. "How long have I been here?"

"Good sir, you have been a quiet guest, and now have great need of food and ale mixed with eggs fresh laid this morn . . . a sovereign sure cure for a wine-soured stomach." He held out the bowl to John, who downed the contents, surprised his stomach didn't reject such a slippery antidote, nodding his thanks and adding another shilling to the coins.

"Come again and find sure welcome, Sir Harington."

"You know me?"

"Aye, from the Accession Day jousts."

"I cannot say that I will pass this road again."

"Begging pardon, sir, but I think you must return this way to solace what wine could not."

John stared at him. An innkeeper who was also a diviner of men's souls. This was truly a miraculous age.

He walked out to a foggy dawn, the sun just rising over low hills. Breathing deeply of the cold, moist air flowing past him, he felt his wine-sodden brain clearing. What strange witchery had he suffered? He had berated Mary for her gentle love and loyalty, the very qualities that had drawn him to her and kept him faithful all this long time. Bitterly ashamed, and without a thought of delay, he spurred his horse back toward Richmond.

He had stopped to rest his lathered horse at a hamlet water trough when a fast rider approached. He recognized one of the queen's messengers.

"Sir John . . . Sir John," the rider called, reining in alongside. "Mistress Mary Rogers sends to tell you that the queen is dying and bids you return at once."

"Is the marriage warrant drawn?"

"Yes, I heard of it."

"Signed?"

"I know not, Sir John."

They both spurred their horses past the small thatched village houses, turning north for the palace of Richmond. Bells had begun to peal in village steeples, and crying dames stood beside the road. A blacksmith, red faced at his open forge, unashamedly covered his face with his leather apron.

John reached the palace mews and stabled his horse. "Does the queen yet live?"

The groom nodded. "But some evil mischief has attacked her tongue and she talks no more, sir."

John rushed past the great fountain and the walled privy garden and into the palace. The presence chamber held small groups of whispering courtiers. The halls leading to the queen's apartments were full of idle, hushed servants as the great palace stopped and waited.

A gentleman usher admitted John to the antechamber. "The queen can see no one, Sir John."

Cecil looked up from a group of privy councilors and nodded a greeting.

Lord Howard looked up and frowned. "I was not aware that you were called, Sir Harington."

"My lord, the queen's Majesty has the service of her champion, whether called or not." He felt shame at that moment. This had not been true when he left the palace, but it was true now and ever.

Howard turned sharply and walked to the far side of the antechamber, meaning his back to be an insult to John instead of the relief it was.

John saw that he was holding a warrant conspicuously in his hand, but could not see if it was signed, though it had a seal and ribbon. He had to know.

"My Lord Secretary," he said, addressing Robert Cecil, "a private word, if it please you."

Cecil, wearing his black robe and badge of office, bowed to his fellow councilmen and approached. "The queen is gravely ill."

"Is there reason to hope?"

"Her Majesty refuses her physicians and her bed, as if she knows she would not rise again." Cecil spoke with pride on his face in the woman he had served as man and boy.

"Is Mistress Mary—"

"At her side, without sleep these two days."

As Lord Howard approached with his head thrust forward to overhear, John lowered his voice and asked, "Is the marriage warrant signed?"

Cecil shook his head and put a hand on John's shoulder. "The succession must be settled. Do not trouble Her Majesty for lesser reasons."

John's body stiffened.

Cecil spoke quickly. "I say it with sorrow, my friend, for I know the warrant is dear—"

"You have no knowing of how important it is to the ruin of two lives."

Cecil smiled. "Do I not?"

"My deep apologies, my Lord Secretary," John said, bowing. He was too much on the edge of despair, but he was done with being hurtful. Striking out did not ease his pain.

The doors to the privy chamber opened and Lady Anne Russell hurried out with a cloth-covered basin. John saw a weary Mary kneeling near the queen seated on her cushions, holding stubbornly to her realm with her last strength, almost at her last breath. They were two of a kind, he saw, both bound to their deepest commitment. He felt great pride that England nurtured such women and renewed shame that he had forgotten for a single hour the devotion he owed to each. It would never happen again.

Mary glanced to the doors as Lady Russell left to fetch more fresh, cooling rose water and saw John standing there in a dusty doublet, the strain of distress lining his face. She put all her glad welcome into her smile, her heart at greater ease on sight of him and wanting him to know it, though she doubted she could hide it if she tried. No reproaches. He had returned at her beckoning, which was far more important to her than his leaving. And it must be enough.

Or it would have been, had not Lord Howard stepped out in front of John, bowing.

"Majesty," announced the usher, probably well bribed. He walked forward and knelt. "My lord Howard presents his marriage warrant."

The queen waved him away, though he moved only a few steps. "This realm no longer has a need of this lord's favor," she said, or Mary thought she whispered the words. Or had she only wanted to hear them?

Elizabeth stirred, and Mary, ignoring the usher, leaned down to speak gently. "Majesty, your Mouse and all your ladies pray you to take some little food and wine."

Her Majesty did not answer, her face in trance, unchanging. She was in some other place, some other time. She opened her mouth, trying to force out words. Mary leaned close to hear.

"Robin." It was less than a whisper, a faint sigh only. Elizabeth's gaze went to her bed table and her ivory jewel box.

Mary rose and quickly brought it. Kneeling again, she saw the queen wanted it opened. Unclasping the lid, she lifted it to reveal a miniature of Anne Boleyn, the queen's mother, a yellowed ivory-handled fan with feathers fallen to dust and a folded paper inscribed with the queen's own faded italic hand: *His Last Letter.*

Elizabeth's eyes held such longing that Mary removed the letter and pressed it against the queen's heart. Her faded blue eyes lifted to Mary and there were memories, longing and sweet quiet . . . all there.

Mary took Elizabeth's hand, urgently holding back tears. The queen found the strength to draw her closer still. "My memories will soon be gone and I am left with this letter." With an effort, she motioned the usher to leave and, from long acquaintance with her temper, he obeyed.

Mary looked to John and nodded. He entered swiftly and knelt beside her. The warmth of his hand over hers was all the support she needed.

With great effort, Elizabeth placed her hand over theirs, the queen's face peaceful, as if she released some care.

In the anteroom, Mary and John heard the sounds of a scuffle as Cecil kept Lord Howard from rushing to the queen. Two yeoman guards took firm hold of Howard's arms.

"Councilor," Lord Howard said, his face swollen with anger, "the queen is not in her right mind."

"My lord, Her Majesty's mind is always in the right. Save your dignity and withdraw."

Shrugging the guards off, Howard stomped to the outer hall, scattering torn pieces of the unsigned marriage warrant along with his dignity.

John gripped Mary's shoulder and she wilted with relief.

She was sure Elizabeth had seen or sensed everything between her Mouse and her Boy Jack. Had Her Majesty planned to bless them all along, or had she changed her heart when it was the last gift of tenderness she could give? Though the queen was rapidly losing this world's strength, Mary thought she saw a question in the darkening eyes. Now that all the queen's choices were gone, would she have preferred a different way for her life, to have married Robert Dudley, had his children and reigned with him? As she clutched Robin's last letter, Mary watched a doubt form in Elizabeth's tired eyes. But Mary would always wonder if misgiving had really been there . . . or only years of gathering sadness.

Cecil approached without being bidden. "Majesty, to content your loving people you must go to your bed."

Elizabeth, still the queen, always the queen, roused herself to new strength at that. "Little man, little man, the word *must* is not to be used to princes. But you know I die and that makes you presumptuous."

Cecil knelt where he was, his hands folded in prayer, keeping vigil with the queen's ladies.

Hours passed as John, Mary and Cecil shifted on their sore knees. The queen's other ladies of the privy chamber stood at the far side of the crowded room, whispering behind their hands.

At last, toward evening, Elizabeth caught her breath and whispered, "Daughter, to comfort you all, we are ready for our bed."

They carried her wasted body to her huge gilt bed, colorful peacock feathers crowning the carved bedstead, and laid her head on her embroidered lace pillow.

The queen called for Archbishop Whitgift of Canterbury, who waited in the anteroom to come and pray by her bed. He began to praise her magnificence in prayer.

"My lord, say nothing more of my greatness," she protested with her last strength. "We have had enough of vanity."

Though her heart was full and heavy, Mary almost smiled at that. Elizabeth, who had never had enough adoration to fill the infinite well of her craving, now approached heaven humbly.

The archbishop prayed for several hours, but when he stood to leave, she motioned him back to his knees as if she would be prayed into heaven. And who would not wish it?

Mary with John at her side reached for Elizabeth's hand, but it did not grasp hers. "Majesty." Mary laid her cheek on the silk bedcover by the queen's hand. "Mother," she whispered, giving Elizabeth a last gift from her Mouse. If Elizabeth heard, she was beyond answering, although Mary prayed she was not beyond understanding.

Later, Cecil approached Elizabeth without bidding. "Majesty, the succession. . . . Is it to be James of Scotland?"

He leaned to her lips and announced on rising, "Her Grace commands, 'Who should succeed me but a king?'"

No one had heard her say it, and Mary doubted the queen could bring herself to relinquish her throne even with her last breath, but she would not dispute Cecil and risk an uprising of every ambitious peer who claimed a drop of Tudor or Plantagenet blood.

The room hushed as Elizabeth finally slept, her head upon her right arm, no longer able to resist the deep rest her now spent body demanded. Shortly after the big case clock struck the second hour on March 24, she breathed a final lingering breath; then her long struggle was done.

And won, Mary knew. The love that she had for her people and her people for her would be remembered. Elizabeth had marked this love herself to her Parliament: "Though God has raised me high, yet this I count the glory of my crown, that I have reigned with your loves."

The queen's long farewell sigh yet echoed in the chamber, and Mary bowed her head to pray for her, though she wondered for just one small moment if Elizabeth Tudor could take second place even in heaven.

Finally, John and Mary rose as one, his arms about her as she shed tears into his doublet.

A physician came forward to arrange the queen's curled body into a more stately pose, while Lady Margaret carefully placed her red wig and crown on her head.

John pulled Mary away into the anteroom. "All is done here. Your duty is spent." He held her tight. "Her father, brother and sister all died in great pain. Hers was a long life and a better end. Be glad of that, sweetheart."

"I am glad of it, John, though I know her pain was of another kind."

"It won't be ours," John said, his arm about her shoulders, giving her his strength.

They walked from the royal apartments through knots of hushed courtiers and others rushing past with gifts to the north and a new king with all his court positions yet to fill.

Others were acting as foragers, pocketing what they could grab. Tapestries had already disappeared from the great hall. Resting against a pillar, Mary saw a servant scooping up pewter plates and knives. Torches had been allowed to go out, and many inner halls were in full dark.

"John, this is shameful . . . unseemly. Is this how they honor Elizabeth? Call the guards. They must be stopped."

"Mary, there is no stopping them. The scavengers swarm."

She had to test John's changed nature one last time. "Will you follow the others north to King James?"

"Only if that is your direction. I cannot blot from memory her goodness to me. It has rooted my love for her as for no other monarch." He kissed her forehead. "And, sweetheart, it is well past time that we began our life together. Did she give us her blessing?"

"Yes, she did in her own way, even if she was unable to say she'd changed her mind."

He looked down into her face, wanting one answer. "You won't miss the court and all its pleasures?"

"Will you allow me time to miss anything?" she said boldly.

He grinned. "Two horses will be saddled and waiting by the south gate at dawn."

They rode south and west to the slow tolling of bells in the distance, villagers and farmers in their fields running toward them calling, "Is our good Queen Bess gone?"

"Aye, this early morn," they cried a dozen times, their hearts saddened anew at each telling of the queen's reluctant leave-taking.

They rode on with the pale winter sun rising higher behind them over the smoke from cottage chimneys, the bells pealing dolefully from parish spire to spire as the sad news spread. Dazed villagers, even those in their older age, had known no other sovereign, and no man alive had known other than a Tudor monarch. "Will it be the Scotsman?" they called, many remembering when the Scots were their mortal enemies.

John answered the first questioners, but soon gave it up to make progress along the dusty road. He knew where he was going.

Just past midmorning as the dinner hour approached, Mary sagged in her saddle. "I am sorry, John. I am undone by the care and worry of the last days."

John rode close, his leg touching hers. "Just a few furlongs now, Mary, and we will rest until you are strong again."

They stopped at the Blue Boar Inn, the courtyard bustling with stable hands. Squawking chickens, having laid their morning eggs at first light, ran between the horses' hooves. John dismounted and helped Mary slide from her saddle, and she wilted into his arms.

The innkeeper appeared at his door. "Welcome again, Sir Harington," he said. "I did not expect your return so soon. Feed, water and fresh hay for these horses," he ordered, handing the reins to waiting hostlers. "This way, Lady Harington," he added, bowing low.

Mary flushed. She was not John's lady yet. They would have to reach his estate, post banns and have them read out over three Sundays. It might be over a month before she was Lady Harington. Still, she delighted in the sound of it, not that she hadn't thought it, hadn't tried it on her tongue and with her pen many times.

John helped her to a table with a tall-backed settle in front of the fire. "Innkeeper," he called, "some hot spiced hippocras for my lady here. And a little of her favorite sharp farm cheese and fresh bread."

Leaning her head against the settle, Mary closed her eyes and thought that John could wait for her no longer, nor could she wait for him. He sat close beside her, and when the wine came, he held the cup to her lips, then broke off cheese and bread, feeding small pieces to her, and she allowed it, loving the way he had care of her.

"You are treating me as a babe," she said weakly. When she looked up at him, she feared that her eyes were red-rimmed, and her cheeks, now washed clear of white paint and red cochineal, must have no bloom. She raised her hand to touch her face.

"Mary, my sweet, you are all sleepy loveliness. I want you always a fresh young maid just as you are."

She laughed softly. "Surely not always a maid, John." Still, if he could read her mind so easily, she must guard her thoughts from such a future husband, especially the thought that kept returning where she imagined their first bedding. Mary looked at him to see how much he now guessed. He was laughing and calling out to the innkeeper.

"Master Innkeeper, we would have your best clean room, with fresh bed linen, a ewer of rose water for washing and ale for drink. And later, much later, a hot meat pie for our supper."

At that the innkeeper called for his wife and a maid, rushing away with John calling after him: "And one more thing . . . we wish you and your good wife to witness our handfasting."

The innkeeper broke into a run.

Mary gripped John's sleeve. "You would keep me an honest woman, when I have shamelessly run away with you?"

"We won Elizabeth's approval. I think Sir William looks down and longs for a grandchild even now . . . as do I long for an heir."

"Hold, sir," she teased, wondering that she could jest so near to exhaustion. "You take your manly prowess as a surety."

He laughed loud this time, sounding merrier than she could remember, sounding indeed very much like the carefree man she had first seen at Elizabeth's throne with Essex in the presence chamber that first day at court so long ago. "You have forgotten one thing, John."

"Have I?"

"The groom's gift to the wife to make legal the handfasting." She shrugged, dismissing her own words to assure him that gifts meant nothing to her.

He slipped two fingers into his purse and drew out a gold ring made of three intertwined circles, which he laid before her on the trestle. He traced round the circles with his forefinger one at a time. "Head," he said at the first circle, then, "heart and hand. I have carried this on my person since within a month of first seeing you."

"John, so long as that?"

"Aye, if we could not marry, I planned to give it to you on a gold chain." He brushed her cheek with the back of his hand, his eyes on her, serious now. "I will yet buy a gold chain to tie you to me."

She leaned into him, closed her eyes and searched along his cheek with her lips until she felt his mouth close about hers. He responded briefly, shifting uncomfortably on the settle. "John, sweet John," she breathed, "don't you know that I am tied to you with stronger bonds than any chain of gold?"

The innkeeper and his wife approached and John rose, handing Mary to her feet. "I will know very soon, sweetheart."

Their hands held fast, they stood before the innkeeper and his wife.

"I, John Harington, knight, do swear," John said, slipping the three-circle ring on her finger, "and plight my faith and troth to join with this woman, Mary Rogers, spinster, in holy matrimony as soon as may be. Before you all as witnesses, I swear this on my oath. This is my legal commitment by the laws of Church and England."

With her waning energy, Mary, very much aware of the new golden weight on her marriage finger, repeated the pledge, looking into John's eyes, aware of no other in the inn.

When she finished, a cheer rose from ale maids, stable hands and a farmer, his scythe at his side, drinking his morning ale at the fireside table they'd vacated, his wet clothes steaming. Scooping Mary up and cradling her against his chest, John walked to the stairs and started up, evoking a new cheer from those looking up at them, their happy faces reflecting what they saw and what they remembered.

"You are committed now, Sir John," she said for his ear alone. "What do the old wives say? Marry in haste . . ."

"Repent *never*," he finished the ancient warning his way.

He kicked open the first door off its latch and walked into a sunny loft room, crushing sweet herbs under his feet. Carrying Mary to the bed, he laid her gently upon the mattress, releasing the scent of lavender mixed into the straw and horse hair that filled the bed sack.

The sheets were rough linen, but she did not feel their prickles for the sense of John's hand unlacing her stomacher and releasing her gown.

He sat down and dropped his boots, the double thumps raising a faint cheer from below. He tossed his doublet after the boots and stretched out his body without quite touching her, except for closing his hand about hers. "Sleep now, Mary. You need rest."

"But, John . . ."

"Ah, wife, you must learn to obey." He turned his head to look into her eyes. "What do the old husbands say? Women and horses must be well governed."

"I doubt you will ever be an old husband, John."

"At this moment, I doubt it, too," he said, watching her lovely dark hair spread upon the pillow, her perfect face in profile, until her eyes drooped and closed and her deep breathing told him she was at rest. Finally, still wondering at his ability to wait yet more hours, the control of desire taking the last of his strength, though the best of it, he knew, John slept beside her.

Mary dreamed long and woke when the westering sun sent long shadows reaching well into the room. For a moment, she did not see the usual sights of the ladies' chamber at Richmond or hear Her Majesty calling for her bitter ale.

John sat by the fireplace in his shirt, his bare legs stretched before him, watching, waiting, smiling.

"John," she whispered, remembering their handfasting, drowning in delight. "Why are you smiling?"

"I cannot rule my mouth."

He rose and came to her, and she saw that his finely muscled legs were improved even over her imagination. *He loves me.* She was his by English law and more his by the ancient laws of Eden's paradise.

"You have bold eyes, Lady Harington," he said, and the name did not make her blush.

"And you have no codpiece, Sir John," she said, wondering at her own daring. She watched his dearest face bend to the bed, his hand untying her shift at the shoulders, slipping it down beneath her yielding body, following its path with his mouth, barely touching her skin. Finally, he removed her garters and unrolled her hose, his lips trailing their descent. Enveloping warmth followed him wherever his lips hovered or touched as light as an April breeze. Mary wanted to beg for their swifter descent, but her throat was too full, moaning her own need.

She was wholly exposed and yet felt never more protected. "Husband." The word filled her with its meaning. He was hers forever. Instead of the cold horror she had anticipated in Lord Howard's bed, this would be . . . well, as unlike that hell as a new paradise. She could only guess at how much.

Mary watched as he quickly pulled his shirt over his head, exposing the place below his neck where the sun had not touched. His strong arms and shoulders that had held lance and sword now reached for her. He had been sculpted by some ancient hand and . . . *He loves me.* The words sang in her head as he stood looking down at her for what seemed a long infinity. His gaze took the path his lips had explored earlier.

Her nipples rose up to meet his as he lay down urgently atop her, their lips meeting with a kiss that fed their hunger as nothing before.

Carefully, he lifted her and entered, pushing slowly, until he met her maidenhead. He hesitated.

"John, now!" It was a desperate plea, a hot command, rising to a gasp.

He pushed through quickly to drown her moment's pain in the molten flood that followed. It was nothing she would not endure a thousand times. She had loved him from the first moment; even her pretend hate on hearing of the wager with Essex had been a kind of reluctant desire. "John . . . John . . ." She could not stop saying his name, inhaling it, owning it.

His eyes opened wide at that moment of releasing his love into her, of becoming one life, one future, one family. All waiting was done and he collapsed against her, drowning in the swollen fullness of her breasts and her cry of pleasure echoing through the small room and back to them again.

At her instant of complete surrender, Mary felt what she had only imagined before: John against her unclothed, kissing her, his weight strengthening her. He was the most powerful and the best of men. She would always feel it into time without end. "My heart," she whispered, clasping him closer still, beginning to believe at last that he was real and not a lonely night's dream of love.

Later, they lay side by side holding each other in the darkening room, the fireplace needing to be fed.

Mary leaned down and kissed the puckered red scar on his chest where Essex's sword had so narrowly missed John's heart . . . and her own. "For so long, I pretended to ignore you, but I saw every time you took breath."

"And I pretended to wait patiently, when every second I was impatient and jealous of my godmother."

"John, no more pretending."

"No, my heart, no more."

She sighed, her body trembling with joy and release.

He mistook the shiver and reached to cover them both with her shift until they were enveloped in lace and Bruges satin.

"I'm not cold," she said. "I was thinking of the queen."

John put up a finger to stop her speech.

"No, John, not with sadness . . . but wonder. I hope she knew what we know. Do you think she ever did?"

John rose on his elbow and smiled down into his wife's eyes. "I'm sure of it, my love."

"How so?"

"When I was a very young man new come to court, I saw Elizabeth with the Earl of Leicester before he died . . ."

"Her sweet Robin?"

"Aye."

"They were in their middle years, yet it was written in their eyes whenever they were together in a room, whenever they touched . . . plain written for all to see. They had loved in every way and carried it always on their faces."

"She never had what we will have."

"No, sweeting, but she never lost him. Whenever his name was spoken in after years—"

Mary touched his lips with her own. "I saw, John. Her face became a mask to hide memory." She sighed a whisper. "Now they have each other for eternity. Will we, John?"

He grinned. "Longer."

Dearest John, he always knew the one word that would make her heart smile.

There was a knock at the door. "Sir John, your hot veal pie has come." There was a clatter as the trencher was placed on the floor.

"Are you hungry, Lady Harington?" John murmured, the words kissing her ear.

"No," she answered, and pulled her shift up and over their heads to make a world for them alone.

The servant's footsteps retreated back down the stairs.

VIVAT REGINA

EPILOGUE

April 28, 1603
Westminster Abbey
Queen Elizabeth's Funeral

*H*er hand clasped firmly against his heart, Sir John and Lady Harington stopped at a small parish church on their way to the abbey to read the carved inscription set up in many London churches by a loving people.

> CHASTE PATRONESS OF TRUE RELIGION,
> IN COURT A SAINT, IN FIELD AN AMAZON,
> GLORIOUS IN LIFE, DEPLORED IN HER DEATH,
> SUCH WAS UNPARALLELED
> ELIZABETH.

Cloaked in memories, they walked on toward Westminster Abbey through increasing crowds. The rain had ceased, though it dripped from eaves and leaves as bellringers preceded the funeral procession, shouting, "Make way, make way!" to part the people. "Your queen comes among you for a last time."

Londoners lined every street and alley leading to the old abbey and hung from their high-storied windows. A great moan rose as the queen's long procession slowly came into view, her crowned and robed effigy lying atop the purple-draped coffin drawn by four matched horses. Muffled drums beat a measured cadence for a following company of pikemen with their halberds turned down.

John's arm went about Mary's quaking shoulders as they pushed their way forward. "We will come through this, sweet wife," he said, his words clear and comforting despite the tumult.

She turned her face up to him, grateful for his words, knowing them to be true, but needing them all the same.

"It's Gloriana to the life!" Londoners exclaimed at sight of the effigy, recognizing her easily, since she had often passed in procession among them. Some wiped away tears, the dead queen's image being so much as she had ever been, even to holding her orb and scepter against her breast. A few made a sign of the cross with a thumb pushed between two fingers to ward off the devil, who was always lurking near death to grab a wayward soul.

"Look on her, boy," said a master haberdasher, judging by his gown, to his 'prentice, pushing him forward for a better look. "Another like our virgin queen won't come again in your life."

"More's the better," the 'prentice muttered. "We got good King James now."

"Hold your tongue, boy!" John said, his grief turned to fury, though he did not lay hands on the lad. "I have basked in her sun as Queen's Champion, and your master has the right of it."

The merchant, eyeing John's clothes and medals, bowed his head near to his knees, pushing the boy low, too. "Humbly begging pardon, sir, for this stupid one." He gave the lad a sharp rap on the head. "You're not with your fellows in a Bankside tavern. The king could still count it treason to speak against her."

"If not the king," John said, still angered, "then I will."

The boy rubbed his sore head and looked sullen and stubborn. "Others do say worse, sir. That she were always a bastard as her father first named her. And more, they say she had bastards of her own in plenty."

Mary nearly choked. "I was one of her ladies, and those who say such slanders speak lies."

The haberdasher bowed hastily. "Oh, my lady, blame me for being a lax master. I spared my sister's boy whippings due, but will not spare him this one, you may be certain."

The master's hand went tight across the lad's mouth. "One more word and you'll end in the Clink Prison and I'll not go surety. Mark you well, boy. One more word and you're just another masterless beggar thieving your bread and ale while the gallows tree waits. Apologize to this lord and lady."

Subdued, the boy dug his dirty toe between the cobbles.

John left the lad mumbling and pushed a way clear for Mary, leading her toward the south entrance. "Do not let your heart break, sweet. There will always be such stupid gossipers. She was a woman beyond women, beyond a man's understanding."

"Yes, husband," Mary said, striving for a seldom attained wifely submission. "Though perhaps," she added, failing the effort, "Elizabeth, being queen, could not be stopped from becoming what she could fully be."

The noise of the approaching procession rose, and John did not quite hear her. Mary smiled. They were but one week churched, and they had a lifetime to reveal their deepest thoughts slowly by the fire of a winter's night, or in the warm twilight of a summer's walk in the extended gardens she was already busy planning for Kelston Manor.

As John pushed their way forward, though still troubled by the hurtful things said against her queen, Mary was warmed by a memory. Lady Katherine Grey always seemed to come to mind to provide her with some intelligence at the right time. "Never underestimate Elizabeth," she'd told the child Mary many times. Now, watching the queen's effigy approach, Mary warmed to that thought. Her Majesty would take care of herself and her reputation . . . from heaven if need be. Mary felt Elizabeth's power and regal dignity still, a part of the queen Mary hoped always to have with her.

They reached the carved high entrance and waited, heads bowed. The coffin's canopy held up by six knights passed into the abbey, their feet crushing sprays of spring flowers laid by mourners. Then Mary stepped forward to join the queen's ladies, the Archbishop of Canterbury, who had prayed at her bedside as the queen died, and a long procession of marching nobles clothed in black velvet. The crowd shouted their approval as white-clad pauper women followed the procession, the same whose feet the queen had washed on Maundy day in imitation of Christ.

As the canopy covering the coffin disappeared inside the abbey's great carved entrance, a collective sigh rose from the crowd outside, so loud as to nearly drown the sound of a thousand pairs of boots drumming at once against the abbey's paving stones.

Inside, John found that thick tapers lit the cavernous apse, fighting the dark through the long sermon and reading of scripture. He smiled in his sadness as he heard the impatient old queen rasping aloud as she had often done of a Sunday morning during an overlong sermon: "Get on with it, good preacher!" Indeed, John thought, had she not been dead this month past, Elizabeth would surely have stalked out at this wordy excess.

At last all ceremonies were ended and Mary joined John as their Faerie Queen, so the poet Edmund Spenser had named her, was laid at the head of her Catholic half sister, Mary Tudor. Near a half century dead, this queen was still reviled as Bloody Mary by Londoners who remembered the smoke and ash of burning heretics rising above Smithfield to drift across the city. If the love of Englishmen had been hers, Mary Tudor would have had Elizabeth's head on the block, as well. Without that love, she didn't dare touch young Bess. Yet here lay the sisters, close in death as they never had been in life.

"King James has ordered this," murmured John, "and is moving his mother, the Queen of Scots, here as well."

"It is a new reign," Mary said, speaking softly, accepting that James's word was now law.

Mourners filed past Elizabeth's tomb reading the inscription: *Consorts both in throne and grave, here we rest two sisters, Elizabeth and Mary, in hope of our resurrection.*

Robert Cecil approached them and they exchanged courtesies. "What think you of this arrangement, Sir John?"

"My lord, I think I hear a *pup! pup!* from somewhere."

Cecil smiled. "His Majesty King James thought this a fitting inscription, and as a new councelor, I could not oppose it."

They all knelt on both knees by the stone sarcophagus inside which Elizabeth's coffin lay, gazing on the effigy.

Cecil remarked, "Her Grace would not like this statue of herself from profile."

Mary nodded. "I think she was displeased with her nose, my lord, and would never allow her portraits to be painted thus."

She and John turned to smile together, remembering their irascible, fascinating Elizabeth. Then, with final farewells, they backed away from the coffin with all court formality, not daring, even now, to turn their backs on this queen.

They walked together down the vast center aisle and out of the abbey to face the silent people yet waiting, heads uncovered, the sun shining now, wet cobbles steaming.

Cecil straightened his bent back to stand as tall as he could. "You are for the west country, Sir John, with your lady?"

Sir John's arm went tight about his lady's shoulders, Mary smiling up at him as the sun lit her face.

"Aye, my lord Cecil, we're for home. Lady Grey's younger son, Lord Thomas William, comes in a week to take his mother's body back to Eltham." He smiled down at Mary. "And we stay tonight at an inn on the road south from Richmond."

"If it please you, old friend, I could gain you an apartment at Whitehall Palace for what rest you need."

John smiled down at Mary. "We thank you, my lord Cecil, but the Blue Boar will be our palace tonight."

"And forever," Mary whispered.

ABOUT THE AUTHOR

*J*eane Westin began her writing life as a freelance journalist, then wrote a number of nonfiction books and finally came to her first and true love, historical novels. She published two novels, with Simon & Schuster and Scribner, in the late 1980s, and after a long hiatus is once again indulging her passion for history. She lives in California with her husband, Gene, near their daughter, Cara, and has been rehabilitating a two-story Tudor cottage complete with dovecote for over a decade. You can reach her at www.jeanewestin.com.

The Virgin's Daughters

JEANE WESTIN

A CONVERSATION WITH JEANE WESTIN

Q. You've written other novels in the past, but this is your first Tudor historical novel. What inspired you to write it?

A. My love of all things Elizabeth I started with my lifelong interest in history, and in particular English history. Though Queen Eleanor of Aquitaine was strong, sensuous and fascinating, she was at best coruler with Henry Plantagenet. Later, Queen Victoria seems to me a shadowy, grandmotherly figure, evoking pity but not devotion. Only Elizabeth Tudor ruled and gave her name to an age that made a small island nation into a great power. She is such a towering personality that innumerable books and movies about her have been created and in today's Web-connected world, entire Web sites and blogs are devoted to her, producing a steady stream of material, both true and false. And yet, our appetite for Elizabeth does not seem to diminish, but grows. With each new portrait of her life we are fascinated again and want to know more, always in search of an answer to: "At heart, who was she?"

Q. How much of The Virgin's Daughters *is based on history and how much did you make up?*

A. That's a tough question to quantify because so much is a mixture. I stay true to what is known about events and what was reported to have been said, but no one knows what the people thought or said in private. A great deal of Elizabethan material, including many of Robert Dudley's letters, was lost during the English Civil War. I confess, I have sometimes shifted or fused time and place to keep this book from running to a thousand pages.

Q. Lady Katherine Grey and Mistress Mary Rogers handle their love affairs very differently and experience very different fates as a result. Did you find yourself sympathizing with one lady over the other? And can you tell us what happened to some of Elizabeth's other ladies-in-waiting?

A. Any reader who has a young daughter will recognize Lady Kate Grey. Her behavior at the time was beyond willful to almost suicidal. Nothing can explain it but her needing love so desperately that she could will herself into believing all would be well simply because she needed it to be. Her young life had been so sterile and loveless that she really had no chance to develop a mature view. How many of us can think clearly when we are young and in love? I do not believe that either Kate or Ned wanted the throne, but there is no way that Elizabeth with her troubled life wouldn't have felt threatened by two people with royal blood having sons so easily.

I am always in sympathy with the character I'm writing at

the time. Both Kate and Mary had problems of defiance and de-layed satisfaction that most modern women experience, although modern women rarely delay satisfaction to the extent that these women did.

Historically, Kate was moved around to several country houses, but for my purposes I kept her in one place. She may have won a slight victory after all, since her second son, Thomas or William (depending on the source), is a direct ancestor of Elizabeth II, England's reigning queen.

As for Mary Rogers, she and John had fifteen children, which, I imagine, kept her busy . . . John, too.

There are good records of one of the queen's ladies: Lady Saintloe. She married a fourth time to the Earl of Shrewsbury and became the renowned Bess of Hardwick, who tried to manipulate her granddaughter Arbella Stuart onto the throne. Failing that, Bess died the richest woman in England. We may owe Bess for far more than her colorful biography. Shakespeare is reported to have seen his first play at the age of twelve at Hardwick Hall.

Q. So much has been written about Elizabeth I. How did you decide on your particular portrait of her?

A. I knew I wanted to write about Elizabeth and her court and looked for a new way to approach a queen who was so well-known and show her in a different light. When I read that she didn't want her ladies-in-waiting to marry and had beaten ladies who'd had af-fairs, I knew I had a different approach to viewing both Elizabeth and her court. Who knew the queen better than other women who were with her?

Q. You strongly suggest that Elizabeth was not technically a "virgin" queen. What led you to this conclusion, and what self-justification do you think Elizabeth made that allowed her to call herself a virgin queen? Do you think she was intimate with more men than just Robert Dudley?

A. Did she or didn't she? No one knows the truth. Many guessed and whispered during Elizabeth's reign. William Cecil, her chief minister, thought she and Robert Dudley were lovers as late as 1572, when she was thirty-nine years old. Now, four centuries later, happily for me, we still wonder: What was their true relationship? We do know this: Elizabeth's love for her Robin and his for her outlasted his life and ended only with her death. Their love triumphed over quarrels, his disastrous marriages, her flirtations with handsome courtiers and calculated political marriage contracts and broke them with most of the foreign princes of the time. For thirty of her adult years she never allowed Robin to leave her side except to do what only he could be trusted to do, or with great emotional pain for them both. Robin's love for her was simply the most important part of his life. Let me ask you: How could such a lifelong, tumultuous, passionate emotional intimacy endure without physical love? The idea defies what we know of human behavior, which has not changed. The answer for me lies in her willing Robin's body servant, Tamworth, a huge sum when she thought herself dying of smallpox. Why, if not to silence him and retain her virgin image for posterity?

Elizabeth could not risk pregnancy and contraception was primitive, so physical satisfaction would have been somewhat less than Church authorized. I'll leave the idea of what that could have involved to your imagination. I think for a queen, as for a recent American president, that was justification for considering her physical contact to be nonsexual, technically leaving her a virgin. In other words: The queen has spoken and wills it to be so.

It is possible that Elizabeth was intimate with other men who caught her eye, and there were several. The most likely candidate is Sir Christopher Hatton. His existing letters to her are wonderfully passionate. Again, we will never know. I prefer to think that her love for Robin was so strong that she was intimate only with him. However, I'm a romantic, not a realist.

Q. You seem to enjoy writing about the Tudor period. What about this time particularly fascinates you?

A. Elizabeth!

Henry VIII gets a huge amount of historical attention, but to me he was a woman hater. If you look deep into his behavior toward women, he used them, politically and physically, but he did not know the meaning of love. He destroyed women when they did not fulfill his plans. His daughter Elizabeth, while having his strength and intelligence, had more humanity. She built England into a world power and kept the love of her people. To this day she is their most popular monarch.

Q. Can you explain more fully what Elizabethans thought of romantic love? The general population seems to sympathize with Kate and Ned, lovers separated by Elizabeth and imprisoned in the Tower, yet much of the court seems to treat romantic love as easily expendable in pursuit of wealth and power. Does either represent the prevailing attitude?

A. Attitudes prevail when they serve. Courtiers and the upper class used marriage to add to their property and titles and to create heirs for both, although neither precludes falling in love. The common people, who had neither property nor titles, were able to be more purely romantic. Since they were largely uneducated they rarely left diaries or letters expressing these feelings. However, they did flock to the Globe Theatre to see Shakespeare's *Romeo and Juliet*. Love ballads were sold on the streets, and Elizabethan love poetry is some of the most beautiful in the English language. For examples of love poetry of the time, read Sir Philip Sidney's "Astrophil and Stella," in particular sonnet 71, "Desire," Edmund Spenser's "One Day I Wrote Her Name" or any of Christopher Marlowe's poems and, of course, Shakespeare's sonnets. Sir Walter Raleigh didn't spend all his time sailing to the New World or fighting the Spanish. He wrote love poems, too, some to Elizabeth.

Q. I never knew before reading this novel that the Tudor court moved from palace to palace as each place began to stink from too many bodies living in too close quarters without good plumbing and with an aversion to bathing. Can you expand on your description of living conditions, and what small improvements began to be made over time? Was the flush toilet really invented during Elizabeth's reign?

A. With our modern plumbing and endless products to make bodies odorless, it is almost impossible for people today to imagine a time when there were no bathrooms, toilets or running water except at public wells. A closestool, which was actually just a chamber pot in the seat of a chair with a lid, served even affluent people. It was screened from the rest of the chamber. Try to imagine a Porta-Potti sitting in the corner of your bedroom without its outer shell and you'll get the idea, although the closestool was emptied more often.

Outdoor privies called closets-of-ease were common, but chamber pots were poured into the street, and strangers in London were warned to walk under eaves lest a housewife dump night soil on their heads. In some more affluent areas the night-soil man came by each morning to collect. A century later, post-1660, Samuel Pepys in his diary describes the contents of his closestools and privies being funneled to a receptacle in his cellar, which was emptied periodically by people who did that work . . . which must be high up on the list of the worst jobs in history.

Sir John Harington really did invent the first flush toilet and installed it for Elizabeth, although it was three centuries later before a newer version came into widespread use.

Elizabeth I had no mistress of the stool, but I created the position for Mary Rogers so that very often she would be near John Harington. I admit the situation is unusual for a novel, but I could not resist it.

Elizabeth was ahead of her time in her habit of cleanliness. She hated foul odors and was clean about her person and clothing and not reluctant to wrinkle her nose at others who were not. She also had a habit of ignoring the advice of her doctors, who at that time believed that bathing was harmful.

Bathrooms as we know them are a fairly recent invention, becoming common only in the early twentieth century.

Q. Medicine was also in such a primitive state during this period, with horoscopes and bloodletting as poor tools against scourges such as smallpox and the plague. Can you expand on the medical misconceptions of the era?

A. Bloodletting was a medical tool until the early nineteenth century, and horoscopes have never gone out of fashion. Very little was known about the body in Elizabeth's time, mostly because religious laws made dissection rare. Early in the 1600s, after Elizabeth, William Harvey discovered how blood circulates, and that began the slow progress toward modern medicine.

A common medical misconception during Elizabeth's time was that the properties of animals could be transferred to humans. One instance I mention in the book is that the powdered heart of a bull would make a human heart stronger. That makes sense if you believe in the transfer of animal essences. A decayed tooth was thought to have a worm in it, and there were many medicines to kill the worm without pulling the tooth, although since the tooth continued to decay, the tooth pullers eventually had to be called. Swallowing gold pills was thought to cure many ills. They were expensive and that made their powers even more believable. For a fun romp through the medicine of the time read *Quacks of Old London* by C. J. S. Thompson. For plant remedies consult *Culpeper's Complete Herbal*.

Q. You suggest that as soon as Elizabeth died, her palaces were ransacked of valuable items and people scrambled to either leave the court or form alliances with the somewhat questionably appointed successor, King James of Scotland. Why was the succession so hap-

hazard and chaotic, and was that true every time a king or queen died? When did the succession become more orderly, and how was that brought about?

A. Until modern times successions were often problematic. Brother killed brother, the little princes in the Tower disappeared after their uncle took the throne as Richard III, only to be killed later by Henry Tudor at Bosworth Field. Nobles chose sides and changed sides.

Though Elizabeth I was hounded to name a successor, she never would name one. Her young life had taught her how dangerous it was for a ruler to have a named successor. Plots and rebellions formed over and over with any disaffected or ambitious group. As Elizabeth grew older, many courtiers began to look north to James of Scotland, hoping for a place in his government. Robert Cecil even wrote to James offering his support. Remember, these were government people who depended on a grateful monarch for power and wealth.

Looting was really minimal, but ongoing. The palace was full of people who took what they could steal, whether the queen was there or not. Early in her reign Elizabeth charged William Cecil with reducing expenses and he achieved better control of expenditures, although graft never ceased.

Q. Can you recommend other books, fiction or nonfiction, about the Tudors?

A. There are so many that this must be a very select list:
    I, Elizabeth by Rosalind Miles, a stunning, blow-you-away

first-person novel, and *Elizabeth I* by Anne Somerset are two of my many favorites, as are any of Philippa Gregory's Tudor novels. Nonfiction works are almost numberless. I have a bookcase of titles I have read and continue to consult: *Besant's History of London: The Tudors* by Sir Walter Besant; *Dissing Elizabeth* edited by Julia M. Walker; *Elizabeth's London* by Liza Picard; *Queen Elizabeth I: Selected Works* by Steven W. May; *The Sayings of Queen Elizabeth* by Frederick Chamberlin, and many out-of-print earlier works.

Q. Can you tell us a little more about your long career as a writer?

A. At thirteen, I wrote a class play and sat in the audience soaking up the laughter; and later a teacher gave me encouragement. It didn't take much more than that to set me on the path of writing. As an adult, I had a job that allowed me to write speeches and work on a magazine, which led me to professional magazine and newspaper article writing. I quickly transitioned to nonfiction books and then, in the greatest leap of faith, to novels. I always read fiction, sometimes several novels at a time, and I determined to write one. After one, I couldn't stop. Writing historical novels is a great escape into the past. I can get through deaths, family illnesses and disappointments by simply going deep into the people and places of another time. It's the best therapy, writing or reading.

Q. You live in a Tudor-style home in California, which you've been refurbishing for many years. Can you share something about that project? Do you secretly wish you lived in England?

A. I love Tudor architecture and gardens and have many books on the subject. My husband and I have enjoyed adding Tudor character to our home. Our latest project was a large leaded-glass window. I picked each hand-blown glass pane, looking for just the right imperfections to age it. I'm searching now for Tudor chimney pots.

I'm happy to be an American, but I'd love to go to England more often and stay longer.

Q. What's next for you as a writer?

A. There are two books I'd like to write about more obscure areas of Elizabeth's life. The first: the duration and power of her ageless, emotional love for Robert Dudley in their middle years and her amazing reaction to his death. She took his last letter and locked herself in her rooms alone for three days without food or drink, until her chief minister, fearing suicide, finally had her doors broken down. What did that letter say, and what did she remember during those hours?

The second book deals with Elizabeth's love, jealousy, loss and revenge against her beautiful, scheming cousin Lettice Knollys, the last wife of Robert Dudley, the Earl of Leicester and mother of Robert Devereaux, Earl of Essex, the queen's two great loves. Elizabeth called Lettice "that she-wolf" and eventually, after Robin's death, bankrupted her and hounded her into obscurity.

QUESTIONS
FOR DISCUSSION

1. Which female character in the novel do you find most interesting and sympathetic, and why?

2. How does Jeane Westin's portrait of Elizabeth I differ from others you've seen in books, onstage and in film? Which aspects of her character most fascinate you?

3. What do you consider to be some of Elizabeth's greatest strengths as a monarch? Her greatest weaknesses? Do you agree that she ushered in a "golden age" for England?

4. Which male character in the novel most fascinates you, and why?

5. There are many references in the novel to people who were executed by one monarch or another for treason. Discuss what might motivate someone to challenge the reigning king or queen, and what factors Elizabeth in particular considered when deciding whether or not to execute someone.

6. Given Elizabeth's past, in which her father ordered her mother's execution and her succession to the throne was often in doubt, do you think her fears of treason were justified? In her shoes, would you have acted differently?

7. Do you think Elizabeth should have married Robert Dudley? What might have happened if she had?

8. Discuss Elizabeth's status as "the virgin queen." What political purpose did that description serve? Do you think she was technically a virgin?

9. Discuss living conditions at Elizabeth's various court palaces. Would you have enjoyed living there?

10. Lady Katherine Grey might be considered reckless, even foolhardy, in her pursuit of Edward Seymour despite the queen's rejection of the match. What aspects of Kate's upbringing and character might explain her behavior?

11. In contrast, Mary Rogers waits years to find fulfillment with John Harington. What in her background and character might explain such patience?

12. Which secondary character do you find most interesting, and why?

13. What do you think accounts for the current popularity of the Tudors?